AGAINST THE MACHINE: MANIFESTO

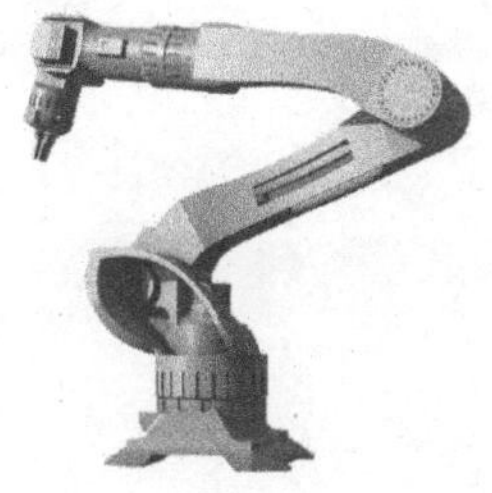

Essential Prose Series 194

Canada Council for the Arts
Conseil des Arts du Canada

ONTARIO ARTS COUNCIL
CONSEIL DES ARTS DE L'ONTARIO
an Ontario government agency
un organisme du gouvernement de l'Ontario

Canada

Guernica Editions Inc. acknowledges the support of the Canada Council for the Arts and the Ontario Arts Council. The Ontario Arts Council is an agency of the Government of Ontario.
We acknowledge the financial support of the Government of Canada.

AGAINST THE MACHINE: MANIFESTO

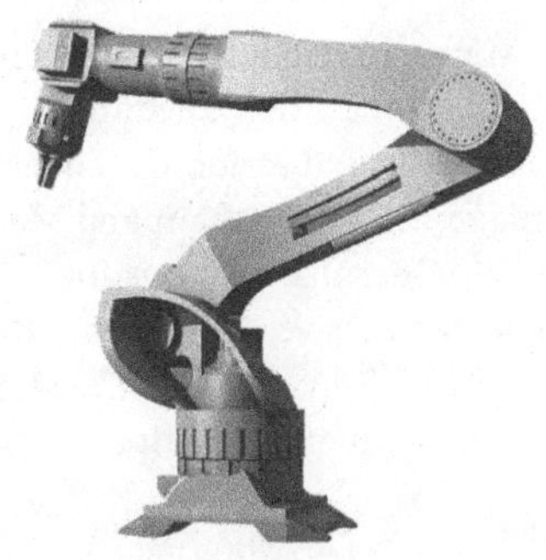

BRIAN VAN NORMAN

GUERNICA EDITIONS
TORONTO • CHICAGO • BUFFALO • LANCASTER (U.K.)
2021

Michael Mirolla, general editor
Julie Roorda, editor
David Moratto, interior and cover design
Front cover Image: Diane Eastham and Made by Photo Lab
Guernica Editions Inc.
287 Templemead Drive, Hamilton, ON L8W 2W4
2250 Military Road, Tonawanda, N.Y. 14150-6000 U.S.A.
www.guernicaeditions.com

Distributors:
Independent Publishers Group (IPG)
600 North Pulaski Road, Chicago IL 60624
University of Toronto Press Distribution (UTP)
5201 Dufferin Street, Toronto (ON), Canada M3H 5T8
Gazelle Book Services, White Cross Mills
High Town, Lancaster LA1 4XS U.K.

First edition.
Printed in Canada.

Legal Deposit—Third Quarter
Library of Congress Catalog Card Number: 2021935737
Library and Archives Canada Cataloguing in Publication
Title: Against the machine : manifesto / Brian Van Norman.
Names: Van Norman, Brian, author.
Series: Essential prose series ; 194.
Description: Series statement: Essential prose ; 194
Identifiers: Canadiana (print) 20210140305 | Canadiana (ebook) 20210140321 |
ISBN 9781771836951 (softcover) | ISBN 9781771836968 (EPUB) |
ISBN 9781771836876 (Kindle)
Subjects: LCGFT: Novels.
Classification: LCC PS8643.A557 A71 2021 | DDC C813/.6—dc23

For Susan

MANIFESTO

Definition (Merriam-Webster)

Manifesto is related to *manifest,* which occurs in English as a noun, verb, and adjective. Of these, the adjective, which means "readily perceived by the senses" or "easily recognized," is oldest, dating to the 14th century. Both *manifest* and *manifesto* derive ultimately from the Latin noun *manus* ("hand") and *-festus,* a combining form that is related to the Latin adjective *infestus,* meaning "hostile." Something that is manifest is easy to perceive or recognize, and a *manifesto* is a statement in which someone makes his or her intentions or views easy for people to ascertain.

While physics and mathematics may tell us how the universe began, they are not much use in predicting human behaviour because there are far too many equations to solve.
—Stephen Hawking

All human beings have three lives: public, private, and secret.
—Gabriel García Márquez

There is something at work in my soul which I do not understand.
—Mary Shelley

WATERLOO REGION 2012

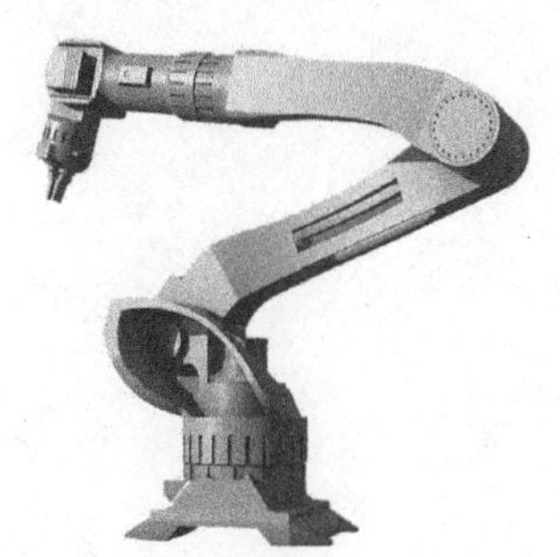

1

WHEN THEY CAME for him he knew what would happen.

He even knows them. Gary Wilson, shift foreman, and Stan Oblauski, Union Rep. They come toward him slowly. Doing this against their wills.

Mel Buckworth lowers the weft wire in his hand, half inch black bar. He brakes the big weaving machine. Carefully. It *is* big. He shuts it down with the job half done. A long train of warp wires trail from the machine's back end like cryonic black snakes frozen in mid-slither. Sliding the weft bar, crimped and heavy in his hand, back into the machine's quiver he takes out his earplugs then removes his safety glasses.

They reveal his eyes. Unusual eyes. Blue, with a singular arresting feature. They sparkle. Like diamonds. Add to them his dark hair, strong jawline, a generous mouth and Roman nose and Mel Buckworth appears a handsome man. He is tall though not remarkably so. His body is solid from years of sports and factory work. His age is beginning to show in a thickness around his middle that he would rather not have.

He steps down from the weaver's platform and faces the two men awaiting him. Oblauski stands solid. Big man. Dark eyes. Maybe six-four at least two eighty. He's in his late forties. Wilson steps forward. Much smaller. Wiry, Mel thinks. That's the word for his friend. Always a friend. Since high school. He has that sad look on his face he gets when he reminisces about the old days, usually when he's had a few. Not now. He's sober as a judge. He touches Mel's arm.

"Gotta come with us, Mel," he says.

The floor noise, big machines belching and hammering, makes him raise his voice.

"Yeah," Mel says, "figured as much ..."

"Ain't easy days," Oblauski says.

Mel looks wistfully at his weaver, knowing he won't be seeing it again. He walks with them across the factory floor. It is a huge building. One hundred metres each way. Green steel girders support the roof. The roof twenty metres up. Rows of industrial strip lights. Fluorescent merciless blue. Gigantic multi-coloured machines hunker in precise rows. Weavers, crimpers, shears, robot spot welders ... there are red and yellow warning tapes glued to the floor around them.

The long wire crimpers line two walls. Different gauge wire spews from their troughs. Weaving machines take up the inside along with the welders, both mechanical and human. The human welders pull down their masks. They look like ancient gladiators doing battle shift on shift. The acrid smell of scorched metal infuses the plant.

At the back taking up nearly a quarter of the floor are the massive shears. They come in different sizes set to cut all gauges of wire, from bar to fence to delicate screen, each woven sheet is sheared to size. The biggest shear has tonnes of pressure with its diamond edge blade easily slicing. It is precise power, from the men who use the lasers to measure and cut, to the glittering edge of the shearing blade when it comes down. There is the shriek of metal and the sharp odour of hot steel.

He'd worked them all. Every machine. Even the loading dock at the back. His first job here was the loading dock. Curt instructions from the foreman. Heavy packets of steel coming in and out. He'd gained twenty pounds in a year. All muscle. Eventually he ran the tow motor shuffling weighty skids around. Then he'd graduated to the interior: first the crimpers then the shears then welding then weaving then ... what?

Twenty-eight years. Twenty-eight years.

2

THEY PASS THROUGH a heavy door. Its grey thickness slides shut behind them. It cuts out the factory sounds. They climb a steep stairway. Their work boots ring on the metal. Another door, this one black. It slides open too, then rolls closed behind them. The hallway where they find themselves is quiet. No people armed with paper moving urgently from office to office. No smell of percolating coffee. No gatherings of gossips. Nothing. The closed office doors line either side of the hall. There are mirrored glass windows for each cubicle. The sound is damped by a rubberized carpet. Mel realizes he can hear nothing of the factory itself in this insulated managerial cloister.

Wilson opens an office door. This one swings like a normal door. They enter. Oblauski goes first, swelling his presence to fill the room. He will not make this easy. Mel follows, then Wilson. He closes the door. It gives an unnerving squeak.

The office is austere. A window with its grey blinds open offers a view of the factory. Triple sealed to inhibit the noise, it overlooks the work floor from above. Grey painted drywall forms ascetic space. The ceiling is dotted white acoustic tiles. In one corner sits a black file cabinet and a grey metal desk with a grey cloth chair. Two card table chairs face the desk. They are black. A black wall clock with white face peers down from another windowless wall. A calendar is pinned below it. No picture on its upper page, just all calendar. Each day of January is crossed off up to this day. Red strokes through each square.

Friday the 13$^{th.}$ 2012.

Mel smirks.

Ironic.

Behind the desk, not rising, sits Herbert Trimble, VP Operations, Kitchener Plant, Erban Industries. Part of the mutable conglomerate which purchased the factory two years ago, he is diminutive. White shirt. Grey tie. Fussy. Balding. His hair salt and pepper. He's permitted himself a pencil moustache. A smidgeon of daring on his tired, bureaucrat's face, he closes a file. He stares at Mel through rimless steel glasses. Mel thinks he resembles a cricket.

"Mr. Buckworth understands why we're here?" he says. His voice is an unpleasant treble. He's been through this before. A veteran of downsizing. Good at his job. That's *why* he's here.

Oblauski's rough voice replies.

"Why don't you explain the process, Trimble? This don't happen every day. Here's Mel Buckworth just like you asked for, twenty-eight years upstanding employment, best weaver we got. Be nice if you told him what you're gonna do!"

Oblauski has faced off with Trimble more than a few times since Christmas. Oblauski is used to wielding his power; the elected power of the union. He likes it. He once relished fixing things for the workers, getting into management's face. Yet now it seems he can do nothing but make things unpleasant, his power diminished.

"It's not personal," Trimble says. Trimble trembles a little, Mel notices. Is the man afraid of Oblauski?

"Please. Sit," he says. His moustache quivers.

Mel sits. Oblauski stands. Wilson waits just behind them by the door. Trimble shuffles his forms and files. Mel knows what's coming.

"This isn't my doing, Mr. Buckworth."

"Just the messenger?" Mel says.

"The what?"

"Nothing."

"I have these forms for you."

Mel stays quiet.

"I need them signed."

"Need to read 'em first," Mel says.

"Signed for tomorrow then," Trimble says sharply.

Oblauski steps forward. He leans on the desk.

"That's all fine an' good, Trimble! What if he disagrees with the terms?"

He is loud. Pushy. Reducing Trimble. This is how he makes it hard.

"This isn't my doing," Trimble says again as if he is somehow removed from the process. "Right," Wilson says sarcastically.

Mel's eyes are locked on Trimble.

"You owe this man an explanation!" Oblauski says.

"What do you want from me?" Trimble mutters.

"The whole deal!"

"What?"

"Say it first! All of it!" Oblauski leans farther forward on the desk.

"I don't ..."

"Why we're *here*! Why this man's *here*!"

"Look, Oblauski, we all know ..."

"Say it!"

Trimble turns to Mel. His moustache twitches again.

"Mr. Buckworth, we're going to let you go."

Despite the foreknowledge it hits him like a hammer. He struggles to compose himself. Twenty-eight years. Gone. *Let you go*. Wiped out as if he hadn't been here at all. Friends here. Even unfriendlies. Relationships from a lifetime. Gone. Erased. Forms in files are the only archaeology that measures who was here. Mel's hands bundle into fists. Does he cross the desk? Stomp little Mr. Trimble? Kill this pen pusher? Twitching moustache.

What Trimble sees is a slight shift in Mel's chair and the sparkle in his eyes fade from fury to resignation.

"Yeah. Figured as much," he says flatly.

"Now the rest of it!" Oblauski says. He has backed off the desk.

"You'll have to sign these papers ..."

"By tomorrow. Yeah."

"Preferably today."

"What about the rest of it!" Oblauski, loud again.

"Surely we don't have to go into detail ..."

You're fuckin' right you do!"

"No need for that, Oblauski!"

"Whatcha gonna do? Fire me?" Oblauski's laugh is merciless and helpless simultaneously.

"Buckworth here ..."

"*Mister* Buckworth! He don't work for you no more, Trimble!"

"Alright. Mister Buckworth."

"What about him?"

"He seems to understand."

Wilson speaks as if from the ether.

"None of us understand, Mr. Trimble."

Trimble pulls off his goggle glasses. He wipes them with a cloth, tries to let things settle.

"So tell me," Mel says.

Oblauski finally sits beside him. He is far too big for the chair.

Trimble puts on his glasses and deliberately turns toward Mel. He twines his fingers together. He rests his hands on the desk. Delicate hands. A thin gold wedding band. Larger Masonic ring. The fingers are too tightly coiled.

Mel looks at him.

His moustache twitches once more.

He is ready now for his recitation. The delivery of the litany.

"As you know, Buckworth, we at Erban are finding it necessary to shift with the times."

"*Mister* Buckworth!" Oblauski half rises.

Trimble blinks, shuffles and studies files for a moment, then returns from where he has gathered himself.

"*Mister* Buckworth, the global economy is driving changes in our approach. You've seen what's happening in the U.S. since 2008. Market forces. Raw materials. Labour factors. Erban is having to retool, contract a little ..."

"What?" Mel stares.

"Shrink, Mr. Buckworth. We have to lighten our workforce ..."

"He means hire Chinese or fuckin' robots," Oblauski mutters.

"Mr. Oblauski," Trimble's gaze shifts toward the big man. His face tightens. His eyes are suddenly steely. How did that happen? From distressed weakling to a man with power. In a single instant he has transformed, successfully girded himself for battle, awaited his moment with professional aplomb by allowing Oblauski to use up his weapons. When he strikes, Mel is surprised and impressed.

"That will be enough, sir! Another word from you and I'll have security remove you from this office."

He uses a high, hard voice. The little shit has grown some bones.

"You can't ..."

"I'm afraid I can, Oblauski."

"We'll strike. Walk out right now!"

"Why don't you do that?" A wry smile grows beneath the moustache. He knows where the true power lies. In this exchange there is only one winner.

"You owe this man the truth!" Oblauski blusters.

"And the truth is, Mr. Buckworth, you're being let go. Not laid off. Not fired. *Let go.* If you sign these papers you will have a severance package befitting your seniority. You will have access to retraining. You will be eligible for employment insurance. You will have a letter of recommendation. And, you will retain your pension benefits though they will not kick in until age sixty-five. You are?"

"Fifty-five."

"I would advise you to sign the papers. Feel free to read them first."

Trimble stands.

"Your union representative here will explain what you need. I'll return shortly. If you have any questions please write them down. There will be no further conversation. I'll leave you to it, then."

He is gone in a whisper. The door clicks shut.

Wilson is silent.

Oblauski is gobsmacked.

Mel Buckworth begins to read.

3

THE SCHLEIERKRAUT TAVERN is crowded and loud. Friday after work. People come from the factories of the industrial basin nearby. Easy to get to, the place is near Homer Watson and Manitou Drive, two major thoroughfares in the city of Kitchener, Ontario, Canada.

The bar itself has a large parking lot, full on Fridays. It's a building from the seventies, done up as a faux chalet from some German nightmare. The inside has been improved from the old days however. Mel remembers creaking wood floors and five-dollar pitchers, the smell of spilled beer everywhere and always one or two drunks at the bar.

Trendiness has made it a sports bar. A good one. Lots of large screens at every angle. Dressy now. Good, substantial chairs and tables. It has a fine craft beer selection. The bar is still there though the drunks are long gone with its gentrification. Kitchener's suburbs have grown up around it to the south and west along Doon Village Road and Pioneer Drive. Now it attracts a new clientele, different from the old days. Less grease, more tech. Way of the world.

Some will stay for a few pints with co-workers and friends, others ready themselves for the hockey game on the screens at seven. There will be a band by ten. The suburbanites will show up, the ones who commute to Toronto but live in south Kitchener with its less expensive housing and 401 freeway access. Mel looks around: just people like any others, good and bad, quiet and loud, though with more money than the old regulars, some of whom still show up after work and are gone by supper.

Not this time for Mel.

There are five stages to grief: denial, anger, bargaining, depression, and acceptance. The first two have been covered fully in the Schleier-kraut with the deconstruction of Mel's loss: the disbelief and fury, the ways to get revenge, the knowledge the job is irretrievably gone, the pride of once having had work, have all been discussed and discarded.

Voices get slurry.

Rounds get bought.

You stay longer than you should.

Mel and Gary Wilson sit at a corner table. Despite the cacophony of voices around them, they talk. They sit close. Mel has a tall glass of lager in hand, Gary sits with an IPA. There are empty glasses in front of them, white foam mixed with dregs of gold in their bottoms. The six glasses make a kind of wall matching the angle their chairs have turned toward each other. It signals to others who might wave a greeting that they should stay away.

Bar etiquette.

"I seen this comin' a year back when the midnight shift got cut down," Mel says.

"Yeah," Gary says. He takes a sip. What *can* he say?

"Shoulda took that foreman job afternoons, then I'd still be there."

"Not so sure of that."

Another sip.

"So what about you?" Mel says. "Your job?"

"It'll go same way as you. They're just keepin' us 'round t' help everybody leave."

"Ugly work."

"Otherwise it'd just be Trimble and Oblauski."

"Fuck that."

"Can you imagine?"

Gary laughs. Drinks.

"So they told you yet when you're gone?" Mel asks.

"Afternoon shift is meeting next Monday. Daytime, not their usual time. Right after that the day shift is gonna be called right from work, like you, only all of 'em."

"What does that say?"

Mel's turn to drink. Half the glass.

"Tells me Trimble, or some guy above him, is tired of one-on-ones. I think this'll be a mass firing. Today was for you 'cause you been there so long. You shoulda been a foreman!"

"Lot of good now," Mel says.

"Can't do much about it. Can't strike. Union's lost, no matter Oblauski's threats and shouts. Can't sabotage the machines either."

"Shit, I never thought of that."

"Cimolino tried it."

"Really? The guy workin' shears."

"Yep. Tried to jam the big ten tonne."

"What happened?"

"You seen the new guys walkin' 'round with clip boards?"

"Yeah, taking inventory."

"Right. Inventory. Jesus Christ, Mel, you can be simple sometimes."

"You mean they're ..."

"Security. Erban Security."

"The Bosses *told* you about them?"

"You think? Nah. I just figured it out after Cimolino happened."

"Fucking bastards!"

"I'll drink to that!"

Wilson downs his beer, slams the glass on the table, followed as hard by Mel's. They sit a moment, both inside their thoughts. Mel sees the server and puts up two fingers. Instead of bringing beer she comes over.

"Are you guys driving tonight?"

Mel and Gary look at each other.

"Take the empties away, Shirley," Gary says. "We'll have coffee."

"Make that one coffee and one beer," Mel says.

Shirley stands there.

"I'll drive him home," Gary says.

"Alright, one black one gold." Shirley smiles and is gone.

"What the fuck am I gonna tell, Pat?" Mel says.

"This ain't your fault, Mel. Just tell her the plant's closing down."

"I'm in enough shit with her. I told you 'bout Christmas. Christ, we barely talk now. Since Dani moved in with that geek boyfriend Pat's moved into *her* room. We don't sleep together no more. She makes supper. We watch TV while we eat. You know how pissed she is I didn't come down on MJ when he quit college."

"What's your boy doing now?"

"Delivering pizza and playing that fucking computer game the rest of the time. He's moved to the basement. Likes the big screen. All I ever see when I get home is blue light comin' up the stairs and guns and bombs and shit nearly shaking the house off its foundations."

"You don't have to take that," Wilson says.

"Oh don't get me wrong ... he does that daytimes when me and Pat are out working. Couple of times I've come home early. Tell him to cut the noise. He does. Then just keeps on playing but wearing headphones. I remember we used to talk."

"Them games are a problem with kids."

"Tell me about it. After pizza delivery he comes home, sometimes two or three in the morning, then he's on his headphones and plays some more. No idea when he sleeps! Slept enough during college, I guess."

"What'll you do?"

"Pat wants him out, wants him on his own so he sees what's going on and goes back to school. I think he's just like me when I was his age, feeling his oats. But it's different now. Gotta have education. He don't see that. Figures something'll come along. At least I left home when I quit school!"

The beer comes, and the coffee.

"Yeah, things are different now."

"That isn't all, Gary. Pat's restless since the kids have grown up. I don't know if its women's problems or I watch too much sports or maybe she's just tired of me."

"You go home and tell her this crap about the job. Should bring her around. The two of you gotta work this out together."

"I got hockey tonight. Ten o'clock. She'll be at home behind her door with her fuckin' puzzles or asleep by the time I get home."

"You should skip the hockey, Mel. It's not every day you get heaved."

"Gotta do it. This is the A league. A few of the guys were Juniors back in the day. A couple even played pro. Other leagues I can miss ... this one everybody wants in. You miss a couple of games, they don't keep you."

"You can't play drunk."

"I'm not drunk, Gary. Three pints?"

"Four."

"I'll quit after this. Grab some burgers out at 401."

"Still it don't seem fair to Pat."

"I'll take her out for breakfast, tell her some place public."

Thoughts of his wife weigh heavily on Mel. They flash through his mind in visions and memories. He has no idea when their marriage began to fail, when they began to grow apart. He recalls instances: fights over his hockey nights, arguments about money, differences over the kids, where to vacation, too much TV, who cleans the house, how to shape the garden, on and on in a crumbling narration of increasing unwillingness to find answers.

Perhaps there are no answers.

Anyway, she's changed. Not the same woman he's known for years. Someone else. Where the fuck was *that* person hiding?

She wanted him to accompany her to a marriage counsellor. He went once. The counsellor was a woman who took Pat's side in every segment of their discussion. She'd accused Mel of not listening, or not listening correctly. What the fuck is *listening correctly*? That was the end of therapy. He thought they could work it out themselves, like adults, like they used to. Pat kept going once every week.

It got worse. He played more hockey in winter, softball in summer in the good, strong company of men. He understood most men: understood their code, the unwritten rules, the right behaviour of guys who respected each other. He thought he'd once understood Mel Junior, his son. Not anymore. Now he's changed too from collegiate champ to a lump on a couch.

He wishes as well he could comprehend his daughter Danielle. She has changed into some other daughter, not the one he raised. Was *that* girl always there deep inside? Did she grow from the soil of experience or just emerge from the dark? Sometimes, he thinks, it's all too complex.

She is with a man now though he is not Mel's kind of man. A little stuck up shit called Stanley as in: "I'm not Stan, sir, please use my name." Little shit. Some big scholarship to University of Waterloo. Computers but not just *any* computers. No. *Nano.* What the fuck was nano? And *quantum*. What the fuck was that? He'd wanted to step on the guy but Dani saw it coming and so did Pat and they both came down on him for being insensitive. He just didn't like the guy! Why was that insensitive?

The beer hits the table half full.

"You're right, Gary."

He has no idea what Gary was talking about just then but he's made up his mind.

"Your coffee done? I'll leave the beer. I don't need it. Gotta be on my game tonight."

"Okay." Gary sets his cup down. "You sure you can drive?"

"Absolutely. All this crap about losing the job. It's got me down."

"It's a good thing to talk it though, Mel."

"Yeah. Thanks for being here."

"You should really go home."

"I'll figure out something. Meanwhile I've got that severance package should last me a year. Maybe I could retrain. Maybe I could do it with my son, get him off his ass. Look, Gary, I know you arranged for all this today. Nobody else gets this treatment but foremen and office staff. I wanna thank you."

"It was nothing, Mel. Just making it fair."

"Yeah. So do you really know when you're done?"

"Like I said, end of next week. There's a skeleton crew to shut the plant down but they won't use any of us. Afraid we'll sabotage things. So I'm gone with the rest, replaced by robots or Mexicans or some guys in China who work for shit. Listen, that don't matter. You and Pat get it back together, eh? Maybe you two and Mona and me can go out for dinner when I'm done. Celebrate our severances. What do you say?"

"Has Mona been talking to Pat?" Mel asks.

"I think on the phone a few times. Haven't seen each other in months."

"You know what they talk about?"

"That's Mona's business. If she wanted me to know she'd tell me."

"Is it about me?"

"I don't know, Mel. Honest. I'll ask her."

"Okay. Listen, I gotta get some food and get to the rink. Good we did this."

"Yeah."

"What's up with you this weekend?"

"The usual."

"You still belong to that book club?"

"Yeah. Saturday afternoons once a month. Good people."

"You read a lot don't you."

"I like it. Wish I'd gone on in school y' know?"

"It was different those days."

"Different from now, that's for sure."

"I wonder what'd happen if I started back in school? All I ever used my brain for was sports. My brother was the real brains in the family. Well, it ain't gonna happen now. I'll get a job somewhere. Let's go!"

In the parking lot they shake hands then embrace, back slaps on thick coats in the January dark. Just enough light to twinkle the ice sheening the pavement. There is a pile of snow plowed up at one end of the lot. Mel has parked there rather than look for a spot. Now he unlocks his F150. It's old but paid for. That's the good part. And no mortgage. Pat had made sure of that. Save and scrimp and pay cash. So he had no debt. Even his sports bets mostly made money. She hadn't liked him doing that even when he'd won but she'd tolerated it, until now.

She sure as hell isn't going to like this news, he reflects. He thinks for a second about going home: turning left up Homer Watson, then onto Highland then Belmont then into Waterloo to his house on Fischer Street. Likely best to get it all over ... have the fight and the tears and the door slams and sleeping alone.

Instead he turns right, heading for Sports World Drive.

4

A COUPLE OF burgers see him through his drive to Ice Sports arena. He listens to classic rock, turned up, Seger and Springsteen driving unwelcome thoughts from his mind. Not quite.

"... let you go ..." from a mouth with a trimmed moustache.

"Someday lady ..." Seger's voice and sudden thoughts of a youthful Patricia.

"... sign these papers ..." the merciless bureaucrat.

Springsteen's "Hungry Heart" and the ache of old days. The days of youth and promise. So simple then. It didn't seem that long ago yet it also seemed like another dimension. Now it's become days with no future. You can't retire at fifty-five! He shakes his head. He needs to focus on the game, prepare himself for these guys. He flips off the radio.

There are three former cities joined together by government fiat in 1973, still known separately as Waterloo, Kitchener and Cambridge which, along with the townships of Wellesley, Wilmot, Woolwich and North Dumfries have morphed into something called Waterloo Region. The Tri-Cities, another moniker for the area, share a Germanic, Scottish, Mennonite and later Portuguese heritage. It's a big sports region though too small for professional teams. The populace makes up for that deficiency with plenty of amateur athletics of every description. In winter there is skiing at a small but popular club, curling in various rinks around the city, then volleyball, basketball, and hockey leagues for all ages. The Kitchener Rangers, an OHL team, is sold out annually. Mel drives to the edge of Kitchener, Sportsworld Crossing, for his Friday night game.

This league is special.

He's played with and against some of these men since he was a kid on Waterloo travel teams. A couple even turned pro for a while and several of them were prospects as Juniors, and then there are the few, the very few including Mel Buckworth, asked to play simply through old friendships and known to have retained certain levels of skill.

He parks in the lot then lugs his bag through the spacious new lobby all dove grey and white tiled floor; deep blue railings line the steps to the concourse. A furniture store has paid for a bright orange 3D icon and multiple posters. Garish, but he doesn't mind. By now he ignores it anyway.

He walks over to rink side in time to see the Zamboni clearing the snow and watering the ice ... its wet path forms a gleaming surface. It is the best ice. Clear and polished like a mirror. A perfect surface before the wounds and scrapes made by skate tracks. It is clear and cold at ice level, the only sound that of the machine and the echoes that bounce off bare walls.

He knows once, in his dad's day and even now in rinks in small towns, ice was shovelled and hosed by teams of rink rats ... the boys who hung out just to get free ice time for their service. Now, like him, they have been replaced by machines. All the old camaraderie gone. Efficiency replacing it all. He turns away. He will watch the Zamboni no longer.

Even his hockey sanctuary is tainted by this day's events.

The dressing room is azure blue and white with polished yellow benches. There has been an attempt at faux woodgrain. Above the benches, spaced evenly where the blue wall turns white, there are clothing hooks. No lockers. Someone always locks the dressing room door when the teams leave for the ice.

As he enters he hears the word "*Bucks*!" from all sides. His nickname. You can't be a jock without a nickname. His comes of two elements: his last name shortened is obvious and then an unexpected hitch to the nickname, his selection skills in sports pools. He's paid for a great many rounds of drinks multiple times with his winnings.

Men in varied stages of undress wave or smile or make jokes as he passes. His appointed place—as all players do he has superstitions—is between Bill Barbour and Tom Turnbull. *Barbs* and *Tommy* as they are better known. Greeting them he doffs his ski jacket, zips open his bag, old style with no wheels, and pulls out a variety of pads. Dressing takes twenty minutes, lots of protective equipment, lines of tape applied, then skates and sweater, ever disrupted by jibes and laughter.

It is an easy place to love, this place. There is an unmistakable bond here. These are men who have lived this ritual virtually all their years. There is no stench of unwashed underclothing. That is for the unenlightened. Their equipment is top quality, not a collection of old used-up gear. Everything has been carefully maintained. They don dry-cleaned orange jerseys with white trim or white ones with black trim depending on their team this night. Sponsor jerseys. Sponsor logos. They have fought for colours since childhood, the uniforms of the game.

At 9:55 they exit the room, their skates on the blue rubberized carpet leading to the ice. They do not speak now. They don't joke. They prepare in the time it takes to walk from the dressing room door to the gate to the ice and then into another world of glistening white gliding steel red and blue lines cool Freon wind as they accelerate to speed. Fastest game in the world at its best.

Pucks are dumped from a pail. The slap of sticks on ice. The blur of black discs. The boom of pucks off pads. The snap of catching gloves as goaltenders warm up. Long ago it would have been a pond or backyard rink. Shovelled and hosed lovingly by a father. No lines, no boards. Shinny games. Short passes. Quick moves. Miss the net lose the puck in the snow. Spend ten minutes searching. Boys steaming in minus fifteen degree weather. A couple of girls wanting to play. Why not? Winter glory.

At fifty-five, Mel Buckworth is by no means a threat to these players. He should be playing no contact/no slap shot but feels that would somehow diminish him. He plays left defence now. If he's good he can hold his own. The younger players in their thirties and forties fly by him like he's standing still. He tries to be smarter. He has the brain for it. Always has had. Like most guys here he knows how to focus, how to bend his concentration to the moment.

He is the one to retreat tactically when the opposing team grabs the puck in their end. His eyes follow evasive routes as men try to get open for a pass. He sees the passes, hears the stick slaps, watches his own guys scramble to back check. He twists to skate backward, blades rasping the ice just as the puck arrives at a speedy right winger. Young guy. Quick glimpse. No one is with him. He can't pass so he'll try a cut toward centre and leave a drop pass or go round and sweep in the short side trying to get past Mel.

Mel watches his feet. Forget the puck. Any weight shift. Any deke.

There! Right left. Up centre. Counter him. Hip to his thigh. Take his leg out.

Done. Guy's down. Puck's loose. Stick. Turn. Look. Pass. Sharp.

Breathe as the play goes the other way.

Glide to the bench for relief.

"Nice one, Bucks!"

Pull out the mouth guard.

"Thanks."

"Oh shit! Look! Yes! Yes!"

"What?"

"Tommy!"

"Yes!"

Puck in the opponent's net. Goalie sprawled on the ice. Tommy Turnbull's stick in the air. The excited huddle of men turned boys for an instant.

Nothing like winning.

5

THE FIRST JIGSAW puzzle was invented by John Spilsbury, a mapmaker and engraver in the mid-eighteenth century. He created his first using one of his maps. The map was mounted on a sheet of hardwood. He created a puzzle by cutting out the countries' shapes with his saw. By the twentieth century die-cut tools were introduced, changing everything. With these tools plastic and cardboard puzzle production increased in both numbers and complexity.

Now they come in multiplicities of form, shape, material and theme, many of them over one thousand pieces, some up to three, four, five thousand. There remains one common element, however: the puzzles come in a box or bag in loose pieces and somehow someone must use cognitive skills, problem solving and intense concentration to decipher and solve them.

Patricia Buckworth lounges in her family room sorting through puzzle tiles. She has a one thousand piece jigsaw of Dali's *The Enigma of Desire*. Long gone are the simple castles and landscapes as she'd graduated from one level to the next. Now she puzzles out the most complex of them: Chihuly glass, famous portraits, Byzantine mosaics, surrealists, impressionists, the greater the challenge the more she craves it. Once she played tennis, volleyball, basketball. She still indulges herself with summer tennis. But puzzles are her pastime now; they offer the challenges of sport while keeping her company by taking her mind off her isolation.

She sips the last of her Chardonnay. She searches amid shades of yellow tiles seeking a shape. Clutching at curves. Perhaps the one with the slight shadow on the inner curl? It is. It fits. A familiar satisfaction fills her.

Victory. Small but significant.

This one piece will lead to a line or a patch of others she has placed in small groupings within the completed edges of the puzzle. She rubs her eyes then, tired from a day's work. She carefully covers her puzzle table, made by her son in his high school shop class, a table with hinged plywood doors flipping up and over the unfinished work, keeping it safe. The plywood is covered in green felt as is the surface on which rests the puzzle. When it is open it looks like a small billiard table.

In the kitchen she considers another glass of wine, opens the fridge and then closes it, leaving the half bottle. She moves about putting things away. Her movements are precise. Just as her puzzle play. Once she was an athlete. Lithe and quick and confident. Volleyball setter. Basketball point guard. Puzzling out the opposition. Placing the ball just so for a strike or passing it precisely to the right girl. High school and college. Until she had stopped attending college.

She'd got married then. Married at nineteen.

She and Mel had once been striking athletic creatures. Prime exemplars of youth and beauty, he the golden boy she the diamond prom queen. They'd dated in school. Always lots of games to attend together. Lots of dances and nightclubs in downtown Kitchener. She was still in school when he'd left it. He was working as a labourer when he had proposed to her. He'd done it with his usual flair: Marty's sports bar, lots of friends, noise and beer and wings and suddenly a thin gold ring with a shard of diamond. At eighteen he had swept her away.

She recalled he'd smiled when he'd asked. He was confident she would say *yes*. He was always confident, sure of himself, smart as a whip at the things interesting to him. Eventually though, they'd discovered that marriage cost money. She lasted a year in college then quit school while Mel looked for a better job. He was hired at Mesh wire; it was steady work for steady money. Eventually it sold to Erban Industries. He had started at the bottom, but with his usual assurance and uncanny focus had progressed through jobs with varied skill levels to eventually become a weaver. She had thought that odd, weaving *wire,* but he'd loved it. Even when he'd had the chance to become a foreman he'd turned it down. It would have been the afternoon shift and would have taken him away from his games.

She had found work as a dental office receptionist. Gerhard Reitzel. Local guy. Reitzels everywhere in Waterloo, this one a young dentist just starting out. Now an old dentist just hanging on. Steady job too though she knows he'll have to retire soon. Still, it has been a very good job, not challenging but busy, not many days passed slowly.

She is fifty-one now, though if she is kind to herself she looks in her mid-forties. She's been told so by several people. She catches a glimpse of herself in the kitchen window, a dark-of-the-night reflection. Certainly not what she was back when.

Still, her shoulder length hair is that lighted blonde which conceals the grey and she has retained her figure, though it has thickened slightly. Her breasts have grown, her hips wider too. Childbirth. Still, she doesn't mind her proportions and knows she remains attractive. She is still active. Aerobics and yoga now. She takes brisk walks home each day after work, lucky to live so close to uptown Waterloo and the Reitzel office. And she keeps intellectually fit with her puzzles.

Yet again she wonders what happened. For so many years it was all so good between them. The two of them in their pleasant parochial world enjoying their sports, their friends, semi-exotic holidays and an athletic love life. They were carefree yet cared about one another. She ponders again why they are not what they were. It comes to her in pieces, like her puzzles, but they are too confused and jumbled to make any sense.

Mel Junior was born in 1989, when Pat had first discovered the strange naming ritual of the Buckworth family. First boy always named *Mellor.* Then came Danielle in '92. Those early years were good years: both working good jobs, buying their house, picking out furniture, family camping, school graduations, birthdays, the kids in sports, the kids starting to date. They had seemed always together. A family.

It's past midnight now and she is alone. MJ is out delivering pizza. Wasting his life. He won't be home until three. Dani now lives with Stanley Best. Just nineteen like Pat had been. Pat could hardly have argued. Still, Dani's such a child, though the only Buckworth to attend university. At least she picked a smart one, Pat thinks. Nerdy but smart. Not like me. I went for the athlete.

And of course, Mel is out yet again. Friday night. Hockey night in the league he's so proud to be a part of, like a boy who never grew up. Why is that? When was the day he stopped being hers and became one of the guys again?

In a way it is more incipient than his having a mistress. She cannot fight this culture within him. She grew up with it as did he, though not to his level of competition. She thinks perhaps it might have started when MJ left for college and Mel lost his scrub game sidekick. Suddenly driveway jousts of one-on-one or backyard beach volleyball for four had disappeared.

Could it have been when their son had returned? Flunked out of college, forty pounds heavier, addicted to a computer game: fat, addled and lazy. She had wanted to punish her son, make him get off his ass get out of the house get a job. Mel had seemed softer, seemed to overlook the very principles he had once sought to instil in his son. Why this way now? How could he have been one way then suddenly another? She had asked him about it. They had argued about it. They still did.

Mel could not or would not explain his lacklustre parenting, saying the boy had to find himself. This from the father who had driven the boy to five a.m. hockey practice or pushed his basketball skills on the driveway or griped over his poor moves in a baseball game. It was all *push* back then. Until the day MJ sat at the dinner table and said he was through with sports. He needed to concentrate on his marks. He was not going to be a professional like his dad wanted. That took the air out of Mel. The thought that he was a father trying to live his dreams through his son. His son had found the chink in his confidence. Mellor Junior had differentiated perfectly.

Dani had evolved too. The pudgy, cute kid in elementary school had developed into a young woman, inheriting her father's lithe body and her mother's face. Yet she too was active: school teams, dance classes, she loved the very things that kept her in shape. She grew tall as well. Five feet nine inches by fourteen. Spiker in volleyball, centre forward in soccer. She was popular and skilled. She had gradually turned pretty, then beautiful. She had dated conservatively, a touch of shyness to her character, and had never defied her parents.

The only exception to her success was her marks. As she'd approached high school she had found it harder to comprehend elementary information. She was tested and found to have ADHD, an issue with brain structure and chemistry which makes it hard to focus. Yet she focused so well in sports, neither Pat nor Mel understood it.

Kids with ADHD have trouble with attention. They struggle with key skills like working memory, flexible thinking and self-control. Many are also hyperactive. What works on the court or the playing field does not in the classroom. They may rush to get things done faster, missing key details not taking the time to think about what they've written or read. They may split their attention to multi-tasking so achieving less in all tasks. Frustration frequently makes them give up. That was Dani's syndrome.

At first she was placed in special classes but complained about being labelled. When Mel demanded she be removed from spec-ed he'd seemed to understand her. Indeed, Pat had puzzled out Mel himself must have suffered the same symptoms as a child. It was the reason he had quit school. It was the secret reason he didn't want to be a foreman. Paperwork.

Mel and Dani had worked constantly on her school work together. What resulted was a growing bond between the two. Dani had learned strategies to focus and stayed in the scholastic stream. She'd worked harder than other students to achieve her average marks. It was clear she did not want to disappoint her father. She had graduated with grades strong enough to be accepted at the University of Waterloo.

Then she'd left her father in her dust. She'd attacked her first year like a general would plan a battle. She had developed skills which damped her impatience. She used a highlighter to accentuate the gist of each page she would read. She came home each night from classes and typed out her lecture notes. She had determined she would not fail. She had never once gone to Mel for help. Something had changed her. She'd completed her first year with surprising marks. A salute to her willpower. She even made the women's soccer team, the family competitive gene ever present. That too was Dani's character.

It was in second year as a sophomore that things truly changed. First and most surprising she had selected History as her major. More reading. Then she spent the summer season working at the university. It was a good job. Gardening. It kept her outside. She looked healthy, tan and lovely. She played summer soccer for the city. Finally, when all seemed going smoothly she went back to school and rather abruptly announced she had a boyfriend. It was only three weeks into class when she told them about Stanley Best, the genius. They had met during summer. She had not told her parents then. She was now. Her first real differentiation. It hit Mel as hard as MJ's had.

Stanley Best was a unique character with a funny accent. He said it was from Yorkshire where he had grown up. He looked young. He dressed strangely, often in wildly mismatched clothing. Once he had appeared wearing different coloured socks. Another time he wore a tie with a T-shirt. The tee shirt said:

$$B>1/n \quad \overset{n}{\underset{i=1}{\varepsilon}} \; x \; i$$

(be greater than average)

He could be comic in a curious way, often laughing at things no one else found funny. He was often dishevelled, his unruly mouse brown hair too long, his pinched face containing miraculous pale eyes of indeterminate colour. A true genius apparently, having solved some unsolved mathematics equation as a child; yet Stanley was no boy.

A young man in post-graduate studies. Fine potential. Over from England on a full scholarship to UW. Apparently he is *the next big thing* in a scholastic world the Buckworths know nothing about. Pat thought he might be using Dani. She and Mel had tried talking with her but she was uncharacteristically hostile. Then, when Dani had moved in with Stanley, it was catastrophic. Pat had hated the idea though realized she had no valid argument given her own age of marriage. She had again talked with Dani, alone, receiving defensive answers and deciding it best not to confront this new demarcation by her daughter.

Mel went the other way. What had been love became judgmental accusations. He obsessed about a daughter he thought was being played. At one point Mel came very close to assaulting Stanley physically. Pat had seen it in his face flushed with anger. His hands curling to fists. A vein in his neck pulsing manically. In particular his eyes were afire. That was when she knew there'd be trouble. She'd got between them. Stanley had had no idea. He'd kept mouthing his platitudes. She had steered the boy away from the confrontation. And when it had passed she had turned to Mel and had seen a very different man. At that point his eyes sparked in a way she'd never seen. She swore she would remember that look. It was a very dangerous Mel Buckworth, one you would not want against you. Again she wondered what undiscovered characteristics lay beneath the man she'd thought she'd known so well.

When Dani had asked Stanley to come for Christmas because Stanley couldn't go home to England, Mel had roared at her in the way he'd once reserved for coaching MJ. Unlike MJ, Dani had answered back. In the end Stanley came to Christmas. Mel wouldn't back down. He had left the family before dinner to join his mother at her nursing home. His brother had gone after him. Apparently George knew that look even more than Pat. There are things even wives do not know.

It was after when Pat tried to fix things. She'd found Mel obdurate as never before: bolstering his lazy son and refusing to see his daughter. It was the start of domestic squabbles becoming more senseless with each passing day. It was as if teams had formed and Pat found herself alone, without her teammate, dealing with a daughter who refused to come home and against two men who had regressed to children.

MJ had found a pizza delivery job to mollify his mother. Mel had found more sports on cable TV which kept him insensate in front of their upstairs flat screen. He gambled more, played on more teams, and drank increasing quantities of beer. He would answer her questions with grunts and mutters until there was no sense in talking at all.

She'd tried to turn things around, let time pass. Nothing changed.

She'd found a counsellor who had helped. She'd asked Mel to go with her; find a way through their crumbling marriage. He came one time only during which he blamed the therapist for everything. There was that ugly spark in his eyes once again.

Pat had moved into Dani's room at first as a punishment, then as a comfort. She was finding the once endearing things she'd seen in young Mel, the very things which had brought her to love him, had become the uncouth habits of an overaged jock.

She'd turned to her puzzles. She had always found solace in them. Yet if she carefully considered the puzzles they were, in fact, her way of coping with distance. A distraction more than a recreation. A pastime more than a passion. They concealed the real question troubling her, deep inside, and the fear to confront it.

Why am I no longer happy?

What is *really* happening?

"There's the true puzzle," she says aloud.

MELLOR JOHN BUCKWORTH, better known as MJ, arrives home early. Fucking car again. Fucking rattletrap. Who the fuck has a Korean car? No wonder it was cheap. No wonder it was in the back corner of Big Bill's lot on Weber Street. Big Bill himself recommended it. Fucking

Big Bill. Dad gives me two grand, says I want a car I gotta raise the rest. Doesn't help me. Doesn't call on his buddies to find me something. Just lets me go out there and get ripped off by Big Bill. Now the thing's jerking all over the road and the heater doesn't work! Can't deliver pizza with no delivery car! What the fuck?

He notices the lights on in the kitchen. His mother must still be up. He decides to avoid her. He takes the side door where the basement stairs are. Unlocking the door, he quietly enters and sneaks down the steps to his place. Outside in the cold a snowplough growls.

It is *his* place now. His hideaway. Not so bad. Wall-to-wall broadloom in taupe. Cream coloured walls. Big flat screen at one end with dad's old analogue speakers attached, a faded grey corduroy couch facing it. The couch was his grandma's but she'd had to give it up when she went into the home. There are a couple of kitchen chairs and a table, fake oak, and a microwave on the table, with a beer fridge beside. The other side of the room contains an unmade double bed in a foyer leading to the bathroom. Shower, sink and toilet in plain white porcelain. Simple. Rent-free. He wishes he could afford his own place. Not delivering pizza. Not with a fucking Korean wreck. *Kia*?

He thinks what kind of name is that. It's as bad as his own. *Mellor*. That's a last name! Who calls their kid Mellor? Even worse: Mellor Junior! Some stupid family tradition. First boy must always be named Mellor John, second boy always named George Mellor. Passed down a bunch of generations from some old bitch who came here from England. She'd lived in England and came to this wilderness? Why in hell would anyone do that? Why in hell did there have to be a naming ritual? Why not the girls of the family? No, wait, Dani's second name is Mary. And then there's Dad's sister, Aunt Mary. He'd only known her as a small boy before she'd got cancer and died. He'd once had a look at a family tree Aunt Mary had kept in a bible. Mellor this, George that, John here, Mary there it was fucking ridiculous. At least MJ is a cool nickname.

He removes his parka, blue canvas material layered with quilted checked flannel inside, revealing his usual black T-shirt and a pair of blue jeans. His gut hangs over the jeans. He is so sure he will lose weight he will not purchase newer, larger sized ones. He takes off his T-shirt and puts on a bulky red sweatshirt. He has the look more of his mother than his father: dark blonde hair, hazel grey eyes, face rounded a little now. He was a handsome boy though the weight shows and has changed his look. He will do something about that soon, he reminds himself often.

He eats some pizza lifted from *Gina's* remainders. The extras the store keeps for employees on breaks. He picks off the mushrooms. Nothing like cold pizza. He drinks a beer, Coors Light, from the fridge. He moves to the couch, puts on headphones, checks his email Facebook Twitter nothing much then goes straight to sign in to Halo IV. Quickly his focus sharpens as he arms himself and guns away at whatever comes at him. He is good at this. Good at most first person shooter games once he figures out what works where, up level to level, playing strangers on the net. He's got great reflexes. They came from his dad. They're all in his thumbs now; the weapons he uses to play his own games; no longer his father's games.

At forty pounds overweight sports are out. He'd had enough as a kid anyway. Had enough competition, instruction, motivation, inspiration, perspiration, evaluation, denunciation and even one or two trophies. Done with that. The trophies sit on a shelf. Glassed in. Dad had made it for him. There's a light that goes on to sparkle them up but it burnt out long ago and he didn't replace it. Dad knows why. Dad knows how you get driven until it's all wrong. Not everybody can be a pro. That's why they're pros.

That's why he and his dad are not.

There is a buzz in his earphones. Text. He's not on his game tonight anyway. He hits his controller bringing the text up on screen. Mother. Can he come upstairs? He considers ignoring her then realizes if he does she'll likely come down anyway. Invade his space. He takes off his headphones, shuts the game down, and then hears knocking at the top of the stairs. The signal someone wants in through his invisible door located on the landing.

"Just a minute!" he calls.

She is already descending. He can hear the brush of her slippers on carpet. He can see her calves then the hem of her pink chenille housecoat and then she is standing at the bottom of the stairs, her blonde hair brushed out ready for bed. She looks like his sister, in a different way, older, in a mother way. She looks concerned. He doesn't like it when she looks that way.

"You're home early," she says.

"Car trouble again." He leans on the back of the couch trying to look relaxed, trying not to feel uneasy. She does that to him.

"That's too bad," she says.

"I need a new one."

"So buy one, MJ."

Why is she so disdainful? Why can't she give him a break?

"Can't afford it, you know that."

"Find a better job."

Always the same refrain. Just him and his problems and her concern. Shit.

"It's not easy, Mom!"

"No one said it would be."

"No fucking kidding."

"You stop that language!"

"Why? It's my place. I should ..."

"No! It's *my* place. Mine and your father's. As long as you live here you follow our rules. Is that clear?"

"Dad doesn't mind ..."

"Well I do! We've had this conversation before."

"Funny how we always seem to have the same talks over and over."

"You know how I feel."

"Oh yeah, you're like dust on a disc stuck on one thing: 'Go back to college!'"

"Well then, why don't you?"

She sits at his table now, crosses her legs. She's not moving. He thinks about leaving then remembers the deep cold outside. The Kia. No heat. He slouches into the other chair. They face each other across the table. Combatants again. He cannot understand why *she* can't understand why he's lost his way.

"Look Mom, I quit because it was a waste of time. Everything but computer class ..."

"So why not re-enrol in that?"

"'Cause I don't have the marks! Why do you think I only made community college and Dani's at Waterloo? I don't have the fu ... I couldn't come up with the marks!"

"She did!"

"I know. You don't need to remind me."

"You spent too much time on sports teams."

"And whose fault is that? Dad pushing me. *You* showed up to nearly every game I ever played! Didn't matter what sport ... hockey, basketball, baseball ... there you were all the time cheering away wearing your team gear having a laugh with the other mothers!"

"I was trying to support you, MJ. Would it be better if I hadn't come?"

"Why can't you support me now?"

She leaves a space in the conversation. Deliberately, he knows. It is the yawning gulf between them. He knows what she will say before she says it.

"You live here rent free, don't you? You eat our food? I love you, MJ, but I don't like your choices. You were never taught to give up yet you did. You just packed in your failures and ran back home. You're twenty-two years old. You should be in school. If you don't go back to school you'll never find work. A career I mean."

"Like Dad, you mean," he says cruelly.

"Those were different times and your father's had the same job for twenty-eight years!"

"Factory work. Not much of that left around these days ..."

"That's what I'm telling you! Do you want to push burgers or mow someone's lawn for the rest of your life? That's why we insisted you go to college! There's nothing wrong with a place that will give you a skill. Your father never had that chance yet he's worked very hard to become good at what he does."

"Yeah. I'm sorry I said that."

"MJ, you can't seem to see past tomorrow! Don't you get the world's changing? You'll have nothing without a skill or a trade. If this were back in my day I would never have got a job with Doctor Reitzel. Now-a-days girls have to have paper, certification, proof they can handle the job. Everyone does! You'll have to too!"

"What if I try for a job at Dad's place? He might be able to get me in."

He leans forward with that, elbows on the table, big smile he knows she can't resist on his face as he thinks he's got her now. He hasn't. He's been too busy with himself to look around at others, especially those who matter.

"You won't like it," she says flatly.

"Why not?" His smile disappears.

"It's a dirty job, a hard job. You won't even shovel snow without one of us telling you."

"I'm not listening to this …"

Half out of his chair.

"Don't stand up. Sit still and listen. I'm trying to help you."

"Lecturing me."

"Okay then. Why don't you be a computer fixer?"

"A what?"

"I don't know the name. You like computers! You spend hours and hours on this one. Why not do something you like? I could ask Stanley. He'd know …"

The hateful geek. Stanley with all the fucking answers.

"Leave him out of this, Mom. You don't understand."

He sits again, gathers his wits. He must explain the unexplainable to his computer illiterate mother.

"I *play* on the computer, Mom! I'm very good at working the software that creates a game, but I don't know how to *make* that software! Just like you at work. You use a computer but you don't know how it works, only that it works for you. What if it suddenly didn't work?"

"Well computers aren't all software, are they? You could become an electrician. You could fix the mechanical parts. MJ, have you any idea what we pay an electrician to come to the house, or a plumber?

Those people make scads of money. Doesn't Conestoga College have apprentice programs?"

"I'm just not cut out for education."

"That's so weak. You're just lazy."

"Haven't got the money anyway."

"We'll pay for it, your father and me. If you go to Conestoga you can live at home and commute. No going off to some other college away from home this time."

"So you can keep an eye on me?"

"We can't afford tuition and residence. If you live here it's just tuition, food and gas."

"My car's shit."

"We'll get it fixed."

"I can't start now. The term's already begun."

"So find some decent work, MJ, to tide you over until next semester! We can ask your dad about the factory. He might be able to get you in there. That's the first good idea you've had since you came home! Good hard work, likely just cleaning to start, but work that will make you some money! Oh honey, will you do it? You'd make me ... us ... so very happy. Just to see you trying again."

"Can I think about it?"

"Really? You have to *think* about it?"

The side door at the top of the stairs opens, then slams shut.

"Looks like Dad's home," MJ says.

There is relief in his voice.

Pat doesn't hear it.

Mel has removed his boots, placed them in the tray and taken two steps up into the hallway that leads to the kitchen/family room. It's a big room, an extension nearly half the size of the original house. The Fischer Street house is ninety years old so most of it is made up of small rooms that served well enough when they were built. Somewhere along the line people decided they needed more space so rooms got larger, then houses got larger; in the suburbs they even gave up their yards for more house. Semi-palatial blocks planted four feet apart. Double garage and driveway taking up half the front lawn.

Pat and Mel took another route. They re-made their old, cramped kitchen into a bathroom and built a new family room/kitchen on the back of the house. Mel had learned the skills required in a surprisingly short time, reading manuals and watching YouTube shorts discovered by MJ. Pat had been both surprised and impressed. He had done a fine job.

Most of their time is spent here: the kitchen all warm pine cupboards and countertops of flecked granite. Outside the kitchen island stretches the remainder of the room with wood floors, big windows, comfortable pine couches and chairs and a fireplace at one end with a flat screen above it. It is practical as well as comfortable. When new cushions are needed Pat makes them herself and replaces the ones on the wood frame furniture. That was the skill she had learned while Mel had studied construction. They have done most of the work themselves, only the plumbing and electrical left for specialists because of code.

Mel sets his lunch bucket on the counter. He remembers his hockey equipment is still in the car. He must retrieve it. Hang it up to dry in the furnace room. Make everything appear normal. He starts down the hall for his boots.

He meets Pat in the stairwell.

"What's wrong?" he asks.

It is what he says to her most times they meet now.

"Nothing," she says.

"You're still up."

"I was talking with MJ."

"Another fight?"

"I'm trying to get him to see the future! Why don't you help me?"

Inside, Mel sags a little more. His plan was to see her tomorrow morning. He's not ready now. He wants to take her to the Checkers on Belmont and sit in a booth and have breakfast when he tells her. Always crowded on weekend mornings. He thinks that way he'll avoid the response he's expecting. For an instant he looks at her in her bathrobe, hair brushed, still very pretty but now so hardened. What happened to make her this hard? He's never cheated. Well, once, but she has no idea. So it isn't that. He wonders why she beats down on MJ.

MJ's just stuck. Mel was stuck once in a dead end job. She never hassled him *then*. She was so happy she was going to get married she never thought of him at that age the way she thinks of her son. And hadn't it worked out alright? Hadn't they both got jobs they still had?

No.

The answer is no. Not now. Not anymore.

"I gotta go out and get my equipment. Left it in the car."

"Just leave your stuff until morning."

"It'll freeze out there."

"It seems frozen in here, Mel," she utters softly. "Why won't you help your son?"

"Just give me a minute. I'll get it, hang it up, then we can talk."

"It won't be a minute. I know how this works. You'll take it downstairs. You'll ask MJ what I've done to him now. You two will have a beer, sit on the couch and talk about nothing. Girls not invited."

"Look, I just need a few minutes."

"Never mind, Mel. I'm going to bed."

She turns and leaves before he can protest. He thinks he should go after her.

And then what?

Tell her?

Tonight?

In that mood?

Not a chance. Not a chance. Not a chance. Not a chance.

7

PAT DEFEATS MEL'S breakfast plan by being up earlier than he expects. He comes downstairs dressed in a plaid shirt and jeans and there she is, pouring pancake batter into a skillet, a small stack already warming on a plate beside the stove. Still wearing her pink housecoat, her hair is brushed back; in the light coming in through the kitchen window he can see the lines of her face. He can see her mouth downturned. Crows' feet at her eyes. She looks her age until she glances up when she smiles at him and it all goes away for two seconds.

MJ is there as well. He sits on the opposite side of the kitchen island. He wears a black hoodie, hood up, like some punk criminal on TV. He too smiles, adds a half wave. Mel dutifully says: "Good Morning." It doesn't feel good. It's if they've been waiting for him. He can sense their anticipation. Who could have told them? He has a brief moment of panic then settles himself. Not possible. Not yet. There would not have been smiles.

He takes his place at the kitchen table. The newspaper is there, the *Record*. He can't help it. He looks for news of Erban's imminent closing. Nothing on the front page. Nothing in business. Nothing in the local section.

"What's up, Dad?" MJ asks.

"Nothing. Why?"

"You just flipped through the whole paper and didn't read the sports."

Caught.

Recover.

"Why, you want it?"

"Nope. Just sayin'."

"Breakfast smells good!" he says cheerfully.

"Ready in just a minute," Pat replies. "Just these last two and the bacon needs to crisp."

"What's this about?" he asks. "Why are you two in such good moods?"

"That's not right, Mel," Pat says. "You're the one usually being moody. Anyway, it doesn't matter. MJ is thinking about going to Conestoga College."

"Mom ... I said I need to think about it."

"That's what I *said*."

"That's not what you *meant*."

"What the hell are you two talking about?" Mel says.

"Time to eat," Pat says cheerily, bringing plates to the table.

"I'll get the coffee," Mel says.

"It's okay, I'm up."

They eat for a while. No talking. After five minutes MJ speaks up.

"Dad?"

"Yeah?"

"What if you got me a job at your place?"

Blank. Sunlight through the window. Dust motes in the air. Some of them briefly sparkle.

What the where the how did when was holy shit why would he's never they must have why now who thought this what do I say? It's as if Mel's brain has broken open and spilled its contents in a glittering ruin his tongue can't dig its way out of to speak. His eyes lower to look at his plate he must not sag must not choke must not divulge why the hell did she have to make breakfast? Three of them together. It should have been two. And not here. Not now.

"Mel?" Pat says.

Where is the plan I haven't thought through, avoided all night in the back of my mind not letting it out and now I'm not ready! Pancakes half gone maple syrup soft golden, the bacon wrinkled and dark on the blue and white plate, stainless steel knife and fork burnished from syrup the coffee steaming black what can I talk about why won't my tongue move?

"Are you alright?"

Pat is inexorable.

MJ waits.

"No. I'm okay. Just had a bad night," Mel says. Stalling.

"You lose the game, Dad?" MJ smiles, one side of his mouth smirks up.

"No. It isn't that. We won."

"Are you hungover?" Pat says.

The new dreaded words. Hardened. Did I do that to her?

"Just a couple beers."

"Just a couple?"

"I lost my job."

There it is. So easy. No lies no divergence no excuses no job. Simple as that. Silence at the table. No one quite knows how to take this news. The breadwinner for twenty-eight years. Solid. Once it was the wife the son the daughter who went to him the husband and father for succour. The man you go to with problems now possesses the biggest of all. Better death. Better remembered fondly than look the fool. All the lessons shoved at MJ. All the self-satisfaction shown to Patricia. All the patriarchal protective reaction piled on Dani.

Where is it now?

Gone in a ten-minute interview. Twitching moustache. Blustering Union. Reassuring friend. Victim of change. Of robots or China or greed or the things that now make the world. Not him. He doesn't have work. He's admitted it at the breakfast table. He has failed.

Then the welter of questions.

"How is that possible?" Pat says.

"They're closing the plant."

"What the fuck, Dad?"

"Stop your swearing. I told you no swearing!" Pat says.

"But Dad's lost his ..."

"They told me at the end of the shift."

"Our house our rules!"

"Okay, I'm sorry. Jesus ..."

"When did you learn this?" Pat says.

"Yeah Dad. They tell you yesterday?"

"Yeah. Yes. Yesterday."

"Just a layoff, Mel? Is that what you mean?"

"No school for me then," MJ says.

"Will you be quiet? Mel, is it a layoff?"

"No. It's done."

"You can't tell me to shut up, Mother!"

"Just get out of here!"

"Why. I wanna know too!"

"I've had about enough of you!"

"I've got copies of the papers I signed." Mel says.

"You signed papers? What kind of papers? Mel, did you quit?" Pat says.

Disbelief in her voice.

"Dad, were you fired?" MJ says.

Disbelief in this boy's voice.

"Mel. Why didn't you say so last night?"

"You walked away. I was going to tell you."

Shift the blame. Take any advantage.

"I didn't know. Oh, honey, I couldn't know."

"I wasn't fired. I didn't quit. They're closing the plant."

"They can't do that!"

"They can do what they want, Son. The world's changing."

Then there is a transformation. The sense of alarm becomes confusion and then a compassion they have not felt for each other in quite a long time. Suddenly they are a family again, all else out there is against them. This is not just a room in a house where they gather; it is a nest and they are within it. They close together in mutual care. They sit at their kitchen table as if in a common embrace. They do not speak for a moment. There are no tears. This is not about death. This is not funereal. It is about life and life's changes and how they will get along through the rest of it.

It comes to Mel how his son is so much a part of him and his wife. His looks are a share from each of them: the dark blonde hair, the once athletic build, the strong features of his youthful face and his mother's eyes. Grey. Or hazel. They are not Mel's eyes.

That is what he and Danielle share. The diamond eyes that show up in old photos of certain ancestors. Glittering even in black and white or sepia brown they stand out. His eyes do that. Dani's do. The eyes looking at him now show sympathy. He knows he is loved but for all the wrong reasons.

"It's not all bad," he says. "I get part of my pension when I'm sixty-five. I get a severance package. Keep us going a while. I get unemployment too for a year. They tell me I'm eligible for re-training so MJ you might not be the only one going to Conestoga. I got a letter of recommendation from Erban. You can read it later. It's a good reference. I might pick up a new job just on that."

"We'd better phone Dani and let her know," Pat says, salvaging her confidence.

"I'll find a better job!" MJ says. Such a boy. Still such care. It seems he means it.

"And go to college," Pat says.

"Mom, let's not do that right now."

"Hey, maybe we could be classmates together!" Mel says. His eyes spark.

"I'll call Dani," Pat says.

"She doesn't need to know." His eyes turn to stone their false cheer gone. This is their marriage dying again their daughter cast out for being imperfect sleeping with a stranger and anyway it could have been anyone other than the nerd because it's his daughter and she has stepped out. The Christmas debacle returns. All three of them think it. No one speaks. The turmoil of the past months overwhelms them.

Empathy vanishes.

Pat gets up from the table. It gives her a chance to break away. The intimacy is gone now. The two men remain seated. She knows certain men have trouble with feelings. It's not they don't feel but showing that kind of depth is different. Handshakes not kisses, backslaps not hugs, consideration more than compassion are built into their culture in a way quite troubling to those who do not comprehend it. She knows Mel will comfort MJ rather than the reverse. He will regain his place as a father. He will calm down once she leaves the room.

She has taken the other side on Dani, on MJ, against him she thinks *he* thinks. She knows he thinks in terms of sides, teams, opponents. He has formed them in his mind. Once their family was a single team against all others. Now it has divided itself. Girls against boys. The old tired persistent sex distinction. It angers her. She turns away.

"So, really Dad, can they do this?" MJ says as his mother leaves the room.

"Nobody seems to be stopping them."

"What about the Union? Why don't they take them to court?"

"I don't know the ins and outs, MJ."

"There's got to be more to it than closing."

"They're moving. Taking the machinery with them."

"Fuckers."

"Yeah."

"God, all those people ... Mr. Wilson?"

"He's still there but expects to go next week."

"Dad, I'm sorry. That job was practically your whole life!"

"I don't need pity, MJ. Really it was just a job."

"It was *your* job, Dad. All my life you've done it. All my life I've known the Wilsons and the Schneiders and the Kawaleckis! All those people you worked with. The picnics and the Christmas parties when I was a kid and just the wonder I felt when you'd take me into the plant with those giant machines. So don't say it was just a job."

"I'm not sure what you mean."

"Don't put it down, Dad. It was your work. And don't hide behind being a man."

"Now I *really* don't ..."

"I know you. I know you'll stew inside and everything outside will look just great."

"Sometimes you've just gotta take it, MJ. It's like a game where the refs are bad. You can't do anything. The system's rigged. You just play along. Sometimes life's a game like that. We'll get along."

"Don't do this to yourself."

"Nothing I can do, Son, just play the game."

Does he really mean it? Can he slough off twenty-eight years overnight? Play the game? Go out and look for a job. Who's going to hire a fifty-five-year-old wire weaver? Two thirds of his life are over, the best is behind it's not a game there are no rules all you can do is survive and then fade away. His life has taken a turn against him: first his wife then his son then his daughter each one in an especially hurtful way. Now his job. He has never felt so defeated; so lost in the weeds.

He isn't ready yet to be sidelined. Not yet. Not now. He has always wanted to make a difference. Perhaps this is a sign. Perhaps now he can start on a new way of life; not fade away.

"Dad, where are you going?" MJ says. His father has just had that thousand-yard stare and then left the table. He doesn't reply. He goes down the hall then upstairs to his room.

It is then that his son cries quietly.

8

DANIELLE MARY BUCKWORTH returns to her bed with her phone in hand. She has a white towel wrapped around her body which, as she flops on the bed, falls away, to her boyfriend's pure pleasure. She has a beautiful body. Rubenesque, he thinks, yet athletic, strong. He still can't believe this blonde goddess with her diamond eyes has chosen him.

Stanley Charles Best—scholarship genius achieving his Doctorate of Philosophy in Computer Science (Artificial Intelligence/Nanotechnology) at the University of Waterloo by way of Cambridge, England where he Mastered in Advanced Computer Science, which he loves to mention and the University of Huddersfield, Yorkshire where he graduated *summa cum laude* Applied Computing BSc Honours which he is not so keen on talking about via Spen Valley High School where he was a social failure and Valley Elementary which is an absolutely *verboten* subject due to the bullying he endured in his formative years—has not measured out his life with coffee spoons, as Prufrock did, but with schools attended. He is a prodigy.

He looks more the part now. He has done what he can, or rather, Danielle has prudently assisted. He no longer wears glasses but sports a complex pair of contact lenses which make his pale eyes less cloudy and more the colour blue. His once blemish ridden face has cleaned up nicely at twenty-four years. His stylish mousy hair is cut by contemporary hipsters from Rodeo Angels Hair Salon on Princess Street. His rather thin body is beginning to expand in pleasant places as he attends the gym with his beautiful Danielle, better known as *Dani*, a nickname which grates on her boyfriend's agile mind like nails on glass. He wants her to be Danielle.

She has made him over not consciously but just by being with him: a part of his life, making new choices, adopting a new set of contexts, expanding horizons he never actually thought were there. He has learned, always a quick study, and has worked consciously as well, acquiring proper fashions and more appropriate behaviours, wanting to be more appealing, to be seen not only to be *with* her but be *part* of her life. Perhaps he was ready for change anyway. He has dreamed of something like this since childhood.

He wants to make love again. Yet she is distracted. Her odd sparkling eyes stare up at the ceiling. Her perfect smile is currently absent. When he touches her she takes his hand and stops him from proceeding. He tries once more with his other hand this time receiving a curt little slap. He curses himself knowing he's shown once again his former odd tendencies. He stops, pushing himself up on one elbow, looking down at her lovely face.

"What's the matter?" he asks. His voice is a touch thin for his liking, an element much persecuted in earlier days though his accent has lost all trace of old Yorkshire affected now with a Cantabrigian exactitude.

"I just got some very bad news," she says. Normally she would share her thoughts. Now she prevaricates. Something, he realizes, has shocked her.

"Can I help?" he asks.

"I don't think so, Stanley."

A tear presses from her eye. It flows down the side of her face.

"What is it, dearest?" he asks, fumbling. Never good at intimacy. Wanting to be.

"I'm sorry, Stanley."

She raises her cell phone. When she'd answered its burbling ring a few minutes previous she'd said nothing but "Hi Mom!" and then "Oh." Then she'd left the bed for the privacy of the bathroom. When she'd returned her face was tragic. She lay on the bed saying nearly nothing. If there is a way to comfort her he must find it despite his own subtle narcissism.

"Please talk to me," he says.

"My dad's lost his job," she says, her voice flat and defeated.

"What ... the wire weaver?"

Stanley possesses a certain resentment toward Mel Buckworth; Mel having a greater resentment toward him. Of course it is about the daughter. She is young, yes, yet he is only twenty-four, not the subversive *older man* he's been painted by Mel. He's a mere one year and a bit older than her brother, chronologically at least; emotionally MJ is an immature child with a vacuous mind. Still, not to think of that now. Her eyes look to him. Diamonds. Her eyes amaze him.

"This isn't funny, Stanley. He's lost his job!"

"What happened? Let me guess ... the plant's ice hockey team lost the big one ..."

He just can't help it—a touch of the Monty Python ...

"You're a shit, Stanley!"

"Alright. Sorry. It's hard to feel sympathy for a man who wants to beat me to death."

"He'd never touch you!"

"Certainly felt it at Christmas. Very glad he departed."

"He did that because he wouldn't do that!"

"Now you have me guessing ..."

"Stanley, my father has worked his whole life at that factory and now they're going to close and they're firing everyone!"

"He told you that? I thought he wasn't speaking to you."

"No, it was Mom."

"You see that's precisely why I can't feel compassion. He has turned you out, stupidly, for simply making your own decision. He thinks of you as a child."

"I *am* his child, Stanley!"

"You are no child, Danielle."

"Can you just forget that for a while? He must be a mess. That job was his life!"

"I thought the sporting life was his life."

"I've got to go home."

"*This* is your home now, isn't it?"

"No, Stanley, I live here with you but it's not *mine*."

"Neither is that place anymore."

"It will always be. It's my family. I'm going back there to try to help out."

"Right then, I'll come with you," he says.

"Why would you do that?"

"Perhaps you might need me? Whatever my feelings for your father, Danielle, I truly love you. If you need me I want to be with you."

"Not this time. It would just make things worse."

"Do you mean you're leaving me? Is that what you're saying?"

Panic. He has ever anticipated this moment and now it is here. To lose this girl would be the worst that could happen. He has never really had a girl before. His odd ways and atypical mind always driving them off. He is an arrogant man, he knows, yet this girl reduces him to humility in the face of her beauty her honesty her care and her choice to be with *him*.

"Of course not. Why do you always think that anyway?"

"I ... love you, Danielle. I want to help."

"It's okay, Stanley. This, us, is important but right now my family needs me."

"Have you grown tired of me? I realize I'm far from deserving. I ... I try."

"Of course not. I love you too."

She kisses him resurrecting his self-assurance.

"You think he'll let you in?" he asks.

"Yes."

"Because I'm not with you."

"Yes."

"Well, that makes it all pretty clear, doesn't it?"

"Stanley, not everything is about you!"

"I'm not saying it is."

"You act like it!"

"No need to raise your voice, darling. Downstairs might hear you."

Stanley does not really own the house but is a senior partner. He lives upstairs: bathroom and three bedrooms have now become an office, a den and a bedroom. The basement apartments are occupied by his friends, colleagues and fellow foreign scholars Will Baker and Michael Selel. The main floor kitchen and living room are common areas. It is a nicely set up place, not the usual student kerfuffle of used furniture and bricks and crates but quite a lot from IKEA and, of course, the latest in technology including an array of advanced devices in the main floor living room, turned into a lab. The house even has a cat named Henry who stalks from room to room like he owns the place himself.

Danielle gets up from the bed and is dressing. Stanley thinks he should say something more. He feels this is a significant moment. He tries to come up with the right phraseology but it is a difficult zone for him. She is upset thus she's not logical. Lack of logic means more emotion. Emotion is good in bed or snuggling or having dinner together but not as tame as Stanley might wish. Yet that too is why he loves this girl. Her character is her own. She has principles. It is why she left home to live with him despite her father's curse.

He decides to remain in bed and watch her. She is entrancing as she twists into her jeans and puts on her bra, then a singlet, then a warm sweater for January. She brushes her hair then puts it in that athletic updo he loves so much. Her neck is sensually long.

"Do you have any idea when you're coming back?"

"When I get through this."

"How long will that take?"

"How should I know, Stanley? He likely won't even talk to me!"

"You'll call me?" he asks.

"Tonight."

"What if he doesn't let you in?"

"My mother's there. She'll let me in."

"Right then," he says. "Be careful."

"I will."

"I mean it, Danielle."

"I know you do."

She has her coat on, her tam, her boots. She looks wintery and fresh. Before she leaves she crosses the room and kisses him once again.

"I'll be back," she whispers in his ear.

9

FÉDÉRATION INTERNATIONALE FÉLINE, with member organizations in forty countries, recognizes forty-eight breeds of cat. Counting among them there are your exotic Abyssinians, your Balinese-Javanese, your Bengals, your Birmans, your Europeans and Orientals, your Peterbalds, Aegeans, American Curls, your Australian Mist, your Brazilian Shorthair, British Longhair, California spangled, Maine Coon, your Chartreux and your Chausie, the Cyprus, the Devon Rex, the Dwelf, the famed Himalayan, Japanese Bobtail, Korean Bobtail, Kurilian Bobtail, the Manx, the Nebelung, the Siamese, the Tonkinese, the Persian, Siberian, Sphynx, Scottish Fold, British Shorthair, Russian Blue, and the hairless cat. There are cats known for their intelligence, grace, big ears, blue eyes and other exotic components. And then there are the mutts, the crossbreeds so complex they have become their own strain, or *stain* to the FIF.

Among the mutts are the tuxedo, the tabby, the calico, the ginger, and on and on in an endless list. How many cat breeds are there? About as many as there are owners inventing one for their cats. There is no actual determined number—just another piece of evidence cats follow their own rules.

There is even a cat that isn't a cat. Schrödinger's *cat* is a thought experiment, sometimes described as a paradox, devised by Austrian physicist Erwin Schrödinger in 1935, though the idea originated from Albert Einstein. It illustrates what he saw as the problem of the Copenhagen interpretation of quantum mechanics applied to everyday objects.

Simply put, Schrödinger stated that if you place a cat and something that could kill the cat, say a radioactive atom, in a box and sealed it you would not know if the cat was dead or alive until you opened the box. So that until the box was opened, the cat was (in a sense) *both* dead and alive. This would place the cat in a state of *quantum superposition.* The principle of quantum superposition states that, if a physical system may be in one of many configurations—arrangements of particles or fields—then the most general state is a combination of *all* of these possibilities, where the amount in each configuration is specified by a complex number.

Henry the Housecat, proud and long lost son of two jungle cats of questionable breed from deepest, darkest Florida, discovered in an animal shelter on Riverbend Drive in Kitchener, Ontario by Stanley Best, is one such quantum cat with a fascinating history.

Born in the Sunshine State in a place called Hammock Park in the town of Dunedin, he was taken up by a very nice man who worked too much and was hardly ever home. Thus Henry accustomed himself to running his house his way. One fateful day the nice man took him north to Canada for a visit with friends and Henry, being quantum, decided to disappear in Waterloo. After days of searching and self-recrimination, the nice man departed south again. Saddened.

As for Henry, he was too busy in the wilds of Waterloo to feel anything but panic as he hardscrabbled his way through nasty Toms, shouty dogs, wily raccoons and a slow but alarming decrease in temperature. (It was October.)

At this point he achieved *superposition* again and somehow appeared just outside the animal shelter's door strategically placed on the stoop. There he was discovered and sheltered. Henry patiently waited for just the right person to come along and pick him out. When he saw Stanley he knew his destiny. He could rule this man with an iron paw. Such a geek! Such a mouse! Such an uncatlike being! As Stanley slowly walked around the cages Henry would reappear in different ones always yammering like a stupid kitten, grabbing at the screens, doing somersaults until the weird human finally got with the program and selected him. Quantum entanglement commenced.

Now he rules the house on Albert Street from various vantage points and even from some invisible ones. He has learned a great deal since he's been with Stanley. He has spent much time lying on keyboards and looking at screens, assimilating the heady, studious atmosphere of the house simply through a process of osmosis. It has affected him. How could it not? The jokes about Schrödinger's cat are alarming but Henry knows who and what he is: so advanced beyond these silly humans he manipulates them like puppets. Want some treats? Do a snout rub. More treats? Belly rub. Define your space. Let no one defy it without payment. Use the eyes. Be disdainful. He has evolved a symbiotic relationship, in his mind, where the humans serve his needs and he, once in a blue moon, pretends to be cute. Still, at any time he may put on and take off his tabby look whenever he wishes and so become ... *quantum cat.*

10

IT IS LATE EVENING. Mel glances out his bedroom window at the quiet of Fischer Street, at the streetlights shimmering off glistening snow, a fresh snow shovelled by MJ. Hard to believe, unless Pat forced him to it. He has watched his son work, carving out the sidewalk and clearing the driveway because he'd refused to leave his den off the bedroom while Dani was visiting. He would not see her despite Pat's pleas. He had principles and was showing his daughter that one lives by principles, that there are consequences.

He is over the sick feeling of knowing his daughter is having sex with that Englishman. He is past the shock of having thought her a virgin. He should have known better and blames Pat for not somehow turning Dani away from the path they had taken themselves at such a young age. Look at them now.

Now the night is clear, the shadows make the world black and white and Dani is gone having stayed the day. MJ leaves to deliver pizza using the F150 tonight. Mel crosses the bedroom returning to a small alcove of precious things. His trophies are there. His medals. His youth. For a moment he ponders something reminisced from a senior phys ed class in high school, on a day the regular teacher was off and replaced by a man more theoretical than physical.

He spoke of the purity of sport. The Greeks advancing athletics to the level of philosophy and poetry. Young men training constantly to represent their cities at games, real games, not the use of the word as it is known now. Pure athletics: running, boxing, jumping, wrestling, most often naked in a state of nature the only thing separating them from the world was a thin film of oil applied to accent their bodies, to limber the muscles and show them off.

Poetry. Motion. Aesthetics. Power. They would compete for crowns ... not gold or silver but perishable: olive at Olympia, wild celery at Nemea, pine for Isthmia and laurel for Delphi. They would wear them for but one day. Only on their tombs would those crowns reappear as carved replicas declaring their glory in stone.

It was the Romans who bastardized sport, according to this supply teacher, by paying professional athletes to fight, gladiators to kill, charioteers to race. Nothing beautiful in it at all but that was Roman culture. He offered no more on Rome or Romans. It was clear he did not like their civilization.

Then the English, with the creation of a middle class, he insisted, had restored sport to a degree. The first society in centuries to possess leisure time, they had invented leisure sports: cricket, tennis, field hockey and of course soccer, or football, as was its original name before being overwhelmed by the American version. A modern Rome the teacher had muttered in passing. Athletes requiring payment.

Mel had been one of them. Boy athletes. He had attempted that shining goal of athletic scholarship only to realize those scholarships did not exist in Canada and North America was filled with millions of other boys trying like him, better than him, so many he was lost in an ocean of athletes. Needless to say, he was once a big fish in the parochial pond of Waterloo. Eventually he'd discovered his glory days had been false ones, even competing in Ontario tournaments. Ontario then was a province of small towns. Even its biggest cities Toronto, Windsor, London and Ottawa were really only enhanced, larger towns when placed against those of the US. His preoccupation, his early life really, had left him little ... trophies, medals and memories ... but there would be no leaves carved on his tombstone and no riches from professionalism, nor even the potential of a College degree ... his school marks too low to enter a Canadian school and an American scholarship just a faded dream.

It is not a subject he wishes to ponder, especially not on this day.

Pat is at the door, peering warily into his alcove. Her face looks strained. They have had words again today over Dani. Why the girl had shown up was beyond him. Did she think his loss would allow her into his good graces? Pat had insisted it was because Dani loved him and wanted to help. He'd said he needed no help.

"Do you want anything?" she asks.

"No. Nothing. I'm fine."

"I'm sorry about earlier. I guess we just don't see things the same way."

"Anymore."

"You think we ever did, Mel?"

"Yeah, I do. At least I did."

A pause. A grace moment in which to think. She comes to him. He watches her. She approaches warily. He is seated. Timidly she reaches out her hand. Pink fingernails. She strokes his hair. He looks up. She leans down and kisses him.

"Would you like to make love?" she says softly.

"What?"

"Would you?"

"Yeah. Sure."

"I'll go get ready," she says. "I'll be back."

"This isn't about pity is it?" he asks.

"Oh, Mel."

"Well it hasn't exactly been a regular thing since you changed bedrooms."

"I needed a change."

"Okay, your place or mine?"

"That's cruel. Why do you act like this?"

"Like what?"

"Like there's nothing between us."

"What's between us is the kids. Seems to me there's not much more left."

"I'm going to forget you said that. It's the stress ..."

"Whatever you say."

She walks out of the bedroom, closing the door behind her.

She does not return.

After twenty minutes he rises and goes to the door of her bedroom. She is not there. He goes to the head of the stairs, walks quietly down, and then glimpses her in the living room, her puzzle table open, a glass of wine beside it and she, the woman who only a short while ago had offered him sex and love, is muttering to herself over her enigma. He returns up the stairs to his room.

She is herself a puzzle, he thinks.

11

"**WHY IS THAT** cat such a little shit?" Danielle asks through her tears.

And there he is. Henry. Perched on top of the fridge one rear leg dangling: emotionless green eyes, vertical pupils showing a pejorative stare from on high. He is a tabby cat. Cute name for a nasty character, she thinks. Where he lies now he shows a snowy white V beneath his chin and four hoary paws so he looks like he just put on the tabby cat outfit, that he's really spirit white and the beige and black strips are for show to be put away once everyone is asleep so he can roam the night like a ghost. He languidly drops from fridge-top to counter to floor in near soundless landings.

He walks oddly for a cat. His head bobs. Up and down up and down as he crosses the floor. You would think it a limp but it's a Henry habit. It should be comical but this is Henry. Each time he walks by he stares straight ahead, one slight movement by anyone and his eyes shift toward the unwelcome action in a sidelong glance. He will not run. He will not play. He will allow only Stanley to touch him and then just briefly, like he's so sensitive each human finger is a scrape on his fur. He bobs dismissively away. She raises her hand. The sideways glance. Like a middle finger.

"Why do you call him Henry?" she says.

"He looks like a Henry," Stanley says. "I was going to call him Qubit but not many would understand it. He has the behaviours of a qubit."

"What's a qubit?" she asks.

"Precisely," he says.

They sit at the kitchen table. It is a wooden rectangle, minimalist, as is most furniture in the house. Danielle has returned from her parents, emotionally bruised from the encounter. She sips her Glenlivet slowly and tracks of tears line her cheeks. He must find a way to comfort her.

Again the father rejection. He would like to hurt that man. He knows how it would turn out should he try and he dare not say such a thing to the loving daughter, but the man is a dolt, a big, blustering, bobble-headed dullard. Does he know what he's doing to his only daughter?

So he's lost his already *defunct* job. Wire weaving. It reminds Stanley of the gutted stone remains in his home town of Huddersfield. Once huge textile mills now lie in ruins reclaimed by nature's vegetation. One time a centre of the *woollens* industry all is gone now replaced by universities and specialty manufactories.

His mother has emailed her weekly missive. There is to be a chrome statue erected at the fork of two roads in Liversedge. Commemorating the Luddites. 1812 now 2012. He recalls his history. Unrest in north England in 1812: a rising, men smashing machines, not at all comprehending the changing world of the Industrial Revolution. Two hundred years and now an anniversary of failure. What did those fools accomplish? This is precisely what Mel Buckworth is *now*: a member of the unskilled; a man in the midst of a new upheaval he cannot grasp; a Luddite in the current usage of the word.

Stanley shakes off his thoughts.

"Henry is just a name, darling," he says. He has forgotten her feelings, failed her once again.

"I've got a better name!"

"I'm sure you do. Look, how can I help you? There must be something ..."

"Mister Walk-On-By!"

"What?"

"I'm going to call him Mister Walk-On-By! He's such a little shit."

When she swears he knows she's not herself.

"Why don't we go upstairs? The lads should be home soon."

"And you don't want them to see me like this."

"Not at all, I just thought there'll be noise ..."

"Never do to have a woman in tears, would it! Especially with Will and Michael! They wouldn't know what to do!"

"That's not fair, Danielle."

"So tell me what *is* fair, Stanley. What do you think of a man who turns on his daughter when she finds her own values? He won't even speak to me, Stanley!"

"He wants you to leave me."

"He thinks I'm a slut!"

"Danielle, I'm sure he'd never ..."

"My mom and he married when she was nineteen! What's the difference? I'm supposed to get married? I should be a virgin? He won't *talk* to me!"

Her final sentence resolves in more tears. Her eyes are so beautiful when she cries. He loves her eyes. He kneels in front of her. She places her arms around him and hugs him close. He almost loses his footing but grasps the kitchen table leg allowing the moment to turn to intimacy.

He feels her tears on his lips. She is so warm. She is so wounded. He can't think of what he should do. He remains in her arms, his lips at her ear whispering softly: "Shhhhh" until she stops crying. She looks at him. Shimmering diamonds her eyes. Suddenly a smile.

"We should go upstairs, Stanley."

"I don't mind, Danielle, if the boys see you."

"It's not that. I think I'm scaring Henry."

"Good. He needs scaring! The little shit!"

She laughs. He has done something. She stands, pulling him upward with her. She holds him very close, body to body, lips to lips.

"I'm not going to break up with you no matter what you think," she says.

"Thank you."

"You take care of me."

"I try."

"You're not like any man I've ever met. You're kind and sweet ..."

"And quirky."

"Just a little. What am I going to do?"

They walk hand in hand up the steps. Henry streaks past them as they ascend, on his own mission to claim his choice place on the windowsill outside the blinds so he's not really *in* the room. There he can observe the gusts out in the cold and the scampering squirrels across the porch roof while keeping an eye on the silly humans he lives with.

He sits on the windowsill like a sphinx.

A tabby sphinx.

A ghost beneath.

A quantum qubit.

12

ACHIEVING A DOCTORATE of Philosophy in Computer Science at the University of Waterloo is a complex and challenging process. It comprises a variety of requirements, each of which must be mastered to achieve the whole. Of the range of research programs available to him, Stanley Best has centred on two fields rather than one: Quantum Computing (with Nanotechnology) as well as a study on the progress of Artificial Intelligence. He is supported in this, what some said was an overarching challenge, by his various scholarships and his already established efforts with the Cheriton School of Computer Science. The school within the University has become the largest academic concentration of Computer Science researchers in Canada and one of the top twenty in the world. Stanley Best is out there on the bleeding edge of the new informational world.

And he loves it.

Not for him the startups of the Velocity Centre. No new games or fibre optic outerwear or the allure of optical display glass or any such thing for which his roommate Will Baker pines. Will is American. California. MIT. He worships capitalism. He searches for the next new thing which will get him a Velocity startup grant which will, in turn, give him the power to expand his planned app or company or secret algorithm or whatever. He wants *not* to retire at age twenty-five, having offered himself the choice by becoming very wealthy while very young. It hasn't been working quite the way he'd planned … so far.

Will is a short, pear-shaped guy. Very American in his dress: mostly a blazer, khakis and dockers but for casual days when he can be found in a hoodie and jeans. His glasses seem an inch thick expanding his deep grey eyes, resting on a pug nose in a round face, ears slightly elfin, topped by carrot-coloured hair. Ayn Rand is his favourite author after Martin Fowler because both will help get him what he seeks. He may appear meek but so does the frog before its tongue snaps up the prey.

And that is the irony around Will Baker. Currently he owes three months on his share of the rent. He no longer contributes to food. Capitalism seems to be working against him. He is so obsessed with his crusade for a magical app that he's losing his tutorial position and running out the remains of his scholarship. As a foreign student he pays what Stanley and Michael do, the premium for international students attending UW. It is beginning to look like he will be going home, taking a job in Silicon Valley in some servile position for a meagre few hundred thousand a year. He has asked Stanley for this thoughts on an app, but Stanley never gets back to him. Will knows he means to, but that is Stanley. Pre-occupied narcissist.

He has asked Michael as well for a loan but Michael lives frugally, his Kenyan background so contrary to Will's American consumer lifestyle. Will would never concern himself with the global philanthropic programs or third world sustainability devices for which Michael Selel is so passionate. Michael wants to give back to the world he has so fortuitously escaped. Michael wants technology to brighten the futures of African youth, bringing them access to the tools they need in order to do as he did, get out and give back. Michael is constantly searching out those who will hear his appeals and provide the resources required to make change for the Third World's poor and untenable.

He looks like a young man built for the long run. Tall and rangy in that East African way, Michael's face is noble, all ebony angles and smooth, flawless skin. His hawk nose gives him dignity, his deep brown eyes offer an air of wisdom and his hands are especially graceful. He dresses modestly, usually a white shirt and coloured sweater with dark trousers. He buys his clothes from Value Village. He places no import in looks. He is a man in search of those illusive altruistic venues to meet humanity's most basic needs. His has been a long road from his village school in Kikima, to Machakos High School, to the University of Nairobi, then to the University of Waterloo. His extraordinary grades and determination have brought him on scholarship to Canada. Michael says he will never retire. Saving the world is a lifetime of work.

The other thing Michael discovered once out of Kikima was the guitar. It seemed as though his fingers were made to draw subtle emotion from each touch of a string. He learned to play the instrument not as others by strumming but with both hands picking and pressing precisely, each note its own piece of information. His guitar is not an expensive one—a Gibson, Ibana or Martin—but a simple old Washburn 200 which he makes sound like an angelic harp. And when he sings his accented baritone harmonizes with his music in arpeggios of melody. As Dani said to him after hearing him play "Blackbird": "I know that song well but I didn't know it was so precise, like a bird's notes."

Will and Michael have been the peripheries of Stanley's home and social life. Yet neither of his friends' ideals appeal at all to Stanley for whom learning is a goal in itself. It is why he selected such esoteric fields of research neither of which will likely see their culmination in his lifetime, yet will fill that lifetime with wonder and rapture and no doubt a few kudos to applaud his exceptional mind. He is cocky. It is hard not to be in this world of education to which he is so attracted and so very, very successful. It turns out the double barrelled challenge has not been perilous for him at all. Hard work, yes. Deep thought, of course. Yet he revels in challenge and quite literally believes in finding philosophic synergies within the algorithmic logic and labyrinthine heuristics of ever advancing technology.

Currently however, none of them is thinking about their work. All three are seated at their kitchen table ruminating on a far more byzantine subject than mere computer science. It is a different science this one, a social science. One in which none of them has had much experience. As they drink their Kenyan coffee (bestowed by Michael's mother's monthly care package) and gnaw on their Nature Valley Almond Crunch Bars, they shift in their chairs, uncomfortable with the problem presented them.

"I'm not sure I did quite the right thing," Stanley says.

"Well, man, when you went off to bed how did she seem?" Michael asks.

"I don't know. She'd stopped crying. Slept well. Got off to class early this morning."

"Listen, dude, you stopped her cryin'. You're golden," Will adds.

"She wasn't smiling when she left this morning."

"She kiss you?"

"Yeah."

"So it's all good!"

"It's going to continue, you know. She's positively *gutted* about her dad. He's a bloody toad. Won't see her. Won't speak to her! He's pissed about her living here. I thought she was going to leave me yesterday."

"But she didn't, did she!" Michael says.

"Yet she will, someday, I'm afraid."

"That's just your insecurity talking," Will says.

"Look at her. Look at me!"

"You better start looking inside her, man," Michael says. "She's a sweet person. She's a wonderful girl. If she leaves it might well be your own fault."

"Nice thing to say," Stanley replies.

"But she won't, don't you see?" Michael says. "She says she loves you, Stanley, and I am sure she means it. That girl doesn't play those games other girls play."

"How would you know?" Will says.

"Alright. I don't," Michael says. "Anyway, Stanley, you look very good! Perhaps not approaching Will's sartorial splendour, but you've got your look together now. I can't see any nerd left under those expensive clothes!"

"What d'you mean by sartorial splendour?" Will says, his challenge ignored in the face of the greater need.

"This is all very nice, fellows, but what can I do to help her?" Stanley asks.

"Beside what you've done?" Michael says.

"Yes. This state of affairs can't go on forever."

"You and the dad," Will says.

"Pretty much."

"Way I see it you've got one way to go. We look at this as a conundrum. You know, like an algorithmic miscalculation."

"Will, this isn't that."

"I see it though, Will's meaning that is," Michael says. "If we make it fit that format we have a better chance of solving it."

"This is ridiculous." Stanley mutters.

"You asked for our help, yes?" Michael says.

"I did."

"So let us help you."

Will has been quiet ... thinking.

"So, this kind of boils down to analytics," he says. "The platform, of course, will be regulated by Stanley's actions."

"Platform? There is no ..."

"Ah, but there is. Yes I see. We must alter the dynamics between you," Michael says.

"The problem is the father!" Stanley wails.

"Exactly! But you've been focusing on the daughter!" Will says.

"Now wait just one moment," Stanley tries to reverse the process.

"Too late for that, my friend," Michael says. "There's an entire new dimension involved we haven't even considered."

"Exactly." Will again. "The actual source of the problem is the father ..."

"Thus the end resolution is the father!" Michael adds triumphantly.

"How is that?" Stanley says.

"It's simple, Stanley," Will says, "you go to the source."

"Oh no!"

"Oh yes, my man." The flat vowels of America lift triumphantly from Will's smiling lips.

"He's an ape! He could kill me! I *sleep* with his daughter. You expect me to approach him calmly and tell him ... tell him ... tell him what?"

"That you're concerned about Dani."

"Danielle."

"Speak in his language, Stanley. You're worried about her, aren't you?"

"He'll just say the solution is for me to disappear. Indeed, he may even take it into his hands to eventuate that."

"Don't be absurd," Michael says. "He loves his daughter. You love her too. Heads together to make her feel better. What finer solution than that?"

"I could email him."

"Ixnay, Stanley!" Will says. "Emails are out. We know he's a physical guy. You've got to shake this guy's hand, share a beer, talk some sports ..."

"I know nothing of sports!"

"Sure you do ... soccer!"

"Of course," Michael says, "Danielle plays football and he himself is a sporting man, he will understand football."

"Wait," Will says. "You call it football you're already fucked. It's soccer here and don't forget it."

"Only an American—" Michael says.

"Here we go—" Will says.

"The *world* knows it as football!" Michael insists. The beginning of another heated and well-worn discussion.

"We are in the doldrums here, fellows," Stanley says. "Not helping my situation."

Both of his friends stand, leaning over him.

"You arrange to see him." Michael says.

"Don't tell Dani," Will says.

"Danielle!" Stanley says.

"Soccer/football, Dani/Danielle ... you have a translation problem to work on Stanley. Better get to it."

"But what do I, erm, how do I ..."

It is too late. They walk away toward the living room laboratory. They argue as they depart. Subject changed. Soccer/football. Dani/Danielle. Apples and oranges.

Binary thought, applied to a quantum question.

13

MEL BUCKWORTH AND Gary Wilson are in a small bar on Highland Road, a retail street lined by old style open air plazas filled with small businesses. To the south are houses built in the fifties. North of it are high density sixties and seventies apartments. Traffic growls up and down the road at one point two lanes building to three with a left turn building to four. It is always busy.

This little bar seating maybe fifty has been around for all of it. It calls itself ONE: a quiet, comfortably used kind of place, the tables wooden, the chairs not quite all the same, the bar itself a U shape, barstools cushioned with cracked plastic tops. The drinks are cheap and the food is good. Mel and Gary have come here for years. A few beers. Steak and chips.

They aren't regulars. The regulars sit at the bar. The angry men sit at the front window.

Mel and Gary are on stools at the raised table by the front window each nursing his drink: rye and ice for Mel, rye and coke for Gary. They watch traffic pass. This evening is their promised reunion. It's been a month since Erban let its last people go. Six weeks since Mel's exclusion. The two are currently celebrating rage. It has not been the best of times for either of them.

Mel spent the first two weeks in shock, finding it hard to conceive this was actually him, his life. He watched Pat go to work each day. Watched her come home. Ate supper when she called him. When she tried to talk about the thing, he would leave, denying his own denial. Otherwise he watched sports on TV played on his hockey teams made calls and received calls from other ousted Erbanites read the newspaper's outrage and felt the anger grow within him as the size of it all sank in. Nearly two hundred out of work. In winter. Just after Christmas.

Then he discovered his severance would be taxed. No one had told him that. Fucking fake friendly Herbert Trimble hadn't mentioned it at all. Despite his bluster know-it-all Stan Oblauski hadn't realized it. Even Gary Wilson had had no idea. It was Wilson's wife, Mona, who had worked it out. He'd phoned Mel about it. The letter from Revenue Canada had put it all into perspective. He had not quite so much capital as he'd thought he'd had.

The only thing true in his mind was his anger.

His next two weeks he worried over money. He watched Pat go to work each day. Watched her come home. Ate supper when she called him. When she tried to talk about things he would leave in frustration. He played on his teams cautioned by the Friday night guys to *tone it down a bit*, watched more sports yet it seemed each game was *rigged* by the refs, made and got fewer Erbanite phone calls most of them empty protestations and it all began to sink in. He felt his wrath build.

It was MJ who got him on the computer to look into retraining. He'd never been good with electronic things. He still couldn't believe they had actually invaded his life. From the kids' calculators to Pat's Olivetti disc typewriter to a family Commodore 64 to personal PCs and Apples to email and internet to Google and Facebook to cell phones and smart phones to robotics and artificial intelligence he understood little of it. Still MJ said this was the best way to go without the demeaning personal interview.

They found the required pages on the Employment Ontario website:

- *how long you have been unemployed, or working your temporary job, and looking for work*
- *places you have applied and positions you have applied for (e.g. cover letters, CV and responses from potential employers)*
- *what level of education you reached*
- *where you worked before, for how long and what skills you needed for that work*
- *what skills you want to get and where you can get trained in them*
- *information showing the skills and job you want to train for are in demand*

So how would he answer these humbling questions: how long this and that, where did and would you, what kinds of education, what nature of skills, who are *you* really to be here on this page? Take a look at yourself you failed fool then provide us with answers. The demand on his privacy disturbed him. Were they seeking an excuse to refuse him? Then came the worst ...

> *To apply to Second Career, you'll work with an employment services agency, where people are trained to help you decide if this program is right for you—and, if it is, to complete your application.*
> *Find an agency in your community and make an appointment.*

Make an appointment bring in your life what are your skills what were you trained for what do you own who are your kin how much is your income where do you live when will you die why are you here sit down there and fill all that out again what is the matter with you make another appointment! No matter which way they searched it came down to that personal interview. They tried another avenue, MJ working the computer, Mel sitting stunned, feeling his anger swell. Then they came to Employment Insurance and the infuriating diminishment of its bureaucratese.

> ***Important Note:*** *to prove your eligibility and to receive any payment you may be entitled to, you are required to complete bi-weekly reports by internet or telephone. Failure to do so can mean a loss of benefits.*

He would not belittle himself with a shameful bi-weekly telephone talk. They selected the internet instead. It was poetic in its officious elegance. It was also impossible for Mel to comprehend its numinous terms. It went on and on every sentence a judgement every phrase a warning each word dripping with condemnation until its culmination reverting to a command to use the telephone and talk with someone and so be further rebuked.

- *If you disconnect or exit the report before completing it, your information will not be saved and you will need to start over.*
- *If your report is missing information, it cannot be accepted for processing. Make sure that you have all your information ready to enter before you begin your report.*
- *If you stay on one page for more than 10 minutes, your session will be disconnected.*
- *Do not leave your computer unattended while logged in to your online report.*
- *When you have finished your report, end your session by clicking on* ***Log Out****.*
- *Each time you access the Internet, your browser automatically saves a copy of the web pages you have visited. Make sure you clear your browser's cache after each session to protect your account information.*

- *If you receive an "error 404" message when you try to log in to the Internet Reporting Service, there could be a problem with your browser; try the following solutions:*
    - *clear your browser's cache;*
    - *delete the cookies from your browser; or*
    - *use another browser.*

Accessing the Internet Reporting Service
Shortly after you apply for benefits, we will mail you an EI benefit statement. The statement includes your access code—a four-digit number which is printed on the shaded area at the top of the benefit statement. You need the access code and your Social Insurance Number (SIN) to submit reports and to get information about your claim.

Keep your access code safe and store it separately from your SIN.

By providing and submitting your SIN and access code, we will consider you to have signed your online report.

If we need more information about your report, you will receive a message asking you to call us during business hours.

"MJ, what the fuck is all this?" Mel says finally.

"Ease up, dad. It's just their website."

"What is this shit? Only ten minutes then they kick you off? What about guys like me? I don't know this crap! Twice a week? You miss, you make a mistake, and they own you?"

"It's okay. I could do it for you."

"I don't want you doing anything for me! I don't want anything to do with this, or re-training or anything else where they try to take your soul away."

"Okay dad ..."

"Second Career my ass! What happens when I show up to some school and there *you* are teaching me this computer stuff, making me look a fool just because I was born too early and didn't die early enough!"

"You need to sit down."

Burbling rage.

"I'm not going back to some school run by people who wanna control me and I'm sure as hell not gonna sit in some classroom with all these kids laughing at me and the teachers half my age! Okay, I don't have paper skills! I've got skills with my hands, my ... my experience, my whole life gave me skills, for fuck sake!"

"I know that, Dad."

"And I'm not gonna take their unemployment ..."

"It's employment insurance, not ..."

"I don't give a god damn what it is!"

Purpling fury.

"Shut that fucking computer off!"

"Dad, it's not the computer ..."

"Then what the hell is it, huh? Why don't you tell me? Tell me why I get canned so some robot can take my place? How is it a guy who paid his taxes, followed the law, raised a family, coached a lot of kids ... how is it that guy's now useless?"

"Why are you taking this out on me?"

"I'm not!"

"Sure as hell seems like it, Dad. I was trying to help."

"I don't *need* your help! You're my son for crissake! You shouldn't be teaching me! It should be me teaching you! What the hell happened while I was living and working every god damned day? Where the hell do we go from here?"

"Tell you what, I'm outa here. You wanna have a hissy fit you have it by yourself or shout some more at Mom, why don't you! What the fuck has happened to you?"

"Don't talk to me like that!"

"Don't like it much, eh? You get mad at me and Mom and Dani and now the whole world because things aren't going your way for once! Things are changing, Dad! Why the hell do you think I deliver pizzas? 'Cause I've got no paper skills, no college, no nothing! I don't want to put myself through an interview any more than you do. So I work!"

"Okay, okay. I understand that. I'm sorry I took it out on you. Still, you see me as pizza delivery boy?"

"No, I don't. And I don't want it either. But now you've seen the alternative. Why don't you call up your buddies? Some of them must have work for you. At least you know people. You've got connections. I thought once you'd use them for me, give me a leg up. You never even thought of it, did you?"

"Yeah, I did, but I thought you should try on your own first. Your mother didn't want me going to friends."

"Well go now, Dad, for yourself."

"I don't know if I could work for a friend."

"After a while you won't be so proud."

And with those words his son ended it. Turned and walked out. He discovered then that his son was no child. He may have dressed like a kid and played computer games and delivered pizza, which is what Mel thought boys do, yet his son clearly knew about his and Pat's troubles. He could parse the family dynamics. He could read his father's character like a book. And in that moment of perception Mel Buckworth felt sudden shame.

In the next two weeks he searched for jobs. He bought newspapers: the KW *Record the Toronto Star the Toronto Sun* he even went to the internet. There were jobs alright ... for five years' experience for apprentices for technicians for journeymen for mechanics for engineers for software software software ... and then there were jobs at minimum wage and commission ... for drivers, cleaners, dog walkers, food services, greeters, meeters, and sales sales sales.

Finally he called a couple of friends only to find times were tough this year, there was a recession happening, but they'd be on the lookout for him. So he watched Pat go to work each day. Watched her come home. Ate supper when she called him. When she tried to talk about things he refused to answer, not until he had some solution and that looked less likely each day.

And he seethed even more.

14

WILSON RETURNS TO their window seats with two more drinks. Doubles. It hadn't been any better for him. He had taken the traditional route: applied for employment insurance, looked into retraining. His face grew more lined and bruised as he told his story.

"All I can say, Mel, you got it right about interviews."

"Didn't go well?"

"If you call sitting in a waiting room with a number in your hand then you get to see some bad-tempered clerk in a cramped little room going well? No."

Wilson takes a long drink.

"So what happened?"

"I had a woman clerk. Sat at her desk, never moved when I come in, never even told me her name. First thing she did, not even hello just asked my name. Then she swivels in her chair so she's facing her computer, her back to me. Then she asked every question for the next half hour over her shoulder and typed it all in. It was like I wasn't there at all. Only needed my voice. Could've done it on the phone."

"That's crap."

Mel drinks as well.

"Tell me about it. So once she's done she swivels back all baggy faced and hard lookin' and she starts going over jobs. She says I got no skills! I say I was a foreman, run 60 men, I got leadership skills."

"How'd she take that?" Mel asks.

Wilson drinks.

"She sort of half smiled like in a nasty way, like she's outa my league, y' know? Then she says what's wrong with Walmart. I tell her my wages the past five years."

"That should've done it!" Mel says. He smiles as he lifts his glass.

"Made it worse, Mel. This woman says those days are over. She says the world's not what it was. She says guys like me, all the boomer guys, had it easy but no more. Today it's *value* of the employee. What the fuck that means I don't know."

"What'd you say?"

"I asked her did she mean I had no value. She didn't answer. She just turned back to her computer and typed a coupla things, then she told me t' expect my first bank deposit in twenty-eight days if I'd gave her the right information. Made me feel like a piece of shit."

"Christ!"

"Yeah. If she'd been a man I woulda clocked her."

"Goddamn right."

"Listen, let's get a bottle before the LicBo closes. I'm about ready to tie one on."

Seething.

"Yeah. And I know where to drink it!"

They each down their drinks, leave cash on the table, put on their coats and depart.

Cold, clear dark of night. Mid-March. Everything frozen. The weak yellow glow of a light pole situated behind Erban Industries. The building looming black as a tomb. Two vehicles sit near the loading dock. A 2007 Ford F150 with motor running, clouds of exhaust in the subzero night, beside it a 2009 Silverado, also running. In the weak light both trucks look black but the Chevy is red in daylight.

The twenty-sixer of CC is half gone. The two men sit in the red truck drinking from plastic glasses. They have been talking for an hour. Heater blasting. They had music but killed it, their words more important. They refill often. It is like adolescence. Neither man has done this since way back in their lives. Teenagers. Drinking outside. Hiding in the dark.

"So you said," Wilson slurs a little, "said you thought they're movin' outa here soon?"

"That's right," Mel replies. "I heard from a friend with the Region."

"What I like about you, you got friends all over."

"Mostly from sports but yeah, they come in handy."

"Some more?"

The proffered bottle is waggled in the air between seats. Mel's glass comes up. Wilson pours it three quarters full then refills his own.

"Fuckin' bastards," Mel says.

"Who?

"You know … Erban."

"Yeah. Fuckin' right."

The glasses touch in their toast, the scrape of plastic on plastic. It is their fury which chimes like crystal.

"I wish we could do somethin'," Wilson says.

"Yeah. Wish we could get in, take the tow motor an' jus' ram everything in sight!"

"Stuff's all likely lined up by the loading door."

"Prob'ly." Mel fumbles his drink, snares it before it spills, smiles like he's scored a goal.

"Whoop! Glad you got that, buddy. Don't need Mona smellin' booze in the truck."

"Wish we could make some mark, Gary. Let 'em know we know what they're doin'."

"Yeah."

Seething silence as they drink. Both look out the windshield at the loading dock in the back of Erban Industries. The light from above makes its struts invisible in shadow but the top is glassy like ice.

"Hey, you still got a pretty good arm?" Wilson says.

"Why? You plannin' a snowball fight?"

"Nope. Just got an idea."

"What."

"We *can* make a mark."

"How?"

"I got gas in the back for the snow blower."

"Wait, lemme guess. The loading dock's made of wood."

"Right and …"

"We pour the gas on it!"

"Yup."

"We can't light it. What happens if we're too close an' it goes up?"

"That's where you come in, Mel, my lad! You're the one with the arm." Wilson dangles the bottle by its neck. Mel smiles.

"Molotov cocktail?"

"Why the fuck not?"

"You know how to make one?" Mel asks.

"Sure! Ever watch History Channel?"

"Alright, how?"

"Gotta finish this first," Wilson says, pouring the last of the booze.

"Save a bit in your glass," Mel says as they drink.

"Why?"

"Li'l toast at the end."

"Right!"

They set their glasses on the dash and exit the truck. It is so cold their faces tighten and sting. Mel dips his hands into the truck bed, finds the plastic gas container and pulls it out. His hands are already freezing. He unscrews the top, pulls out the yellow spout then screws it back on. Wilson has rags. He holds the bottle as Mel pours the gas. Not well. Too much spillage. Wilson tries it himself. Right hand holds the bottle left hand the pour. Comedy of errors. They laugh like children. The bottle finally fills. Mel stuffs a rag into the neck.

"Mel, that's a mistake."

"What. I seen it like that on TV."

"You're watchin' the wrong shows."

"Huh?"

"Yeah, History channel, like I said. You light the fuckin' thing an' it's burnin' so you try throwin' the bottle then what if the rag comes out?"

"What then?"

"Rag I was holding's got plenty gas on it. Cap the bottle. Tie the rag around the bottom. Light it up. Throw the bottle using its neck. Like a German potato masher!"

"Yeah. I get it. More direction and farther."

"Let's get our trucks outa here first. Down the lane in the shadows."

They leave the bottle. Return to their trucks. They pull into the side of the plant away from the light. The vehicles vanish in shadow. They walk back around the building. Wilson has brought the two plastic glasses from his truck and sets them on the ground a good distance from the dock. Then Wilson takes the container, climbs up the loading bay steps and pours gasoline all over the wooden surface. Walking backwards he starts from a corner back to the steps. The container empties as he reaches them.

He walks down the steps and back to Mel. Mel has the bottle in hand by the neck. Wilson pulls out a Bic, lights the rag, it flares quickly. From twenty metres Mel throws: the bottle arcs up turning and turning bright flame in the air hits the loading door smashes and drops then a white whoosh of combustion. Blue fire grows yellow as it climbs the air. The fire turns to conflagration as flames follow the gas down the cracks down support poles scorching more blue into yellow. For a moment the two men stand frozen in the radiant beauty of revenge in the heat of their fury made manifest.

They touch glasses. Toss down their drinks. Throw the glasses into the icy snow. Crush the glasses with their boots.

"Let's get outa here," Wilson says.

"Before someone sees."

They start up rev up get out of this place. They drive too quickly. Adrenalin. Wilson in the lead suddenly slows. Mel jams the brakes. He knows why. Wilson feels too suspicious. Still, there's likely no one around to see them in this wasteland of mausoleums of twentieth century industry. But there might be a night watchman somewhere in the boneyard.

Change? Yes. There has been change. They have wrought change and a measure of retaliation. Mel glances back through his rear view mirror. Flames lick the sky. He looks forward again. Wilson's truck is weaving.

It looks too much like panic.

By the time they have stopped in a 7-Eleven parking lot on Ottawa Street they are frightened. The triumph of revenge is fleeting. Now they are just two terrified men looking goggle-eyed at each other as the trucks sit back to front so the drivers' doors are side by side. Neither of them has ever stepped outside the law before, even as youngsters or adolescents. Perhaps lifting a candy bar but this, this is uncharted terrain legally ethically personally. They have glimpsed that part of their untamed selves despite their social training, their good solid lives, their responsibilities to sons daughters wives friends society, all the expectations of others. It is a strange new attitude for them.

Mel's many encounters with the adrenalin rush of athletics come to his aid now, despite the fear. All the way here, following Wilson, he had had his own dread and knew if Wilson were stopped, they would be done. He'd pulled out and passed his friend, slowing him down from in front. Signalling them into the 7-Eleven.

"You okay? You gotta get straight, man. Drive home. You were all over the road back there. You wanna get busted?"

"Jesus, no. I just couldn't get my mind to stop racing. I wanted to go back."

"We can't go back."

"What if we left somethin'?"

Mel gets out of his vehicle, looks in the back of Wilson's truck and returns, smiling.

"You can relax, bud. The gas can's in the back. The bottle's in pieces. We're good."

"We left the glasses. What about tracks?"

"We crushed 'em. The fire'll melt our footprints. Take 'er easy, man. We better split up in case somebody saw us."

"Christ, Mel, I can't believe we just did that! It was crazy, unbelievable ..."

"I know. Take it easy, Gary."

"But that was ... was arson! What if we left somethin' behind? What if we left tracks?"

"Easy. Just breathe. Calm down, Gary."

Wilson breathes slowly in out. He has lost his red flush. Mel gets into his truck. He too wants to return but knows it would be a mistake. He's seen TV shows where the fire bug returns to watch. Not going to happen.

"Okay. We should go home. It's almost three. So whatever you do, don't tell Mona nothing, alright? And when you get home take your coat off in your garage. Smells like gas. You okay now?"

"Yeah. Yes."

"You gotta focus, Gary. You're only five blocks from home."

"Yeah. Sorry, Mel. Not somethin' I normally do with my nights out. I'm good now. Kinda sobered up. I'll make it from here."

"Yeah. Time goes quick when you're having fun! Drive slow and safe."

"You too, man."

"Remember. Not a word. This is just for us."

"I know."

Mel gets home easily, no traffic this time of night. He drives a straight run, then left off Ottawa to Homer Watson Boulevard, two quick turns, then goes north along Belmont through Kitchener. He passes St. Mary's Hospital, then crosses Highland Road then Victoria Street. He drives through Belmont Village and the invisible border of Kitchener/Waterloo. On the narrow streets in Waterloo he tries to pull into his driveway. Pat's and MJ's cars are there ahead of him. He blows out an expletive. Leaves his truck on the road. Grabs his extra keys from the truck's glove box, moves the two cars out, opens the garage, pulls the truck in, pulls down the door and replaces the cars where they'd been.

Before he goes in he removes his overcoat, leaving it in the truck. He opens the side door leading down to the basement and up to the kitchen. Inside he can hear MJ cursing the way he does when he's playing his games. Obviously he's wearing headphones. Mel goes downstairs takes off his shirt sniffs the sleeves then soaks the shirt then his jeans and his socks for good measure.

He returns upstairs, shuts off the lights, then continues up to the second floor trying not to make the floor squeak. He passes Pat's room. The door is closed. He takes a shower in his ensuite bath then puts on some boxers and climbs into bed. All the troubles of the past weeks are abruptly gone. All the might have dones should have dones could have dones all the whys and why nots all the pity and blame are diminished. In the end he has accomplished what lay beneath every minute of every day since his termination. He has stolen victory from a hard loss. He's still drunk, he knows, yet cannot help but smile at this night.

He has done something.
He has struck back.

15

AMRIT KHADRI HAS been a constable in the Waterloo Region Police Service for sixteen years. He has served in uniform in every Patrol Division: the North Division serving Waterloo, to the Central in Kitchener, to the South located in Cambridge, Doon and the Trillium Industrial Park, and even to the Rural North Division serving Woolwich and Wellesley townships.

He has operated often in the Community Resources, Communications, and Media Relations departments mostly due to his easygoing, relaxed and friendly personality. He has handed out tickets, pulled apart duelling husbands and wives, solved robberies, and performed other active police business but has never been involved in a car chase or used his firearm, currently a police issue Glock 17. He has handed out one famous citation for reckless operation of a vehicle to a fifteen-year-old Mennonite boy weaving all over Floradale side road as he tried to hold off his opponent, another fifteen-year-old in a second buggy with a much faster horse.

By and large Amrit Khadri considers his work interesting and enjoyable. He has not developed that cynicism which often comes from dealing with the unruly or unfortunate of the Region. He thinks people are basically good though some can be brought to certain choices more quickly than most. He takes pride in the uniform and what it stands for and is careful to maintain a positive image both on the job and off.

That uniformed, clear cut arrangement has been somewhat altered by his being assigned the position of detective in the past two years. He has found increased incentive from the more analytical, investigative side of policing, if not the increased number of hours he puts in *off* the job. But for a slight gain in weight, some investigations often involve lengthy periods of being seated, he has aged well and loves his work.

He is tall and slightly paunchy though keeps himself in reasonable shape knowing it's not only good for his health but good for his ego as well. He has an interesting face, at once cheerful and open. His face is a series of planes. He possesses a fine bone structure. When he smiles, which he does often, his teeth gleam. He has dark brown eyes which contain a charming glow. He wears his hair short and though he shaves daily always seems to possess a slight swarthy shadow.

Born in Gravesend, England he is fifty-one years old. The son of a traditional couple who emigrated from Mumbai (then Bombay) to the centre of the Empire, he grew up as an English boy: football, video games, pub nights, and girls. He did well in his new home until the day the old traditions infected it. His parents had come to him on his sixteenth birthday informing him they had made a match with a lovely girl, good family, fine dowry, from India. Everyone would return to the old country in two years' time when he and the girl would be married.

There were other kids whose ties with India could not be severed and stories went around, mostly about girls departing for marriages they neither agreed with nor wanted. He hadn't expected it in *his* life. He'd refused. The family had quarrelled bitterly. In the end Amrit had chosen to leave home, cursed by his father, guilt-ridden from his mother's tears, to find a way to continue his life on his own. He knew his father and knew the man would never back down. So he had decided, with money he'd saved, to immigrate to Canada.

He was fortunate. He had an uncle on his mother's side living in a city called Brampton. The uncle was a successful teacher at Sheridan College. He took the boy in and ensured his education, instilling in young Amrit a strong sense of principle which led to an interest in law enforcement. After the necessary courses which led to Aylmer Police College and the process of recruitment at Waterloo Region Police, Amrit was accepted and began his new somewhat solitary life.

When his mother died he returned to England for the funeral. His father never spoke to him. He decided it best to leave things that way and after a week of visiting friends he returned home to Waterloo. He had lived in a number of apartments and town houses throughout the tri-cities, depending on where he was stationed. As a detective those Divisions took on less definitive meaning as he would follow cases to any area of the Region.

He finally settled in a fine condo complex in Waterloo on Willow Street called Waterknell Place. Lovely setting, expensive but comfortable, he found others living there to be friendly and highly educated. Normally multi-habitation buildings are so mewhat anonymous but this place proved different and a fine asset to the outgoing, social Amrit Khadri.

He has never thought of a family. Occasionally, he supposes, he has recognized the damage done by his parents and their culture. Though he looks East Indian he acts as any Englishman, or Canadian for that matter, might. He has dated often and even developed a few long term relationships but something, somewhere would always emerge to veer him away from the track of commitment. Perhaps he was too relaxed for some women, perhaps in their ways they knew he was not a marriageable man. He felt he did well enough on his own. He had hobbies: tennis, which kept him reasonable in shape and reading, at which he was voracious. He was also an excellent cook.

When he wasn't working.

This day he is at Columbia Street, in a small office, going over some notes on a targeted assault he'd followed up and concluded. A local and a university kid, a girl, and lots of beer. He discovered the boy had planned it. Soon, he hoped, it would go to trial. As Khadri prepares his materials Sergeant Robert Reinhardt knocks softly on the glass door. As he enters Amrit rises to shake his hand. They have been friends for years.

"Don't stand, big guy. I got something for you you're not gonna like."

"I've just been going over ..."

"I know. It's been adjourned until next month."

"How did you ..."

"I'm a detective, aren't I?"

The Sergeant smiles. He is a wiry man, very fit. He is older than Amrit yet looks ten years younger. "So, I'm afraid you've caught a date with the Fire Marshal's office. Some factory out on Trillium. They're sure it's arson. I need you to take a drive down there, see what's up. I thought you could use a bit of a break."

"I've got other assignments, Rob."

"Yeah, so now you got this one."

"Now?"

"Pretty much."

In the parking lot he finds his grey Crown Vic, 2011 and ensures everything is in place. He does this by habit. He is a careful man. Really, he uses this car almost exclusively as a detective so isn't much worried. Still, the check is regulation. He follows the rules seeing their sense. It takes him twenty minutes to get to Trillium Drive and the Erban Industries place, a For Sale sign on the property. He recalls something about its closing. He sees the Fire Marshal's vehicle in the drive and parks in front of it. A guy is sitting in the driver's seat filling out a form.

Khadri flashes his badge. He knocks on the window. It's bright but cold for March. The guy looks up. He rolls down the window. He doesn't want to leave the car's warmth.

"Detective," he says. He doesn't look like a happy man; been here a while, obviously, Amrit thinks.

"Amrit Khadri.".

"Oh, uh, Bill Hendricks."

"What d'you have?"

"Bottle shards. Molotov. Kids likely fooling around. Sale sign in front's a good invitation. Don't think they meant to cause this much damage though."

"You going to show me?"

"I guess. Yeah. You English? I thought you were an Indian."

"It's a long story," Khadri says, stock response to the usual passive racial ignorance.

Ruefully Hendricks opens the door and steps out. He puts on

gloves. His boots look dusty. He leads the way to the back of the building. Once investigators have narrowed the origin of the fire to a small enough area, they can lay down something like an archaeological grid to help when sifting through the debris. The top level of fire debris may need to be blown off to find physical evidence beneath. The loading dock is the source of the ash. It is virtually gone. The grid stretches out across the parking lot. There is still a fire truck parked, two firemen inside drinking coffee. They don't get out.

"Call came in after three this morning. Night watchman over across the street, coupla buildings down from here. By the time the trucks came the loading dock was lit up like a bonfire. But the fluid leaked inside the building, set some wood skids on fire. Only thing saved the building was all the metal on the skids. Machines, y'know. Area seems contained but I've got two guys looking. They're inside."

They pass the remains of the loading dock and enter a steel door up a set of metal stairs. Inside is cold and smells acrid with smoke and something else Khadri can't quite place. It is a huge empty shell but the corner where they entered has a number of big machines squatting useless and filthy on the cement floor. Two firefighters are poking systematically at the walls around the door. They are very careful. The insulation has burned. Not all fires are out when they seem. Khadri approaches the skids with the machines. The mysterious smell is burnt rubber.

"You don't think it started inside?" Khadri says.

"No forced entry. You can see the light at the bottom of the lift doors. Right there, see. Some of the rubber melted but it's pretty obvious."

"Okay, glass shards?"

"Base of the building. I figure somebody threw a bottle, hit the door."

"And that burned the dock?"

"Nope. They spread gasoline on the dock. Guess they didn't wanna get burned when they lit it up."

"That says to me it might not be just kids."

"How's that?"

"This place closed down some time back. A lot of people lost jobs. Maybe some of them took it personally. Embittered employees. This seems like a message. I doubt they knew about the cleft in the doors."

"Didn't find nothing."

"Let's try it again outside."

"Fuckin' cold."

"I realize that. Still, we should take a good look."

"In my car. Found part of a plastic glass in the grid. They must have been drinking. Foot stomps all round it."

"Any clear prints?"

"Partials."

"Is it bagged, the plastic?"

"'Course it is. I been at this a long while, Khadri."

"That's fine. Just asking. It might be of use. Anything from the glass shards?"

"Not enough. Smashed to smithereens."

"Fine work on finding the plastic though."

"Thanks."

"Listen, you've been out here half the night. Why don't I look around a bit? I saw you filling out your report."

"Yeah. I'd like to get that done."

"If I find anything further I'll let you know. Go ahead. You look cold."

Hendricks thanks Khadri and returns to his car. Khadri goes with him. He wants a look at the front of the building, in case someone missed a break-in.

A second car pulls in. Nice sedan, conservative beige Ford Fusion. The driver is a small man, his head just above the steering wheel. When he exits the car Khadri notes an expensive, textured wool coat, dark grey with black pants and a pair of black galoshes. His hair is salt and pepper. He wears a silly pencil moustache. He looks at Khadri through rimless steel glasses. Khadri thinks he resembles a cricket.

It appears the man is going to ignore him. He has keys and is about to enter the front office doors when Khadri steps up. The man turns sharply.

"Yes?"

"May I ask your name, sir?"

"Herbert Trimble. VP Operations for Erban."

"You do know this is a crime scene?"

"Eh. Of course. I was here earlier with the fire trucks. And you are?"

"Detective Amrit Khadri, sir." Khadri shows his badge. He holds out a hand to shake Trimble's. Trimble ignores it and turns around. He unlocks the door. Khadri, uninvited, follows him inside.

"Why are you here now, Mr. Trimble?" Khadri asks.

"I'm here to assess the damage out back and I have some files to retrieve."

Trimble keeps up his small-stepped, quick-paced walk down a hallway forcing Khadri to follow in his wake. He enters a spacious office though there is only a wooden desk and a single plush office chair along with a grey file cabinet remaining. Trimble removes his coat and galoshes. He wears a white shirt and striped blue-on-blue tie. He begins working as though Khadri didn't exist, pulling open a file shelf, running a finger over the tabs, removing one thick manila folder and setting it on his desk. Khadri notes he ensures the folder is as close to perfectly squared on the desk as possible. Trimble sits down and opens the sleeve.

Khadri steps in front of the desk and slowly places his right hand on a corner of the folder. Trimble looks up, slightly outraged at this public servant's nerve.

"What is it, detective?"

"A few minutes of your time, Mr. Trimble, and some manners might help."

"It seems there's little to say. Teenagers playing with fire, I'm told."

"I have another thought on that subject, Mr. Trimble."

"Oh?'

"This company closed down not long ago. You're moving equipment out."

"Yes."

"Erban employed over two hundred people, did it not?"

"Yes."

"You were the person responsible for terminating their employment, yes?"

"Yes. How did you know?"

"Just a guess. How'd they take it?"

"Well enough. They were given generous terms of agreement."

"No one got angry?"

"One or two ..."

"No one made threats?"

"I suppose ..."

"I require a list of your former employees, Mr. Trimble."

"That can be arranged but surely you don't think an adult did this, do you?"

"If I asked you to name three employees who might have, could you tell me?"

"If you put it that way, then yes."

"Why are you not co-operating, Mr. Trimble? Have you been terminated as well?"

The words bring Trimble to his feet. He is still a head shorter than Khadri.

"Of course not! I am *Management*! What can you possibly mean by that inference, sir?"

"Name one then," Kadri says. "Off the top of your head. Who might be a loose cannon?"

"Name one what?"

"Someone you'd suspect."

"Stan Oblauski, the Union Representative!"

"Your reason?"

"He was rude, insulting, irregular, pushy ..."

"Doing his job, you mean?"

"There are ways and ways, detective ..."

"Khadri, if you've forgotten. I think I see what you mean, however. You have a strong code of business conduct, sir, do you not?"

"Of course I do. That man had none. He was a brute."

"I see. Anyone else?"

"Well, if I had time ..."

"Oh, you do Mr. Trimble. I would like a copy of your list from cleaners to workers to management and I would like you to highlight another copy with the names of those you suspect might have done this."

"I am preparing for a move, Mr. Khadri. I haven't the time ..."

"Might I remind you again that this is now a crime scene? It could take time for investigators to go over everything. Months even."

"That's ... that's ... not possible! We have a timetable. I have a timetable!"

"The faster I get what we need the faster the investigation will go."

"Who is your supervisor?"

"Here is a card for calling in a complaint, Mr. Trimble. Please feel free. Detective Amrit Khadri. Meanwhile, I'll need that list, and your annotated version tomorrow."

"You said highlighted! Good heavens!"

"I think you are being purposefully obtuse, Mr. Trimble. You could accompany me to my office in Waterloo. We could go over the list together."

"No. I haven't the ... listen, I'll get you a list. I'll go over a copy of it tonight. If I think of anything I'll highlight ... annotate the list! Why would anyone risk this kind of thing at all?"

"Did you personally dismiss them all?"

"Of course. It was my assignment before I move on to Head Office."

"Yes. I thought that."

"Are you insinuating I had something to do with it?"

"Not the crime, Mr. Trimble. Perhaps as part of the motivation. At any rate, please bring me that list and I'll be on my way."

Amrit Khadri, a thick folder of names, addresses and work histories tucked under his arm, departs the building. He is smiling. *Turd* is the word he is thinking as he reflects on Trimble. His thoughts turn then to other subjects as he begins a search that will eventually take him to truly unexpected places, both in his work and his life.

16

ANNA JEAN BUCKWORTH spends much of her time looking out her window at the little forest on the other side of the glass. Above the treetops is a bright blue sky. It is a sky full of memories. This is what she does best now. Remember. Glaucoma has taken part of her vision. Her years in Butler Textiles have taken most of her hearing. Her age has taken her vigour. She is eighty-three. Her increasing ill health has landed her here at Pinehurst Nursing Home. Yet she still has her mind. And her memories. A great many memories. The sky and its clouds are the tablet she reads from, on the other side of the window.

She feels something coming on again. She has a cough that will not go away. She recalls often, as though it were yesterday, her children Mel, George and Mary through each of their journeys from toddlers to adulthood, until Mary developed breast cancer and wasted away. Some memories she would rather not have. She is confused and sorry over it and has heard neither son speak of it in the years since it happened. Her sons have always been distant from each other, particularly after Mary's loss. She was the glue which held them. Anna cannot fathom what would bring her sons to be like magnets unable to touch, an enigmatic force holding them apart.

She shifts her thoughts to the boys and their differences even from birth. Mel a squalling baby, an adventurous climbing toppling stout little man with his father's eyes and a kind of half smile on his face, as though he were conscious of the mischief he was causing even at two years old. Then George, the quiet baby who had slipped into the world with a minimum of discomfort and continued in that vein through his childhood. Much different from Mel, he followed his older brother constantly even when rebuffed, yet never aspired to be like him.

Mel gravitated to his father who taught him his skills in building, in sports, in fixing his old Ford Fairlane. Only in school did Mel lose his shine with marks coming in that reflected a mind not focused on the work. All other things he would have considered a challenge but Mel seemed to take school or leave it. He accepted his low marks, particularly in Reading and Writing though he seemed to have an analytical mind in mathematics and shop classes. It was just, as Anna had been told by so many, that Mel either could not or would not focus on things which did not interest him. The boy's safety net was his charm and his skill in sports from kindergarten to high school graduation. Teachers tended to overlook the missing homework or too-quickly submitted tests. This was the boy who led the school to its lofty morale and its sports championships and though he was adored, he was always humble ... taught that that was a man's proper demeanour by his father.

George, of course, went the opposite way. Shying away from sports he found freedom and challenge in books and excelled all through school. George could concentrate his intellect on advanced subject matter beyond what teachers would give him. He too became a kind of school leader, the kind every kid didn't want to be and whom every teacher and parent worshipped for his uncanny mind and polite deportment. He went on to university and a stellar career while his older brother married his high school sweetheart and got a job in a factory.

Their age difference, but more their difference in interests and skills, distanced the brothers from each other. Anna had tried several times and Mellor, their dad, did the same to get the boys involved in common projects but invariably their two distinct characters would disagree and the project would end with one or the other withdrawing.

And as children Mary would be their interlocutor, young as she was they both adored her. Mary was a soft-spoken child who could toss a baseball with Mel and build a snow castle with George. When both boys had left home Mary helped her mother take care of her ailing father. He hadn't made it past fifty.

It was the smoking mostly. He was always seen, except perhaps while in bed, with a thin white tube glowing between his lips. His breath got short, he got heavy and then came lung cancer. Mary had stayed with him until he'd died and it seemed to Anna that the generous Mary must have caught something of what was killing her father for after that she seemed to fade herself. She found work in an office and remained home with Anna. It wasn't long really until the breast cancer and not long after that when she passed.

Anna turns away from dark thoughts and gaily recalls Mel's and Pat's wedding. Anna got on well with Pat. It was easy. They were the golden couple. Poor George with his thick horn-rims and scrawny body had never really dated. He hadn't seemed interested. He was interested in technology, not an area at that time where girls tended to find interest. It was years until Grace appeared and then merely a matter of months to their marriage and the shock of a black woman in her family allowed Anna to recognize that perhaps George had always dreamt of a bigger world than Waterloo.

As for Anna, she is happy where she is. She knows she won't be living much longer. She knows why she is here in the home. She doesn't mind the social events and the people maintaining their cliques though she is disconcerted by the mumblers, mostly male, who wander the halls and the gossips, mostly female, who can find anything wrong with anyone any time anywhere. Which is why she tends to sit in her chair and gaze out the window.

She lets herself drift. She recalls when Kitchener removed its streetcars in the fifties. She has flashes of Oktoberfest nights with Mellor: *gemutlichheit*, dirndls and lederhosen, litres of beer, *Prost*, the polkas, the crowds and the big tent at the Concordia Club. Then she thinks of fall fairs and the strangest of all, the Rockton World Fair in a piddling village partway between old Galt and Hamilton. Fun though. Those fall fairs were fun with their midways and show rings and races and always the chance of meeting a boy.

Then the rising sun over the Grand River at Kauffman Flats in the old days when you could swim in that river. Frigid winters of skating and toboggans. Hot, humid summers of bicycles and popsicles and cool lemonade. Fine blustery autumns and the Mennonite Farmers' Market out near St. Jacobs just north of Waterloo, the smells of meat and cheese and flowers. It has been a fine life, fading now, but with few regrets. A simple life but one well lived.

If only Christmas had not happened.

17

HOCKEY NIGHT. FLASHING blades in halogen lights, puck booming off the boards, the cold breath of ice, men shouting encouragements, colours of jerseys, the thud of pads from blocked shots, equipment rattles as men body check. Mel is on his game tonight. Playing almost up to the rest of them. He has had an assist. Some games are like this when you are focused you see it all as it seems to slow down. No one can take time and space from you just flow with confidence skate with the puck marvelling at the skills you've acquired loving this moment in your hockey life.

Just where he wants to be on this night. After another fight with the wife suspicious of why he'd washed his own clothes. Who is he seeing where did he go why can't he talk to her! Each time it happens it drives him out he can't face the battle he has other battles burning inside. Still looking for that illusive job he has made the rounds of his friends once again with more of the same: it's a bad year or try me in a few months or I'd hire you but insult you with the pay. More often now he finds his way to bars. He would like to visit his Erban friends but doesn't want the sympathy. He'd like to go to Gary's house but he can't now, since the fire.

Once he went to George, his brother's place, but as usual George was away on some technical call for Hitachi. George was Mel's opposite. Smart, laid-back and very successful. He'd got into tech early, into IBM out of university. He was posted all over for 15 years with varied tech firms while climbing the corporate ladder. He existed through a litany of deals as larger companies bought out smaller ones: Sand Technology became National Advanced Systems which became Hitachi which on its own was too big to be bought. George shone there as he did everywhere. He went to conferences in exotic places. He'd married Grace Anne Wesley, a native of Antigua, and lived with her in Cambridge, the third city of the Waterloo Region, because it was on the 401 and he was now responsible for Southwestern Ontario. Easy commute to Toronto or anywhere south.

Interesting that everything Mel never was George always was. A scholar, he didn't involve himself much in sports. He liked golf which Mel admired but did not play. George had married later in life so his kids, Mary and Melissa, were still in high school. There wasn't much common ground between brothers. When they did meet there was always an edge to their encounters. It was never spoken aloud but subconsciously everyone knew George was a satisfied man and Mel was the elder son who hadn't turned out as planned.

When Mel arrived at George's house, in the obvious wealth of the big old homes surrounding Victoria Park in Galt, Grace was just getting home from work. It was cold but sunny that afternoon. Mel was struck once again by Grace's charm. Her ebony skin stood out from the snow in perfect contrast and her long, slim body even in a ski jacket was beautiful.

She made coffee and they sat together in her home office. She was a travel agent but really a teacher. She taught at Conestoga College. Sometimes words she used Mel did not quite understand. They talked about his job loss of course, they talked about their kids of course, they talked about the weather when they ran out of other things. It was bad enough to be out of work and bad enough with a younger brother who'd made it beyond you and bad too that Grace was so subtle about it, trying to comfort him, but he was not going to make it her business or anyone's for that matter.

"You don't need to leave, Mel," she says. Her long Caribbean vowels empathetic.

"Yeah, I just came over to see George."

"I'm sure he'll be back tonight. Mel, Pat seemed worried about you."

"What do you mean?"

"She called last week."

"She shouldn't involve you," he says.

"We are all one family, Mel. Pat thinks you're upset. Perhaps drinking a little much."

"I'm not."

"Of course. Any luck on the job front?"

"Not really."

"I could help you write up your resume, Mel."

"What?"

"You'll need a job history to apply for work."

"Grace, I had one job all my life! How you gonna blow that up into something, huh?"

"But you've done so much else ... coaching, mentoring ..."

"Come on! I coached kids! That other thing ... what? Mentor?"

"Those things show leadership."

"Grace, I don't even know what the fuck it means!"

"Please don't get angry, Mel."

"So just please stay outa this, okay! I'll find something. I'll do it my way. Now, I gotta go. Tell George I'll see him when he isn't busy."

He didn't return though George called the next day. George sounded concerned. Mel didn't like it. They didn't talk long. George asked a lot of rhetorical questions and when Mel wouldn't respond dropped the conversation.

Tap on the shoulder. Hit the ice. Leave the drab thoughts behind as you skate like hell just to keep up. The puck comes your way. Fast and hard and just a slight reach then glance around to see Davey Isley going strong down his wing. Lead him. Shoot a pass a foot high over reaching sticks catch him on the move. He curls in. Defence tries to check him. He swings behind the net. You're at the blue line. Clear. Isley passes back then turns in front for the screen. Get it. Line it. Slap shot. Off a shin pad. Thunk. Where did that guy come from? Bounces behind you. Reach for it. Chats Chatsworth already has it. Other team. Young guy. One of the ones who played OHL. Leaves you in his snow. Watch as he shifts a shoulder shoots five hole. Fuck! You look like a fool like the old man you are like the guy out of work out of gas out of options. Go to the bench. Smack your stick. It breaks. A hundred bucks for a new carbon. Now you really *do* look like a fool. Head down. Don't talk. Your fault. This sucks.

"What's the matter, Bucks?" Isley asks him.

"Fuckin' game!"

"Only a game, Bucks. Take it easy."

Does this man not realize nothing is *only* a game? There are mistakes you make that can be forgiven, then there are the ones that make you look an idiot. *Only* a game. He is losing. He has no job. He has no real wife. His kids go right past him as they leave him behind. He's too old for this league. That fury bubbling beneath his surface rises once more. He loses sight of the game playing out before him. In his mind there is only the injustice of life; the game which pretends to have rules. He has played by the rules. It seems rules are for losers. He has that one time stepped outside the rules with Wilson. Together they took the rules and shoved them aside even if only for a few minutes of bright, hot light and the joy of actually having done something remarkable.

Game over. They've lost. Losing hurts. Showing your age and weakness hurts more. Mel sulks. In the dressing room guys come over, try to cheer him up crack some jokes make some fun of it; men helping one of their wounded. If only it could be so easy with Pat. Of anyone she has grown old with him, shared his triumphs and losses and yet now it seems she cannot understand what the loss of his job means to his self-worth.

Once the men are dressed and out at The Moose and he has a beer in hand, guys around the table, he begins to feel better. He has other things on his mind now, something he is good at, something his peers value in him ... he is, after all, Bucks Buckworth and tips them off on his choice of point spreads for the NHL games next week.

He is chatting with a small group either side and across the table leaning in when he hears the news. Despite his foreknowledge it shocks him. One of the players is a firefighter for the Region. Doug Asher. Muscular guy. Handsome. He could be one of those half-dressed calendar firefighters they print out for charity. Once the gambling talk runs down he turns toward Mel. No one hears them beneath the music, laughter and social talk.

"Didn't you work at Erban Industries, Bucks?"

"Yeah. Not anymore. Dumped everybody. Movin' the plant, or something like that. I did okay though. Severance package. Kept my pension. Other guys didn't have it so good. "

"So I gather. Well somebody's real pissed off about it."

"What do you mean?"

"Got a call last week to go out there. Big fire at the back of the place."

"Really?"

"Fire Marshal's calling it arson. Somebody set it. Burned so well 'cause they used an accelerant. Hell of a blaze."

"What happened? Somebody get hurt?"

"No, nothing like that. Turns out the accelerant was gasoline. It leaked inside under the loading bay doors. Old building y'know. Bunch of stuff on wood skids caught fire inside. That set the insulation on fire. We forced a door and caught it just in time."

Shock. Outside the rules; *way* outside. He suffers a moment of panic, covers it by drinking his beer. He sets the stein down.

"What's gonna happen?"

"Fire Marshal brought in the cops. If it was kids they're in for it. If it was somebody lookin' for revenge they got it, until they get caught. Coupla hundred grand damages. You think of anybody might do this?"

"Christ no, Dougie. That's crazy!"

"Yeah."

"Anything else?" he asks.

"I wouldn't know. Should be in the paper though. Hell of a blaze."

And there it is the brief moment of rushing adrenalin revenge and joy all cut down to the rudiments. Fire Marshal, cops, damages, investigation. He should tell Wilson should tell him tonight no, not tonight, go over tomorrow when it's all sunk in and you can be calm.

Go over tomorrow.

18

AFTER PAT HAS gone to bed Mel searches the recycling box for the local section of the *Record*. Sure enough it is there in one of the papers he hasn't read that week. ARSON AT ERBAN is the headline; then the story of the closing, the loss of so many jobs, the economic repercussions to the Region. After that came the story of the loading dock and the inside damage and the realization of what he has done and where it might take him. Yet even now, with the shock of the thing, he finds satisfaction in reading the story, digesting its significance, knowing so many others will read this with approval. He tears out the piece to keep it. It is another kind of trophy. He discovers then he has taken the lead in this life game by *not* following the rules. He thinks how so many successful people *became* successful because they did the same.

Outside the box. Bend the rules. Break the rules. Be beyond them.

And he thinks of what it would take to be one of them. The Outliers. As things stand now he is merely an outlaw. He hears the side door open. In a split second he makes a decision. He can't be what he is, so must be what he needs. He would have to become two beings at the same time. Two totally different entities somehow sharing the same life. Or perhaps a different life now. Crucial for him to survive. His thoughts set him on a track, on a conduit really, leading he knows not where. As it is, in that instant he surprises himself. He is somehow new. An invention of himself, un-purposed by society or rule of law or simple custom. He is somehow ready now, as he has never been before, to take on a new character, to be two versions of himself. He drives home enmeshed in such thoughts.

MJ comes home from pizza delivery. He is looking to get to his game and get playing, leave all this shit behind for a while in the focus and freedom of stalking and killing on the internet. He is startled to see Mel up so late. He turns to go downstairs when his father calls him.

"Son?"

"What?"

MJ is surly. Mel recalls the computer squabble.

"Mind if I join you downstairs?"

"I don't know, Dad."

By this time Mel is facing his son in the stairwell. He is two steps up. Big. His son looks up to him literally as he once did figuratively in his life. He remembers the boy's face in its varied emotions from triumph to shame. Now it is a smirk. He does not want to lose his son as he has his daughter. He needs to return to the man he was. Play him. Play the other later.

"How about a beer?" he says.

"I guess."

They go downstairs. At the bottom MJ removes his coat. The sight of his softness disgusts Mel, but he is not here to admonish. He must apologize. He is not here to be a teacher but to become a student. He is here to learn the things he must from his son which will allow him the gateway into the world he does not comprehend. He has resolved now to leave the old ways behind and strive to make himself somehow significant once again, someone his world will never fathom, something beyond the pale. Still, he must play what he was, the person he was, to become what he yearns to be and though he has no idea precisely of what that looks like, he knows he must work for it as he never has in his life.

"Look, I'm sorry about the computer. I blew up. I've been stressed with the whole job thing. I took it out on you and that was wrong. I was angry at being so ignorant."

"Dad, it's okay. I'm just tired. Lots of driving tonight."

"It wasn't okay, MJ, and I apologise. I want to ask if you'll help me learn it."

"What? The computer?"

"Yeah. How to use it. How to get online, right? How to search for things, find things out. I'll need to know stuff if I'm going to get myself to a better place."

"Sure, Dad. It's pretty easy. On YouTube you can learn anything."

"I don't even know what that is. Music or something?"

"Nah. Way more than that. Everything from music to medicine to whatever you can think of. Most of it's just showing how to do things so you're not scanning manuals all the time. I know you don't much like reading. Come on, grab a couple of beers and I'll show you. It's easy once you get the hang of it."

MJ is suddenly energized. His father has actually apologised. He can't recall the last time that happened, if it actually ever did. Here is the chance to prove himself not in athletics but with a skill set his father does not possess. MJ feels empowered. Confident. All the diffidence of the past months drains away as he powers up the hard drive and logs himself in. This is something perhaps they can share as they once shared sports. Something perhaps in which he the follower can at last lead.

He resolves to accept his father's occasional tantrums. He knows what it's like to have to train to evolve a skill from the years of apprenticeship under his father. He knows what it is to fail. He resolves he will not let his father fail. He will offer the patience he never received. He will deliver his father a new set of aptitudes just as his father once taught him. He knows now his father is imperfect, has seen it in the arguments with his mother, in the foolish banishment of Danielle, in the way he is so old school not prepared for the world in the now.

He will get him there.

And to Mel, like magic his son is with him again, roles reversed, his son the teacher cajoling, praising, pushing, and he finds it doesn't matter at all.

As long as it gets him where he wants to go.

19

NEW MONTH, NEW puzzle. Pat Buckworth finds herself aligning the outer shards of another thousand piece event. This time it is *The School of Athens* by Raphael. Less weird than Dali. More subtle and detailed. Multiple characters, costumes and, of course, a background so complex she knows this will test her.

It is always the backgrounds: the cloudy skies, starry nights, veined marble arches and pillars, desert sands or tundra snows and the sea, always the sea. The sea is ever the hardest to solve. There are depths to the sea no one can recognize. There can be turmoil beneath the calm water. There can be joy in the rage of waves.

She thrills to the challenge of this complexity stretching her skills to find the right piece, the key to the rest. She has not failed yet. Every so often stopped in frustration, she has put puzzles away for a while, coming back with fresh eyes and a cleared mind; she has never given up. If she could just do that in life.

Life is like the sea.

The arguments with Mel are more frequent now. They are seemingly about nothing, little things, yet *always* about what lies beneath. Somehow MJ has convinced his father to learn to use the computer. Over time Mel has become obsessed, she feels, spending as much time there as he does at night with his sports, live or televised.

He has not looked for a job, not applied for employment insurance, not even kept up his physical fitness. His eyes have retreated. No longer can she discern that diamond flash so unique to Danielle and him.

She misses Danielle as well. Dani won't come home at all since the last time she was rebuffed by her father. Pat calls her daughter often, however. They meet for coffee. Dani doesn't invite her to Stanley's house. She says she's too new for the other guys to feel comfortable with her mother. Pat feels abandoned. At home she is equally alone. Her husband and son spend their time together on the computer. Mel seems to have formed a bond once again with his son, this one the reverse of sports, this one where the child coaches the father.

Pat finds it disconcerting. She cannot comprehend what Mel is trying to accomplish. He comes upstairs when MJ leaves for his pizza job. He eats a silent supper punctuated by her questions, prying only succinct responses from him. He descends to the basement again or goes out to watch or play hockey.

MJ has even taught him that game he plays. She hears them cheering and swearing, discovering manifold methods of killing each other. Something Freudian in that. Yet it is more what he does when his son is not home that troubles her. Each time she comes downstairs he quickly flicks the screen from what he's been looking at, back to a Canada Manpower site, which is all she ever sees.

Recruitment Consultant
William Pew CA
Toronto, ON
via LinkedIn

General Labour Workers
Total Staffing Solutions Inc.
Brampton, ON
via LinkedIn

Construction Project Manager
Skilled Trades Agency
Toronto, ON
via LinkedIn

Site Supervisor—Toronto
Skilled Trades Agency
Toronto, ON
via LinkedIn

Plant Manager—Guelph
JP Recruitment Ltd.
Guelph, ON
via LinkedIn

The trouble is Mel doesn't realize it's the same page every time. When he tells her he is doing a job search she feels she cannot strip him of his dignity by telling him what is so obvious. And that is the puzzle. What lies beneath his perplexing behaviour? What has become of the man she has loved?

The School of Athens is halfway aligned when she is overcome by fatigue. She can puzzle no more this night. If she can sleep.

She doesn't sleep.

She is awakened by a crash downstairs. She hears Mel's curse. Her bedside clock reads eleven-thirty. She gets up, puts on her robe and goes downstairs.

He sits at the kitchen table. There is a bold coloured box on the floor. A beer bottle lies beside it leaking liquid from its open spout. Mel's coat is half off. Clearly he swung the wrong direction knocking everything off the table. He tries to extricate himself from his coat sleeve. Perceptibly, he is drunk.

"Are you alright?" she asks first.

"Yeah. I'm just ... fuckin' coat."

"I don't think it's the coat, Mel," she says.

"Just ... wait ..."

He yanks at his coat sleeve tearing the cuff but pulling it off. He drops it on the floor. He sees the bright box. His eyes widen with shock.

"Oh fuck ..."

He grapples with the package nearly dropping it again. He sits heavily into a kitchen chair. He opens the box. It is sealed at the ends but he rips at the seal and jams his hand inside. He withdraws the Styrofoam sleeve which brackets a new laptop. HP Pavilion. He sets it on the table gently. He's forgotten the beer on the floor. There is relief in his eyes. He hasn't ruined the computer. Pat cannot credit this picture.

"Jesus, I thought I broke it," he mumbles.

"You're drunk."

"I'm not drunk. I just had a few with the boys. Really good game tonight."

"Who was playing?"

"What?"

"Who was playing the game? What teams?"

"It was Pittsburgh!"

"And who?"

"The Kings ... no ... Anaheim ... shit, one of the Hollywood teams."

He is muttering again. Anger burgeoning. Beer in control.

"You're drunk. And what is that?"

"My new laptop! Got it at Best Buy before the game! Best you can buy!"

He laughs at his little joke. A moment of diamond flash in his eyes gone as quick as a shooting star. Dull, drunken eyes. Now it is she who begins to anger.

"A computer? You? What on earth are you going to do with it?"

"I'm gonna use it. MJ needs the desktop."

"To play his stupid game! You hardly know how to turn the thing on!"

"That's wrong! You're wrong! I know things now!"

"And now you're defending MJ's game? For God's sake, Mel, what's happened to you? You're becoming exactly like your son … a good for nothing …"

"Shut the fuck up!"

"What did you say to me?"

"He's helping me out!"

"You speak to me like that again, Mel, I'll walk out."

"My son's helping me!"

"To do what? You play his game and he always wins. You go out every night to play or watch hockey. You drink all the time now. When was the last time you looked for work?"

"I'm lookin' for work!"

"Right. On Manpower, right?"

"Yeah."

"I don't know what you're really up to, Mel, but I've got that same page of Manpower memorized. Recruiter Consultant. General Labour. Site Supervisor. Do you think I'm stupid? Whatever you're doing it's *not* looking for work. And now you come home with that thing. What did it cost? You know your severance is going to run out? Faster, if you buy toys!"

"Not a toy."

"What?"

"It's not a fuckin' toy! It's a tool! I'm learnin' how to use it!"

His voice is loud now, harsh. The way a drunk thinks he'll win an argument. She counters with spite.

"Great. You're going to go to Conestoga now, with MJ? Is that it? Is that the great plan? Father and son geek fixit inc. We could call it millennial/boomer, or maybe Mil/Boo!"

"I don' need t' take this!"

"Stop shouting."

"My house. Shout if I want!"

"You'd better think about what you're saying. You've driven your daughter away with your stupid pride. Are you trying to drive me out too?"

"Don' talk about Dani ..."

"What is *wrong* with you, Mel? You're barely here even when you're home! I make you dinner you sit like you're alone. You won't talk to me! You drink downstairs with your son playing that game. You know he's just using you? Getting back for all those times you beat him in sports. He's laughing at you, Mel! If I didn't know better I'd say losing your job drove you crazy! What is wrong with ..."

When it comes the slap stuns her. A hard big flat hand on her face. The concussion inside her ear the sting on her cheek the pull of muscle as her head twists then losing balance a vacuum as she falls through space and time and history and love and hate and childbirth and deaths and all the moments she so clearly remembers until the floor comes up slamming into her like a pile driver. She sits in the stink of spilled beer. She is wet on one side. The side that hurts. The side that hit the floor.

Her eyes focus. She looks at him above her his hand on the table holding him up. He has never, ever done this. Never, ever in their lives together. Never, ever to a woman. Never to his children. Seldom in athletics. Yet now he has. Done this to her. How can this be? She must get up. He cannot help her. She must do this on her own. Rise. Grasp a chair. Her ear rings. Her right elbow throbs.

She stands.

Her eyes rise to his. His are cloudy. Dull. Stupid.

She wonders why she ever loved him.

"You okay?" he says.

"Just, stay away from me."

"I'm ... I'm sorry."

"Just go downstairs. Wait for MJ."

"I'm real sorry, Pat. I don' know ..."

"I'm going to bed."

"Let me look. Did I hurt you?"

"Get *away* from me!"

"I'm sorry ..."

"Goodnight," she says as she leaves the kitchen, walks the hall to the stairs, climbs the stairs, goes into her bedroom, walks past the bed and into the bathroom and turns on the light and locks the door.

Something has just shifted in the universe.

20

GRACE ANNE WESLEY can hear the Sunday bells. St. John the Divine Cathedral peals out its call to worship from atop the hill across the valley. She doesn't attend the Big Church. She returns home from Sunday school at St. Boniface Anglican walking the colourful side streets of St. John's toward Valley Road to the outskirts of town where she lives. She can glimpse the indigo of Deep Water Harbour to her right and to her left the rise of the Shekerley Mountains. The metal doors of shops slide up with grating noises. There are greetings and brief conversations as she passes the shops. Laughter echoes in side streets. The merchants prepare for the first of the cruise ship tourists who will fill the streets of St. John's by noon hour.

She is a child, leggy and awkward, walking home in her Sunday best looking forward to swimming today in a little known cove west of Jennings where tourists don't go. She is happy on this beautiful Antiguan day. Her friends chitter beside her. The sky is azure. The single storey shops and houses exist as a rainbow of colours along each side of the street. She smells bread baking. She smells fish frying.

She is happy in school, her last year of primary anticipating the vaunted Antigua Girls' High School. She works the big Saturday market for spending money but her mother will allow her no more. She has good grades and her mother wants to keep things that way. Yet working the market has shown her another side of the world outside the island. While she works she studies the tourists who shop for her father's driftwood carvings.

They come from all over the world. They come from all races. She is especially interested in those of her colour with so much money, usually American or Canadian, as they descend from their cruise ship palaces or taxi in from the resorts that block off so many of the island's beaches. She thinks she would like to be one of them, those tourists.

Some people have told her she is pretty. She knows looks get tips so she buys better clothing with the money she earns at the market and makes sure she is clean and comely each day. Her teachers believe she has a chance for a scholarship. She knows her destiny is likely to serve tourists. She studies hard so perhaps she won't have to. She loves the island but not enough to be a servant who can never leave it.

She has no idea as a child that she will eventually depart her beloved Antigua for the changing seasons of Canada. She has no idea she will achieve a degree in Hotel and Tourism Business Administration, be employed at Sandals, meet George Buckworth, a Canadian technologist at a business conference, meet him again when he returns on his own, eventually take him to meet her parents, then fall in love and marry him in her church of St. Boniface, then move to Cambridge Ontario Canada and discover snow, and wealth.

In this dream she cannot know these things. She cannot be in two places at once but this dream, this dream makes it seem so, this dream about the bells of Antigua on a Sunday morning. Yet she wonders why won't the bells stop.

They keep pealing and echoing through her mind until she awakens to the insistent ringing of her front doorbell. It is not Sunday, it is not sunny. It is Saturday. Glancing at her alarm clock she sees five thirty in the morning. It's dark out. Someone is at the door. She feels sudden fear that something has happened to George but he is asleep beside her. He too awakens but she is up slipping into her robe.

"What's going on, Grace?" he mumbles, half awake.

"Someone's at the front door." She pronounces 'the' as 'thee', and a long 'o' in 'front'.

The doorbell again. It is insistent.

"I'll go," he says.

"Nonsense. I am up. I'll go and see who it is."

"I'm getting up. Look out the window first, Grace. This time in the morning ..."

"I will."

She walks down the stairs, the stairway slightly curved to the vestibule. There are narrow stained glass windows on either side of the door. She glances through an amber shard and sees Patricia Buckworth standing on the front terrace. There is a suitcase beside her and what looks like a folding card table. She opens the door.

Patricia sits in the airy kitchen all white and grey and gleaming chrome at the bistro table which George and Grace use for breakfast. The kitchen is larger than Grace's family's entire house in Antigua. She has grown accustomed to it now, not that she takes anything for granted, just that she is the type who adapts. She seems to possess that rare kind of life with few regrets. Her hand is on Pat's hand which rests on the table.

The left side of Pat's face is slightly swollen and her eye is slowly blackening. She has stopped crying, the tracks of tears remain but she is more composed, enough to talk over her declaration at the front door.

"I've left Mel."

She pauses to drink from a teacup. Her hand is no longer shaking. The hot tea steams up into her face. It is soothing. Grace and George have been soothing as well though mortified by this turn of events. Grace has told her daughters Mary and Melissa to stay upstairs so as not to embarrass Patricia. They are old enough, both high school girls, to comprehend.

"He hit you?" George says, yet again. He is quietly furious. He sits at the table as well, his face flushed from his wrath. "He actually hit you?"

"Slapped," Pat replies. "I don't think he even thought about what he was doing he was just so drunk and I pushed him, taunted him. I asked for this."

"No one asks for this," Grace says firmly. Her voice remains calm and quiet. She is trying to mollify *two* people at the table, her sister-in-law and her husband. She is trying to assimilate the extraordinary circumstance which led to the three of them here in her kitchen.

George had wanted to drive to Waterloo to confront his brother. She has prevented that. Not if Mel is violent. When George had wanted to call and give Mel a piece of his mind she had stopped that too. No confrontations. One already. That is enough. She has always possessed a slight fear of Mel's outsized personality his big body his athletic dexterity his very vitality. It was never the thought that he had rejected or resented her or considered her different. It was just his ability to project himself in a room with a strange charisma his brother did not possess. Much of it had to do with his eyes ... the most unusual eyes she has ever seen ...

He is a force, though he doesn't seem to recognize it. His job loss has wounded him badly: that part of him which is so charismatic, that part of the confidence in himself. She has seen it evolve from shock into panic and now, it seems, into something else. George ignored it as he always has, except for this Christmas and that had just made things worse. And now Patricia herself has felt the vexation which Grace considered inevitable in Mel's decline.

"We've been having trouble for nearly a year," Pat says. "I think he's tired of me. He spends so much time out now ..."

"Playing his games," George says.

"He goes out to watch them too now, with his friends at sports bars. At least I hope ..."

"You don't think he's having an affair?" Grace says, knowing he is all too capable of it. Knowing his charisma. Knowing his impulsiveness. *Feeling* his attraction.

"I don't think so, Grace. Oh, I hope not."

"No, of course not," Grace says. "Just a fleeting thought."

"For all his flaws, he's not an undisciplined guy," George says, not knowing at all what kind of guy his brother is since he left high school. He has memories of his brother and the vivacious Patricia. There were other girls flocking about, of course. His brother was an athletic all-star. Even after he'd walked out of school he was still popular. He'd become a bit of a hellion which made him fashionable in his day. Yet he never took any of the girls seriously. It had always seemed to be Pat. It was Pat. By that time George was in university and returned home for the summer wedding.

It was a simple affair. A small church and a Legion hall, her dad paying for the food his dad providing the booze. It was enough for them. Neither had money. Neither expected much more. By then Mel was too old to entertain thoughts of professional hockey. By then Pat was too young to expect a house or expensive accoutrements. But both of them were beautiful. Both of them were healthy. Both of them excelled in sports. And both were very, very happy.

It occurs to George then that things fade: beauty skills emotions even marriages, even brotherhoods. He resolves in that moment to pay more attention to his own marriage and family. To lose them would be unbearable. And to think his brother has driven his wife away. His resentment of Mel returns once more: the golden boy the big brother the *presence* at any gathering the pride the trophies the ignorance the lack of sensitivity and finally this last awful Christmas. It all comes back and he knows now why he has purposely pushed his brother away.

"So what would you like to do?" Grace says. "You are welcome here, dear, until things settle down."

"Oh, I wouldn't want to impose—" Pat says.

"You won't be imposing," George says. "Better if you meet him here anyway. I can't believe he actually hit you!"

"I don't know how to fix this, Grace. First to go was our sex life. I hope you don't mind me saying ..."

"Of course not," Grace replies.

"I should leave," George says.

"No, George. I need to be honest. You need to know everything. It became a routine, just a habit. It never used to be. Then we kind of quit being together. I wanted to play non-competitive sports but Mel flat out refused. He said he hadn't lost his edge. Then all the staying out nights 'til late, then MJ comes home from failing college and Mel does nothing to try to fix things, help his boy, just lets him go to waste in our basement. I couldn't believe it.

"That was when we started arguing. Sniping at each other all the time, knowing each other's weaknesses and playing on them. I'm as much to blame as he is. Then his blow up with Dani. I still don't know what happened that night, George, between you two but the next day he told her not to come home until she'd ditched Stanley. *Never come back* he said ... and now his job. Gone. It's like he's lost his drive for living. That's what started the drinking. He's like a wounded animal. He's behaving in ways he never did. He's learning to use the computer from MJ ..."

"What?" George is surprised.

"He said he needed it to look for work but now he's not even looking and he's refused job offers from his friends he's too proud and suddenly he comes home drunk with a new computer saying it will solve all his problems! I just can't understand him anymore. He plays games with MJ on the computer just like they used to play basketball in the driveway. He won't even speak about Dani, let alone talk to her. When he lost his job she came home to see him. He stayed up in his room 'til she left. He hardly talks to me and when he does it's an argument."

"Did you say *his* room, Pat?" Grace asks.

"We've had separate rooms since Dani moved out."

"Good lord, that's months!" George says.

"Why didn't you tell us?" Grace says.

"I couldn't. You just don't go around telling people ... We went to a counsellor but after one session Mel just refused and wouldn't go back. I'm still going. The therapist gives me strategies for dealing with him but Mel is a wall now. Doesn't listen. Doesn't talk. I don't think he loves me at all anymore!"

She cries again, sobbing desperately in a way neither Grace nor George have seen. Suddenly it is as if she is alone in the room her sobs so deep each one a new torment. Grace embraces her. George, not knowing what to do, leaves the room. He thinks about calling his brother again. He rejects it. No preaching phone call will fix this. His brother will not be lectured. He has always been the *alpha* wolf. George imagines how Mel's vanity has been upset with the loss of control of his family the loss of his job and even the loss of his physical powers as he ages.

He can hear Pat settle down with the comforting words of his wife. Grace is good at this. Being a teacher has given her skills and a confidence she did not possess when he'd first met her. She came to a new country a new job a new life and taught herself to be accomplished. She has helped him as well to see past his own ego. She has displayed her strength with the girls too, both of them self-assured. She has lived a previous life which taught her to value each moment of this one.

From that day in the lobby of Sandals Antigua when he first caught sight of her lanky beauty and all thoughts of a meaningful conference fled his mind, when he stayed on after to get to know her away from the resort, when he returned again and again and got to know her family and her secret island places and finally when he found she loved him, he has worshipped her. He knows he is a lucky man.

Pat is exhausted. She has been up all night having been betrayed in the worst possible way by the man she loved. For all his vivacity and charisma, Grace thinks, there was always a strange negativity to Mel, particularly when the brothers got together. A huge accent on the *when*. It happened too seldom for two men who lived in such proximity. A mere half hour drive apart. They gathered their families infrequently. Christmas, of course. Thanksgivings, erratically. Anniversaries once or twice, birthdays, then kids' birthdays only, then long weekends each fading into other priorities. Even when she and Pat became close they seldom visited each other's homes preferring café lunches or shopping excursions.

Their last Christmas will be their last together, Grace knows. The Christmas of Dani's boyfriend's appearance and Mel blowing up and leaving for Anna's nursing home with George following him saying *Anna was his mother too*. Everyone else remained at the house subdued and confused while MJ got drunk and Stanley and Dani finally departed.

When the men returned they were hostile, not talking. Mel entered the house and said George was waiting in the car in the driveway. Grace gathered her girls and quickly extricated them. Pretend kisses. False hugs. Escape from the toxic environment.

George never spoke to her of that night. She knew better than to ask. Eventually it would come out. George did not keep things from her but he did tend to wait while he worked out a clear resolution. Grace does not think that will happen this time.

Grace remembers how Pat's pursuit of puzzles has grown. Now Grace knows why. Once Pat and Mel had been active together. Once they had been an unstoppable pair always strong in tennis, badminton, volleyball, slow-pitch anything where they could play together. They both had that instinct to seek victory and the skills and style to find it.

Grace and George, early on, would hear of their sporting exploits. Later, as George became busier, they lost track of all the parochial play until one day there was no Pat and Mel playing, only Mel's bravado with his men's teams and the increasing complexity of Pat's puzzles.

Grace wishes that could be altered somehow. She has, despite their friendship, no idea the depth of Pat's troubles. So much can be concealed inside lives. Those secrets which stay within one until one works around them or learns to live with their consequences.

George watches as Grace leads Pat upstairs. He follows them bringing her bag and her puzzle table. He wonders at the puzzle table when it dawns on him its importance to her. It makes him think Pat might be staying a while.

She might not be going back at all.

21

STANLEY PUTS DOWN his book and sees Danielle in a towel, her long blonde hair loose and tangled from the shower. She will brush it now using a little oil to bring it to its lustrous best. It is real blonde hair in its variant shades of honey to flaxen to glittering gold. He loves to watch her do this. He loves to watch her do most things. At this moment, however, she does not brush her hair. She pulls it aside and looks angry. Her eyes spark.

"What's wrong?" he asks.

"That cat. Why won't the stupid thing just let me pet it? It acts like I've got a disease. Mister Walk-On-By just gives me the side glance then strolls away."

"He's still getting accustomed to you."

"After six months?"

"Well, he's like that."

"Maybe I should bring in my own cat?"

"Not a good idea, Danielle."

"And why not?"

"Henry reacts rather poorly to other cats."

"What, stares them down like he does me?"

"No. More terrorizes then disappears into thin air. Once Michael brought in a friend's cat for a week. The friend was off to a conference and asked him a favour. He thought nothing of it. At any rate we saw *neither* cat for the entire week. Howls and screams in the night but no cats. We hauled Fluffy out from behind the furnace in the basement. We found her there at the end of the week. It took two of us to extricate her. As Michael took her out of the house we saw Henry sitting at the top of the steps glaring down. Not the best of vacations for Fluffy. So please, no other cats."

Danielle brushes her hair. He sits and watches for the magic moment when she straightens and flips it all back in a blur of blonde. Then it can be his turn …

"May I brush your hair?" he asks.

"Only if you give me an explanation."

"What? What about? Henry?"

"No, not Henry."

She points to the windowsill with the books.

"Stanley, what are those?"

"Books, my love." He states the obvious in a comic dead pan. She doesn't pick it up.

"Sports books? Stanley, you're not interested in sports."

"Who's to say I can't be? I'm expanding my horizons. I did grow up with football, you know. I've also tried my hand at cricket! I have a working knowledge of sport."

Dani picks up *Hockey 101: Rules of the Game.* She waves it in front of him.

"You planning on taking up hockey?" She smiles.

"It's *ice* hockey to the rest of the world, my love. There is another version ..."

"I know, Stanley, I've played field hockey. This isn't that. What's going on? Oh, look here, *Football for Dummies, USA Edition*, and oh, here's *An All American Game—Baseball Explained!* What are you up to?"

She has set down the books and removed her towel, a breathtaking moment for Stanley, one of which he never tires. She dons underclothes, jeans and a sweater as they talk.

"God, Danielle, you're so beautiful!"

"Thank you, but that won't get you off. What about these sports books?"

"I tried YouTube, not enough detail."

"You mean you've read all these? When?"

"This past week."

"How could you possibly read that many ... never mind. I should know better."

"I've retained quite a lot. Bit of a talent of mine."

"Yes, but why?"

"It occurred to me I should augment my knowledge of Canadian culture."

"This is about my dad, isn't it? Forget it, Stanley, he won't change."

"I have many interests, Danielle."

"Sure you do. Look, this is sweet but you know the situation. My dad won't speak to me unless I stop living with you and I'm not going to do that."

"You're sure?"

She grabs her gym bag from the closet's upper shelf. She folds vibrant coloured sports garb into it. She smiles at him. Her eyes light. She has the most stunning eyes: luminescent, sparkling, like diamonds. Then he remembers her father's eyes.

"For such a smart guy you're really insecure, Stanley. I'm not leaving you."

"I can only hope."

"I love you, stupid! You've given me a whole world I knew nothing about. It's not just computing. Every time you take me to that professor's house ..."

"*The Musical Room*, yes ..."

"Well I've never listened to classical music before. I didn't take music in school."

"It's not actually *classical*, my love, more *chamber* music ..."

"Whatever. It's beautiful. I look forward to every time we go. Imagine, sitting ten feet from a string quartet in a man's house! They play Saturday night at Roy Thomson Hall for all the Toronto muckety mucks, then here they are for us at that house, audience of fifty. And those movies at the Duchess Theatre. Not the usual Hollywood stuff I grew up on. I'm even used to subtitles now. And you have a view of the world, Stanley, which makes you so fascinating and bold and the people I get to meet through you ..."

"Yes, though I'm not much for people ..."

"But you are! People *like* you, Stanley. They find you enthralling just like I do. And they're all so interesting on their own. I feel so ordinary with most of them yet almost all of them take time to talk with me ...

"Danielle, you're not exactly ordinary ..."

"I'm just trying to explain. Not even my father will make me leave you. I want you to understand that and not worry about it. We're good together. For a while I had trouble getting past a few things ..."

"You mean my arrogance ..."

"I didn't say that, but that too. I really think we've come a long way since I moved in."

"You've changed me, Danielle. I'm proud of you. I now enjoy sports, in moderation, and dance, something I never really considered, and food. I once treated it as fuel, simply whatever would keep me going. Now I feel far more creative and interested in food. We have *our own* accomplishments, darling, discovered together!"

"Thank you for saying."

She zips up her gym bag.

"Where are you going today?"

"Soccer practice."

"It's freezing out!"

"Indoors, silly. Got to get training for the season."

"The season's over."

"That was the university. This is indoor five on five."

"Of course. Should have known. Silly me!"

"So what are you doing today?"

"Oh, I just thought I'd return those books to the library," he says, lying.

"Can you drive me?"

"Yes, of course I'll drive you."

"Will you kiss me?"

"You'll not have to ask that twice. You know you kiss wonderfully."

"So do you, Stanley."

And they do.

22

IT TAKES SOME time for their Volkswagen Golf GTI to heat up. Most of the warming goes on in the diesel engine. Passengers use the electric seat warmers. Both Dani and Stanley are bundled up. It is a clear, cold, sign-of-spring day. Stanley drives up Albert Street to Columbia then west to University Avenue and farther out to Fischer Hallman Road. There is still dirty snow on the ground. A west wind rattles the branches of trees. The trees are bare, the cars grimy white from winter road salt. The roads are clear, however, and Stanley makes the trip to Forest Hills Collegiate in under twenty minutes. Along the way Dani has asked again what Stanley will do. He has forgotten his first excuse, lame as it was.

"I'll drop by the campus."

"I thought you said you were going to the library."

"Oh! Yes. That too. The *university* library! But I'll check on some platforms running new algorithms. Just a favour for some friends."

"What do you mean?" Dani laughs, ignoring the lie.

"Well, we're looking at chatbots and digital assistants and how AI can be of use with natural language processing."

"English please, Stanley." Dani laughs again.

"Yes ... well then ... I'm helping a couple of friends as I said. They have secured a two million dollar grant to develop their company."

"Wow! What's its name?

"Maloona."

"Funny name."

"These fellows are fortunate and very smart. Will Baker would give his left arm to have been one of them but he won't work with them."

"Why not?"

"Well it's his ego, you see. You know he dearly wants to found his own *start up*. He's positively obsessed. I worry over him."

"Why?"

"At the end of the summer semester his scholarship terminates. He hasn't been doing well: spending more than he has, grabbing at straws in his quest for the magic *app*, his work at school unattended. I've decided to lend him some money."

"Please don't do that, Stanley."

"Why not? A friend in need ..."

"He's not your friend, Stanley. He's a nice guy and he's lived with you longer than me but deep down Will has a sense of entitlement that's a bit sad. I know I shouldn't judge him but I don't think he's the type who would pay you back. I don't know, I just don't really trust him. Never mind. You do what you think is best. I shouldn't interfere."

"Danielle, dear, that is precisely what you *should* do. I've put him off several times now and clearly I need to listen to myself. I know what you mean. It's not a deep negative, I do like him, but you've just told me what I realized months ago. Something utterly strange is driving him. For the life of me I couldn't put my finger to it. It *is* that sense of entitlement. And I know his parents are wealthy so why not simply ask them for the money?"

"So you're not upset ..."

"For advice? I may seem arrogant, my love, but I *do* know good advice when I hear it."

Their change of subject has made him feel increasingly guilty. She is so honest with him, so upright and loving. He feels like a worm. He worries once more over Michael's opinion that he himself might cause her to leave him. Yet he cannot be honest with her now. He has bubbled himself to a boil over Mel Buckworth and cannot back down. He tries to find a way back to his latest excuse.

"At any rate Sam and Kaheer asked me to look in. That's my plan. They really do have something extraordinary. It's all about finding a method which allows the human voice to issue instructions and the application to learn from them."

"So it's artificial intelligence software?"

"Yes. The beginnings ... just a moment ... we're to make this turn here ... why does that man keep waiting when nothing is coming? Now the light will change!"

"Easy Mister Fast and Furious! We're early anyway. So? I really don't get AI that much, Stanley, apart from the movies."

He is pleased with himself to have brought back the impersonal. Today looms before him like thick smoke. He does not know what he will do if it becomes fire. He tries to appear offhand and confident.

"Yes. Well, it doesn't exist at the levels portrayed in fiction, though it may someday. Really, AI is simply artificial neural networks composed of the equivalent of neurons connected by synapses layered at every level, so increasingly abstract information is being modelled.

Deep neural networks observe and learn from data rather than merely following instructions, you see. Essentially the software writes itself."

"Of course! It's all so clear to me now!" Dani shakes her head. They make the turn onto Fischer Hallman and go south. The traffic is heavy but smooth over four lanes. Once past the Superstore Plaza they turn right, into the school. Stanley drives through the long parking lot to the front entrance of Forest Hill C.I. It is a yellow brick building. The brick is showing its age.

"Why here, anyway?" Stanley asks.

"This is a city league. They don't use the PAC building. That's university only."

"I see. Well, take care, darling. Call when you want me!"

A quick kiss and she is out the door walking up the steps of the somewhat strange Torii Gate trellis sidewalk to the school's entrance. She waves once before opening one of the glass front doors. Fortunate in his little lie, Stanley concentrates now on a quite different problem. Not hard to drive to, just down Queen Street then left on Belmont then back into Waterloo. It is the *end* of the journey which poses so much trepidation.

The time has come.

Stanley has listened to his friends and determined upon a man to man talk, hoping ever so much it will not turn *mano a mano.* As he drives he considers the options. Ring the doorbell. Big Mel opens. Fills the doorway a step above the cowering Stanley.

"*Sir, I would like this chance to …* no. *Sir, I've come here to discuss a mutual …* no. *Hello Mel, I was in the neighbourhood and thought …* absolutely not!"

Will he slam the door in my face will he reach out and grab my shirt will he actually punch me knock me off the porch pick me up and throw me into the bushes call the police spit on my shoes he could do anything he hates me he hates me believing that I molest his daughter believing I've stolen her away perhaps I should come another day. I'm depending on Pat to forestall him but what if she's gone off shopping, then what do I do in the face of such physicality, such animosity, such abhorrence, such a parent?

So, Mr. Buckworth, here I am to face your judgement … no, that's awful … the Mr. Buckworth is good though … *I'm here to talk about Danielle …* too fast, too fast … *I'm here on a matter of mutual concern* … oh heavens, that's just ridiculous … perhaps call him on my cell, arrange a meeting … coffee shop, beer joint, that little place on Belmont, The Checkers where he likes to breakfast … no, you've made up your mind now just do it you … geek!

He is there. Arrived. He has followed the route without being aware, gone with the traffic completely distracted in a near comatose state and yet somehow he's made it. Parked in front of the house. It is a comfortable little home: the front yard showing a garden rather than a lawn. There are patches of snow on the boulevard.

Terrified. Sweating intensely. His bundled winter clothes now too warm with driving and he having grown too ardent with his thoughts. He opens the door. The icy breeze hits him like a wave washing over him. His sweat turns cold. He stands by the car.

He stands by the car.

Unable to move. He stands by the car.

23

IT IS ALL she can do now. Anna Jean Buckworth lies in her bed weak with pneumonia and stares out the window. It is Christmas Day evening and she has new memories. Because of her illness she has not been able to join her family for the day. They came to her.

First Mel has come with Patricia, Mel Junior and Danielle. They came in the morning. They brought cranberry muffins. They brought coffee from Tim Hortons and a nice tea for her along with a fine poinsettia plant all bright red and green. They stayed the morning leaving just before lunch.

After lunch George arrived with Grace and Mary and Mellissa.

They were on their way to Mel's for Christmas dinner. Grace had made a rum cake. They each had a piece on paper plates and stayed until mid-afternoon. George read to her. The Nativity from Luke. She became tired from all the excitement so the family left early.

She slept for a while but now she awakens. The sky is dark now. Sometimes that is the very best canvas upon which to paint her memories. Lately she's been composing the time when she was newly married, newly pregnant sharing tea with her mother-in-law, learning the rules of Buckworth baby naming.

"If it's a boy, dear, then you must call him Mellor Junior, after your husband."

"But why would I do that, Mother Isabel?"

"Oh, I thought the same, dear. It's a family tradition. The first boy receives that name and something else. Have you any idea?"

Anna recalls resenting the constant testing by Isabel, as though Anna were somehow beneath the old biddy. She put up with it, of course, for Mellor's sake, all the quizzes and questions and proper attire and special dishes and the rest made her furious, but this time she had the answer.

"Mellor's hammer!" she said brightly.

"Why that's right, dear. How did you know?"

"Oh he's told me about it, Mother Isabel, many times. It's a family heirloom, isn't it?"

"It is indeed. It goes back to the first Mary Buckworth."

"When was that?"

"Mary Buckworth came here from England in 1813," Isabel pronounced.

"It's actually that old?"

"It is. That's its only value."

"She came from England?"

"From Yorkshire. It's written on the last page of the family bible. That will be yours when I pass on."

"Thank you, Mother Isabel. I'll treasure it. But who was her husband?"

"I'm afraid I don't know, dear. The family tale starts with her. She must have lost him early in life. Not unusual in those days. Perhaps that is what made her come to Canada. At any rate, if you have a boy he will be given that hammer when his father, your husband, passes."

"What if I have a girl?"

"Her name will be Mary."

"Because of that first Mary?"

"I thought it strange too, Anna dear. I lost my only girl. I could have no children after that."

"I never knew. I ... I'm sorry."

"It's not something one speaks of. Not in my day. At least"—Mother Isabel cracked a smile and touched Anna on her belly—"at least I had no more of the Buckworths' ridiculous naming issues."

It was one of the few precious moments when Anna had shared a laugh with Isabel.

It is a good memory.

Broken abruptly by Mel's arrival. His second arrival that day. Her son.

He is glaring. He is huge in the doorway and bigger as he approaches her bed. It is something which swells him somehow quite beyond his actual physical presence. She has seen this only a few times in his life. Like a cat's fur extended when it is angry to make it appear larger than it is. Mel was usually an easygoing boy, except for his athletics of course, but when his temper rose it swelled him like that, not only in her perception but particularly in those upon whom his wrath had been raised.

"What is wrong, Mel? Why are you angry?"

She watches him forcibly quell the hobgoblin within. She can feel his aura dip. She can feel the constriction in her chest begin to ease. He is not smiling but is no longer huge.

"Some trouble at home, Mom! Dani brought her boyfriend."

An offhand comment but she sees past it to the fury he is trying to quell. She attempts to make it easier for him.

"Oh, that young scientist. His name is Stanley! Yes. He seems nice. Rather shy."

"I don't want to talk about him," Mel says, his aura once again swelling.

Then George enters. He is flushed. Out of breath. It all happens so quickly. He does not even greet his mother.

"I need to talk to you, Mel. Now."

"What are you doing here?"

"Chasing you."

"Go on back. I'm with Mom."

"Hello, Mother, did you get some sleep?" As George acknowledges her, he is distracted she can tell. He has always been able to centre on things intellectual, much the way Mel focused on athletics. George does not expand when angered. He becomes very calm until he can work out the cause.

"You wanna stay, stay," Mel says bluntly to his brother.

"Can we just go outside a minute? You left a bit of chaos in your wake."

"Outside then!" Mel says.

They never make it. They get to the door, not the other side of it.

Anna hears.

"What did you think you were doing walking out like that?" George asks.

"It was that or smack the little shit. I thought you'd be proud of me!"

"All of it was uncalled for, Mel."

"Just wait until it happens to you!"

"What the hell does that mean?"

"He's *fucking* my daughter. He's *fucking* my Dani. She's nineteen years old and she's shacked up with this doofus!"

"Easy, Mel."

"Easy? Easy for you to say. Who's *fucking* Mary without you knowing, huh? Who's *fucking* Melissa, your baby girl? You think your girls are *hot*? Think they'll bring their *fucking* boyfriends home for your *approval*? Think that, *Georgie*?"

"Stop right now."

"Make me."

"This is ridiculous."

"Yeah. You are ridiculous!"

"You sound like a child."

"You know what I remember, Georgie? Speaking of children. You know my clearest memory of you? It's you at the bottom of the basement stairs crying like a little girl and holding Dad's saw in your hand shouting at me not to come down, don't dare come down or you'll use it. What the fuck was that, huh? Crying like a baby and holding a saw!"

"After you'd beat me up!"

"A bit of rough house ..."

"Stop it, Mel."

"Like I said ... make me!"

"Alright, I'm leaving now."

"You scared again, Georgie? You gonna cry?"

George is halfway out the door when he freezes, turns his head, speaks.

Anna hears.

"Do you remember at all why I was like that, *big* brother? Do you have any clue? You'd spent that day shoving me around because mother asked you to *babysit* while she went to her IODE luncheon meeting!"

"I didn't wanna babysit!"

"Of course you didn't. I remember it much more clearly than you. Just as I recall my life without need of the prerequisite trophies! Isn't that your life? Trophy to trophy? Isn't that who you are now? A middle-aged man playing childhood games of bully. Acting like a *child*. More of a child than your children!"

"Fuck off."

"I intend to, Mel. And if you ever refer to my girls in that manner again no matter what it takes I *will* make you stop. If it takes a saw I'll use a saw. Stay out of my life from now on. You've made enough mess of yours. Now goodbye."

He leaves and the door clicks shut. Mel seems momentarily frozen. The huge aura is dissipated now, leaving a shadow against the blonde wood of the door.

Anna speaks.

"Mel, go after your brother. You apologize. I never raised you like that. I'm shocked to hear you say things like that. Your poor brother ..."

"It's not his business, Mother." Mel is still facing the door.

"Go now. I mean it. Go now."

Without looking back, without a goodbye, her eldest son leaves her adrift. He opens the door and departs.

The sky outside is somehow blacker.

Anna weeps.

24

STANLEY RINGS THE doorbell of the house on Fischer, a narrow neighbourhood street near Uptown Waterloo. The house itself is far from foreboding: cozy two-storey with old, worn red bricks and white shutters. The white door has a half moon window near its top. On such a sunny, beautiful day it all appears so welcoming. Stanley mounts the steps of the front porch. He knocks on the door. He waits. He waits longer. A minute passes. He turns to leave when he hears the dead bolt lock click.

MJ answers the door.

"Stan? What are you doing here?"

Where is Pat? A whole new set of problems are raised with the son. Stanley shuffles, unsure what to do next. His mind is computing like crazy accessing memory files finding emotional code roaming into the ROM of his brain trying to instantly reprogram the RAM so as not to be so afraid and unsteady. File after file within folder on folder the unconscious process proceeds at the speed of light. Yet it is so much more than technology this mind which is not a device but a being with self-awareness, emotions and the primordial *fight or flight* instinct battling within.

"Something wrong with Dani?" MJ asks.

It takes a moment to register in Stanley's already overtaxed mind. *Dangers of the OS failing. Find something quick!*

"Hello MJ. I, erm, no, there's nothing with Danielle. She's at soccer. I drove her there. She's fine! I found myself in the neighbourhood ..."

"Stan, this isn't your best move," MJ says.

"I thought perhaps if you got to know me. That is, your parents ... and you, of course! May I speak with your mother?"

"She's not here."

"Oh, that's unfortunate."

"Look Stan ..."

"It's Stanley, MJ."

"What the fuck difference does it make?"

"I just prefer my real name," Stanley answers.

"Why would that matter?"

"Yes, well ... What would you do if someone decided to call you Mellor Junior instead of MJ? I doubt you would respond positively."

"Yeah. I get it, but now *you* listen. This is a house of nicknames. You'll have to get used to it with Dad."

"It's just I don't want to be one of the *Stans*."

"You're the only Stan we know."

"Yes but there's Afghanistan, Kazakhstan, Kyrgyzstan, Pakistan, Tajikistan, Turkmenistan, and Uzbekistan. I have no desire to be Anotherstan."

He can't help it. The opening was just too prescient. A Monty Python instant.

"What the fuck does that mean?" MJ says.

Normally the joke would be the perfect launch in a room of strangers. MJ doesn't comprehend it. Stanley finds himself deep in the mire still standing outside the front door, freezing.

"Oh, nothing really. Just an observation."

"Of what?"

"Rather, it's a rhetorical statement."

"What?"

"Sorry. Just a lot of mumbling. I'm rather distressed at this point, MJ. I came here to see your father. Is he at home?"

"This isn't the best day, Stan."

"It's ... never mind. Is he ill?"

"In a way. He had a bad night. Now he's trying to set up his new laptop. Hey! You're a techie! Maybe you *should* come in? Maybe you can help us."

"Perhaps I might," Stanley says, grasping at the one lifeline left him despite MJ's awful description. *Techie*! He steps through the door as MJ stands aside. Stanley removes his scarf his toque his gloves his boots and unzips his coat as MJ talks.

"I can do the basic stuff but all the different programs and loading are kind of beyond me. Dad seems to want a lot more than I know. I like gaming. He wants more. He's been spending a lot of time online on our old desktop. Now he's got a laptop. Latest thing. So we're using YouTube for instructions. It's slow. Like he wants a sports stream, for instance ..."

"Streaming sports? I can do that."

"Yeah, but more than that. He wants a VPN. He wants the best security. I don't know where he's got all this but he's been on the desktop whenever I'm not. I think he's becoming an internet junkie. He's been hard to figure out lately. Maybe now's a good time after all."

"I do hope so."

"He's down in my room. We're using the desktop to look things up."

"Thank heaven for YouTube," Stanley says, joking.

"No kidding," MJ responds. He has missed it again.

The two advance down the front hall toward the steps. At the top MJ halts Stanley, grasping his arm. Stanley looks at him for some reassurance. It is not there.

"Look, if Dad gets mad get out quick. He's not good today. A lot's happened. And for shit's sake don't ask about Mom."

"Thank you, MJ. I appreciate you letting me in. Perhaps if I can help him ..."

"And he'll call you Stan. Don't complain. It's his way."

"Of course."

They descend into Hades. An errant metaphor from Stanley's data base.

25

THE DISARRAY IN the room is disconcerting to Stanley who is a *clean desk man* demanding order. He picks his way over a yellow and blue bag from Best Buy, past an HP Pavilion box and piles of styrofoam and cellophane plastic not to mention the half empty pizza box, cans of beer, bottles of water, wayward clothing and finally the table where sits his nemesis.

Behind the man is the desktop, lighting the room with its digital glow giving Mel a pallid appearance not helped by his two-day-old whiskers, going grey at the chin. There are age lines on his face brought out by the overhead strip lights. Yet when he looks up it is those eyes, Danielle's eyes, diamonds in luminosity, which simply overwhelm the computer and LED lighting and mesmerize Stanley.

"What's this guy doing here?"

The eyes spark. Mel's is the voice of doom. There is nothing kind or warm in it.

"He showed up at the door, Dad."

"Show him out then," Mel says.

"Dad, I think we could use some help."

A momentary click of courage rises in Stanley's mind. Rather than doubt it he acts upon it, stepping toward the table, extending his hand.

"I am here, sir, to speak with you about Danielle. And I may be able to help you set up your laptop to fit your needs."

Giving Mel a very clear choice. He is slow this day, the hangover taking its time expiring, the hard truths of last night burning his mind, yet the loss has not quite settled in. She is gone. He is sorry. She will come back. Like Dani. Forced away. *Both* Dani and Pat. He has driven them out. But Pat will come back. She always has.

And here is the man whom he once considered assaulting standing before him like a lamb at the slaughter. Here is the fellow who rides the bleeding edge of technology, the thing which has stolen his work his pride his confidence even his daughter and now his wife. Here is the person who represents all the terrible things which have happened. Here he is ready, it seems, to receive what is thrown down upon him. Mel knows what it must have taken to bring him here. Mel is no fool. Stubborn. Not stupid.

When he hears Stanley's second sentence his mind quickly rolls through his options. He needs help in his quest at this very moment and Stanley Best is offering. Mel is a competitor. Sport teaches much about life. When to strike when to lay back when to get mad when not to. When to pass when to shoot, kick, throw, hit; when to do the right thing at just the right moment. This is one of those freak opportunities appearing when someone falls on the ice bobbles the ball stands away from the plate. These conjectures run through Mel's mind as he stands and extends his hand. Use the chance. Time to *play*.

They shake hands. Just like a game.

"Okay, Stan. Let's see how it goes." Mel sounds doubtful. "MJ? You can't do this?"

"No Dad. Not like him. You gotta remember he's a genius."

"Oh, not really ..." Stanley offers, burning once more from becoming a stan.

"Guess we'll find out," Mel says.

"Thank you, sir, for your time. It is much appreciated."

"You want a beer, coffee ..."

"I don't suppose you would have any tea?"

"I know where Mom keeps it. I'll get a couple of bags. You guys sit. Back in a sec!"

MJ disappears up the stairs leaving an uncomfortable silence, momentary but critical as each man wonders whether and where he should begin. Just as Stanley decides to broach the subject of the computer, saving the hard part until later, Mel speaks. His voice is less doubtful. To Stanley's mind he seems to have become suddenly co-operative. Stanley is not at all clear how this happened. He does not comprehend a *game face*.

"How's Dani?"

Again the nicknames. Stanley's teeth grate. He answers quickly.

"Very fine, sir. Currently at football, erm, soccer that is."

"How's school?"

"Well, sir, I don't consider what I do as school ..."

"I meant Dani."

"Oh! Yes. Of course. School. Danielle. She seems to be doing well, sir! I don't mean she can't improve but at this point so close to the end of the year she is ready for final exams and papers. Indeed, most of her papers are in. Only two exams this session."

"What do *you* actually do?"

The pinwheel spin of topic takes Stanley off base.

"*Do*, sir?"

"Cut the, sir, call me Mel."

This is a huge concession further shaking Stanley's equilibrium.

"Of course. Ah. Mr. Buckworth."

"It's Mel."

"Mel." Softly.

"That's right. Easy enough, eh? So what do you really do then, Stan? Where does your money come from? How do you support my daughter?"

"I have grants, sir ... Mel ... scholarship grants and research commitments."

"You have more than one subject?"

"Fields of research would be more accurate."

"What are your fields?"

"Well, in a nutshell, I am hypothesizing that neural networks, given large quantities of data and powerful computer chips, will give machines new powers of perception and, working on the potential of certain algorithms to join AI with quantum computing, along with crafting nano devices to self-learn."

"Robots."

"No sir, ah, Mel. More cloud computing. It's the coming thing."

"Clouds? What?"

"An example. What would you say if I told you that desktop there, your laptop and my handheld device could all access the same deep web information through a new miniature machine? A machine combining the capabilities of all three while learning your preferences at the same time?"

"Deep web?"

"The *whole* of the internet, not just the surface."

"You can do that?"

"Not yet. It's coming. Sooner rather than later. Google has made it a priority."

"The search guys!"

"Yes. Search engine to be precise. Google wants to craft self-learning devices in future."

"I thought artificial intelligence was robots."

"Not really."

"Robots replaced me. How do you explain that?"

"Was your work repetitive?"

"I was a wire weaver."

"Oh. I see. Yes, it's possible. Robots currently work on repetitive tasks."

"Yeah, but what if a warp gets tangled? The fucking robot ..."

"I'm sure that would require a human overseer."

"But not me. Why not me? I was asked to be a foreman!"

"I'm sure that was an honour, sir, Mel, but you would require retraining in robotics."

"How hard is that?"

"It's a very specialized field ..."

"So what's gonna happen when my wife, my son and daughter can't find jobs?"

"Yeah, I'd like to hear that one too!" MJ says. He has come down the stairs with the teapot in one hand and a cup in the other. He's neglected a saucer. He joins them at the table.

"Here's your tea, Stan."

"Thank you, MJ."

Stanley notes the lack of milk. Still, under the circumstances he pours himself a steaming cup. Tea is the backbone of the English, he notes silently, good from births to deaths and all occasions between. He takes a brief sip, then begins.

"Automation has historically, inevitably improved the lifestyles of societies embracing it. It does eliminate jobs in the short term, often with painful consequences, but for any economy as a whole automation drives down the prices of most goods and services."

"So what happens to us when we lose our jobs? Or can't find a job," MJ says.

"I would say retraining, MJ. You're in a perfect position to do that right now. At your age ..."

"You say he's the perfect age?" Mel says.

"I ... well, yes. He already has the requisite basic knowledge."

"And I don't!"

"I'm afraid not, erm, Mel. You are different generations. Yours was analogue whereas MJ's has been generally more digital. No one's fault ... march of time and all that."

Mel reaches into his shirt and withdraws a small object on a chain around his neck. He holds it in his palm so Stanley can see it: a small hammer. Stanley looks up at Mel in confusion.

"This is a family heirloom, the same as our names, Stan. Our family came over here in 1813 from Yorkshire. I'm not big on history but Dani is. She says she believes the Buckworths were driven out by the industrial revolution."

"Actually, Danielle has told me quite a lot regarding your family. She misses it ... you."

"We'll get to that later. Meanwhile we're talking robots."

"The industrial revolution likely did drive them out, Mel. Your ancestors, I mean. Steam power. Then came electricity and the internal combustion engine. Those three inventions combined, and their applications, moved people from rural to urban lives, off the farm and into factories or clerical and service work. New technologies today will do much the same but more quickly."

"So what happens to us?"

"The industrial revolution led to compulsory school systems to deal with *those* technologies. That increased literacy and numeracy enabling multiple new occupations and careers never seen prior to their advent. Before 1800 people rarely travelled. They knew nothing of the world and had no way of knowing. Yet they can now drive and fly anywhere in the world. With electronics they can learn of the rest. We have entered an informational, technological revolution, Mel. In your youth did you ever envision that you might communicate via cellphone or email with someone anywhere in the world? You see my point."

"Yeah, kind of."

"The point is, MJ, *your* children may not go to school at all, or schooling will be a socializing process as students self-learn through access to knowledge from the deep web and cloud computing."

"I don't think that's gonna happen," Mel says bluntly.

"I bow to your opinion, though as you see I hold my own."

"It's gotta be stopped. You're talking about all the good things it brings. What about nuclear weapons? And these viruses that stalk your famous internet! Or the terrorists who use it!"

"It seems you've discovered quite a lot, Mel. You're already using what this revolution provides."

"I can hardly get him off it, Stan!" MJ says.

"You talk about machines learning to serve us," Mel says, "but what happens when they learn too much, when they know more than us, when they turn on us and make us serve them?" When he finishes there is a pause. Stanley knows he must be careful.

"That is a future I cannot surmise. I can only base my opinion upon a factual basis. Anything else is speculative."

The two are frowning at each other. MJ notes things going downhill. He changes the subject. Despite his scholastic failings his emotional awareness is very well tuned.

"Speaking of machines, let's get to Dad's laptop, eh? You guys can talk about this other shit anytime. Right now we've got a mission! Get Dad going on his machine!"

"Of course ..." Stanley quickly backs down. There can be only one *Alpha*.

"What's the deep web again?" Mel says, pressing his advantage.

"I'm sorry?"

"You said we can learn from the deep web."

"Well briefly, search engines like Google and Yahoo explore and index websites because of links. They use links to rank results. This is the so-called surface web. But the internet doesn't stop there. The deep web holds information invisible to most search engines: personal email and information as well as online banking accounts, corporations' private data bases, all materials which can be reached if a link is known. When you check your email or your bank account you are actually in the deep web."

"How do you find out these addresses, links?"

"Word of mouth, usually, or instructions from owners, advertising, sometimes even accidental traffic surfaces."

"What's the dark web then?" MJ asks.

"An intensely dangerous place," Stanley answers. "The deep web contains mostly harmless digitized data. The dark web is home to criminals, factions and those who build websites without DNS."

"Huh?" Mel mutters.

"The internet has a structure. The root servers act as a master directory for the internet. The Domain Name System or DNS, which converts complex Internet protocol addressing codes into the words and names, relies on the servers to tell computers around the world how to reach key internet domains. One rung below the root servers in the Internet hierarchy are the servers that house internet domains such as dot-com, dot-biz and dot-info."

"Whoa! Jesus! Slow down!" Mel says, holding his hands in the air.

"The dark web is anonymous. The Onion router, now called Tor, is free and open-source software for enabling anonymous communication. Can you envision that? You can't *browse* the dark web. You have to have prior information, mostly via chatrooms, to set your destination."

"So hackers? You must have been there some time Stan, the dark web."

"When I was young and rather stupid."

"I doubt you were ever stupid, Stan!" MJ says. "How did you do it?"

"You won't try it, MJ?" Stanley says.

"I'll make sure he doesn't," Mel says.

"The ends are not the best, Mel. Pornography. Black hats. Drugs. Guns. Stolen information for sale. Anything. There's one site right now, called Silk Road, on the FBI list. Drugs of any and all kinds are sold there anonymously. I have a feeling it's going down soon. But I digress.

"Look, if you try navigating without a guide someone will follow you back to your device. Then it's curtains: anything from taking control over your information to blackmail will follow. Never go there."

"Shit," MJ says, "it sounds scary."

"It is," Stanley says.

"But you can go there if you want, if you know how," Mel says.

Game on.

26

STANLEY AND DANIELLE listen to Michael play at The Bombshelter Pub that Saturday night. It is inside the university's Student Life Centre. It isn't much, a place to go but never *the* place to go; it is a beat up room in a beat up old building for undergrads in the midst of the campus. Its name derives from its weighty appearance, square pillars all over, brick walls, big round tables. Yet there is a small stage and the meagre stage lighting enhances Michael's dark skin beneath his white shirt and black trousers. His aged, beat up Washburn 200 seems to glow as well. Light shines on his agile fingers as they coax the complexities of *Benga Beat* from his guitar.

He has chosen not to sing this night but introduce new rhythms and styles to his audience. East African. West African. South American. Some call it World music. At times people stop drinking their beer, stop talking, stop everything to listen to the sounds as his fingers fly up and down the frets and tickle the strings in the reverberations resonances echoes timbres suggestions meanings within his instrument. His guitar seems an extension of his body. He plays the sounds of his soul. There is enthusiastic applause after each number. He is magical.

When he takes a break, The Bombshelter regains its normal clamour: more beer, more burgers, more talk of the man who can capture their attention as he has the past forty minutes. Danielle is excited. Dressed in white jeans and a blue linen shirt she uses the lightest of makeup and simple turquoise earrings. The sparkle is in her eyes and her smile as she beams across the table at Stanley. Stanley wears his horn-rimmed glasses this night with jeans and a grey chambray shirt. He too is smiling. Michael joins them.

"That was wonderful, Michael," Danielle says. "So complicated. It must be hard enough just to get your fingers to do those things let alone remember all the music!"

"I practise every day, Danielle," Michael says. "Just an hour but it's good to keep up. Let it go any length of time and you find you have lost your touch."

"I hear you once in a while downstairs but not often."

"That's because I play softly. I have an *aficionado*."

"Really," Danielle says, rolling the word, teasing her friend suggestively. "A girl?"

"No, he's a boy."

"Oh. I'm sorry."

Danielle is nonplussed. She was not expecting Michael to come out. She had no idea what to expect. It wasn't a problem for her but a rather fat surprise. She takes a drink from her beer watching as Michael and Stanley laugh.

"No, no darling," Michael says, his long vowels so melodic. "It's *your* favourite boy."

"Stanley?"

"Not quite, love!" Stanley dissolves in a paroxysm of glee.

"Why are you guys laughing?"

"It is Henry!"

"The cat?"

"Indeed," Michael says. "He curls up on my bed when I practise. Sometimes he sits very, very still and watches my hands. Sometimes, when I pause, I can hear him purr. He likes it quiet, you know, the music."

"Does that cat like everyone in the house but me?"

Stanley nearly spits up his beer.

"No. No. Not you alone! Henry hates Will! Haven't you noticed? Of course not. You've been busy nursing your own animosity. Believe me, if it came to a vote whether he stays or goes Henry would only scrape by."

"It seems," Danielle says, "it would be two—two. A stalemate."

"You're forgetting, love, Henry has a vote too."

Danielle says nothing, then smiles.

Michael rises. He too is smiling.

"I'm going on again. Something you'd like me to play?"

"Something African!" Danielle responds, smiling back.

Michael approaches the stage. When the lights come up he picks up his guitar, adjusts the mic, tunes the strings, sits on his tall stool and pulls the mic toward him.

"Just for a moment I hope you will indulge me, good people, with a song of Africa and one close to the heart of a friend who sits through my rehearsals each and every day."

He plays differently from the rest of the night strumming a pop rhythm, not introducing the song; the laughter introduces it for him.

A-weema-weh, a-weema-weh, a-weema-weh, a-weema-weh
A-weema-weh, a-weema-weh, a-weema-weh
A-weema-weh, a-weema-weh, a-weema-weh
A-weema-weh, a-weema-weh, a-weema-weh

Without falsetto, his voice is clear and happy, his accent lending the song authenticity.

In the jungle, the mighty jungle
The lion sleeps tonight
In the jungle the quiet jungle
The lion sleeps tonight

He shouts *Everybody!* And they join him!

A-weema-weh, a-weema-weh, a-weema-weh, a-weema-weh
A-weema-weh, a-weema-weh, a-weema-weh, a-weema-weh
A-weema-weh, a-weema-weh, a-weema-weh, a-weema-weh
A-weema-weh, a-weema-weh, a-weema-weh, a-weema-weh

He quiets the crowd by dropping his volume, then goes again from soft to raucous.

Near the village the peaceful village
The lion sleeps tonight
Near the village the quiet village
The lion sleeps tonight

Then a loud, grinning look toward Danielle and Stanley: *Ha! Ha!*

A-weema-weh, a-weema-weh, a-weema-weh, a-weema-weh
A-weema-weh, a-weema-weh, a-weema-weh, a-weema-weh
A-weema-weh, a-weema-weh ...

And as they all join in beers swinging side to side, feet tapping the floor, hands providing percussion, barmaids swinging hips with abandon, laughter holding it all together, he begins to riff wildly on the Washburn bending notes sliding others letting the boisterous rowdies go softer into a whisper behind their mugs then growing to growls and squeals and the final crescendo cascading around the pub and ending with an arpeggio that brings a standing ovation.

Danielle is standing, laughing, eyes sparkling. Waving a finger at Michael.

You dog!

Or in this case ... *friend of Mr.* ... you-know-who!

At night's end when they exit the pub they cross the campus going through the Math buildings to the ring road, then join the Iron Horse Trail which, if they kept walking, would take them through Waterloo and south to Kitchener following an old, defunct rail line. They stop at University Avenue, however, making two lefts which bring them to the Mongolian Grill in the University Plaza. It is a restaurant where customers select the foods they wish to eat and take them to the huge "shield" grill where chefs in black shirts and bandanas take over. It's a popular place to eat for students. You can return more than once with multiple choices of meats and vegetables. They order another beer each, a coke for Michael, and settle in to enjoy their food.

Their walk home afterward is an easy one: east on University then north on Albert to get home. It is warm for early spring and a pleasant walk, though they still wear either a coat or sweater against the night's cooling temperatures.

Dani's phone rings while they walk and she answers.

"Hello?"

Silence.

"MJ? Shouldn't you be working?"

Silence.

"He what? Why?"

Silence.

"Jesus. Did you see it? Is she okay?"

"Oh God," Stanley says.

Dani waves him away.

"Let her be, man," Michael says, calming Stanley.

"When?" Dani asks. Her voice is cracking.

Silence.

"Packed and left for where?"

Silence.

"I know what this is about. I couldn't tell her myself," Stanley says to Michael.

"Uncle George? Cambridge?"

Silence.

"Ask Stanley? Why?"

Silence.

Dani shuts off her phone.

She glares at Stanley.

27

MIKE LAZARIDIS WAS the innovator of Research in Motion, maker of the Blackberry phone. A generous man, for years his corporation expanded and took Waterloo along with it into the twenty-first century. Always intrigued by physics, Lazaridis funded the Perimeter Institute for Theoretical Physics, soon a leader in contemporary quantitative science. Following that, his charity expanded to the University of Waterloo, his *alma mater*, with the creation of a new five-storey edifice housing the Mike and Ophelia Lazaridis Quantum Nano Centre.

The building is a marvellous symbolic glimpse at the future, its exterior distinguished by a honeycomb of structural steel, a pattern inspired by the hexagonal carbon structure of the nanotube, while the Quantum half possesses windows which are either transparent or translucent depending on the angle of perception. The facility itself is considered the most complex scientific building ever constructed by the university. As Lazaridis said upon its opening: "*This critical nexus of quantum computing and nanotechnology brings the world closer to the cusp of previously unimagined solutions and insights.*"

Stephen Hawking was there at the launch.

Inside are quantities of futuristic equipment, highly specialized labs, white boards and glass windows covered in algorithms and equations, high tech classrooms and airy *mind spaces*. It also houses some of the best scholars on earth to make use of this unique environment. In some areas there are chairs and bistro tables along a glass wall looking south and to these are attracted those taking lunch, working on a problem, or just sitting to talk as Stanley and Will do on this bright sunny Monday.

"I tell you, Will, it was nearly preternatural. I couldn't believe the man could change so much so quickly from wanker dad to welcoming father."

"That's because you helped him," Will says.

"Yes, I understand that. Yet it's more. The man seems obsessed with learning how to navigate the internet. He is positively burning with this need for information."

"What did you give him?"

"I loaded him up with protection protocols though he'd already done some research and wanted to know about the deep web."

"You're kidding. I thought he wasn't that bright."

"As did I. I've seldom seen someone apply his powers of concentration the way he does. He *drinks* data. I introduced him to Facebook's private page and then to Sci Hub and finally to what I think he really wanted ... Keybase and Hidden Wiki."

"What's he want with those?"

"That's just it, I have no idea. MJ, the son, told me as I was leaving that his dad was searching for a new job and though that seemed a bit weak, MJ believed him. I personally think the father already knows far more than his son about internet interface. He wanted *Tor* though I told him it would be difficult for him, then he demanded at least *Duck Duck Go*."

"What happened?"

"I downloaded it. Now he'll play with it. At least he's off *Tor* for the time being. He's in a big hurry for some reason. He offered to pay me for weekly tutorials. I've no time for that!"

The seeds of a concept burgeon slowly and often from unlikely sources as they do now. First they exist as scattered kernels with no apparent pattern or purpose. One must mull them over, perhaps plant one or two in the mind, let them burble and sprout, take one's time before taking action. Gradually, if they are valid, they will take root and flower.

Will Baker, on the other hand, is impetuous. His concept comes as a physical jolt. He is drinking coffee one moment then spilling it on the table the next. As he and Stanley use their napkins to soak up the fluid he internalizes what he has heard. When the table is clean he pushes Stanley to farm his thoughts.

"He wants a tutor?" Will says.

"Well he asked me."

"What about me?"

One seed sprouts. A crucial source of money.

"I suppose I could introduce you. You'll have to govern him though."

"I'll make it easier for him," Will says.

Second sprout. An unaddressed need and an introduction.

"I'd appreciate that, Will. But what about your own work?"

"One day a week with the old guy. That wouldn't interfere."

Third sprout. The time to solve his indigence.

"I could take you there. I'll visit again soon if Danielle will allow," Stanley says.

"Why not give me his number, his email? I can introduce myself."

Fourth. Remove the competition.

"Alright. Let me text it. I'm off downstairs now and over to Nano. Apparently they're building something rather special in the lab. Are you home tonight?"

"Not sure yet. I'll text."

Fifth. Time to put these entities together. Make sense of the equations.

Allow them to grow.

Create fruit.

Apple is a fruit. Blackberry too. Tangerine Computer Systems. Apricot Computers. Raspberry Pi Foundation. All good names. All good fruits. All very profitable. He should name his new app after a fruit, something of benefit to everyone, something everyone knows about or will at least recognize. It has to do with something you *peel* like a banana, no, too domesticated. *His* fruit must peel must seem daring must taste good when properly prepared.

Will Baker thinks it through: sifts his seeds and grafts his sprouts and nurtures them as they grow in his mind. Swiftly, as all acts of genius seem. Unexpected, as no one suspects what he plans. Quietly, so his concept will not be pilfered.

A need that the Everyman wants ... the deep web. Who doesn't want more access? Who would not pay for a portal? This could become the biggest protocol since Google Search, he thinks. A brain to help them get there. It was all in the conversation. It was all in Stanley's mind and yet not even Stanley was able to see it. Only he, Will Baker, has made that reach. For so long he has been reaching and now he has grasped the required concept to actually start.

Next comes the milling and manipulation. He can work with Mel Buckworth, being paid for just keeping him out of trouble, all the while farming his seeds with sites, encryptions and algorithms along with the data mass required to build his new application. A portal to take Everyman where he once could never go, its functions as simple as possible. Mel will test it. If he can operate it anyone can. So while Buckworth pays for Will's service he will also serve as Will's beta lab rat.

Stanley has told him that Mel isn't answering his phone. Stanley texts. Upon its arrival Will texts Mel.

Mr. Buckworth
i have heard u need help
i am Stan's colleague
i know the deep web
weekly tutorial daily talk or text
imbursement in cash
complete anonymity
reply asap
will baker

Texting done he sits back, looking around the space of the Quantum Centre. He makes a further attempt at creative naming. Must peel must seem daring must taste good when prepared. Not banana too safe. Not cassava too strange. Prickly, must be prepared, must taste good, and must have an instrument to open it.

Pineapple.

The word for money.

That fast.

28

THERE ARE NO tears left. Danielle has cried herself out. She's not sure she will see her father ever again. She looks up at Stanley, her eyes dull and red, and glances at Henry lounging just outside the room. One eye is on her from beneath that crossed paw.

"Why does that damn cat keep looking at me?" she says crossly.

"Well you *have* been making some noise," Stanley says. As the words come out he knows he's blown it.

"That's what you think? Fine Stanley, I won't bring my troubles to you again."

"No, that's not it, love ... I, erm, I was just commenting on the cat's behaviour."

He turns to the cat, waving his hands.

"Henry ... shoo! Shoo!"

Henry uncurls and saunters into the room. Always the unexpected.

"Just look at that sideways glance! It's like I'm out to get him or something!"

"I'm sure that's not it. I know Henry pretty well."

"I wonder what he thinks," she murmurs.

"Cats do not think, Danielle. They are simply instinctual. Their conduct can be modified in a vague Skinnerian manner, food and such, petting ... you know. You shouldn't let Henry bother you. But enough of Henry. Are you feeling any better?"

"This isn't easy, Stanley. My parents breaking up. My mom's left and I never had the chance to see her and all this happened the night before you were actually there! And you *lied* to me when you went! You didn't notice anything strange?"

"I noticed he'd changed toward me. I am here, undamaged, aren't I? And I believe he appreciated my work. I did notice one thing ... he kept asking for more and more protections so I stacked the machine for safety. I'm afraid he'll do something stupid while searching. I do know he intends to learn about something that seems quite important to him."

"Learn what? My dad hardly reads, unless it's the sports pages."

"MJ said your father was improving his skills! That was it! MJ told me your father had taken control of the desktop the past few weeks which is why, I assume, he purchased the laptop. Very robust one, I might add. MJ must have advised him."

"MJ didn't own the desktop! That was the family's, for everyone. My lazy brother just used it all the time for his game."

"Well I believe your father has affected him. He was quite perspicacious when I was loading your father's machine. Followed everything closely. Actually, both of them. Are they always so focused?"

"Just when they play their games ... my dad with sports, MJ online."

"Very impressive though, darling. I mean it. Watching father and son work together like that, brainstorm together, push their limits. I was astonished, actually."

"Stanley?"

"Yes?"

"Why did you go there? Why didn't you tell me?"

"I'm sorry, Danielle, I just thought it best to meet him alone. I needed to straighten things out after Christmas. Amazingly, he seemed open. I had no idea what had happened. MJ said something but not your father. It's as if he is capable of rather adroit compartmentalization. There was no mention at all of your mother."

"Now I'm not so sure I want to see *him*. Ever."

"Don't jump to conclusions, love. We don't know exactly what happened between them."

"He slapped her! He assaulted my mother! They've been having trouble a while now. So tense with MJ cooped up in the basement, Mom in the kitchen and Dad upstairs. I couldn't stand it. Always a squabble. It was like a Big Brother house with people knowing each other's flaws and aiming right for them. I couldn't live like that."

"That won't happen with us," he says.

"I know. I knew it when I met you. Just don't lie to me Stanley, ever, even if you want to protect me. I want to be part of all our decisions."

"And you will. Would you like to rest?"

"No. Let's have supper. I think good old Mister Walk-On-By's food bowl is empty. At least I can try to *Skinner* him!"

Downstairs Will is making supper while Michael assists as sous-chef. Will has made an American chili and Michael a Kenyan pilau, the fragrance of cumin, cardamom, cinnamon and cloves infusing the kitchen. All three men are adequate cooks. When Danielle had first arrived she'd doubted she could compete. Then a few of her mother's recipes found their way to the table on her nights to cook: spicy meat loaf, chicken and dumplings, veal schnitzel and an amazing mac and cheese gave her a place among them. They ate together four nights a week if they could and the other three nights had take-out or went out to eat.

Henry sits mournfully by his bowl. His fur has that odd look of a T-shirt worn beneath it, the white V at his neck which Danielle finds so amusing. His face is unreadable. His tail curls around his left front paw. Stanley moves toward the cupboard but Danielle reaches for the cat food and measures it into the bowl. Henry flinches. She sees it. She moves toward him. He dives under the kitchen table. Gone like smoke. Danielle left in his wake again.

"What is wrong with that cat?" she cries.

Michael laughs, his long vowels soothing.

"Oh man it took me months before he'd be in the same room. I thought it was blatant racism! Then I played him some music."

"Cat's aren't supposed to like music, Michael."

"This one does!" Stanley says.

"Don't worry, darlin'," Will chimes in, "he'll come around someday, or not. Do you know he once shit in my shoe? He still won't let me near him."

"I'll get the plates, set the table," Stanley says, avoiding another exchange with Danielle.

"I heard you were helping out Sam and Kaheer," Will says, somewhat critically.

"Just attenuating one or two algorithms ..."

"You need to help *me*, Stanley. They've got their thing."

"You mean help you with ..."

"On my app ..."

"Don't say it!" Stanley says. "You know how I feel about games."

"This one isn't a game."

"What is it?"

"I can't say right now."

"So how can I help you?"

"A touch here and there."

"Without seeing the architecture?"

"That part's not done yet. Look I just need an algorithmic muse!"

"I am no muse, Willis."

"You're the closest thing!"

"You need to converse more with like minds. What about Matt Miner and Brad Keys in the Velocity residence?"

"Gaming analytics? Yeah. That's an idea. Think they'll talk to me?"

"I'm sure they will. That's the concept of the Centre isn't it? Brainstorming?"

"Man, why don't you move away from your get rich app fascination? Do something for the world?" Michael asks. "Clearpath for instance ... developing mobile robots, automating dangerous jobs."

"Not my style, Michael. I'm an entrepreneur from a long line of them."

"Californians?" Stanley says. "Let me see now ... inventions, yes ... blue jeans!"

"Don't start ..."

"McDonald's!" Michael says.

"WD-40!" Stanley says. It's a game often played.

"Hula hoops! Danielle says.

"Alright! Enough! I'm gonna burn this chili!"

"What will you do when you get filthy rich?" Danielle asks. She's forgotten Henry. He's forgotten Pineapple. Right now they are all simply best of friends. None know how that will change in future. None know the strife awaiting.

"Well darlin'," Will says, breaking into his best Texan accent, "ah jus' might buy you 'n yor fella here a brand new fancy-dancy pure-bred Ashera kitty t' replace what's his name?"

"Mister Walk-On-By," Danielle says.

"Yep! Looks kinda like him except it's an Asian leopard cat."

"A what?"

Will attempts an explanation, then gives it up and goes for his iPhone. He types in a phrase on Google. He hands his device to Danielle. She reads the internet display aloud.

"*The Ashera can cost as much as a whopping $125,000 because it is an extremely rare breed. A Los Angeles-based firm produces only 5 kittens each year. This exotic breed is a hybrid of the Asian leopard cat, a domestic housecat, and the African serval. Personality-wise, it is loyal, affectionate, and very intelligent. Despite the controversy about its genetics, the Ashera is the most prized pet cat in the world.*"

"Well that cuts out Henry, both price and personality!" Michael says, laughing.

"Where is he anyway?"

"Under the table?"

Everyone bends to look.

Not there.

Quantum Henry.

29

THE GAME IS on for Mel Buckworth.

He ignores the NHL playoffs the basketball baseball volleyball soccer skiing tennis track and field swimming diving boxing fencing cycling golfing gymnastics weightlifting rugby and Australian rules football which have always passed the time for him and even made him a little money when he chose to gamble.

Now he spends increasing time spans with his laptop online, searching out new things. He is retraining himself. Pushing himself into the next generation as much as he possibly can. He has never worked this hard on anything not physical before in his life. He knows none of it will be easy. He wishes he had his brother's brains. He knows he will need someone like Will Baker. For some reason Stanley's colleague has texted him, offering help, requesting a visit.

Still, he has found his purpose. He has been through the phases of grief and seems to have recognized all but *acceptance* of his place in the world. He realizes he is outcast, a casualty of this new revolution, this new way of thinking, the new society evolving so quickly, the systems he cannot aspire to grasp.

He has, however, recognized that brave new world, listening to Stanley explain its existence. He has gained a new appreciation of young Stan as well. Stan is an outlier: an exceptional individual beyond normal expectations of achievement. Mel knows a pro, a talent, when he sees one. The skills with which Stanley has taken Mel's laptop from conventional to extraordinary have been astounding. He has accomplished it in a matter of minutes, minus the download time, and achieved even more. He *explained* as he went.

Of course Stanley employed the technical terms which Mel, and even MJ, could not really comprehend but he would clarify them as best he could, the way a professional player would elucidate to a couple of amateurs. He was not impatient. Patronizing, yes, the way Mel was when he'd coached his son or kids' teams.

Mel recalls meeting Darcy Tucker and Shayne Corson in 2008 just after Tucker had left the Leafs and signed with Colorado. Mel was at his cottage that summer and had decided to visit Port Carling. He'd stopped into the hillside bar for a beer and caught sight of the two hockey players. He'd walked over and introduced himself. They were quite friendly. Tucker told him he owned a cottage on Lake Muskoka.

Mel bought them a beer. They asked him to sit down. After some cottage conversation, lake levels and fishing spots, he told them he'd played way back in the day and still did in the old boys' leagues. They laughed when he offered one or two of his stories. He asked them what they felt was the biggest difference for a player reaching the NHL. Corson said it was physically tougher. Tucker told him it was time and space. Both of them insisted their years of training took over in the end. Action and reaction were just too slow until one recognized that it really became about training and instinct.

He'd wanted more but it was difficult for them to explain and equally so for him to ask the proper questions. You can't ask what you don't know and he knew enough to know that he didn't know much in comparison. He'd left them after one beer, not wanting to bother them further but he'd reached a kind of comprehension with something Tucker had said about passing or shooting decisions ... *it just looks right, Mel, in that second* ... a life of hockey, the skills and training and struggle and all of it condensed to a single *second* when everything comes together, intuitively.

That was Stanley: in another way.

He had grasped as well the thing Stanley was so afraid to say when he'd explained societal changes. That he, Mel Buckworth, is a victim. That he has been playing defense all this time (but for one moment of arson). That he has not accepted it until the day he understood it actually is all a game. That was the day he tried to set up his computer, the momentous day when Stanley had appeared. The day Mel stopped his old life and began to create a duality. For weeks afterward he'd explored, barely pausing to eat or sleep as he'd learned new skills and adopted a new character.

The internet was a trove of ideas, ideologies, information, invention and iconoclasts. He found after a few false starts that he could manipulate this monster, bring to the screen reams of knowledge, anecdotes from social media, narratives of news coverage, photographs and films from pornography to Pac-Man, reports on sport, rumours of conspiracies, buzzes of popularity, legends of revolution, articles of instruction, statements of manifestos, yarns from history, tales of daring, scoops of data, items of any and all interests and, most particularly for Mel, accounts of others like him in similar situations and how they found ways of achieving reprisal.

He discovered Neo-Luddism and thus the theories of vengeance:

anti-materialism, minimalism, anarchism, eco-terrorism, anarcho-primitivism and dystopian futurology. He found Chellis Glendinning's "Notes toward a Neo-Luddite Manifesto" then The McKinsey Report then Jaron Lanier then George Dyson and Nicholas Carr. These were things, of course, he would never have read or even thought to read before, simply because he'd had no idea of their existence. Opinions from brilliant people: difficult to understand yet finally, after highlighting and re-reading and even studying ...

They gave him the *why*. Then he discovered the *how*.

Theodore Kaczynski, the Unabomber.

Mel came upon him by accident. A search on Neo-Luddism brought him this:

> *Between 1978 and 1995, Kaczynski mailed or hand-delivered a series of increasingly sophisticated bombs that cumulatively killed three people and injured 23 others in an attempt to start a revolution by conducting a nationwide bombing campaign targeting people involved with modern technology. In all, 16 bombs were attributed to Kaczynski. While the bombing devices varied widely through the years, all but the first few contained the initials "FC," which Kaczynski later said stood for "Freedom Club," inscribed on parts inside. He purposely left misleading clues in the devices and took extreme care in preparing them to avoid leaving any fingerprints. He issued a manifesto opposing industrialization.*

Mel knew that the current world, the one Stanley had described so offhandedly, had played him effortlessly. Now he would learn to play it. He was realizing he'd have to find ways *beneath* the technology in order to engage in it. Stanley could have been a hacker, attacked it on its own ground, employed the technology against itself. Mel was a Luddite. Came from Luddites. He had researched the Luddites in one very long night of revelation. He examined his tiny hammer, the one he'd worn with ignorance after his dad had died. *Enoch*. That was its name. So much more than an heirloom. So emblematic. So significant beyond its meagre size.

It offered a symbol in this new world and a strategy for playing. Unknowingly he and Gary Wilson had, with their arson, repeated history. Now he would use Luddite ways and means when planning his second move. There *would* be a second move now. History reassured him. No more defensive play. He would use Kaczynski's methods. He would go on the offensive. He would play this game bequeathed him, a game without rules. It was all in how you played it.

He was good at games.

It is just at this point in his thinking when Will Baker shows up as promised. It is evening. MJ is gone for the night. The knock on the door then this short paunchy guy in hoodie and jeans is on the porch. He looks a bit shifty beneath his veneer. He comes in takes off the hood and reveals carrot hair all askew. Weird. Unlike Stan he has no fear of Mel although Mel has 50 pounds on him and nearly a foot of height.

Will sashays around the front hall all confident and inspectorish then turns to Mel with a quizzical look and takes a seat in the living room. Mel never sits in the living room. It is all antiques. It's Patricia's room. The puzzle room. Still, the guy kind of forces him in his own home, to sit.

"So Mr. Buckworth ..."

"Name's Mel."

"Alright, Mel. I'm Will Baker. Call me Will. I assume I'm on time."

"Yeah."

"So, how can I help? The deep web, the *dark* web ..." Will accentuates the word, giving it a chilling application. He expects a laugh. He doesn't get one. Mel Buckworth looms across the room. Will begins to comprehend Stanley's trepidation.

"You said one day a week plus daily calls. How much?" Mel asks.

"You recognize I am an accredited expert in this field, Mr. Buckworth, and will be taking from my own time to help you."

"How much?"

"Three hundred a week."

"Nope."

"What?"

"You heard me. If you know about me you know I'm unemployed.

That's why I'm doing this, to get more skills in the field to make myself marketable ... and a few other things."

"I understand but ..."

"One fifty."

"Mr. Buckworth ... Mel ... that's not even reasonable."

"Neither's three hundred."

"Two fifty then."

"Two hundred. Take it or get up and go. And you'll have to sign a paper."

"What kind of ..."

"Non-disclosure agreement. Employer/employee. As well as an agreement never to use my computer without my presence along with a written guarantee never to hack it."

"That's a little stiff, Mel. If you don't mind my asking where would you find something like that? There are no contracts regarding hacking."

"Maybe you're not as good as you think then, Mr. Baker. Maybe we should just give this up. I don't think you're gonna be what I need."

Will Baker is stunned that this big jock is going to reject him. This Waterloo bumpkin is turning him down the money is gone just like that he will end up going home in shame this can't be happening. His parley with an unemployed labourer who has even now gained the upper hand turns Will's meticulous plan to smoke. It can't be true it can't be possible surely there must be a way to come back!

"What? Wait. Mel. Two hundred is fine. I'll take you wherever you want. I'll use my own computer. There's no problem here. I'll sign. I'll sign."

"Okay then," Mel says. Now he is smiling. Now he looks normal. Will Baker cannot comprehend what indiscernible force has been levelled on him.

He has just been played.

"So in this case, then," Will slows down his rate of speech, deepens his voice, "I will require while instructing you that I be enabled to work on my own developing application and that *you too* sign the equivalent agreement regarding *invention* in conjunction with my signing your *employer/employee* document. You will not look at my screen without my presence and my agreement. You will not disclose anything you might garner during our tutorial sessions or in our telephone conversations. You will not even mention to anyone, and I mean *anyone,* about our current relationship. Am I clear?"

Mel is no longer smiling. His tactic has been made. He had the kid for a few seconds. He saw it behind those shifting eyes. Then it's right back in his face. This is the guy he needs alright, the one who will offer the subtleties of a pro with the soul of a mercenary.

"What's *garner*?"

"Learn."

"I thought I'm *supposed* to learn."

"What I teach you."

"When do we start?"

"Why not now?"

It has been a successful meeting. He has taken a step. The world will change. Mel Buckworth has a coach named Will Baker and a playbook by Theodore Kaczynski.

30

IT WAS THE chase through Fairview Mall that finally did it for Amrit Khadri. The day had begun as days generally do. He'd reported in around eight-thirty, read through his calls from overnight, reviewed his assigned investigations and prioritized them for the day. That took him to notes from his interviews with the owner and staff at the Schleierkraut Tavern regarding the fire at the Erban building. He still couldn't shake the idea it wasn't just a kids' prank and deduced the tavern's denizens might be talkative over their beer. It hadn't panned out.

Yes, there had been groups from Erban, drinking. Yes, they were bitter. Had there been any loose talk of revenge? No. Any overarching rage, bar fights? None. Still, he carefully finished the notes and saved them to his Erban folder then changed screens and completed a Crown package for the court on an upcoming date involving an Amber Alert he'd resolved.

It hadn't been hard. A divorced couple. Arguments over custody. Ex-husband kidnaps the child on a custodial visit. Khadri had tracked the guy to his parents' place where he was told they'd refused to take the child in, then to his girlfriend's place for more of the same, then to the guy's own place. Khadri had made a deduction the guy would, by that time, have needed gas to drive far away. Sure enough. Gas station on the corner of the street at Pioneer Drive and Homer Watson.

There was the car, a blue Toyota, right licence plate, the child inside, the man pumping gas ... Khadri pulled his car up six inches from the guy's driver door. No way was he getting into that car. The arrest had been simple. The guy was just desperate and lonely. Khadri had cuffed him then radioed for a patrol car to take the child home. Then came the reams of paperwork he was finishing now. This was not the part of investigation he particularly enjoyed. He would rather have been in the field than filling out forms.

Finishing up he decided to drive back to Erban. It was too coincidental that the arson had happened just after mass firings. By this time in his career Amrit Khadri had grown to believe there were no coincidences.

And then one presented itself.

He had, as usual, checked over his car then decided to turn south on Weber then down to Erb, one-way street, to take the Conestoga Parkway around to Ottawa Street saving himself time crossing through the city. No sooner had he arrived on the ring road just coming off Erb, easing into traffic, when a black Mercedes blew by him. He was calling it in when he saw the patrol car, full lights and sirens, roar out the Bridgeport Road entrance on the tail of the Mercedes maniac.

Amrit Khadri accelerated and followed closely behind the police Crown Victoria, letting the guy ahead do his job which was to watch the Mercedes make its moves in and out of traffic and when it was safe put the pedal down and catch the speeder. Khadri would follow as back up. He knew there would be more patrol cars joining in, heading the sucker off and if it got out of hand, like a chase down a residential street, they would terminate the pursuit and form a grid search pattern. Still, few thoughts of that now as the Mercedes cut off another car with a quick jump right and into the flyover at King Street leading it out Highway 8 to the 401. This was going to get ugly. The guy nearly flew down 8.

Then as two more cruisers came up the ramp from Fairway Road. The Mercedes driver saw them, veering three lanes into the off ramp. Now a different set of circumstances confronted the pursuers. The Mercedes entered Fairway Road, filled with traffic, blew through the light, turned right and sped into the huge parking lot at the Fairview Mall. The Crown Vic with Khadri on its tail followed, though slowing. More police were converging at Wilson or Manitou to block the speeder. He had streaked through the parking lot and screeched to a halt in front of the Sears store.

There he jumped out.

The Crown Vic stopped behind the Mercedes. Both officers exiting quickly, moving up the sides of the vehicle hands on their side arms. Khadri had another idea and swung past them and round the corner to arrive at the Walmart entrance. He got out. Locked his car. Moved quickly into and through the Walmart. He saw nothing strange. He continued into the mall itself through the food court's aromas, up the corridor between clothing and shoe and lifestyle stores. He started to doubt his hunch. Then he glimpsed movement at the T junction leading from Sears. Someone walking too fast. Young guy. Greasy blonde hair. Leafs sweatshirt. Black jeans.

He went after the guy. Walking quickly, dodging shoppers, dark looks from civilians not knowing what this guy in a cheap suit was doing but he was too pushy. Khadri kept on. Gaining but breathing hard, the young guy heading for the Hudson's Bay store. If he made it in there he was gone: multiple exits. Khadri knew he had to spring the guy somehow, reveal if he actually *was* the perp.

"Police. Stop! You there. Blue sweater!"

Right guy. He took off in a sprint, Khadri after him. Not a fucking chance of catching him. Huffing, puffing, every bit of his belly tire weighing him down. Then a uniform passed him, flying by, full stride going faster than the perp. When the perp hesitated at the escalators he gave the uniform two precious seconds. The perp started down an aisle to an exit. The cop crossed through ladies wear and exploded out of the multi-coloured spring dresses to tackle the perp.

Khadri arrived, nearly purple. Still enough energy to help pin the perp, turn him over, cuff him. Once done, Khadri sat on the floor wheezing hard, sweat running down his back, his chest heaving. The cop had his knee on the perp's back.

"You okay, sir?"

"I ... I ... yeah." Rather than talk Khadri pulls out his badge.

"Hey, you were driving that grey ..."

"Yeah." Breathe. Breathe. "I was."

"Good thinking goin' past Sears. How'd you know?"

"Just ... a guess. Didn't really want to get out of the car," he said, joking.

The young cop laughed then radioed the arrest. Two more uniforms arrived. They grabbed the perp and stood him up. They were efficient, though not gentle. This jackass could have killed someone.

"Help you up, detective?" the young cop said.

How is it when I'm right there in the midst of the action, the place I want to be, the very nub of being a cop, the reason for my being, I turn out looking like a broken down hack? Okay, that's it. Gym time every day before work. No more Tim Hortons. The young guy's got his hands out, both hands, look at him, he's expecting dead weight! I'll show him!

"I'm good now, Constable. Just fell off my fitness wagon."

"But not off your senses."

Be nice to the old guy, Khadri thinks. I'm not old! Just weak. Get up now. Come on.

"So, I hope it was a clean collar," Khadri says.

"Stolen car. All I know, sir."

"Loved watching you come out of those dresses! Colours like butterflies! Hah! Guy never knew what hit him."

"You okay then, detective?"

"Yeah. You go on. Central Division?"

"Yes, sir."

"I'll follow along. You'll need my report."

And then it was over. *Coincidence?* Why'd I take Erb Street? Would have missed the whole thing. What's not coincidence is the shape I'm in. Time to suck it up. Tennis is the answer. Maybe up in Waterloo Park. It's spring and they'll be open now. I can start on the treadmill tomorrow. And some weights. When did I become a *tourist*? This is my *work* for God's sake!

As he drove to Central, his adrenalin dropping, he felt very tired. Ordinary people can get soft. Most do as they age. They run from danger if danger appears. Or waddle. But a police officer has a duty to head straight for it not knowing precisely what it will be but the possibility of physical contact is always there. You don't pull your gun to stop a fist fight. You don't Taser the woman porch pirate. But you might have to chase someone and to lose that kind of race matters more than simply winning or losing. You've let a perp get away through your weakness.

Time to change the equation.

31

HE'D KNOWN WHERE she was, of course, Grace having called the night after she'd left. Grace had been cold toward him. That was when he'd realized this time would be different. There was no attempt to get them back together: no "ask" for him to come over, no arranging a time, no plan for her to return. When he'd asked Grace to put Pat on the line she'd told him she didn't think Pat was quite ready. He knew what he'd done. He had never done anything like it before. Of course they'd had tiffs, one or the other leaving to cool off, but he had never, ever struck her. He wonders at himself and a character seeming the reverse of the man he always thought he was.

He is ashamed. He remembers the encounter through the drunken haze and resultant hangover. Despicable. He has brought it upon himself, found a harsh duality within his character and strangely—simultaneously—he has begun activating that otherness. How else to explain his new grasp of the digital: minimal at most but growing exponentially.

So he has waited for her, not wanting to trouble her more, eventually so enwrapped in his cyber studies when she calls he is surprised. The call comes on the home phone. Land line. He knows it is her. Everyone else uses his cell to contact him.

"It's me," she says.

"I'm sorry," he says.

"I know you are."

"Are you alright?"

"The bruising's gone now if that's what you mean."

"I meant are *you* alright."

"No. I'm not sure."

"So ... you're not coming home?"

"Not yet, Mel. I, we both have a lot to work out. I haven't felt this way in a long time."

"What way?"

"Free, I guess. Released. We've been in trouble, Mel."

"You mean me ..."

"No. I mean us. Our marriage. Neither of us is the same anymore."

"We can work it out."

He does not sound convincing. His is *not* convinced and recognizes he might not want her back in his new, dual life. He has chosen a path. He has taken the steps, created the plans, made the arrangements to see himself along that tenuous path. Patricia's return would be a diversion. He must focus with all his capabilities now to explore, comprehend and control his new life, his new purpose, his newfound character. He waits for her to respond. Her silence on the other end of the line makes it feel as though she feels the same. It takes a moment until she speaks.

"Will you come with me to see Nancy?"

"The psychologist? You know how I feel about her."

"I just need you to try, Mel."

"I've changed. I've stopped drinking. I haven't signed up for summer ball yet. I don't think I will. I'm learning new things, Pat."

"So am I, Mel. Nothing's the same."

He pauses.

"You're right. It's all different."

She pauses too.

He finds he cannot really talk with his wife. All his research and learning and new motivations have filled him up and pushed her aside. The way things come out he sounds like he isn't sorry at all. He has other priorities. He is building his game plan.

"I'm gonna go up to the cottage, Pat. You should come home here. I'm making some changes and I can't do that here in this house. I need another scene. I won't bother you. I'll stay away. Give you some space. There's lots I can do at the cottage to keep me busy and have a place of my own for a while."

He does not want her living with Grace and his brother. He does not want his brother involved at all. He can see George in his mind's eye. Ever soft. Ever delicate. Ever arrogant. Yet his brother has something, a kind of radar, allowing him glimpses into others' minds. He will not go near his brother. This relinquishing of his house is Mel's first move. He *must* achieve distance from the old ways, yet must appear reasonable. He can have no one question his behaviour, particularly his brother, George.

"You mean this, Mel?"

He can hear her voice crack.

"Yeah. I think so."

"A trial separation?"

"Do us both some good."

"Thank you, Mel."

She sounds suddenly stronger.

"For what?"

"Meeting me halfway."

"Sure. I feel the same."

"When would be good?"

"Friday. I'll pack some stuff and leave Friday morning. Thursday night I've got a tutorial I can't miss."

"A class?"

"Sort of."

"You don't want to see me?"

"Better not now, Pat. Make it a clean break."

"Okay ..."

Her voice is quavering again. He can feel her distress. He must not fail in this, not his first move, not with her. He must find a diversion to distract her. He must offer something slightly out of character but not imprudently so.

"I gotta clean up the house first. I done all the monthly payments. You'll have to take that over. I'm gonna get internet at the cottage. I'll spend more time looking at retraining; maybe find something that fits. And I can get odd jobs up there especially in the spring: opening up people's places, maybe repairing some things ... docks, driveways ... you know. I'll be spending some money on tools and stuff."

"Dani told me about your laptop, Mel. MJ said you're using it now. I'm sorry I said anything about it that night."

"Don't be. That was all my fault. You're right, Pat. We need time apart."

"Do you love me at all?"

"Of course I do ..."

She does not reply. Never before was there any *of course*. He tries to settle; compose his words. Why did she have to ask that? He puts the phone to his ear, his apology already on his lips.

She is gone.

32

IN HER NEAT private room in the nursing home Anna Jean Buckworth rises from her bed and crosses unsteadily to her closet. The pneumonia she thought would take her has not. She is strong enough now to don her housecoat though unable to fully dress without help. She wonders again, as she has each day she since she came here, why God won't take her. She has trouble lately understanding God but her gospel tells her to have faith in his works, that his works are mighty and beyond comprehension. She has seen God's work in the spring time as everything, including herself, seems to come back from winter hibernation. Still, she cannot but feel that her time should be over having become so helpless. She quickly retracts those thoughts in a prayer to Jesus for faith.

She does not pray kneeling. If she tried she would never get up. And she does not attend the services provided each Sunday. She has done with the hypocrites of religion. She has no religion now but faith. So her chapel is her room and her nave the rolling blue and white sky out her window.

The knock on her door disturbs her prayers. She is not troubled. She can pray later. She makes her way without her walker to the door and opens it.

"Mom, you're up!" Mel says, surprised to see her out of bed. He hasn't been around, not since Christmas. She won't think of that now as she leads him to the single chair by the window. She turns her walker and makes it a chair, carefully locking it into place.

"I recovered again. Glory be!" She laughs.

"I'm so glad to see this, Mom!"

"Thank you, Son. Grace and George have been by. They haven't said much about you. That tells me there's something. Are you and George fighting?"

"No, Mom. I came by to tell you I'm going away for a while."

"Moving? After all these years?"

"I lost my job, Mom. I'm trying to find something else."

"How is Pat taking it?"

"Well, there's no easy way to say this … I've left her, Mother. Her and the kids."

"Oh, Mel, don't break up a family. There is nothing worse."

"I have to, Mom. We're not getting along and I know it's my fault. I don't want to upset you. You'll hear the details soon enough. It's just I … I … have to leave."

With those words the pent-up rage and sorrow rush to reduce him. Suddenly he is sobbing. He tries to stop himself but can't. All the imprinting of his mother helping him, making things better when they were bleak, all the hope and the aspirations they have shared together since he was a toddler have turned on him and made him the worst kind of failure. He leans forward, his head in his mother's lap, as it would have been in the old days, and simply cries until he can cry no more. Her hand has stroked his head as it always has in these moments. Her voice has cooed long remembered phrases. His trauma slowly dissolves with his tears.

When he is finished she hands him some tissues. She utters no further words of shortcomings. She can sense her boy has reached his limit. Grace and George have mentioned some things in passing. Finally he is here and she will get the truth. The way it has always been.

"My job's gone, Mom. They just took it away," Mel says.

"There will be others. You're well liked, Son. You'll find something."

"That's just it though. I won't. I've tried. The world is changing, Mom. It's becoming something I don't understand. My kind of guy's not welcome no more. I'm a relic, Mom. I'll be replaced by a robot. Since I figured it out I haven't been the same. It seems I been doing this all for nothing. I don't seem to fit anymore."

"I understand, Mel. How did you think I felt every time you'd come over to get my channels back on my VCR? You showed me and showed me and I never got it. I just don't think that way. Maybe the same thing's happening to you."

"But I'm fifty-five years old. You were in your sixties!"

"So the world moves faster now," she says.

"Pretty much."

"Do you have to leave your family? Can't you take them somewhere it's not so bad? Where you can live plain and ordinary?"

"The kids won't go. They got their own lives now. Pat and me, well, things have been rocky. I'm not even sure I love her anymore."

"Oh, you do," she says. "You just don't remember it. Maybe you're right, Son, to go away, I mean. Just for a while. Have you thought about where?"

"Yeah. The cottage."

"I think there's a better place."

"Where would that be?"

"You remember when you were still a boy, we went to the St. Jacobs? Back before it got all commercial. Remember that?"

And *that* quickly she lifts him from his place in this world to another, finer one. He a boy of twelve. The market a warren of stalls and the open backs of black horse-drawn wagons from which Mennonites in odd looking clothes would sell food and other homemade merchandise. He had wondered at the horses and wagons. He had wondered why some drove black trucks, dressed sombrely but more conventionally and were more comfortable with the shoppers. Yet there was this strange tribe of believers. They seemed connected to everyone like them. They seemed at ease. Still, they were different.

George found them so intriguing he did a school project on them. It turned out they were far more complex than even his twelve-year-old mind could conceive. The first white settlers to arrive in numbers to the KW area, then called Sand Hills, the Mennonites were a tightly knit Protestant sect having migrated from the United States, their pacifist beliefs incurring the anger of their neighbours after the American Revolution. Over years the Mennonites spread west and north of the Grand River owning much of the best farmland in Upper Canada.

With their traditional beards, black suits and broad-brimmed hats with dark blue shirts, with their women in ankle length dresses and matching bun hair veils over the years many modernized, or reformed.

Though all shared their Anabaptist origins some changed with the times. But the Old Order Mennonites did not. Rejecting technology they refused all modern machinery and any use of electricity. Their farms were run by human muscle and horse power.

Mel and George were given several car rides into the country to glimpse them with their big horses in the fields, or large groups brought together to raise a barn in a day, or the tiny churches dotted throughout the countryside and on Sunday a host of horses and black wagons parked there for most of the day. They saw Mennonite children play softball on Sundays. They saw young couples stroll the edges of church yards. They visited a farm. They saw in a field three men throwing forks of hay up into a wagon hauled by two giant horses.

It was fascinating. Flowers, maple syrup, summer sausage, apple pies, the farms would sell products by gravel roadsides. Not all of them would journey to St. Jacobs to join the big market there. They preferred isolation. Young Georgie was much more fascinated by their culture than Mel, who had really just wanted to play softball with them. Test their skills. He was refused this by his father, however, who told him never to interfere.

Mel returns from his reverie thoughtful and quiet. His mother has found yet again a way to comfort him. He is calm. He even laughs when she reminds him of his attempt to cross a creek using a split rail fence up in Wilmot County, his vaunted balancing skills counteracted by a sudden break in the ancient grey wood and a clumsy tumble into the creek. Georgie had never let him forget that one.

So there *is* an answer to this conundrum of technology! He recalls then stories from the seventies of farms hidden in the depths of Perth and Huron counties populated by people who once had been hippies. Back to the land and all that. Could he do it? He wondered how they would be getting on now, then realized the flaw to his plan. He would have to either be accepted by Anabaptists or old hippies who had lived together for their adult lifetimes.

Yet if he backs off, accepts it all, ends up eventually in another place, as his family did long ago crossing an ocean. Perhaps he might go far away, somewhere off the grid of the nascent system.

Maybe there is an answer.
But first there is a responsibility.
And somehow, he has been chosen, or chosen himself, as a warning.
Someone to ring the alarm of inhuman progression.
He knows he will never see her, his mother, again.

33

THE COTTAGE WAS a lucky buy when Mel and Pat were young. Ironically, it was sold to them through a divorce. A guy Mel once worked with. On the northeast shore of a small lake near the old railroad town called Mactier, it is a quiet place nicely distant from its neighbours with thickets of hemlock and pine between. No beach all rock one big rock the Canadian shield deep blue water no crowds few boats too damned good to ignore.

It isn't a big place. It has three bedrooms and a simple bath. Rustic. Cedar boards on the outside glisten with a varnish finish, green trim and green roof shingles complete the woodsy look. It has a single kitchen/great room with a wood stove its black metal pipe rising between wooden beams to a cathedral style ceiling. The kitchen/great room is furnished in pine. The inside is bright with big windows facing west for spectacular sunsets across the lake.

They'd been looking for a beach cottage on southern Lake Huron when this place came up. It wasn't winterized. That would have been too expensive. They bought it at a bargain price and have owned it nearly twenty-five years. They have kept it maintained, as most cottagers do, with their family labour.

Within a week Mel has an internet connection through Bell Canada complete with a rolling VPN along with the best anti-virus anti-malware anti-phishing cyber security programs possible, courtesy of Stanley. Mel was issued a warning to use only SSL certificates and never click on inviting links. It was as if Stanley knew Mel was embarking upon a strange voyage into a digital netherworld. No one said anything. Not Mel. Not MJ. Certainly not Stanley. Yet all three knew Mel would need protection.

That week Mel purchased supplies in town as well. A grocery store and a hardware store make up the majority of merchants on Front Street. For more discreet purchases Mel will travel north to Parry Sound or south to Barrie. All part of the evolving game plan. He settles into his regimen: running and weights each morning, then errands and maintenance on the cottage, lunch, then afternoons evenings and into long nights with his digital study.

He is astonished at his own acumen. It is as if the intellect which he'd thought was exclusive to his brother, George, has been living inside him until he has finally matured sufficiently to discover it. Once he had focused on sports, in a way he never had with school work. Now he has altered that equation. With equal concentration he begins to develop augmented skills. The more problems he encounters the more accustomed to his device he becomes.

He watches YouTube to give him computing basics and surprisingly soon advances to more complex operations. As he continues he unearths a burgeoning dexterity he never thought to possess, never actually knew existed, until he'd embarked on his journey. Once involved in this learning he never swerves. There are hours and even days when he is consumed by his newfound powers. Will Baker continues to earn his wage from a distance. He is on the phone with him often. Twice already Will has come north to work with Mel. They have been invaluable days.

He is not an accomplished digital thinker, *yet.* He has purchased a printer and in neat stacks or file boxes close to hand has created an analogue library on aspects of coding hypertext protocols, domain name allocation, browser capabilities, App uses and methodologies with a plethora of acronyms like GIGO IMAP RADCAB SDRAM and on and on through the alphanumeric world.

He goes beyond his lessons however. More than skills he needs strategies.

He uses the life of Kaczynski as a primer. The *Unabomber* is all over the internet even sixteen years after being arrested. He'd evaded arrest for seventeen years before that. A brilliant man with something to say, Mel believes: a kind of prophet. Mel's lack of scholarship leads him to credit Kaczynski's manifesto *Industrial Society and Its Future*, as a set of truths to live by.

Mel has studied the manifesto meticulously, believing it describes what he himself has experienced. He has never done anything like this before: scrutinizing a large, complex document in search of its meaning. He employs Dani's solution by highlighting passages, returning to them to check their validity within the entire document, and thinking about the ultimate queries and solutions posed. He has trouble at the beginning with all the references to the Left and the different kinds of Left but muddles his way through the jargon until he begins to comprehend. In particular one passage rings in Mel's mind as inevitably true:

> *The ever-increasing acceleration of Technology will lead to the creation of nano-cyborgs that can self-replicate automatically without human intervention ... The conclusion of technological advancement will be pathetic, Earth and all those in it will have become a large gray mass, where intelligent nano-machines reign.*

There before his eyes is the proof not only of his own demise but that of his children and generations beyond. He never considers the words of Kaczynski deranged at all. The subtleties of the language still escape him and, like most new readers, he takes them at their literate value. He does not attempt to search for rejoinders. He simply cements in his mind the resolution that what he is set on accomplishing is the right thing to do and this document is his guide. A second extract provides a strategy:

> *Any kind of social conflict helps to destabilize the system, but one should be careful about what kind of conflict one encourages. The line of conflict should be drawn between the mass of the people and the power-holding elite of industrial society (politicians, scientists, upper-level business executives, government officials, etc.).*

The rambling manifesto provides him with warnings against technological evolution, ideas with which to hinder it, limitations to his actions and additional techniques to incorporate into his budding Luddite crusade.

For he *is* a Luddite: his present circumstance, his family's history, his society's neglect, even his single rebellious act conspire to reinforce this feeling. He not only represents himself but all those who have been discarded by an unforgiving, hostile world which cares only for the bottom line and the nebulous future. It is this thought which decides him to take symbolic responsibility for each of his future actions using the moniker *LUD*. Like the *Enoch*, symbol of his family's history which dangles from a chain around his neck, this new identity will allow him to make his declarations in the name of a greater power, an ideology operant in the oppressed masses through two hundred years of technological tyranny.

Mel believes he can emulate Kaczynski despite sixteen years of silence: the Unabomber entombed in a supermax prison. Silence no more, Mel thinks. Things are playing out just the way the man forecast them. Now current society will have *another* to write about, try to snare and arrest, making it ultimately examine itself in the process. Mel is no writer. Mel is a man of action. He will turn words to deeds. That is his strength. FC was the signature Kaczynski used. He will not use that. It is sacred to him. Instead, he will be LUD.

34

"I'VE CONVENED THIS meeting so we might discuss a situation regarding the house," Stanley says. The others: Danielle, Michael and Will sit restlessly at the kitchen table. They have finished dinner, done the washing up, and are ready for their evenings but for Stanley's insistence on this consultation.

Henry sprawls on top of the fridge looking bored. The usual single leg dangles. The tail curls up then down in a lazy fashion.

"Henry is getting too chubby," Stanley announces to groans and laughs.

"I thought this was going to be about rent or repairs or something! He looks perfectly fine to me!" Will says, pointing to the furry one. "Anyway, I don't feed him!"

"And that is precisely the reverse of the problem," Stanley responds.

"Meaning?" Michael asks.

"Meaning that three of us *are* feeding him!"

"I thought that was your job?" Michael says.

"It is. That's my point. Please don't tell me you don't fall for the ankle rub when you see his bowl is empty, Michael, or the secret to your secret Henry concerts is that Henry consumes multiple treats during the process! Oh don't bother to interrupt. I've discovered the pack of *Temptations Tasty Chicken* in your room!"

Stanley produces the half empty bag, yellow and red, bright kitty face smiling, holding it forth as a piece of evidence. On the fridge, Henry's eyes widen and his ears prick up.

"And no, I did not enter your room. You left your door ajar the other day and Henry himself shoved it out through the gap!"

"I'm sorry, man." Michael's long vowels and baritone voice give the apology depth. "I simply cannot help myself. I suppose I require the audience." His sombre mien gives way to a wide, white grin and twinkling eyes as Danielle giggles.

"And you, my girl, you claim not to feed the cat?" Stanley says, turning to her.

"Mr. Walk-On-By? Why would I do that?"

"Precisely because you do not wish him to *be* Mr. Walk-On-By but rather Mr. Cuddles or Mr. Purry-Furry or some such thing! Tell me truthfully now ... you have never placed food in that cat bowl?"

"Well, maybe once or twice, but I didn't mean to make him fat," Danielle says, then chuckles along with Michael and Will. Stanley is at his most comic when outraged.

"The devil you say! We've all been outwitted by a cat. His *life* is food, don't you see. He is a parasite. Cats have always been since the days of the Egyptians! *Worshipped* for heaven's sake and now he's turned this house into the Temple of Henry! It will not do! No more laughing now. I mean this. We'll kill him otherwise."

"Stanley, I am with Will on this one," Michael says. "He doesn't look so bad."

"That's because you haven't properly examined him!" Stanley says.

In a flash, taking Henry completely by surprise, Stanley whips around grasps the cat hauls him off the fridge folds him into his arms then, with one arm under his forelegs and the other holding his backside, allows Henry's rather ample belly to fall open to the world for observation. It doesn't help that Henry's fur tends to have a part in the middle of his belly, making the offending body more obvious. Henry's eyes bug out as he rolls a growl. His tale switches back and forth while he bends and twists but cannot free himself from the straitjacket of love holding him so convincingly.

"Exhibit two!" Stanley says. "Note the size of this paunch! We'll be forced to change his name to Falstaff unless something radical is done!"

With his greatest *yowl* Henry twists himself free then digs his rear claws into Stanley's stomach pushing off launching himself through the air onto the kitchen table, all three sitting there shocked by the sudden landing in their midst, then leaps completely over Danielle no side glance this time and skitters around the hardwood corner to disappear from this Inquisition. By the time everyone looks back they find Stanley writhing in pain on the floor holding his stomach and begging for antiseptic and bandages. Michael is closest. He opens Stanley's shirt to find three delicate red holes each dripping small blots of blood.

"It seems you yourself might be a bit paunchy, Stanley," Michael remarks. "But I do see now what you mean about Henry."

His head now in Danielle's lap, Stanley's eyes bug out as he peers down to evaluate the damage. He looks very much like the panicked Henry, if just for an instant.

"Good God, look what he's done to me," Stanley says, moaning.

"It's not that bad, man," Michael says.

"You're not feeling it! Those holes must be half an inch deep!"

Will is back in a minute with iodine and bandages. He unscrews the bottle tips it up holds a cotton ball to the mouth and watches it brown then applies it to Stanley's wounds.

"Ghhaaaaaa!"

Stanley coils like a wounded worm in a foetal position around the now excruciating points of agony. He cannot speak. He can barely breathe. He pants like a, well, like a cat.

"Why'd you give him iodine?" Danielle asks.

"It was handy!" Will answers.

"Surely there was Polysporin?" she says.

"I thought it was an emergency!"

"It's just a bloody cat scratch," Michael says.

"Give me the bandage, Will," Danielle says.

Will hands it over. Michael slowly pries Stanley out of his *catatonia* telling him to breathe slowly. Danielle applies the bandage. Stanley begins to relax as the sting dissipates.

"Nice touch, Dani," Will says.

"It's *Danielle*, if you don't mind!" Stanley's human foibles return as he rises from the floor helped by Michael and Will.

"Just sit him down here." Danielle pulls a kitchen chair around.

He sits.

"You want some water?" she asks.

"No. I'm ... Good God, Will, are you trying to kill me?"

"I thought it was worse the way you were acting! Anyway, the iodine was in your meds cabinet. I thought it was an English thing!"

Stanley pants yet another moment, then recovers.

"Never mind. Punctured like a balloon. Everyone! Please sit down. Danielle, would you open that delivery box please?"

Danielle opens the cardboard Amazon box and withdraws the contents, a flat rectangular box with colourful label. She quickly opens the next box, withdrawing its contents and placing them on the kitchen table. A round plastic dish coloured beige on the bottom and green on top with a single beige pie shaped opening. A heptagon. Stanley opens the top to reveal seven other pie shaped depressions, enough room in each for a one cat meal. Everyone laughs. Danielle stands and gestures like a model displaying a feature for an audience. She does it well. More laughter. Stanley takes it from her and flips open the top within which is a simple turn mechanism with timer.

"Look, can we just get this over with?" Will says, disgruntled. He does not feed the cat.

"I can't believe it! You're automating Henry's feeding time? " Danielle says.

"Look, this is my solution. Absolutely no one but I shall feed the cat. This, as you see, is a programmable pet feeder. I will program it so Henry receives his food morning and evening. As you see, one portion is always open with the rest tucked away neatly under this lockable cover. If Henry eats his entire portion he will be out of luck until the next portion appears. I am placing it here, beside the refrigerator and his auto feed water bowl. You see me now filling it with dried cat food. No one is to place food into an empty portion. Henry must learn self-control."

"Let him eat cake, I say!" Michael shouts, grinning.

"He's already done that!" Stanley retorts. "And that reminds me ... no snacks left open in anyone's room. The little chuf will steal them and you all know it! Please, please, let's just co-operate in this. Now if you don't mind I need to go upstairs for a while. I am still in some pain."

Stanley departs, theatrically hobbling up the stairs. Henry, from the living room/lab, concealed beneath the worktables filled with laptops, monitors, CPUs, speakers, portable hard drives, flash readers, keyboards, mice (not his kind), a maze of coloured wires and a couple of pads of paper, watches him go. Balefully.

35

BY THE END of May Mel is ready. He has taken his cue from neo-Luddite essays. He has learned to search the deep web and has found significant information to formulate his game plan. He finds the addresses of the offices of the corporation called Erban Industries and, with a deeper search, some executives' homes.

He considers his first steps warnings, a portent of things to come. He possesses the perfect weapon. Two years previous one of the cottages on the lake had become abandoned, posted *No Trespass* by the Sheriff's department. Something about a disputed inheritance. He had explored it anyway, careful not to enter the building but looking around beneath for something useful for his own cottage. He'd found nothing: a few cement blocks, a rusted lawnmower, cans of dried paint, greyed over cedar boards, plastic bags of rusted bolts; all the detritus of a cottage not yet removed to the dump. Still, he recalled one thing in particular which would make the perfect agent for his opening gambit.

Rat poison.

The Roman Empire invented courier service during the reign of Augustus. It was quite successful. Yet post is not always pleasant to receive. Besides the *overdue payment* letters, the term *poison pen* refers to malicious anonymous letters likely carried by those first Romans.

Initially the *poison pen* was usually personal: generally filled with insults and threats toward the recipient. Sometimes there *must* have been poison: a snake in a bag, toxic pins stuck in parchment, cloth rubbed by a leper, even some types of venomous ink. Eventually, however, the poison pen became the chosen tool of *social media* and lost its cachet in the analogue world.

It was 2001 when anthrax attacks, labelled *Amerithrax* from the FBI case name, occurred within the United States. Anonymous letters containing anthrax spores were mailed to news media offices and politicians. Five people died, seventeen more were infected. The case was never solved.

In 2003 another campaign was created by someone identifying as *Fallen Angel*, mailing letters to the White House filled with ultra-deadly ricin. Fortunately, no one was harmed as the letters were intercepted. This case as well was never solved.

Then came Kaczynski who turned parcels and letters into bombs, killing two people and maiming others over seventeen years until he was finally arrested, but only after publishing his *Manifesto*, his own brother having recognized his writing style and turning him in. Mel will create no written manifesto. He has no skill as a writer nor as a chemist and is sure, though the ricin formula looks to be simple, he would kill himself before anyone else should he attempt the chemistry.

He decides to retrieve the box of rat poison from beneath the abandoned cottage. He drives to a stationery store in Barrie, a large one, the kind that sells everything so he can't be noticed purchasing envelopes and a ream of paper. He is careful, wearing a black peaked ball cap and nondescript clothing for whatever cameras might peer down on him. He wears work gloves so no fingerprints will be left behind. He pays in cash. He has parked in another lot away from the store so no one will see his truck.

He possesses the address of corporate headquarters for Erban Industries and two personal addresses of executives careless enough to use Facebook or LinkedIn. He has searched mainly for the critical information of one Herbert Trimble and found it under a service club of which Trimble is an officer. The rest of the power people won't matter but for the publicity they will bring, Mel thinks, though Trimble will likely open his own mail at home. Revenge. Finally. Tumble Trimble.

Now it becomes delicate. Mel dons powderless latex gloves. He lays a line of rat poison on rice paper used for rolling cigarettes then folds the paper flat. He uses an ancient crayon from his kids' cottage stash of years past ... he likes purple ... and scrawls on a sheet of paper *RICIN* then below, his symbol: *LUD*. He folds the paper with the rice paper inside ready to pop. He has found a typewriter at a flea market on Highway 400. He'd made sure the ribbon and every key worked. He uses that instrument to print the names and addresses on the envelopes.

Next come his evasions. He takes three days. With his camping and fishing gear and a waterproof bag he drives five hours north to Sault Ste. Marie. He buys Canadian stamps in a Pharmex. He mails his letters to the Canadian addresses. He buys an old fishing boat with a ten horse motor. A few hundred bucks. He trailers it to Belle Marina. He goes fishing for the day. He manufactures an engine problem for anyone watching, border patrol or drones, then takes to the oars and at dusk he lands on the US side near a holiday camp. No one comes after him.

He phones for a taxi, gets it from the camp's gate and takes it into town. He pays cash. He buys stamps at a Walmart. He mails to the US addresses. He has dinner and buys some food for next day. Gets another cab. Back to the camp he pitches his pup tent in the weeds by his boat. Next morning finds him out on the river fishing at dawn. He actually nets a trout, spends the day on the river then lands at the marina and trailers up. He drives back home. Along the way he sinks boat and trailer in a deep river on a dirt backroad off Highway 108 north toward Elliot Lake.

Then he waits.

He searches the internet daily, hourly, aware that he would have missed the Erban arson had not a friend told him about it. He has the arson newspaper article stored in a folder hidden beneath his mattress. It is important for him to have trophies. He secretly hopes Trimble will sicken from the rat poison. He has read that ricin takes two days to show signs and then produces an awful death. He wants Trimble and all those others to quake with fear for two days. They must feel the consequence of their actions.

Question their lives.

Question themselves.

He misses the final line in his towering imperfect syllogism.

Therefore ... question himself.

The game can't be played with self-doubt. It must be done with training and instinct. Above all, instinct.

36

USING THE EXPERIMENTAL search system, Will Baker's beta version of Pineapple, he combs news sources across the internet mixing the best of Google with DuckDuckGo for security, Yippy for depth, Tor and Onion links for the obscure.

His first inkling is a local newspaper ... the KW *Record* online. It mentions a local man, one Herbert Trimble, having reported mail tampering to police. The story is brief, only that Mr. Trimble had opened a letter to find a white substance. It made clear Trimble was an executive of Erban Industries, currently relocating from Kitchener. It mentioned the arson of March. It made no conclusions.

It is enough, however. Mel uses his imagination to fill in the blanks left by the report. The powder puffing out into the air the folded page with RICIN the call to police the trip to emergency the panic of not knowing the heartache of his family, all of this he visits upon Herbert Trimble with the trembling moustache. Then, of course, would have come the final touch: LUD. The mystery. The symbolism. It instils in Mel a feeling better than the arson. It strikes at the heart of the crisis—not machines but the men who manipulate workers. It sends a signal to these selfish bastards that they are on notice and they all, every one, will know why.

Then come the reports from distant destinations. *The Atlanta Journal-Constitution* prints a headline in its crime section: Erban Executives Under Attack, this time listing the RICIN and the mysterious LUD, this time a brief interview regarding corporate re-adjustment. It does not list the names, only the positions of the victims. It says office clerks suffered some effects but doesn't say what these are. Mel has a moment of remorse, then shoves it aside as collateral damage in his ongoing battle with the future.

There are more reports from other sources: newsmagazines, blogs, TV news and websites. The neo-Luddites get hold of the signature and begin to create a storm in the deeper parts of the web. There are anonymous postings of a rising. Several outlaw groups claim responsibility, however, and this upsets Mel. This is *his* battle and their staking claim destroys his aim.

He prints the reports and blog addresses, copies videos and even fake claims and places them in the file folder beneath his mattress as well as saving them on encrypted files in his computer. He knows he should not keep records but finds his need for these trophies essential. He knows this will be a long lonely fight against technology and its heartless masters. He knows others will try to steal his thunder. It makes him alter his strategy.

He has learned much from Kaczynski.

He has learned to play a new game.

One of the things one knows in sport is the necessity of a good offense. If you attack you have your opponent reacting, moving backwards, being too careful, often wrong footing. That way leads to defeat. Whatever the defensive tactics, strong offense will eventually break them down. Mel cannot rest on his ricin laurels. He must change his tactics to a more locally based offensive thus disconnecting the false claims of others. To be noticed he must up his game, strike before his opponents can organize, find another way through their defences and deliver a little more punch.

His first thought of course is to recreate Kaczynski's pipe bombs but he is not the Unabomber. He cannot purchase gunpowder in Canada without producing his driver's licence. He does not have the skills to make gunpowder nor the talent to steal it. He doesn't want to kill anyone anyway. He wishes only to grasp their attention. He finds another way.

Mel's internet research takes him to varied places describing the amounts of gunpowder and flash powder used in various fireworks. Though useful for Canada Day celebrations they do not contain what he is seeking and there is little doubt they could be traced to wherever he might have purchased them. He needs something other than fireworks—a more frightening shock.

There are types of firecrackers long banned in Canada and most US states. With a little more search on DuckDuckGo he finds them. Cherry Bombs, Silver Salutes or M-80s have one thing in common: they possess more grams of flash powder than can be legally sold in most places. Invented by the US army to simulate battlefield noises, the resulting rate of property damage and personal injury when released to the public brought a ban down upon all of them.

Using *Pineapple* and an address he found on his regular search engines Mel comes across the illegal versions rated by the ATF with statistics and pictures for each:

M-80
Average Size: Five-eighth inch diameter, 1.5 inches long
Average Load: Approximately 3 grams explosive mixture
Risk Factor: Damage to fingers, hands, and eyes

M-100, Silver Salute
Average Size: 1 inch diameter, 2.5 inches long
Average Load: Approximately 9 grams explosive mixture
Risk Factor: Severe damage to face, arms and body

M-250
Average Size: 1 inch diameter, 3 inches long
Average Load: Approximately 13 grams explosive mixture
Risk Factor: Severe crippling, disfiguring injuries

M-1000, Quarter Stick
Average Size: 1 inch diameter, 6 inches long
Average Load: Approximately 25-30 grams explosive mixture
Risk Factor: Extremely severe injuries to body; has caused death.

The three Ms, he sees, are made from red cardboard tubing of varied lengths depending on their explosive power with a visco fuse extending from each. The Silver Salute is different; it is cardboard painted silver which, once lit, shoots out spangles. As he reads these figures the momentousness of what he is doing sinks in. Rat poison disguised as ricin is one thing. Mail bombs are another level. He breaks away from his computer as though it were a diabolical engine.

Outside is early May. The black flies flit invisibly. The mosquitoes are starting up. It has been an early spring, warm, thus they multiply into their millions. Yet there is a full moon glowing over the lake, its reflection glistening silver from the water. The moon is so close he can see its face, its mountains and craters, its glimmering aura. The night is still and clear. Trees shadow everything. He smells hemlock. Crickets' chirps fill the air along with the soft lapping of water on the shoreline. He dons a bug jacket over his T-shirt and takes the steps down to the lake.

He remembers building the steps, constructed on top of the rock upon which the cottage sits. He remembers Patricia holding the pressure treated boards, measuring precisely for him, the kids doing their part as well fetching tools or drinks or making lunch, the inevitable peanut butter sandwiches—and he sighs. Those days are gone.

He finds himself a different man. The other half of the duality he had envisioned. Once a husband, lover, partner and father, provider for the family, proud of his small sporting triumphs, happy with his kids, still in love with his wife, he feels now more machine than man. Less *feeling*. He has had to be to raise the power within him to act, to provide him the strength to battle against the new culture intractably sweeping society into its maw. An uncaring dishonest immoral vicious and unstoppable evolution. Is that what it will become? What Kaczynski says? Slaves to machines? All the newest, smartest technologies requiring the service of humans? That thought is hard to bear, he finds.

No matter what our dreams of the future we are carbon based lifeforms. Carbon is well-suited to form the long chains of molecules which serve as the basis for life as we know it: the proteins and DNA. Sixty percent of the body is water. We require water to stay alive. But what if the earth starts to die or worse, we continue to make it unliveable?

The silicon chips in his laptop require no support. Given the right algorithms they will become what we make them. But will they be a new species? The product of humans? What is a human anyway? What makes humans so sure we are impervious to extinction?

What will happen when silicon based artificial intelligence becomes self-aware or when nanobots think beyond their instruction? Is that evolution? Is the human race creating its own elimination? Will we become slaves or simply vanish? Will technology use up the planet, and us, and then leave for more fruitful pastures?

If this transplantation remains unchecked then there will remain nothing human. Stopping this erosion or evolution requires not regulation but the creation of a *different* world view. *How is it people cannot see this*, he thinks.

He strips off his clothes and dives off the dock deep, deep into the cold waters of a May lake in Muskoka. The shock takes away his thoughts. He swims to the surface, subconsciously hoping never to surface. He has never had these kinds of thoughts before.

In that instant Mellor John Buckworth envisions his trek. He cannot change history. He is the Luddite of his own life caught in an overwhelming System of *progress*. Still he must hamper or at least warn the world of this replacement of humans. There will be consequences, he thinks, if we do not temper our dreams. There will be future consequences no one seems able to envision.

Yet he *can* do something. He can smooth the path for those who come after him, perhaps even the lives of his children. If he can convince someone significant of the purpose of his quixotic quest perhaps that message might pass on until someone, some day, might generate the change required to preserve humanity and distract it from its headlong rush to perdition.

Himself. A Manifesto.

Sometimes our thoughts run too deep and our dreams reach too far.

37

PAT'S NEW PUZZLE is appropriate to her circumstances.

She has solved two others throughout the month. Her time has come down to empty ritual: wake up check the phone get ready for work check the phone walk to work check the phone work have lunch check the phone work check the phone walk home open a wine bottle talk with MJ, sometimes, check the phone prepare supper eat with MJ, sometimes, check the phone clear up the dishes check the mail check the email check the phone open a second bottle call Dani, sometimes, work on her puzzle work on her puzzle work more on her puzzle get ready for bed wake up in the dark take clonazepam work on her puzzle ... wake up in the chair in the livingroom check the phone go back to bed somehow fall asleep dream about being lost in a puzzle wake up ... re-run the cycle.

She makes an appointment with her doctor. Her doctor is stern, a touch frightening. She drinks too much, he says. Sometimes she talks with Grace. Grace is comforting and calm. Sometimes she reaches Dani. Dani is tearful and brave. Sometimes MJ will eat supper with her. MJ is aloof and quiet. Once a week she visits Nancy Silvain, her psychologist. Nancy is warm yet professionally opaque.

And Mel, of course, is gone.

He has not called. He has texted her not to call him. He says he is working things through. He is doing odd jobs and retraining himself, he says, using YouTube. *Mel using YouTube*? When she questions MJ he tells her Mel had had a session with Stanley. *With Stanley*? Setting up his computer, MJ says, the day she left. *With Stanley?* Had Mel contacted MJ? No. When she called Dani she discovered her daughter was troubled. Stanley had worked with Mel but hadn't told her about the visit. *Mel and Stanley?* Had Mel contacted Dani? No.

Her puzzle this time is a wall of wine corks. More than two hundred corks pictured, each with its own inked stamp, all of them positioned tightly together. Even the edge pieces are just partial corks so there is little advantage there. Still, she follows her method. One begins by trying to find the edges then searching for clues to various images then placing pieces in their proximate positions. Gradually one area will grow and one will dwell unsolved while another will suddenly reveal itself. One thousand pieces. She has never given up on any of them. She simply finds more and more complex puzzles. Inside her focus she forgets other troubles. It is challenging, this solving of riddles, a sojourn of calm in the otherwise fleeting life she now lives. There are so many ways to attain the picture, find the whole, complete the journey, find solace in the finish, then place the puzzle on a backing and file it away with her other trophies.

Her current life, however, is an enigma she finds she cannot solve. She has not even found its edges. Nothing lines up anymore. There seems no pattern. It is as if she must construct this puzzle by working it from the back, on the opposite side from the picture. No matter which way she approaches it, nothing offers a clue. The drinking muffles her pain for a while but not her misgivings. She is down to a glass at dinner and one with her puzzle in the evening. Doctor's orders.

She decides she needs to get out more, be less alone, see some people detached from her personal problems. She joins summer tennis. Waterloo Park. Clay courts, comfortable old clubhouse. She starts playing doubles twice a week: once for women only, once mixed doubles. Soft June evenings, the pop of the ball off the racquet strings, the laughter of women playing together. Time away from her troubles, the subtleties of meeting new men, her partners for an evening of tennis.

She spends more time with Dani joining her for restaurant suppers, sometimes alone, sometimes with Stanley. She finds happiness in her daughter's joy. She finds delight in Stanley's oddities. She discovers why Dani loves him. Inside his peculiarities she encounters a brilliant, gentle, kind man.

MJ is his usual self. It seems he has subconsciously sided with his father. He was there with Stanley and Mel on that strange, fateful weekend when everything changed, yet he won't reveal anything. *Mel and MJ. and Stanley? Together?* So she mostly leaves MJ to his own devices then discovers, quite by accident, a page left open on his computer: *PRE-ADMISSION AND MATURE STUDENT ASSESSMENT REGISTRATION FORM* for Conestoga College. Whatever happened that weekend wasn't all bad, she thinks.

She finds herself, after the first few weeks, comfortable with her own company. Without realizing it she has begun to collect pieces for the edges of the thing she thinks she cannot comprehend. She finds she can re-construct memories from childhood and adolescence, everything up until Mel. She recalls camping trips to Algonquin, holidays with her parents, sports tournaments with her friends, goofy family get-togethers with cousins, going to the CNE, Christmas presents, birthday presents, even Oktoberfest. She'd been a contestant for Oktoberfest Queen. She finds some solace in faded pictures. They are the pieces of her life. Yet it is an incomplete life, without edges, as so much of it had become influenced by Mel. *Those* picture albums she does not visit, not even the ones with the kids. They are too painful. The puzzle remains incomplete.

Then a surprising breakthrough occurs in a counselling session.

The room is Scandinavian in its simplicity. Warm grey walls with sharp dark trim. White ceiling with inset lighting. Mahogany desk and chair. Mahogany doors conceal patient files. A beige microfibre couch and easy chair with yellow ochre and India red patterned pillows providing colour. A similar patterned Persian carpet covers the floor. The requisite scholastic degrees are displayed in simple metal wall frames. A single window is covered by a sheer. A single painting, palette style, of an autumn maple hangs alone on one wall.

Nancy Silvain is the reflection of her room: stylish skirt and blouse, short cut blonde hair, long legs that cross easily as she listens and engages. She exudes a calm of professionalism. She sits in the chair angled facing the couch. Patricia sits on the couch. They have been talking for half an hour.

"You seem to be doing all you can to work your way through this," Nancy says.

"I hope so. I just wish I could get closer to MJ."

"That will come with time."

"He's not bad, you know. He isn't spiteful. He just seems to have picked Mel's side."

"He'll come around. Be patient. It's very good news about Conestoga."

"I know. I hope it's true. I mean I hope he follows through. I wish I knew what happened that weekend with Stanley, the day after Mel hit me. Somehow that day affected Mel. When I called him he told me what I've told you already, about separating, but he seemed preoccupied, emotionless, yet underneath it all kind of driven."

"You think he meant it, all he said?"

"Yes. I think he did. He was just, not all there at times, you know?"

"How did you feel?"

"Oh, you know. I've been over this."

"It's okay to go over again. Perhaps find a different angle. Something about *your* feelings rather than being concerned over Mel's."

It comes to Pat then that she has never actually looked at the event from her own point of view. Experienced it, but not examined it. She'd worried about Mel's feelings, how she must have goaded him, how he had been so oddly distant yet purposeful beneath. She had been astonished that he would strike her! Her decision to leave had been necessary. Then her phone call to Mel. The separation. The sense of being somehow in a vacuum.

Now, in the shelter of Nancy Silvain's office she finally begins to speak of herself, parse her feelings not just from that single awful night but from further back, years really: the joys of the marriage the rapture of children the loving companions buying the cottage worries of mortgage planning kids' futures sometimes success sometimes trouble sometimes victory other times loss most times just getting on with life with the families the friends the colleagues the parties the births the birthdays the holidays and the funerals. The work of living from day to day depending upon one another.

She looks up to see the clock has gone past her hour.

"Oh, Nancy, I'm sorry. I should be getting home."

"Not now, Pat. I have no appointments. I'd like to hear more."

"I've been rattling on ..."

Nancy says nothing.

"I think things started to change five years ago. Mel wanted to continue sports but he's so competitive, while I began to just want to enjoy the people and the games for themselves. It was around that time he pulled out of our mixed leagues and we had different nights out after that. I played less, I admit. It was around that time I discovered jigsaw puzzles. Mel would be out so often I thought I should stay home with the kids. Both of them were in high school then so the puzzles gave me something to do when they went off on their own, or had friends in to visit. Mel and I have never been readers, books, I mean. So the puzzles were like mysteries to me. My mind was active while I worked on them. I think they allowed me *not* to think about what was really happening."

Pat looks up.

Nancy says nothing.

"We grew apart," Pat says bluntly, as if for the first time comprehending this. "Oh, it wasn't an affair, at least I think not anyway. It was more subtle. Men behave differently when they're together. Mel would come home all charged up or angry or just oblivious from work or hockey or ball not really paying attention to us. When he was home he watched sports. I remember he bought the cable sports package. He said everybody would like it. He didn't realize the kids weren't that interested in watching sports and I was doing my puzzles. So he bought a big screen and watched downstairs, alone.

"Then MJ went to college. I had my volleyball nights and Dani her school sports. Oh, Mel came to *those* games. Dani's. He was different though. He got frustrated by coaching decisions or referee calls or the way some kid was playing. Sometimes he was embarrassing. He was turning so much of it into himself. It was really all about him.

"I didn't see it. I was disappointed but I didn't know what it was. Then *we* started having trouble. We'd snipe at each other, always on edge, waiting for the next fight. I'm fairly sure that's why Dani left home. She could have stayed when she got into Waterloo but she didn't. She's never told me why. She loves her dad and she loves me and I think we were both trying to make her choose sides. God, that's awful.

"When she left home Mel went out even more and I got more complicated puzzles. We both drank more, but never together. The arguments got louder. Each of us would walk out on the other, lots of times, just to cool down or get away from each other. We stopped trying to solve our differences and just lived with what we had each become.

"We moved into separate bedrooms. Sex was just sex when it happened. Not love at all. We went through the motions of marriage. I came home once early from work, just a feeling, and found Mel packing to leave. I begged him to stay and yet to this day I realize I didn't really want him around anymore. That's when we came to you. I thought maybe if we talked about it with someone else we could get back to where we were. Well, you know what happened."

"I'm glad *you* stayed, Pat."

Patricia is crying softly now. She is inside her deepest feelings.

"When he lost his job things got very strange. Other people had the same thing happen yet they kept going. I'm sure I don't know all the things other people kept secret but Mel just couldn't accept it. I know it was his job for most of his life but he got all twisted up. He started blaming everybody and everything for what happened to him. Then this thing with computers. He hated them now it's all weird. He's obsessed. The night he bought the computer was the same night he hit me; the night I left.

"I wanted to leave! He gave me the excuse! I wanted to punish him so I didn't call him for three weeks and then when I did I still didn't want to come back. He told me we needed time. He was going up to the cottage alone. He didn't want me back either! I see that now. He got mad again. I hung up on him, Nancy. I don't love him and he doesn't love me. I don't want him back but then I've betrayed him just when he needs me the most. I'm sorry I don't know what to do. I'm sorry I'm so, so sorry ..."

Nancy rises crossing to the couch. She sits beside an exhausted Patricia. She offers tissues then a long, warm embrace. She holds Pat until she stops weeping then pulls away, her hand still in contact with Pat's shoulder.

"You're not betraying anyone, Pat. The important thing is not to betray yourself."

"You think so?"

"I know so. You've just given me the truth, your truth, as you never have before."

One edge reached.

38

HE DOESN'T KNOW which side to take. He wishes there were no sides at all. What happened to his life after high school? If he hadn't gone to that fucking college he might have kept his parents together. All he knew was he had to get out from under the density of their failure. And once gone he had failed *himself* by somehow becoming another person: the person his parents feared most, the rudderless careless causeless unfocused fat MJ he knew himself to have become.

Loser.

And when he returns from that fucking school it's all a mess; now he's in the mix of his own fiasco and his mother and father are a catastrophe. They don't sleep together they fight all the time their marriage goes downhill faster and faster. His sister has left for the same reason he did and now it's worse without her. Then all their lives change in a few short minutes in the heat of a fight in the shout of an insult in the slap of a face in the slam of a door.

And now he haunts his basement domicile afraid of the mother who has returned. She has now a kind of confidence he hasn't noticed before. It has taken a while to find herself with drinking and puzzles and sometimes tears but those things have passed. She talks with him now when he surfaces. She cooks him meals she cleans the house she goes to work she goes out with Dani she has found some new friends. She is not the same woman who lived with his father.

He too finds himself changed. That day with Stanley and his dad was astounding. The day after his mother had left, his father ignoring what he had done, so concentrated on cajoling Stanley to reveal his knowledge. MJ had watched his father absorb it as though his life depended on it. Then there was the drive-by reference that took MJ by surprise; having come downstairs with Stanley's tea and into a conversation he wished now he had never heard, yet knows was the most significant of his life.

The next weeks were a whirlwind. His mom and dad splitting his dad leaving for the cottage not talking to him except *hand me this* and *hand me that* and then gone with the dawn without even *goodbye*. Then Mother comes back and she tries to talk about Dad but he doesn't actually *know* anything. He calls Dani. She comes over to visit Mom. MJ is sure she knows how to comfort her. He stops her on her way out.

He too needs her.

It is a warm, soft evening. The sunset glows on the pretty front garden on Fischer Street. The blooms are coming: the tulips, hyacinths, lilacs, and forsythia. His dad had laid out the stonework back when MJ was ten, letting him help, giving him the rubber hammer to tamp a stone into place as his mother and little Dani planted perennials: his sister with dirt smudged on her face, his mother smiling as she looked up at Dad, his dad patting his shoulder.

The sun rides the garden shadows softly crossing each bed of plants, each wrought iron ornament, washing the red brick and white shutters of the house into gleaming beauty. There are robins in the trees and the delicate smells of the blossoms.

"Dani, what's going on?"

He stands in front of her on the porch.

"I don't know, MJ."

"You just talked with her!"

"You live with her! What's she said to you?"

"Nothing."

He leans dejectedly against the wrought iron rail.

"Come on," Danielle says.

"Can we sit for a minute?"

"Yeah. Okay."

They take their places on the top step of the porch, the places they have always taken when growing up together, when talking together, when sharing their secrets. This step has heard all the truths and losses and adolescent misgivings from both of them. It has always been their place to be level and never to lie. There are places like that in most lives if we could just remember where they are now.

"Really, she doesn't talk much to me, nothing important anyway," MJ says. "She works on her puzzles. I think she goes to that shrink still.

It's like she wants answers from *me* about Dad but she's afraid to ask and I don't know what's up with Dad anyway. What did she say to you?"

"She said she was fine but she drank half a bottle of wine saying it. She said Dad was working things out, said he needed to be alone, that he'd texted her not to call him. She looks so tired, MJ. Have you noticed?"

"She's up in the night a lot. Kind of crazy about her puzzles. I hear her come to the kitchen."

"We've got to help her," Danielle says.

"What do you think about Dad?"

"He called Will Baker this week. I overheard. How do they even know each other? If he does it again I'm getting on the phone I don't care if he hangs up or not! Why don't you go and see Dad?"

MJ shifts toward his sister, leaning in, hand on her knee to steady himself.

"It's like I don't know him after the thing with Stanley. He's changed. It started out alright but then Stanley got talking about the future and kind of hinted it had no place for Dad."

She looks at him, those diamond eyes spark. She places her hand on his.

"Help Mom, then. She's here. Dad isn't."

"I don't know what to say to Mom."

"Just be nice, MJ, be pleasant. Stay out of her way and don't ask for things you might not want to hear. I'm going to come and see her more often."

"You should move back home."

Her hand abruptly removes itself. She walks down the steps then turns to face MJ. Her face in the evening light is beautiful, her hair glimmers. For the first time in his life MJ looks at his sister as a woman. Another change he will have to deal with.

"MJ, I love Stanley. I might have left because of Mom and Dad's problems and then of course Dad didn't like Stanley, but I won't leave Stanley now, not for anything."

"He blames me, Dani!"

"Dad? How do you know that? Did he tell you?"

MJ stands, takes the two steps down to the patio and faces his sister. "You weren't there that day, Dani, it's as if a light bulb went off in Dad's head. Stan told him he was too late for real change but me, I have a chance because I'm young. Dad shut me out after that. Then he left. No explanations."

"So you blame my boyfriend."

"No. Of course not. I would have thought that before but not anymore. He just told the truth! Anyway, Dad maybe opened a door that day and stepped through and left us behind."

"What's Will got to do with it? Why would Dad phone him?"

"Honest, Dani? I don't know. Dad said he had a computer coach before he left."

"Will Baker? Teaching our father metrics? Doubtful."

"Why?"

"Will is a snob. An intellectual shithead. He's on a campaign to create some wondrous app that's going to make him mega rich! He wouldn't waste time teaching Dad. Maybe Dad was calling Stanley."

"On Will Baker's cell?"

"Oh shit, I don't know MJ. I'll ask Will when I get home."

"We need to find out what's going on."

"I'll have a talk with Stanley too. Maybe you can get Mom's side of things."

"She hardly speaks to me."

"She says you hardly speak to her."

"I don't know what to say!"

"You've got to try."

"Can I come by and see you once in a while?"

Dani touches his fingers with hers.

"You know you can, MJ. But what about Stanley."

"I changed my mind about him, Dani. He's a smart guy. He's strange alright but I'd like to know him better."

"I love you, MJ," Danielle says, and kisses his cheek. They hold their embrace for another moment. It has been a long time for each. Something strong and beautiful passes between them.

"I'll drive you home," MJ says.

39

AMRIT KHADRI HAS gone through the list provided by Trimble. He's tracked most of the former Erban employees. It has not been easy. Often he has been met with resentment and sometimes outright bitterness. He has found a few hotheads who might be candidates for arson but each had an alibi for the night of the fire. This isn't the criminal world. Though he should be accustomed by now, it is not a comfortable feeling to intrude on these people for somehow, this is different. This is the world of honest workers traumatized by a reality they had never anticipated.

The interesting element is their varied progress. Some have already found new work, some are on employment insurance, a few have gone back to school, some sit at home trying to keep busy with renovations or household chores. Finally, there is a number who have departed. They have either left the city with their families or just gone off alone to get away.

His investigation has therefore been incomplete. He spends his days on the phone trying to follow up on the absentees. Some have left forwarding addresses, some have not. Some have come home and have called him. He has narrowed the suspects list to twelve names, seven of whom remain unaccounted for while five are hunches brought on by their behaviour, either aggressive or fearful. He is due for another drive around tomorrow to check the seven not yet interviewed.

He is about to move on to review other cases when Sergeant Reinhardt opens the door. His face is hard set. His stance almost military. Khadri knows something is wrong.

"Amrit, some major shit's happening with that arson case."

"What? I haven't got to everyone yet."

"Well someone has got to that Trimble guy."

"The executive?"

"Yeah. It's bad."

"Fire?"

"Poison! Ricin. Heard of it?"

"Yeah. A powder, isn't it? Made from castor beans or something. Who in hell would do that?"

"He got it in his mail and he's not the only one. A bunch of mailrooms in local tech firms are reporting the same. We got people going to hospital, placed in isolation in case they might have breathed any in. Seems a breath or two can kill you."

"Christ, this is insane."

"You're tellin' me! Public Health is on it, protocols are in place but we haven't got enough hazmat teams to deal with this."

"What would you have me do?"

"I don't know why but Trimble is the only *individual* so far to have one of these mailed to him personally. He and his family are in isolation in Grand River hospital. I got a Hazmat team out at his house."

"Can I interview him?"

"Yeah. Get to the hospital. Ask for Dr. Magnuson. He'll walk you through."

It takes fifteen minutes from North Division to Grand River Hospital, a massive multi-layered confusion of halls and wings and stairways. As he enters Khadri catches the jumbled smells from the cafeteria and doughnut shop then walks into the aromas of heavy duty cleaners used in the hallways. He doesn't like hospitals. They serve a purpose in the community but he just can't help himself. He asks for Dr. Magnuson at the information desk and a volunteer takes him through a maze of corridors to Administration.

Magnuson, a tall, bespectacled man with Nordic features, is waiting for him. He wears the requisite white coat but his blonde hair is a little long and his face tanned from spring skiing in the mountains somewhere. He possesses a very deep voice that seems to come from his feet. He shakes hands with Khadri. Strong grip.

He walks Khadri through another labyrinth. As they continue the hallways become increasingly quiet. Fewer people. They pass through several *restricted* doors. And then there are nurses wearing N-95 masks. Wearing disposable gloves. Wearing safety shields. Khadri starts to worry but Magnuson continues on to a large window. On the other side of the window is a small ward. It is immediately clear to Khadri that he cannot enter or exit that room from where he stands. He sees a door at the other end. Teal curtains creating pseudo-privacy for patients are drawn all the way down each side of the room.

At the window is Herbert Trimble in navy coloured pyjamas and a turquoise hospital gown. He is pale as a ghost. His eyes are grey marbles. The moustache is slightly untrimmed. Trimble's face is a mass of lines and creases. Khadri thinks he might soon be investigating a homicide. He turns to Magnuson.

"How can I speak with him?"

"Just here. Corner of the window. A speaker. Rather old style but it gets the job done."

He presses the button, says into the mic: "Mr. Trimble. Do you remember me? Waterloo Region Police? Khadri?"

"You have to release the button, Detective," Magnuson says. "He's still in shock so you might not get much."

The voice that comes back is tinny. The tone of that voice tries for command but is overwhelmed by obvious panic. Khadri, despite his initial distaste for Trimble, feels sorry for him. At the Erban office he'd met a man relishing control, yet here is that same man victimized.

"I remember you, sir. Detective Khadri. You had the idea first, didn't you, and I didn't believe you. Lord, I wish I had now."

"Sorry?"

"You had me give you a list of employees. You told me to note anyone I thought was suspicious. The man who did this is sure to be on it. Why didn't I believe you?"

"It's difficult, Mr. Trimble. No one expected this. Did you open the letter?"

"Of course I did! That's why I'm here. Why my family's here! You realize all of us might die because I didn't bother to complete the task you asked of me. Can you get me that list? If it's the last thing I do I want the person responsible!"

"Yes, sir, of course. But while I'm here, did you note anything odd about the envelope?"

"Never looked at it. Just saw my name. Typed. Had a stamp. No return address. I opened it with my letter knife. Ripped the top off and the powder puffed out. Oh, God. Jesus. Doctor Magnuson? When will the test results come back?"

"Just speak with me right now, Mr. Trimble, please. I'll be brief."

"You have no idea what we're going through here!"

"No, I don't. I do want the person who did this as well. I'll only be another few moments. What can you recall? Time stamp on the stamp? Any writing inside?"

"Yes! Yes! *Ricin*! The paper said ricin. And it had something in crayon. LUD. That is all. Fool that I am I pulled the page out. More of the powder. I'm a dead man."

"There have been several cases of this kind before, Mr. Trimble. Most often the powder was nothing. Baby powder."

"But there are other cases, aren't there?"

"Did you notice anyone near your house recently? Somebody follow you to the factory?"

"Nothing. It was almost done. Finished. I'm simply awaiting reassignment! Who would be monster enough to do this?"

"No one actually stands out, sir?"

"Oblauski! I told you that once! Him."

"He's a union representative, Mr. Trimble. Perhaps you resented his mannerisms. I've interviewed him. He is a bluff man."

"Interviewed? Why?"

"He was on the list. I've interviewed nearly everyone on that list regarding the arson. Mr. Oblauski has a solid alibi regarding the arson ..."

"But not this! No! Of course not. You need to arrest him!"

"Believe me, sir, after this, I will be back at them all, even those I haven't yet talked to."

"You didn't get to everybody? Why in heaven's name not? You're the police!"

"Some are on holiday. A few simply moved. I'm still catching up with them either when they return or if they left a forwarding address."

"What kind a cop are you? If you'd caught them by now this wouldn't have happened!"

"I'm sorry, Mr. Trimble. We haven't established if the cases are connected, though I agree it seems highly likely."

"I don't wish to speak with you any longer, Khadri. And I intend to make a formal complaint about your laxity in this circumstance! Now move away and let me talk with my doctor!"

"That is your right, sir. I'll see you get a card ..."

"Did you hear what I said?"

Khadri leaves Magnuson to continue. He has a nurse escort him to the front entrance, marvelling at her sense of direction. Once outside, he sits in his car, door open. The sun beats on the parking lot the heatwaves shimmering just above the asphalt. He senses real trouble. He knows he hasn't put enough time or energy into the Erban case, not at all sure of his own suspicions regarding the arson. He is sure now. He needs a way to get ahead of this rather than simply react.

Later that week comes the news that the ricin letters are more ubiquitous than originally thought. Mailed in both the US and Canada to a variety of tech firms and, in particular, to Erban Industries. Not ricin but ancient rat poison with no potency. No fingerprints. No way of tracing the letters. Typewriter printed. Again not traceable. Nothing tying them together but Erban and emerging technology. And the two words: Ricin and LUD.

The first word Khadri understands. The second in crayon, LUD, he is sure this is someone creating a signature. Though there was no sign of it at the fire it could have been missed or melted. He resolves to prioritize this case. Find out about LUD. Initials, nickname or acronym? He is sure a signature means more crimes to come.

He does not know it yet, but his investigation will lead him to within two seconds of his own death.

40

WHEN MICHAEL DEPARTS for his night tutorial, Will Baker decides to work on some irregularities in his Pineapple app. He cannot use the house lab's machines, the best of the latest technologies, for his project must have absolute security. He knows Stanley's inclusion in the process would have it working with far fewer bugs than currently. Still, no one can know of it. It is the *nether* side of the technology world.

He has taken other steps too, since Mel's move north. His biweekly phone calls are scheduled so Mel and he can speak openly using their phones and Teamviewer connecting their computers. Twice he has borrowed the car and driven to Buckworth's cottage: all day events with an increasingly demanding and conversant Mel. He is staggered by the progress of the man he once thought a dolt. Mel has manipulated Will's Pineapple app adeptly. The rows on Mel's database tell the story: he has visited numbers of sites: Dark.0de, Exploit.in and others without DNS.

In the meantime, no one has looked at the house vehicle's odometer. Will has been careful to fill the gas tank each time he returns. Three hours there and three hours back he travels up 400 North until the Mactier cut-off. It is beautiful, his drive, as the car passes Barrie and enters the southern part of the Canadian Shield. Someone told him this portion of his travel is the most expensive length of highway ever built in Ontario. Blasted through granite, winding past lakes, the striated beauty of pink and black rock and glimpses of so much water so deep blue on sunny spring days are stirring. The rock and water are often concealed by pine, birch and hemlock forests and so long as it isn't a weekend, the traffic is not so bad, making the trip a pleasure. Once he even glimpsed a moose standing in shallow water but he was going one-twenty and couldn't stop.

He wishes it could be easier. He wishes his algorithms were more effective. He wishes Mel Buckworth was not part of it. He wishes he knew what he doesn't know about the bugs in the platform. But wishes aren't horses or beggars could ride and Mel could safely surf the deep web. As it is each time Will arrives it takes an hour to de-bug Mel's machine. He is pondering this circumstance when he is accosted by Dani, the last thing he needs.

"Will, do you have a minute?" she asks.

"I'm just about to get some work done, can it wait?"

"I don't think so."

"You sound serious."

He does not really take her seriously. He wonders what this pretty *girl* is actually thinking. He gives her a moment, leaning on the newel post of the stairs. He is accustomed to pretty girls now. In his youth they despised him but with a growing reputation as a man of the future more of them seek him out. Normally he overwhelms them with his intellect and once in a very long while, actually has sex with some.

"Last week I overheard you take a call. You said, "Oh, it's you, Mel."

"I don't recall that."

"I do."

"What's your point, Dani?"

"There aren't many Mels around, Will. Was it my father?"

"My calls are none of your business. Even ones you've *overheard*."

His sarcasm clear even to her, he turns to leave, a step up the stairs, then is forced back by her challenge.

"And that gives me my answer. What were you talking about?"

"As I said, none of your business."

"Have you become a computer coach, Will? Perhaps I should ask Stanley? I wonder what he'd think of it."

The bitch will involve Stanley Best. Of course she will. But he can't afford Stanley knowing. So many ethics being broached here. He must shut this down. He responds icily.

"You don't have to do that. You're wrong anyway."

"I may be blonde and I may be an undergrad, but I'm not wrong. Maybe I should call my father. Better yet, I'll have Stanley call him."

Things have taken a startling turn for Will. The lightness of Dani's tone coupled with the tough tenor beneath stab into him. He has underestimated this, this Amazon girlfriend of Stanley's. She has seemed so soft to him until now, so blithely accepting of them all, so seeming in awe of their powers. Now she has shown a little of hers and Will Baker is not accustomed to quarrels with women. The bully style didn't work. He tries his charm.

"Okay. Yep. It was your dad. Stanley hasn't got time to help him. I thought I'd give him a couple of pointers. He's a bit of a rookie, Dani.

I think that call was about some virus he'd picked up. I told him how to remove it. He's a good guy, Dani. Just in over his head."

"I see. So your *coaching* is just a couple of phone calls. My brother made it sound more involved than that. He also sounded much more authentic."

If it comes out what he's doing with Pineapple, if it comes out he's using a citizen as a lab rat, if *any* of this comes out, he is finished. How is it girls get so powerful? How is it this one isn't at all what she seems? What can he do to evade her? Nonchalance!

"I'm helping him, okay? Anything wrong with getting the old guy up to speed with technology? He's trying to retrain himself ..."

"There are courses for that."

"He wants it private."

"Will, are you taking money from my father?"

Oh God, how did she deduce that? No weapons left. Wait ... shrugging honesty.

"Occasionally, yes," he says. "He's grateful for my help, even if you're not."

"How much?"

"Huh?"

"How much is he paying you?"

"A couple hundred. Not much. He insisted."

"So why aren't you buying groceries again for the house?"

How can she twist it to him and his skipping his responsibilities? She has turned it all back on him and now she attacks. Good God, what now? Throw yourself to her mercy. That's it!

"It's not a regular payment," he says. "Oh, Dani, I wish I hadn't done it but it was just a couple of times. I wanted to help him. I need the money! I want to stay here. I don't want to end up in California again. Give me a break!"

"And I just want to know the truth, Will. I'll call Dad."

Now she is in more defensible territory. He knows his client. He knows Mel wants things kept secret. He knows this girl and her father haven't spoken since Christmas. Her father will stonewall her. He will call Mel to warn him.

"Go ahead then. I've got nothing to hide."

"So why did you *try* to hide it?"

"I didn't."

"Not five minutes ago you told me it was none of my business!"

"That's not hiding anything?"

"So why couldn't you say it was Dad right away?"

"'Cause it's none of your business!"

Will turns on his heel and mounts the steps. He smiles to himself as he departs having clearly prevailed in the argument. Sometimes women are so troublesome. He'd wished once he could have had this one; not anymore. Good luck, Stanley.

"Will!"

He stops and turns on the step looking down upon her.

"What?"

"Something's not right here. You know my parents are separated. You know my dad is vulnerable. I know you need money. I *will* get to the bottom of this."

"Don't be a dumb-ass, Dani. There's no bottom. There's nothing. I just help him out."

He disappears up the stairs.

Leaving Danielle to wonder why Will was so evasive, then dismissive, then hostile. And his last statement ... *help him out* ... indicates he's still doing it, not that it was a fleeting thing, not that it is past. He used present tense. She knows he is up to something nefarious regarding her father; likely involving money. She knows his financial troubles and knows a great deal more of his character now she's lived in the same house for months.

She does not want to call her father. She does not, after their estrangement, wish to restart their relationship with questions of money involving Will Baker. She considers she might be overthinking this, then recalls her conversation with her brother. She thinks again of Will's last words.

She sits on the steps. She is so tired of it all. Why did this have to happen? Once her mother, her father, MJ and she had seemed the perfect family. Sometime, somewhere in her past, spring was beautiful.

Daffodils then tulips then big balls of hydrangea coloured the garden with cardinals singing their bright songs and she on the grass among flowers and the fluffy blue and white marbled sky she would watch in her father's arms as he kissed her forehead while mother dug peat moss into the flower beds and everything was slow and peaceful.

Somewhere, sometime she held her mother's hand in the living room awaiting a prom date: so nervous so joyous looking forward to the boy and the dance and the friends who would gather in washrooms to giggle their gossip and her mother was her rock and her father was beaming telling her she was so lovely and even MJ gave her a whistle.

Somewhere, sometime she rode in the back of the car with MJ who listened to his earbuds while Mom and Dad talked about chores to be done when they all got up to the cottage and she would think of leaping off the grey cedar dock into cold deep water, down and down feeling the thermocline as she would sink beneath it almost out of breath and then kicking up to the surface. And her father would be standing on the dock. Lifeguard. Protector.

Somewhere, sometime she had once felt safe.

41

MEL BUCKWORTH'S NEXT steps are to acquire the Ms, these mini-explosives termed firecrackers. He has decided to limit himself to M-80s. He knows they will cause collateral harm if one goes off in someone's hands: fingers gone, possible burns. He tries not to think too much about it. Yet this is a message he must deliver to save society from itself.

He spends night after night deep into the internet searching for vendors who might hint at selling the illegal shots. He employs the surface net to find advertising then the deep web for further information finding his way onto Dark.0de for particular addresses, staying on the dark web as briefly as possible in the only chatroom which has accepted him. He gets addresses. He does not ask if they are valid. His adrenalin pumps as if he were playing in a final game of something. His heart is in his throat. He uses Tor again and tries for the Silk Road. He gets off when he sees the site does indeed only sell drugs.

On the web he emails to three addresses. He feels like a man on a tight wire. Balanced but always in danger of falling. He doesn't know whether to trust them. He punches out his request then shuts the laptop. Because it is four in the morning he knows he's unlikely to hear anything back right away. Exhausted from his dip into the dark side he takes a shower and goes to bed.

He is met in his dreams by his conscience. He wanders a Daliesque desert, a surreal space with skeletal creatures, the remains of old machines all green and rust red and iron grey against shades of mustard and ochre. Robotic creatures roam through canyons and men with flames for hands bleed black fluid leaving footsteps in their wakes which turn to puddles of oil soon igniting into fire. The dust in the desert is gunpowder blowing black across the landscape. There is only the sound of a wind howling with sudden explosive gusts as the air ignites. A single stone path weaves around the puddles of oil and fire.

He wonders why he follows this trail through ancient, gigantic machines: the huge scarlet shear with its silvery blade, the long robin's egg blue crimping machine that disappears in the distance its iron black wires ejecting, falling beside it in impossible lengths. He moves around a huge metallic weaving machine and finds Dani, an eight-year-old Dani in her scarlet soccer outfit with yellow numbers. She wears an 8. Or is it an infinity sign? She does not recognize him. She turns on her heel while holding a white ball in one arm. She walks ahead of him pointing out buildings on the edge of the grassy soccer field in the midst of the yellow desert. She looks back. She has a devilish smile. She punts the ball at a building, the Erban factory; it hits and explodes ripping the building apart. He watches it burn. When he turns to her she has aged. She joins hands with Stanley. Yet Stanley is an old greybeard. They exit the field together, the two characters disappearing between structures of architectural wonder.

He cannot follow. They move too fast and are lost to him in the tangle of buildings. He turns to the desert. It beckons him with its blustery voices and there on a scarred wooden crosstree hangs his tiny hammer: his memento, his token, his history. Yet as he approaches he realizes his misperception. As he closes on it, it increases in size until it is huge. He lifts this hammer from the hooks holding it and it weighs so much its head hits the ground and cracks the ground, the fiery cracks streaming out all around him. He summons his strength and lifts the massive sledge and turns searching out a target. There is the weaving machine all grey and green and black wires and he swings the hammer up over his shoulder leaving a gunpowder arc in the air and smashes it down on the weaver which shatters into a ruined jumble. He swings up and around again, a huge fire wind circling him and slams it down upon the machine this time fragmenting it totally leaving him strong, jubilant, and victorious.

Stanley appears once again with Dani. They come from between glassy buildings. Where they walk the desert is replaced by greenery. The two examine the smashed machine. Together they work to reassemble it but, when it is done, it is not a weaver it is something else: a grey box with silver cables extending from its interior. Stanley touches the cables together and there is a flash and a thousand small nanos scurry out of the flash and carry the box and Stanley and Dani away. Dani waves. Smiles. Her eyes spark like fire.

Mel awakens.

Sweating from the dream.

His laptop calls him. *Ding.* Email.

He gets up and goes naked to the kitchen. He opens his email. A skull fills the screen, white on black; a small *enter* at the bottom right. He clicks on the link.

Everything opens up at once his malware protection his spyware protection his virus protection his ransom protection the protectors of all of his protections and encryptions. He tries to get out but can't. Backspace. Escape. Control-alt-delete. The chicklets are useless. Things are lighting up all over the screen. It is like watching a battle play out before him. He panics and once again tries to shut it all down. He pulls the machine's electrical plug but the battery keeps it running. He turns the laptop over and rips the battery out.

Dead.

He is sure this time the trolls of the web have destroyed his machine.

But no.

After a while he reinserts the battery and turns on the machine.

His protections are working it seems. No need to call Will Baker. He steps away from the screen so he won't be tempted to intervene again. This isn't the first time he's battled hackers though it is the worst he's faced. One by one the flares of warnings are removed from the screen, each skirmish a victory for his defences. It is a soundless battle as the protections step up one by one to reveal their existence, evaluate and probe the furies. Then the furies begin to disappear.

No blue screen of death. No black screen of shutdown. No apology for his lost materials. No demands for bitcoin. There are lists of messages: this one is removed, another prevented from opening, still others are quarantined. Soon he is following prompts and cleaning up his screen working closely with the technology. He tries his email program again but it flutters in and out. He shuts down once more, waits fifteen minutes while dressing and making coffee, then turns the machine back on.

Good to go.

He has another email. A different one.

He steels himself for a second onslaught of hacks, threats, Trojans and DDos'rs. He has been warned of all this by his son, then by Stanley then finally by Will. He is to watch himself, guard against what has just happened to him in this ugly digital world he seeks to disrupt. It has fired back. It has failed.

Victory is sweet.

For a moment the dream revisits him. He tries to parse it, comprehend, but it is too close. It has been a night of the inner self. Then he laughs. Such a jock as him trying to understand these anomalies, both subconscious and real.

He opens the email.

<u>2012 FIREWORKS SUPPLY SCHEDULE</u>

AQS Fireworks Supply *promises* to have all the fireworks you want for May 24, the 4th of July, and New Year's!

Firecrackers, Bottle-Rockets, 500g Cakes, Mortars, Family Packs & More!

<u>LOCATED IN THE SHADOW OF THE CASINO</u>

Hours of Operation:

April 1 to May 31—10AM to 4PM

June 25 to July 1—10AM to 10PM

July 2 to July 3—10AM to Midnight

July 4—SPECIAL HOURS—8AM to 8PM

July 10 to August 31—10AM to 4PM

November 10 to December 30—10AM to 4PM

December 31—SPECIAL HOURS—8AM to 6PM

He assumes he should know what AQS means. He pops up a new window to find the acronym's meaning. It shows up as a casino on a native reserve straddling the border between the US and Canada, only a few hours' drive from the cottage. Yet it means taking a risk, another, bigger than his previous foray with the faux-poison letters. This will require him to cross the Canadian border onto Native land in the US, purchase the M-80s, then return with the contraband in his car while going through Canada Customs.

He acquires the address of the casino, then just before he closes out he notices a tiny link to a message site. *Please Indicate Your Shopping Date.* He clicks on it and finds a form. He fills out the form: name, cellphone, licence plate, date of arrival, then closes out, wondering if he's just ascertained his arrest.

He rolls his chair away from the table and begins to plan. A boat would be too much risk among the Thousand Islands of the Saint Lawrence River. He knows by reputation there is a great deal of smuggling in that area. He is sure both US Homeland Security and Canada Customs are aware. So that is not the way. It will have to be by vehicle. They expect him to arrive by vehicle. He's given them a date and a licence plate number. If he does that, using his truck, he will have to use his passport.

His passport is at home. He cannot go home, cannot see Pat. It would be too painful for both of them. She knows him too well and will know he has changed. And worse, he is now a criminal since the night of the arson. That would have been shameful, had he been caught, but the letters, what he is planning, these are felonious actions with repercussions not just for him but anyone close to him should he be apprehended. Pat will be suspected first. The kids a little less likely but they will still feel the fallout. They do not deserve what might come.

He cannot retrieve his passport so it must come to him. He cannot send Will Baker to ask for it despite their working relationship. It would be far too suspicious. He cannot ask Pat to mail it. That would involve her even more. Dani is out by default. So he comes to his son. So long as his work here is concealed he thinks he can ask MJ to bring him his passport. He will tell the boy to keep it a secret from his mother. MJ has had years of obedience trained into him with a father as his coach. He will not waver.

The long weekend is close. He will ask his son to join him at the cottage: a father/son get-together. Fishing. Beer. Steaks. Normally it would have been a family thing but with his burgeoning quest there can no longer be a family attachment in any way.

It hurts to think it. Yet he has set his course. He will be vengeance. The LUD of reprisal and retaliation. A modern neo-Luddite. He is alone in his mission to awaken people to their impending doom, to destroy or disrupt the subjugators, to become the man/machine which makes terror.

He phones his son.

42

VICTORIA DAY ON the Monday of or before May 24th is a statutory holiday in Canada. Many call it the May two-four weekend because beer is often sold in 24 packs in Canada. Initially named because Queen

Victoria's birthday was May 24, 1819 it morphed into something else. Most Canadians consider it the unofficial beginning of summer: opening their cottages, going camping or attending civic celebrations which involve much drinking and viewing of fireworks displays.

This year it is early. Rather than fight endless lines of traffic heading north on Friday, MJ has told Mel he will arrive Saturday morning, the 19th of May. When he walks into the cottage he sees nothing unusual. Mel has concealed any evidence in his bedroom and closed the door. His son will not enter his father's bedroom. Not with the door closed. Still, Mel has packed his files in a trunk at the foot of the bed used for extra blankets. He knows he must be careful here. He knows his son is no fool despite his adolescent behaviour. So when Mel greets MJ with a hug and pours him a morning beer to mark the weekend, MJ is a little dazed.

"So, how you been, kiddo?" Mel powers over his son with his enlarged presence. His eyes spark with subtle aggression. MJ removes his jacket. It has been raining all morning. Mel has a fire going in the wood stove to keep the cottage interior dry. Outside on the lake the rain splashes down like quadrillions of pebbles.

"Good, Dad. What about you?"

"Me? Oh fine! Just fine. Did you bring my passport?"

"Yeah. Here." MJ fishes it out of his plaid shirt pocket. "What do you need it for anyway? Going somewhere?"

"Might have an opportunity in the US," Mel says, smiling the lie. "Pay's not bad. Not what I was getting but not so bad. Thought I'd drive down and check it out."

"Where is it?"

"New York."

"The city?"

"Upstate. Small place called Ogdensburg."

Mel is careful to keep the lie close to the truth. He will cross the Saint Lawrence River at Cornwall, find the fireworks outlet on or near the Native Reserve then return by a roundabout route which will return him to Canada via the Ogdensburg-Prescott bridge. Far enough, he hopes, for Customs officers not to assume he is smuggling.

"Doing what?"

"What is this, *Sixty Minutes*? You sound like you're grilling me."

"Sorry, dad, just curious. I guess this means you're not coming home."

The bleak sound of his son's voice troubles him. He goes gently now. Less assertive. Despite his new self-appointed LUD status he must remember his family. In his new duality he has left his initial persona behind. He must use it now for his family. Their well-being remains essential to him. He sits at the table next to the kitchen area, a big eight-seat wooden slab, carefully stained to look rustic.

"I'm still not sure, Son. I need time. So does your mother. This job may not pan out. I may have to find work outside Waterloo anyway. That whole area's losing its base. Tire plants are gone, more factories closing, it's all up in the air. I'm sorry to put you through this, MJ, I really am, but it's been building with your mother and me a long time. Then you knew that, didn't you?"

"Yeah, pretty much. Listen, I brought someone along. She's waiting outside. A bit nervous about coming in."

"What, you got a girlfriend now?"

"Not exactly."

MJ moves to the door and opens it.

"Hi, Dad."

"Dani!"

The rush of feeling shatters his contrived plan. It is so delightful to see his daughter. She is lovely her long blonde hair peeking out from her raincoat's hood, her pretty face and lively eyes. He always forgets she is so tall. He is proud of her and embarrassed at the same time for having treated her as he has. She saves him with her humility.

"You told Stanley I was forgiven. Is it true or should I leave?"

"No, no … of course not. Come in out of the rain! Give me a hug! So glad to see you."

He speaks the words but they sound hollow. He knows she can tell. He tries for a different tone.

"The whole thing was blown out of proportion. It wasn't you, Dani, it was everything: troubles with your mom, worries over work, and I'll admit I was angry you chose to live with Stan. I didn't like him. I didn't see what you saw in him. I think I do now. He's a brilliant guy. A great catch! That boy's gonna be very rich someday!"

"You make me sound like a gold digger, Dad."

Again he's made a mistake. Her eyes flash. He curses himself for being transparent. He must keep his new self hidden from his children. For an instant he yearns for his origins, for the old days, when nothing was ever concealed, when truth and joy were mainstays of the family. He recalls his little girl with scraped knees returning from softball with the boys. An Erban family picnic. That was it! And her older brother bragging how she had shown up the sons of the men from the night shift side when they told her she couldn't play. She had played alright. They had pushed her around. Then she had pushed back. A slide into second base with a kick to the legs of the player above her, so shocked he dropped the ball. Remembering this, he focuses on his daughter the way he might assess an opponent on a sports field.

"I didn't mean it that way, Dani. I'm sorry. I like the guy. He's been generous with me, helping me out with the computer."

"I know. He told me. Thank you for letting him do that, Daddy. He was so scared of you. He didn't even tell me he was going to see you."

"Nonsense!"

"He's still uneasy about you. I asked him to come with me here. He wouldn't."

"I don't know why! I thought I'd made it clear how I felt."

"You can be pretty hardline, you know. People who don't know you ..."

"Well you know me, and your brother knows me, and we're gonna have a fine weekend—the three of us. I got steaks, I got fish, I got veggies and the grill's all tuned up!"

"Can I have a beer, please?"

"Of course! I'm sorry. It's just the surprise of seeing you."

He goes to the fridge. He is old school, a trifle shocked by his daughter's drinking. He grabs a Molson Export. He twists the cap and hands his daughter the bottle.

"Why don't you two get your things? MJ you have the guest room. It's all set up for you. Dani, you take the front bedroom, I'll just get some sheets on the bed and a blanket. It's still getting cold here at night."

They set down their beers and leave together. He watches them walk down the steps to the driveway, unload their packs. His children. Adults now. Hard to believe. Hard to believe almost anything after his past few months. He has his passport; at least that is done. He's explained his need for it. That went well.

He's seeing his daughter after five months. He is stunned she looks so like a woman now. The kiddie he used to dance with around a room, read to at bedtime, comfort when she cried, praise when she succeeded, cheered on when she played her sports, watching her grow and gain grace as a teen, then worried over her despite expelling her when she'd finally differentiated.

It feels so good to have her back yet he knows he must maintain a distance, as with his son, as with his wife. Keep them safe. But not this weekend. This will be his grand goodbye without them knowing. After this he will begin his triumphal *descent*. Inevitably, he knows, he will be arrested. He will leave them this weekend with a glow in their hearts and some fine final memories of the man who was once their father.

It stops raining by early afternoon. A watery sun mists through high cirrus. They put the dock in the water as they always have, each one knowing what has to be done. Then they haul the boat to the boat ramp across the lake. Mel drives home around the lake with the trailer. MJ and Dani choose to take the boat back together. Mel notices cottages coming to life after winter. Docks are in, windows open, often the happy shouts of children echo along the shore. He arrives home from a slow, sweet drive drinking in the springtime.

He is on the dock to meet the kids. They have taken longer than normal. They should have been back before him. He goes on alert as they come in. There is something furtive about them as they tie up the boat. He worries his caution will spoil the weekend. He tries to think of how to adjust when MJ from the boat tries to lasso his sister and to his surprise succeeds and to his even greater surprise his little sister yanks the rope and tanks him into the lake. After that all is laughter and teasing and their stealth abandons them.

They clean the boat, bring out the canoe and the paddleboard; set everything as it should be on the dock. They rake winter's detritus from under the cottage each pitching in, have a supper of grilled steaks, then return to the shore again after sunset with a fire going and plenty of insect repellent. They make s'mores. They relive their years at the cottage. They even talk about Pat but only as an inclusion to each of their stories; never a story about her, only a story with her inside. They carefully avoid the pitfalls which could so easily cripple their vulnerable mood. Mel is relieved to see his daughter's vibrant eyes and hear his son's laughter. He goes to bed happy that evening.

And suddenly he misses Pat.

It can't be helped. To keep her safe he knows what he must do.

43

THEY SPEND SUNDAY sweeping the roof of its winter leavings, mostly sticks and a carpet of rust-brown hemlock needles. They take down a dead hemlock just back from the lake. It is riddled with woodpecker holes. A stiff breeze coming off the lake keeps the insects down. There are buds on the few hardwoods in their forest. The daffodils Pat planted years ago have come up bright yellow in the sunshine. In among the trees wood violets peep purple through the detritus of tree needles; a mix of hemlock and pine and, in the deep places, the beauty of a carpet of trilliums thrills them. Dazzling when the sun lights on them blooming so early. They are lucky to see this divine display. The air smells so pure the trees sing as it passes through them.

The riddled hemlock comes down where they'd wanted, between other trees. And then the familiar cottage sound of a chainsaw ruffles the air and fills it with the fragrance of oil and gas; the smells of work in Muskoka. Mel rips through the tree, MJ splits the chunks into quarters, and Danielle stacks them until they have come to the end of the day and the end of the job.

Satisfied.

Sweaty and hot they strip down to their underwear (once they would have been naked but the kids are adults now) and dive, all three, into the frigid lake. Then he splashes them and they splash back. Shocked to pink as they climb the steps out of the water they each grab towels and their dirty clothes and, just before they ascend to the cottage they pause, look at each other, two pairs of gleaming eyes, one pair reflecting their sparkle, and come together holding each other in an intimate circle. One person is missing. All three feel it yet no one says anything. Still, it is a kind of joy.

They are at supper when the emotional holiday comes to an end. They have finished a bottle of wine and are on their second, nice dry whites to go with the fish, when the talk turns from the day's events to something else. Mel notes a look pass between his children.

"So, what time do you think you'll leave tomorrow?" he asks. "If you'd like you can stay longer. Go home Tuesday morning, miss the traffic."

"I'm sorry Daddy, I've got early classes," Dani says.

"Just one more day with your dad? Can't you miss one day?"

"No Dad, I can't. I'm not that smart. You know better than anyone! You're the one who got me through high school!"

"I knew you had it in you. Your limitations weren't disabilities. You proved that to everyone by the way. I'm proud of you."

"And you'll soon feel the same about MJ," Dani says.

"Oh? Meaning?"

"Meaning I've decided something," MJ says.

"And what would that be?" Mel asks jovially. A little too much wine in him.

"I took the Academic Upgrading Assessment and, well, I aced it. It's all I needed to get back into school. I'm going to start Conestoga College in September."

"Wow! I'm impressed," Dani says. Mel thinks she sounds rehearsed.

"Me too!" Mel says. "What courses?"

"Computers. I have to take the Hardware and Software Essentials first. After that I'm going to try to become a repair technician. I think if I make it I'll try to work for Best Buy or someplace like that."

"Whaddya mean, *if* you make it?" Mel says. "You put your mind to something like you did in sports and you'll make it alright. I'm glad for you, Son. Glad you've got yourself going again. Makes me feel good."

"Nothing like Stan or those guys. Shit, they're geniuses. That day Stan came over, Dad, the day he put your computer together I was, like, blown away. But I recognized things I'd done myself on our desktop and it started me thinking. I might be able to do some of that. It's the future alright like Stan said. I don't wanna be a pizza boy or whatever. I want to get something good. A transferable skill."

"Makes sense to me."

"What about you, Dad?" Dani asks. Mel wonders where *that* came from.

"Well, I've been lookin' for work, y'know. Might have something too."

"How's the computing coming along?" MJ says, rather clumsily.

"Oh fine, fine. I bumble along."

"Really?" Dani says. "I would have thought with *Will Baker* coaching you, you'd be beyond bumbling."

Silence. An awful pause. Finally …

"Where'd you hear that?"

"He told me."

"The fuck."

"He told me you paid him."

"The little fuck. I'm gonna punch his lights out."

Mel's eyes are flames brighter than those of the table's candles. They reflect the blaze in his mind. That that bastard nerd would break his secret. That of all people Dani would find him out. He wonders if she has talked to Stan. But Stan couldn't have known about Will. So how does *she* know? Then he comprehends all this has been planned. The *surprise* arrival of Dani, the boat ride they'd taken together, the stealth he's detected: a conspiracy. They have plotted it through. He has been ambushed by his own children.

That they would turn on him in this way, just when he'd thought he could relax for one weekend, one final memorable weekend, now all but terminated by what his response will have to be. There is no choice. He must drive them away no matter the damage. He must set them free of him. All he wants to do is hold them, his children, but he is no longer the man he was and they have become sudden strangers.

Dani breaks the silence.

"It wasn't actually Will's fault. I kind of waylaid him. Still, if I hadn't got to him did you think MJ wouldn't have told me? You've been strange lately, Dad. You kicked me out of the house because I finally stood up to you. You treated Mom badly. You started drinking too much. You never bothered to look for work. Then you assaulted your wife, our mother, then you left her behind. Why is that? What are you really up to?"

This from his children wounds him deeply. What happened to the bright angel of this afternoon? What happened to the industrious boy? Why would she come here after months of not seeing him to play nice, the sweet young daughter, then turn on him like this? Why would his son lie to him about it?

"Your mother put you up to this, didn't she?" he says.

"She doesn't even know I'm here."

"Why did you come?"

"To bring you back home."

"That's not going to happen."

He swivels in his chair toward his boy.

"Why did you lie to me?"

"What?" MJ is shocked by the sudden shift.

"About Conestoga!"

"I didn't. That part's true."

"Sure. You've always been a liar, always been lazy, always ..."

"That's enough, Dad!" Danielle says. Her eyes match his now. MJ looks at them both in fear. He wishes he could just leave the table but he'd promised Dani his support.

"You don't tell me what to do, young lady!"

Voices are rising. Temperatures too.

"Don't call your son a liar. *You* are the liar! *You* are the coward. You left your wife for what? What, *Mister* Buckworth? What the hell are you doing? Do you even know? Do you have a mistress?"

"No!"

"Okay, it's the job then!" MJ shouts, triumphantly.

"What about it?"

"What about it?" Danielle says, harshly. "Other men lost their jobs. They haven't become this monster you are! I live in a house with guys who study quantum particles, Dad. Quanta can be in two or more places at once. That's a perfect description of you."

She is coming too close.

"What the hell do you mean?"

"It means a man can be several men: a father, a son, a husband, a brother and you are all those but a man can be a guardian *and* a menace at the same time as well. You're like trying to trap water. You're so fucking evasive."

"You don't know anything about me!"

"Who can really know anyone? Call it my quantum character theory. The more I seem to know the more I know I don't know. You changed when I started dating Stanley. That much I *do* know."

"I just didn't like the guy."

"Then you lost your job and started this something with Will: fraud artist, parasite, just plain creep! What are you two doing? Where is your laptop? What are the secrets you're keeping from us?"

"Never mind."

"I'd like to see it."

"Yeah," MJ says, "I would too."

"It's pass protected. You'd never get into it."

"Don't be so sure, Dad," MJ mutters.

"Oh I'm sure. I'm not the dumbass you think anymore. Will Baker's a very good coach. You see, you're not the only one changing. I've decided something as well."

"So what is it?" MJ asks.

"I can't tell you," Mel mutters.

"Typical," Danielle says.

"I'll tell you this much ... that boyfriend of yours insulted me that day he came over to the house. Talked to me like I was a *nothing* in his world of techno somethings. Every word of advice he gave your brother was a slight against me. This from a kid half my age! So I made a decision to prove him wrong and I will prove him wrong. You just wait!"

"And watch?" Danielle says, taunting.

"You won't be able to."

"Sure."

"Dad, maybe we can help you?" MJ says.

"I'm so far past any help you could offer you wouldn't believe it."

"So show us then!" Danielle says.

"I can't. I won't."

"So you can't."

"Shut up!"

"No. I won't shut up," Danielle says. Her voice, normally lilting has taken on a monotone. She perches on the edge of her chair. MJ wonders where she found this toughness. He gets ready for his part. This will not be easy.

"I'm going to leave now and go back to Mom. MJ is coming too. We're going to work together to help her in any way we can. We're going to make especially sure that *you* don't get near her or any of us. You're a bully, Mel Buckworth. You're a sad, wretched jock and underneath that smooth good sport bullshit we all know the bully has always been there. So we're done. MJ get your bag, get mine too."

MJ moves quickly. This is precarious. One misstep and anything could happen. His father's and sister's eyes shoot diamond darts at one another. He does not want to be hit by one. It would likely maim him forever. He wishes now he had not agreed to serve Dani's plot. For a while it seemed she'd left it behind. He'd been blinded by her sweetness of the afternoon, just as had his father. Then the look across the table and he had started, on cue, with the truth. For a moment his dad had been proud of him then Dani stepped in and it all went downhill.

He is back with the bags stuffing his feet into his boots his sister and father still not moving, just ... looking ... at each other.

"I'm ready," he said.

Danielle rises from the table and backs to the door. Beside him she dons her sneakers. Their father seems frozen in place, not a muscle shifting on his face; like a dead man but for the flash of his eyes.

Then they are out the door.

MJ expects him to come to the door. Expects a taunt or perhaps an apology.

Neither happens.

They can see him sitting at the table in the candlelight. They get into the car.

They drive off down a lightless road, down their cottage road, knowing it from the years of using it. No more. Not again. Neither one speaks.

The next morning Mel calls Pat.

He tells her she should plan for divorce.

44

MEL SETS OFF one morning the week after the long weekend. He takes highway 141 to Bracebridge, then 115 to Carnarvon, goes south on 35 which turns into a maze of roads through Peterborough then farther south on 28 until he hits 401 and from there it's a straight, fast run northeast to Cornwall and across the Seaway Bridge over Cornwall Island into the US. The usual questions are posed at Customs ... passport please where are you from where are you going what is your purpose a glance back into the bed of the F150 and thank you, sir, hope you win big.

He takes highway 37 through the reservation. He is in a unique jurisdiction now, one which does not necessarily recognize the laws of Canada or the US but those of the Mohawk. The natives police themselves, use indigenous law and are quite adept at self-governing through tribal councils. But the rules are not quite the same in this place.

Mel stops for gas. It is tax free. Liquor and cigarettes are tax free as well but he chooses not to purchase either. He drives directly to the casino, an upscale resort, and then tries to find a fireworks store *in the shadow of the Casino.* It is not an easy task. He drives around the parking lot and finds nothing but casino buildings. He decides the place must be off the grounds so drives out to a gas station, enters and asks the clerk about fireworks stores.

"There aren't any, sir. You have to wait 'til a couple weeks before the Fourth of July. They set up tents then."

"I found a website that says I should look in the shadow of the casino! What does that mean?"

"I don't really know, sir. You're too early is all."

He leaves the kiosk and walks to his truck, cursing his own stupidity, fooled by some internet troll. Chalk it up to experience. So what about a Plan B?

He unlocks his truck and opens the door when a burgundy jeep pulls up beside him. The man in the jeep is hard looking. Pale grey eyes evaluate Mel from a cadaverous face, grey and blue shadows beneath a black Stetson, thin lips set in a permanent frown, hawk nose that gives him the look of a predator. He wears a worn black leather jacket. He reaches inside it. Mel readies himself for a gun.

Instead the man produces a sheet of paper. He hands it to Mel. Mel sees his information on the sheet. He looks back at the man.

"Caught your licence plate in the casino. You give up quick, don't you?"

The voice is like rolling rocks over gravel.

"Follow me. Keep up."

Mel starts his truck and follows the jeep down the highway then onto gravel roads twisting and turning until he is completely lost. He thinks again about robbery and considers turning around but knows he could never find his way back. He has no idea where he is, on or off the reserve, and there have been no signs to tell him. There is no option but to commit. He has known all along there are going to be risks. He keeps his eye on the jeep as it turns into a tree-lined dirt drive which takes them five hundred metres off the road and into a forest clearing with two decrepit mobile homes set in an L. Three trucks of varying quality and age, all facing different directions, are parked in the middle. The jeep pulls up close to them. Mel does the same.

When they are out of their vehicles the man jerks a thumb toward one of the homes, a rundown place, yellowed vinyl peeling off gypsum walls, a part of the roof has a blue tarp covering it. The trailer is like a dying flower.

The hard man opens the door. Mel steps through.

Inside is a detonation of colours: packaging of every kind showing silver, cherry, hot pink, royal blue sprays of sparkling cascades, their names reflect the brilliance: Yankee Doodle Salute, Flying Saucer, Mars Rocket, Opening Flower, Burning Bush, Neighbor Hater, Dixie Delight, Raging Raptors, Mighty Atom, Lucky Star, Tears from Heaven, Big Bang, Fire Eye, Whirly Wheel, Mystic Rain ... they are stacked to the ceiling down the length of the trailer on both sides.

When he recovers from the pigment blitz and the waft of flash powder Mel asks: "Where are the M-80s?"

"Need to see your driver's licence first, and your passport."

"Why?"

"You could be anybody."

"No copies," Mel says as he hands them over.

"Don't worry."

"How do you know I don't have fake identities?"

"Then you wouldn't be here."

"How's that?"

"You're new at this, ain't ya?"

Mel says nothing. The guy glances at the photos, reads the info, looks up at Mel, hands them back, turns and walks back outside with Mel trailing. They cross the clearing following a path behind the other mobile home, equally dilapidated, and eventually enter a glade in the midst of which is a red steel container, big enough to fit a small car, padlocked shut. It stands out from the budding green of the forest like blood.

"What is this?" Mel asks.

"Outdoor Type 2 explosives magazine. Bullet proof, fire proof, weather resistant, theft resistant and ventilated. Can't be too careful with this stuff."

The hard man says this as he opens the lock, then the door. Inside the container is all plywood lining, including the door, with shelves down each side, each shelf filled with crimson tubes, different sizes for different shelves. Mel recognizes some Silver Salutes near the back.

"You said M-80s?"

"Yeah. Maybe 40? And now I see them, maybe five Silver Salutes?"

"Alright stay where you are. Don't come inside. I'll get 'em for you."

Mel stands and watches as the hard man picks the articles off the shelves and places them in brown paper bags, then puts those in a cardboard box and steps out of the magazine. He hands the box to Mel, shuts and locks the door, then leads the way back to the mobile homes. This time he opens the door to the second home. Inside is a kitchen table, grey arborite to match the walls, and some beaten up chairs. There is a small flat screen TV on a metal stand. Farther down is a decrepit kitchenette. A cast iron frying pan sits on a burner and a browned coffee perk beside it. The refrigerator looks rusted shut. The hard man takes the box from Mel and sets it on the table.

"You bring anything to carry 'em?"

"No."

"Shoulda brought a plastic container. Something spark resistant."

"I'm sorry."

"Okay. We'll package 'em up nice and safe with this box. When you get home put 'em in plastic containers and seal 'em shut. You don't want these things getting damp."

The hard man makes sure the tubes are secure, adding some paper to fill the box tightly, then grabs a tape gun from a shelf above the table and quickly rolls out the tape sealing the box shut. He turns to Mel and names his price, cash, US dollars.

Mel has at least come prepared for this. Somewhat shocked at the price he opens his wallet and peels off hundred dollar bills, then fifties, then twenties. Counting. The man counts them again. He is fast. Like a card shark. Like a bank teller. The bills riffle so quickly Mel can't follow.

"Okay. That's good. Now you'll stay the night at the casino. Buy some cigarettes and some Indian trinkets you can claim to be for your kids, the wife or whatever. Maybe get a carving. Something you have to declare."

"Where should I hide the box?"

"In plain sight. If they got dogs you're done anyway."

"How do I explain a box?"

"Buy a Mohawk quilt. Wrap it round the box. Put it all in a gift shop bag, they got big ones at the casino. Make sure part of the quilt's sticking out so the guy can see it. If there's room put the other gifts on top, if not, use more gift shop bags. Make sure you keep the receipts. Make sure you declare all the gifts."

"How the hell do I stay at the casino? I haven't got any money left!"

"They take credit cards. Don't try to be cheap, don't stay anywhere else. You were gambling. You won a bit so you bought souvenirs. You got a wife and kids?"

"Yeah."

"Try to stay breezy, like you're happy. Get a shave. Buy a new shirt. They ask you how much for the merch you tell 'em exactly. Don't hesitate. You spent most of it buying the gifts. Show the receipts. How much you got left in your wallet?"

"Forty dollars. I didn't imagine your prices."

"You expected Walmart?"

"No, just ..."

"And if you get busted you say you got these from a guy. An Indian guy. Came to your room at the casino. You called a number from your room. Find one in the phone book, write it on a casino matchbook."

"*Any* number? Somebody could get in trouble."

"Not your problem. And remember, I get trouble you get double trouble. I know where you live. You feel me?"

He has moved close, his planed face inches from Mel's. There is no mistaking the meaning of his words or in his eyes as he speaks. Mel suppresses a feeling of dread hoping his face won't betray his fear. The hard man means business.

"Yes."

"Good then."

"Ummm ..."

"What?"

"How the hell do I find the casino from here?"

Hard man laughs. His laugh is rumbling rocks cascading.

"I'll take you out to the highway, then you turn right."

Canada Customs turned out to be easy. Mel crossed as planned at the Ogdensburg-Prescott International Bridge. And he'd whisked through Customs with a smile on his face and humble Canadian attitude. His drive back north was smooth and sunny and he felt like he'd won a particularly close game, won it with a gamble. All the way back to the cottage he thinks of where he will send his M-80s.

All Canadian this time. No one stealing LUD's thunder again.

Research in Motion. Waterloo

Open Text. Waterloo.

Descartes Systems Group. Waterloo.

Google. Kitchener.

Algorithmics. Toronto.

Softchoice. Toronto.

Zarlink Semiconductor. Ottawa.

Maplesoft Group. Ottawa.

Soroc Technology. Woodbridge.

Gennum. Burlington.

Enghouse. Markham.

OnX Enterprise Solutions. Thornhill.

Compugen. Richmond Hill.

And, of course, Herbert Trimble. Kitchener.

A Silver Salute for him.

45

A SOFT SUMMER Sunday in the early morning garden. There is dew on the clusters of pink peonies overflowing their wrought iron stands their heavy heads drooping with the weight of water, dew on the green-going-white hydrangea budding out through their fences and dew on the purple clematis gleaming at the peak of their climb, high on the garden trellises.

Patricia Buckworth loves this kind of day: the early daylight refreshing, the aroma of air and earth, pottering in her garden, the new morning gleaming off plants, the sharp chirps of robins and cardinals' trills and the squirrels scampering along the back fence.

It is an unusual garden. Rather than lawns she and Mel had decided years past that they preferred a cobbled look, based on a Spanish style garden they'd seen in Puerto Rico while on vacation. So Mel had done the work: fencing in the garden (they had wanted brick walls but the expense was too much), dividing the sloping land into terraces, wheelbarrowing sand and screening and setting the stones then lining the levels with six by six beams to create garden boxes where Pat planted her flowers and trees. It was a work of months and some expense but both had been pleased with the result. Mel was especially exultant when he gave away his lawn mower.

As she threads through the walkways she recalls her mother showing her, the tomboy, the intricacies of gardening. She was ten and had wanted to get out and play. Her mother had stayed her gently. She cannot recall a time when her mother was openly angry. Patiently she had shown her only child the world of women in those days of barely budding feminism. Still, she thinks, without Paula Wells, she would not have learned the arts of the kitchen the garden the housework the fashion but more significantly as she grew older, how to depend on herself and how she should know to treat others.

Patricia Wells was lucky enough to have been a pretty girl. Even as a child she was what older women called "fetching." Her behaviour was not quite so lovely. With boys as neighbours she naturally joined their games. They were rough and tumble but she loved to play hard and get dirty, to the dismay of her mother.

Even as she grew older she continued her sports but by then boys were interested in her in other ways, and she in them. It was Paula, her mother, who had offered some badly needed self-awareness, while athletics had given Pat confidence. In her teens she had differentiated, wanting to prove she was her own woman yet in so doing attaching herself to Mel. It was not that Mel was dominant, it was that she had allowed it. Somehow she had missed the feminist movement in the midst of sports, dating, sex, love, and then family. She knew her mother hadn't been happy when they had married so young.

Pat focuses again on her clipping. She tends her plants almost as closely as she once tended her children. She uses her snips judiciously to cut away errant twigs, give the plants shape, providing each bed with its individual look. There is a peace to gardening: time seems to slow and thoughts seem to drift. Beneath the big spruce are the variegated greens of ferns, hostas, the broad leafed spikes of Jack-in-the-Pulpits, and trails of Virginia creeper she is forever cutting back as it fights to fill her garden. In the sunlit parts colours appear. She has planned her plantings so that something is always in bloom from May daffodils to October aster. Sometimes she sits on a wrought iron bench for a rest and some tea and her thoughts.

For once she is not at her puzzle. For once she has found a modicum of peace as the sun lifts above the surrounding trees and begins to heat the back yard. A month has passed since she learned of her children's trip north to their father. They have not told her much, only that Mel is physically fine but emotionally estranged. She had known that already. Mel's telling her to get a divorce had been clear enough. The shock of that was worse than the night he'd slapped her. She had reeled from the suddenness, the cold, the bluntness.

Both her children had come to her house straight from the cottage. They spent the next day comforting her, saying their father had turned his back on them too. None of the three could comprehend what he was actually doing up there but the kids had said he was enigmatic and emotionally cold. They'd related to her their weekend, how well it had started then how quickly it had descended into dispute and departure. It was as if their father had purposely driven them off.

The question still troubled them ... why?

There have been changes, however, since that day. MJ has quit his pizza delivery and just as quickly found a good summer job. Landscaping. Hard work for a boy softened by a year of computer games. The first week she would salve liniment over his aching muscles. He never complains. Not anymore. He is home for supper most nights. He still plays his game but only after helping her with chores around the house. He has even cleaned his basement room. He smiles much more often. He never swears in her presence. He has asked her to help him begin a diet. It is as if the estrangement from his father has somehow freed him.

Dani has her university job, landscaping as well, which she has always loved. She plays soccer in a city league. MJ and Pat try to make each of her games. Stanley is there as well. Without Mel as an intimidating presence Stanley becomes much more open. He and MJ speak often. MJ believes he can learn a great deal from his sister's boyfriend. Once he'd informed him of his acceptance to Conestoga in computing, Stanley became a fount of knowledge, almost a tutor for her son and certainly a flourishing friend.

Tonight she is going to Dani's for dinner. Her first time there. She looks forward to it. She wants to know more about Stanley Best (*please don't call him Stan, Mommy*) and the friends her daughter has lived with for the past ten months, Michael Selel and Will Baker. MJ is invited as well. There is a new bond between brother and sister, an affection she has not seen in years.

There is just one thing wrong in her life.

It brings a memory of a cathedral in Montreal. A camping trip with the family lost in the midst of the city, Mel driving car and trailer through narrow streets, impatient horns blaring at them. They had found a parking lot to escape the stress of the traffic. As Mel looked at a street map trying to find a way out she had taken the kids around the corner to give him some peace. They found themselves across from a beautiful massive old church in the heart of the city right on René Lévesque Boulevard. She'd returned to find Mel but he had not wanted to come with her. He had thought to have lunch at a hot dog stand and of course the kids followed him for a treat.

She'd decided not to join them and returned to the church. The building had a magical quality about its architecture: its grey stone and weathered green domes and steeples, Marie-Reine-du-Monde cathedral. It was not the famous Notre Dame but was enough for her. Entering had calmed her. Its beauty and size and the hush, once the huge entry door swung shut, were remarkable. Inside, Pat had walked up the aisle approaching the massive ciborium directly beneath the building's dome. She took pictures. The ciborium itself was a brilliant work of art, Neo-Baroque twisting columns above the altar, all copper and gold leaf. It entranced her. Yet on the way toward it she had begun to notice the place was not simply a tourist attraction. She saw people in the pews on their knees praying while others sat glassy eyed looking inside themselves and still more in a corner chapel in deep contemplation. One woman had her head resting on the pew in front of her, exhausted from her troubles.

Pat could *feel* the pain of these people. It was a climate of grief. She knew she should not disturb their devotion. Instead of continuing toward the high altar, she backed away down the aisle, through the entrance and outside the church where it was sunny and she found she could breathe again. She has never forgotten that moment.

She and Mel never travelled much other than to play sports. They were a parochial pair respected in their community. They were very good at what they played and usually led their teams to victories. So many trips by car or by bus. Their churches back then were arenas, their gardens the groomed greens and browns and limed lines of playing fields. They never thought much beyond them. They never explored anything outside All Inclusive Resorts preferring the tennis courts or the pools to the foreign cultures neither could comprehend. They never observed the poverty and pain outside those placid hotel grounds with their polite staff and subtle security on the beaches. Perhaps as a bus took them to and from a resort they would look out the windows and be reinforced that their way of life was superior, that their choices had been the right ones.

Seldom did they take time to sit in the shade of a palm on a white beach with turquoise rollers reaching the shore. Seldom did they consider their luck. To them it had never been luck. They had been the golden couple, the ones to be envied, the peak of suburban culture. Pat would never forget their prom. She was queen. It was expected, of course, but she had carried it off quite well. And afterward the drive to Niagara Falls, five carloads of kids, plenty of liquor, and the raucous party in five rooms of the Lundy's Lane Inn. It was carefree and careless and celebratory. No one thought of a future which might bring adversity. It had all been so easy then.

There was one other church Pat would never forget: the First United on William Street in uptown Waterloo. Her family's church. Where she was married. They were all there. Her parents, her uncles and aunts, her relations from farther away, their friends, their acquaintances, his parents and family all invited to attend the wedding of the exquisite bride in her white taffeta to the boy whom everyone knew would go far. It had been perfect. The weather, the flowers, the bridesmaids, the sweep of the church which lent her wedding the distinction she'd felt it deserved.

So long ago.

The Mel and Pat show.

How could she have been so naïve, such a fool to believe mythology could remain real?

Over now.

This is her church now. Her garden. Glistening in the morning sun. A garden of rejuvenation as she stands and moves toward a small bunch of bleeding heart beneath a cedar hedge. Their blooms are small pink bells.

The bells of her garden cathedral.

46

AFTER A SHOWER and a light lunch she dresses in her tennis outfit: an argent and yellow Adidas dress, white leather Nike shoes, a white sunshade and sunglasses with white frames. The outfit flatters her. It fits nicely on her figure, goes well with her blonde hair and shows the length of her still shapely legs. It is her best outfit because this is Sunday and the Waterloo Club's mixed doubles social. She wants to look good as the newly single woman. She picks up her racquets, both Dunlop Bio 200 Lites and bags them.

She knows too many folks at the club from years past. She knows they will know about Mel. Some of them might even know more than she does. She hopes not. Meanwhile she maintains her dignity and throws in a little cougar sexiness just to show the gossips she is not defeated.

Grace is there looking beautiful her ebony skin shining in the sun beneath a sea blue outfit. Pat quickly joins her knowing George is not there. His only game is golf. He was never a guy for the rough and tumble.

Grace and Pat hug. They smile as they drop their tennis bags. The two of them standing side by side are a picture so many appreciate. They are not oblivious. It feels flattering. Then the names in the hats are drawn: one hat women's names one hat the men's. They do this so married couples will not necessarily play together. The point of the afternoon is to mix. Play a set get a drink have a rest on the clubhouse balcony and wait for the next draw. The *thwock* of bright yellow tennis balls back and forth against the green of clay courts the whites of the lines the bright colours of players' outfits then the textured greens of Waterloo Park in the background and cheers from the distant cricket pitch all mix in the sunshine of the day. On the balcony there is a hum of conversation with bursts of laughter; then the clink of glasses and the call of players' names and once again the scraping chairs as everyone rises for the next round.

She meets her partner. He is called Amrit. He has a warm, firm handshake. He is Asian, his brown skin enhanced by his tennis whites. He is tall and slightly paunchy though she notes his biceps beneath his sleeves. He has a most interesting face. When he smiles his teeth gleam and his dark eyes possess a softness unusual in most men. His face is a series of planes though not harsh ones for he possesses a fine bone structure. He wears his hair short. He dons a set of aviator sunglasses. Overall she thinks he is good looking and wonders why she has not seen him before. This is new territory for her. She wonders if she should engage with him or just play the game. She introduces herself then asks about him, why she hasn't seen him. She is a little shy, unaccustomed to being single.

"Amrit Khadri! So pleased to meet you, Patricia. As you can see I'm a touch out of shape and this is a way to ease back in. I'm afraid my work sometimes gets the best of me."

He has a mellifluous voice with an English accent. She finds it comforting.

"Oh?'

"I'm a policeman, that is, a detective."

"Isn't that dangerous?"

"TV shows have us running around shooting off guns though I've found the job requires more research and sitting than action, thus my middle age spread. I have never had to draw my firearm. I hope my reactions are fast enough to keep up with everyone in this game. And you, Patricia, you're a regular?"

She loves to hear her name in full; it sounds out so beautifully in his voice.

"Yes. We've belonged here some years. It's a lovely club."

"We?"

Suddenly she sinks. Stupid. Stupid. It comes from a habit she must learn to quit.

"My husband and I."

"Well, shall we?"

He leads the way through the gate to the court. The court is hot in the afternoon sun, the clay getting dusty. This time Pat faces Grace and her partner, Bill Deane. Pat knows Grace is good, as fast as she is. She knows as well that Bill likes to hit the ball hard. An intimidating man. Not the nicest of manners in mixed doubles tennis but Bill is the kind of person, like Mel, who needs to win. Still, she knows he will watch his manners. She has earned his respect.

The two couples meet in the middle, spin the racquet for first serve, and take their places on the court. The sun is high so is no encumbrance. The wind is light, no advantage there. As they walk back Amrit says: "Any tips?"

Pat speaks softly.

"Grace is quick, she gets nearly everything, but her balls come back flat. Bill will try to drive it through you. He serves an American twist."

"Yikes! I thought this was for relaxation."

She truly enjoys his accent.

"Hit to Grace if you can, or if they're both back drop the ball over the net on Bill's side. He's slow coming forward."

"How about us?"

"What you got, stranger?" she asks, smiling.

The set starts out active, both couples fresh and closely matched. When he serves Bill does not hold back against Pat. His twist serve loops over the net cuts the clay and flies up and outside. Amrit is more a gentleman. His serve, a flat serve depending on speed slows a little when he faces Grace. Finally, the score is five-four with Pat serving. Amrit walks back to Pat.

"Bill's lost control. He's frustrated. Hard as you can, first serve."

She does so. The ball ticks off the net tape. Fault. She glances at Amrit. He smiles and nods his head. She understands. She hits her second serve with the same force as the first and it goes for an Ace right down the centre court line.

"Out!" Bill shouts.

"No, Bill," Grace says. "It was on the line. Look here, it's left a mark on the tape."

Bill is fuming. Pat's fourth serve is returned sharply by Grace. Bill rushes forward and punches the ball in a volley but he runs into the net, falling over it. Normally it would be a comic moment but one look at Bill Deane, tennis whites now clay green, extricating himself from the net, and Amrit moves forward to help. He is shaken off.

They have won on Bill's fault. A good set but for Bill's seething undercurrent. Everyone is careful to be genteel during the handshakes. They quickly move off the court leaving Bill to brush himself off.

"Ladies, may I buy you a drink?" Amrit says. "I think we all need to cool down."

The three mount the stairs to the balcony bar.

"Bill seems to be having a difficult day," Grace says, smiling.

"He's like that," Pat says.

"Yes. Remember the mixed final last year? Of course you do."

"Not a good memory," Pat responds. She does not want to take conversation there.

"May I ask what happened?" Amrit asks.

Grace picks up the story.

"Pat and her husband were in the final against Bill and, who was it?"

"Jenny Albrecht." Pat says. She wishes the subject hadn't come up.

"At any rate Bill was playing *no prisoners*. At one point he took an overhead smash at the net and aimed it directly at Pat."

"What?"

"Indeed," Grace says, her accent lulling the subject of her tale. "What Bill forgot was Pat's husband, who might be the best older player in the club. Bill had the next serve. He used his American twist but he's known for it. Bill was expecting a backhand. Mel is a fine athlete. Poor Bill realized too late Mel had actually run around to his forehand and smashed the ball back again. I don't think he meant it, did he, Pat?"

"Don't ask me," Pat says, laughing.

She is loving the accented lilt of these two. She relaxes, knowing what's coming.

"Well that smash went straight to the testicles before Bill could raise his racquet. The match was delayed while Bill hobbled into the clubhouse. When he returned he was a lesser man, so to speak, his play so weak Pat and Mel won the last set six games straight."

"Sounds like quite a man, your husband." Amrit smiles at Pat.

So suddenly her enjoyment turns sour. She pauses a moment. This is the first time she will say it in public. The hurt of the loss comes so quickly she can barely speak.

"Ex-husband. We're separated."

"I'm sorry, none of my business."

His tone has changed too. She can feel his sympathy.

"You couldn't have known. Are you married?"

"No."

Surprising her. A man like this. She cannot help herself, she pries when she shouldn't.

"Not ever?"

"Well, when I was young there was an arranged marriage planned with a girl in India. I was born in England; Gravesend actually. Though my Indian culture was clear from my parents I didn't live it. I was an English boy. I refused the marriage. My parents disowned me. I left England soon after and came to Canada. I suppose I just haven't found the right person yet."

"That's a long time looking," Grace said. "You're in your forties, yes?"

"Fifty one, actually."

"Well you don't look it," Grace says, smiling.

"And you two are what? Thirty-one, thirty-two?"

"Don't be smart, Mr. Khadri."

"That is *Officer* Khadri to you, ladies."

He smiles. His smile is gentle.

Pat likes him.

"I'll get those drinks," he says.

47

BECAUSE IT IS a warm evening the supper has turned *al fresco*. There is a grilled chicken turning on a spit under the auspices of Danielle, a rice and spinach salad creation by Michael with red beans, green peas, onion, tomato and peanuts as a garnish, and for dessert a delicious cherry pie recently unwrapped from its Zehrs packaging and plated by Stanley.

The back of the house on Albert Street isn't much. None of the inhabitants have time for gardening. There is an old cedar privacy fence as is normal for most Ontario back yards. One Norwegian maple in full glorious green rises in the corner and towers above the house. There is a deck coming off the back door to the kitchen. It runs maybe two by four metres one step up from the ground.

The grill sits on the deck. The grill is a little beat up, its black coating having faded to grey with rust spots here and there at the joints. Winters have been hard on it. Beyond the deck is a good sized back lawn. Normally the lawn is weedy and long but Stanley has found the lawnmower beneath winter shovels and an old tarp and actually got it gassed, oiled and running. The lawn is now weedy and short except for the edges where the mower can't go.

They sit on garden chairs, a recent purchase from Home Hardware, made of white plastic/resin. They drink Shramsberg Blanc de Blancs with watermelon juice. With the drinks there is a charcuterie board on a side table, actually a wooden folding TV table, perched precariously on the back lawn. The chairs are arranged in a sort of circle with the three men and Pat seated around the table. Stanley gets up to steady it every few minutes.

An old picnic table is covered by a cheery plastic tablecloth in sun splash yellow pinned in place. Red plastic cushions sit on the benches to prevent slivers seeking out picnickers' skins. The IKEA kitchen dishes sit gleaming white on the table surrounded by tableware and glasses. Two bottles of Ulysses Napa Valley Cabernet Sauvignon and two of San Pelegrino look like green columns each at a corner. Five places are set.

"Will has been called away," is Stanley's reply to Pat's question. He wears linen trousers and a light cotton shirt. "I believe he's returning to California. His grants have run their course."

"He left a note," Michael says. Michael is wearing a collarless blue shirt and darker blue jeans with sunglasses perched on his head. "Didn't say goodbye. Typical of the man."

"I believe he's embarrassed by his financial state," Stanley says.

"But he left his teaching responsibilities! Who does that?" Michael says.

"My dad's going to be disappointed," MJ says, then realizes his mother is sitting across from him. "Oh, Jeez, I'm sorry, Mom."

MJ has come in his usual attire. T-shirt with some obscure band's name on the front and blue jeans ... the T-shirt so faded the band must have faded too, long ago.

"It's fine, MJ," Pat says. She has felt the jolt but less now than before. "It's something we can't skate around."

She wears a pink sundress. In the heat it is perfect. It is also a perfect fit. Michael, having just met her mother, now sees where Dani got her looks.

"What do you mean, MJ?" Michael asks.

"My dad was paying Will to tutor him on computers. You didn't know?" Danielle says, standing by the grill, her voice suddenly brittle. Up to this point she has been relaxed, casual, in her purple kaftan with gold inlay, her outfit perfect for a summer's day.

"No. Not at all," Michael answers. "Though I wondered about his leaving sometimes for whole days ... gone in the early morning and back very late at night." Michael's soft Kenyan drawl conceals his concern.

"Our cottage is three hours from here," MJ says. "I bet he was going there. Maybe he's there now. You never know."

"Can you ask your father?" Michael says.

A short hiss from Stanley brings Michael up short.

"It's alright, Stanley," MJ says. He turns to Michael. "We don't speak to him anymore. Dani and I had a run-in with him at the cottage last month. He wouldn't give us any answers then so I doubt he would now."

"I'm sorry to hear this," Michael says. "Stanley doesn't keep me up to speed."

"I thought it a family affair, Michael. I'm sorry."

"Well whatever it is, Will's gone, Dad's gone, and here we all are having dinner together!" Danielle says. "It's a beautiful day, let's talk about other things!"

The steel in her voice belies her apparent light attitude.

"How was tennis, Mom?" MJ says. He and Danielle are in sync. He knows to steer conversation away from his father.

"Oh, you know … the usual." Pat stumbles a bit, preoccupied.

"What is the usual, Mrs. Buckworth?" Stanley asks, trying to bring her out of her funk.

"Sunday mixed doubles. Please call me Pat. Everyone does. Do you play?"

"I'm afraid not, Pat … may I call you Patricia? It's a lovely name."

"Of course. Actually someone called me Patricia today. One of my partners. He is from England as well."

"Oh? What part?"

"I think he said Graves or something. I wasn't really listening."

"Gravesend?"

"Yes, that's it!"

"It's a town in Kent, east of London."

"I liked him. He was a gentleman. Like you, Stanley. Patricia must be an English name, it runs off both your tongues so well."

"Actually I believe it originates from the Latin *Patrician* meaning nobleman. It *is* a popular name at home."

"Are you from Kent as well, Stanley? You sound much the same as Amrit."

"I'm a Yorkshire lad, Patricia, though I lost my accent long ago to Cambridge."

"His name's Amrit?" MJ says. "But he's English?"

"Of course, dear. His heritage is East Indian but he's never lived there. Never even visited as far as I know. He moved to Canada as a young man. He's a policeman. A detective."

"Wow! What'd you do, Mother, pin him down and question him?" Danielle laughs.

"It came up in conversation, Dani. Your Aunt Grace was there as well."

"I didn't mean anything ..."

"Of course not. I know."

"I'm sorry."

"Back to this again!" Pat breaks the spell herself this time. "Time to change the subject. Michael, what is it you do at the university? You're in computers as well as Stanley, aren't you?"

"Well, Patricia, it is quite a stretch to compare Stanley's fields to mine. I work in robotics. Our paths cross occasionally when I apply AI to robots, engendering learning processes. Right now my efforts are in agriculture."

"Farming robots?" MJ says. "Sounds like science fiction!"

"I can assure you it's real. At the heart of my work is the need for increased production yields. The UN estimates world population will rise from seven billion today to ten billion in 2050. The world will need a good deal more food and farmers will face the pressure to keep up with demand. Agricultural robots will increase yields for farmers in various ways. From drones to autonomous tractors to robotic arms, we are searching out best solutions."

"Goodness, that can't be easy," Pat says.

"Indeed, Patricia, these applications can be difficult to automate. Take a robotic platform designed to pick peppers. The device must navigate natural obstacles to grasp, pick and place a pepper in a hopper. This is much different from a robotic assembler in a factory line. The agricultural robot must be flexible in a dynamic environment and accurate enough not to damage the peppers as they're being picked. And though farmers want them badly, they are currently far too expensive. I am attempting to create inexpensive robots for ordinary farmers. I think of my home and the good they would do there."

"Wouldn't they cost people jobs?" Pat asks.

"On the contrary, they would free up people for other, more constructive work."

"I see. I admire you, Michael. I guess it made me think of my husband's situation."

"So much for back yard baseball talk!" MJ shouts.

"How about soccer talk?" Danielle says.

"Now you're gonna boast about your two goals last week! Stanley, you gotta get this girl's ego under control."

"I'm not sure that's necessary, MJ," Stanley says, laughing.

"If you'll excuse me I'd like to use the ladies' room," Pat says. She knows by bringing up Mel she has shuttered the pleasure of the party.

"Mom, go upstairs to our bathroom. The one off the kitchen's not so great," Danielle says. "It's more Henry's bathroom than anyone else."

"Henry? Another partner?"

"Kind of," Danielle says, grinning. "He's the house cat."

"Oh! I'll do that then, dear, up the stairs."

She departs, crossing the lawn to the back door. Everyone awaits its closing.

"I am so sorry," Michael says.

"Not your fault," MJ returns. "It's Dad's fault ... the whole thing."

"Have you any idea why he's at your cottage?" Stanley asks.

"We went up to find out last month," Danielle says. "That was when I told him I knew Will was helping him."

"Of course," Stanley replies, aware of the story.

"He was crazy mad, said he'd punch Will's lights out," MJ says.

"Yes, but what's he actually doing?" Stanley asks again.

"That's when he shut us down," MJ says. "One day it's all peaches and cream, he's like our dad again, then the next he turns into a stranger."

"It was like he set it all up!" Danielle says. "When I think of it now he was playing us. First he was our dad from the old days. We had a great time with him. The next day we cut down a tree. Not much time to talk so we waited 'til supper. That's when he turned. He went back to all the old insults from before, he started on MJ again." She turns to Stanley. "He even told us the day you were there at the house you'd insulted him."

"I thought I'd made progress!" Stanley says, his voice slightly defeated.

"Dad said he was going to prove you wrong. He said we'd see. Said we would watch but he wouldn't tell us what he was doing. He was awful. Like he turned on every insult he could use to drive us away. I've never heard him like that ... in my life."

"When we asked him what he was doing he told us we wouldn't understand," MJ says.

"I wanted to talk to Will about it when we came home. But he'd left," Danielle says.

"When exactly did he leave?" MJ asks.

"The Wednesday after you and Danielle returned," Stanley says. "I found a note on the kitchen table. It said he was going home. It said he had prospects for his new app, this *famous* secret app he's been working on these past months. I suppose he's going to pitch it to someone in Silicon Valley."

"Why wouldn't he do it here?" Michael asks. "The Velocity Centre ... even you or me."

"Afraid his ideas would be stolen, I assume," Stanley answers.

"By us?"

"Or he's involved in something unethical," Stanley says, half to himself.

"Wait a minute," Danielle says, "he left the day after we got back? We went to mom's place and I didn't come here until Tuesday evening. I told Dad I was going to ask Will some questions when we didn't get any answers from Dad. He must have called Will after we left. Warned him!"

"Well it is clear to me they're involved in something together," Michael says.

"For the life of me I can't comprehend what it would be," Stanley says. "I mean, Will Baker and Mel Buckworth? Two more different worlds there can't be."

"Yet he bought a computer the night he had that quarrel with Mom," Danielle says. "And before that I'd overheard Will on the phone with him."

"This doesn't make sense," Michael says.

"Will needed money," Stanley says, "your father paid him for help, but why?"

"Because I quit working with him," MJ says. "He was so pissed all the time: first at the computer, then at me, I told him I couldn't do it anymore! I guess he got his own help."

"He's angry at computers yet he goes out and buys one?" Danielle says. "You won't work with him so he finds Will Baker. Will Baker of all people! How would he even know him?"

"And then he plays us at the cottage! He turned on us like he turned on Mom," MJ says.

"Listen, we've got to stop. I don't want Mom hearing this."

"You instructed her to go upstairs, Danielle," Stanley says. "She couldn't possibly hear."

"She'll be back any minute. Let's get off this subject!"

"Your guitar, Michael. Pick it up," Stanley says.

"Huh?"

"Music. Play some music!"

Michael crosses from his chair to the deck. He sets down his drink, a tall glass of fruit juice, picks up his guitar, quickly tunes it, then begins to play.

48

PAT, AGAINST HER daughter's advice, is in the kitchen bathroom. It smells a little of used cat litter but its window is open onto the back yard. She has washed her hands and stands at the counter in front of the mirror looking at the woman staring back at her. This woman is not the same one she saw this morning. This one is ageing. This one is full of doubts and cares.

She has heard everything. Those poor kids outside trying to comprehend. As smart as they are they lack the experience that comes with age. She has listened to their arguments, their claims and revelations and examines them now, one by one, in her mind. It is not an easy thing to do. To think how the day began and now come to this.

Something as innocent as Michael talking about agricultural robots turns to who will suffer because of them. She knows she did that. A knee jerk reaction. It happened to my man. It will for others. Does Michael even think of this?

It seems Mel has decided to alter his life. Not only will he divorce her, he is driving his children away. As surely as a man bent on self-destruction he is shedding all that is good in his life, leaving it behind as though it was an encumbrance.

This can't just be about losing a job. Other men and women lost theirs. As far as she knows they are coping to greater or lesser degrees. She cannot know them all. She cannot peer into others' lives and know what lies beneath. There could be all sorts of problems she hasn't heard of. Mona Wilson hasn't called her in months. At one time they were great friends: she and Gary, Pat and Mel. She resolves to make that call tomorrow if only to satisfy herself about what has happened in *their* household and why Mona seems to have dropped their friendship.

So, as with the increasingly complex puzzles she continues to solve in her living room, she tries to decipher this plethora of secrets created by her husband. Former husband. This is the enigma she works through each week with Nancy Silvain. The puzzle of herself.

If she becomes objective, listening at a window, she can begin to grasp clues not so much of herself, but of Mel. He is pushing everyone away for a reason. Perhaps he's decided to end his troubles. Yet she cannot conceive Mel capable of suicide. He is not that kind of man at all. Suicide would be an admission of failure and Mel Buckworth hates to fail. This much she knows. Mel was born to win. It is in his genes.

So it must be the future. The past is gone and he is thinking about things to come. But what *are* they and why does he keep them secret and why does he drive his family away? There is no reason to it.

If she could be with him she would try to discover his thinking. She would question him, piece together the puzzle that he has become.

Does he remember his past? Is it only this stupid job? He never fell apart after a loss. He didn't like to lose but he never dwelled on it. He was always the smiling one even if that smile was pasted on, helping his teammates through their defeat, being the rock they all looked to, we all looked to, his family as well, and now is the time he falls apart leaving us bereft. What does he look to gain from all this? What is in there among his secrets provoking him into becoming another man?

Does he never think of days at the beach with the golden sand and the dunes behind us? We would spread our blankets and towels on the sand and watch the children wade into the water, so young then that even the wavelets would knock them over but they didn't stop, they didn't let falling down impede them. They got up again and looked back for reassurance and we would wave them on and out they would go until they were up to their necks and then he would run in to join them his muscular body rippling as he ran splashing up founts of water jumping the waves and then he would be with them, one on each arm, wading ever deeper, letting one or the other slide off to swim a few strokes beside him, always there for them to hold on to.

Does he at all retain memories of us in our youth, so full of promise so pumped with joy we would come together and he would kiss me and whisper to me his tongue sliding down my neck to my shoulder where kisses would bring goose bumps and how we so easily fit each other? Making love in the long grass out on Snyder's Flats Road on warm summer nights, nights like this one.

He loves us. She know this with all her being. There must be a danger so imminent he expels us from his life, not as a punishment more as a hindrance as if somehow we might hold him back from something. He is doing this to protect us.

Yes.

He is embarking on some kind of journey which could end in disaster: the earth burnt around him and everyone, everything, all that once mattered must be kept safe by keeping them distant. Is it he plans a future which has no future, yet still exists in a stasis of danger? Oh, Mel, my man my lover my husband my friend you think you have nothing left. I think I understand you.

And a second edge is attained.

49

AS SHE TURNS TO leave she hears the creak of the bathroom door. A head pops around the corner. A small tabby cat peeps up at her. Big green eyes. Hesitant. Curious. Pat does not move. The cat does not move. She knows she should return outside or her children will worry. Michael will think he has caused her withdrawal. Yet for some reason she feels a need for something to take her mind from her troubles if even for a few moments.

She squats with her back against the counter. The cat responds by moving through the doorway. A comical little cat with wary eyes. She holds her hands open in front of her. The cat shies away, *don't touch me* in its face. She coos. The little cat pauses then walks slowly forward. It has a funny bobble headed walk, its head moving up and down like one of those things on cars' dashboards. It turns back, passes her a look over its shoulder and begins to leave.

"Ohhh?" she says, disappointed.

The cat stops, its tail twitches, then it turns back walking toward her.

Rather than pick it up she allows it to rub against her knee, then sniff her knee then come into her hands where it sniffs a little more. Slowly she moves her fingers and scratches behind each ear and as the cat looks up at her she moves her fingers down both sides of its face, rubbing the fur, reaching under its chin. The cat makes a silly grimace and raises its chin for more. Her hands hold behind its ears and her thumbs rub over its eyes stretching the face just a little. An amusing little face.

The cat breaks off. It shakes its head so quickly the movement makes a *brrrrrr* sound. And then she is stroking its back. It curls. The little thing purrs. So sweet.

"What's your name, darling?" she asks.

Purr.

"Of course, it's Henry. I've heard of you. Good boy, Henry."

It falls on its side presenting her with a tabby belly and some white fur near the back of its legs. Such a small little fellow. She softly trespasses, her hand moving up and down the belly, not too close to his rear legs but softly up belly and chest, back and forth. Unusual, she thinks, for a cat to enjoy its fur pushed against the grain.

Purr.

The cat has calmed her. This brief interlude on the floor of the bathroom with this little tabby has taken the ache from her shoulders, the dart from her temples. Her body slumps a bit more, the little cat looking up at her. She is held by his beautiful eyes: their green, their dark pupils, the lines around them and knows he has helped her. Then she picks him up.

Error.

There is a meow and a growl and he squirms, tail slashing. Yet she so wants to share him with everyone outside. Something else to speak of, something to change the subject and mood. She knows how to hold him. She crosses the kitchen, then pushes on the back door and steps into the sun with her furry surprise.

At last she is smiling.

She holds the cat up.

"This is Henry?" she asks, not ready for the looks of shock, astonishment, wonder, and horror as everyone's eyes stare back.

"Henry!" Stanley shouts.

His shout stirs the cat. Henry hisses. Primordial grimace. Incisor teeth. Then the infamous yowl and he wriggles and squirms and with one paw pushing off her breast he ejects himself out away from her five feet in the air landing on the lawn scrabbling away fast as light into the deepest weeds he can find in the uncut base of the fence. Everyone jumps up from their chairs, the chairs scattering, drinks spilling on the lawn as they make the futile run to catch him.

With Henry's leap from Pat's arms the group on the lawn shifts left following the streak of tabby. Stanley, Michael, MJ, and Danielle make their turns almost simultaneously as though choreographed by the cat himself. Michael, closest, makes a dive at Henry trying to intercept him. No chance. Henry is past him before his feet leave the ground. Still, certain *laws of physics and gravity* continue to drive Michael's dive right into the lawn where certain *principles of textile colouration* assume control as Michael's blue shirt and jeans connect with the grass and the grass does its level best to stain the wrists elbows belly knees and even the toes of his dapper *Dockers*. Then the inevitable *Murphy's Law* as Michael's Ray-Bans jog off his head and Stanley running behind him steps on the shades obliterating them with an expensive crackle while Stanley, unfortunately shoeless, receives several shrapnel-like pieces in his right foot.

The *laws of pain and reaction* rear themselves as Stanley lifts and grabs his foot while hopping to his right backing into Danielle who has already leapt over two downed lawn chairs to reach this moment of impact where *Newton's Third Law of Motion* occurs as Dani connects and goes down with Stanley so back to the *principles of colouration*, this time adding blood red to the green for more amusing stains on the lovers' clothing resulting in the application of *Manson's Law* by MJ who, now in much better shape and more nimble due to his summer job, leaps over Michael's prostrate body (*Newton's Second Law*) does a near *double Lutz* but doesn't quite make it, drops (*gravitation*), rolls (*Newton's Third Law*), skids (*principles of colouration*), hits the fence (*Newton's First Law*) thus achieving a *classic triple Newtonian with a Manson twist* and full marks for *colouration*!

Henry would hold up a 9.2 were it not that he lacked opposable thumbs.

Pat is left standing on the deck unsure what to do. It takes a moment for each to recover but when they do, finding their injuries minor, the laughter begins. When they each look at the shambles one small cat has created, there is nothing else to do but laugh. They help one another up, have a second look for injuries, comment on the dye jobs each has so creatively fashioned then try to organize the search for Henry.

"I can't see hide nor hair of him!"

"He's a tabby. He's got built-in camouflage."

"Jeez, there's a lotta weeds."

"I'm not a gardener."

"No, it's just ... it makes him harder to find."

"You've got to look past the weeds."

"What?"

"Hunters look past things to find their prey."

"Is this a Kenyan thing?"

"In the corner down here, there's a hole in the fence!"

"Oh shit, not that!"

"What?"

"He's never been out before. He's a housecat."

"Oh, I'm so, so sorry I brought him outside."

"That's alright. We should have warned you."

"I'll go around to the other side and see if he's there."

"He couldn't have made it that far that fast."

"Pardon me but did you note the speed he actually achieved?"

"Henry!"

"Here, Henry!"

"Come on, boy!"

"Try clapping your hands."

"What good would that do?"

"Well he's a cat. Maybe he'll get curious."

"OMIGOD!"

"What? Are you alright?"

"The chicken!"

"Where are you going?"

"The chicken's burning! Smell it!"

"Nothing back here!"

"Try the entire perimeter, look for more holes."

"Wouldn't he just freeze with fear?"

"Obviously, he didn't."

"At that speed he could be down the block by now!"

"Oh, I do hope not. The poor thing ... I'm so sorry ..."

"Somebody get some water!"

"What?"
"The chicken's on fire!"
"I'll get it!"
"In the kitchen!"
"Not enough time. Garden hose!"
"Watch out it's already turned on ..."
"Noooo! Aggh!"
"I'm sorry!"
"It was the chicken, not me!"
"Yes, well, I got the chicken!"
"It's called a ricochet, isn't it?"
"I'll get you a towel."
"HE'S NOT ANYWHERE OUT HERE!"
"Come back inside. I'm sure he's here!"
"Holy shit!"
"What's wrong?"
"Grab me. I'm coming over!"
"Wait!"
"No time!"
"Help me here! Somebody!"
"I got his elbow."
"Pull for crissake!"
"What is that smell? Gad!"
"Skunk!"
"PULL!"
"Watch out!"
"He's tumbling!"
"I can't!"
"Uggh!"
"Heavens, are you alright?"
"Just ... give ... me, a minute."
"The chicken is ruined!"
"Let's not worry over that. Where is Henry?"
"If I catch him he's gonna replace the chicken!"

"Oh, dear, you don't mean that."

"The little shit."

"You got skunks back there!"

"Damn that was close."

"What a stench!"

"Thank God it's not on me!"

"What about dinner!"

"We'll get takeout."

"I'm soaked. I've gotta change."

"I think we all do."

"I just realized I've ripped my sundress."

"You were Henry's take-off platform. He did it!"

"I'm so very sorry."

"I've got his food bowl. He'll come back when he's hungry."

"What if he can't find his way back?"

"Let's get changed and we'll look again."

"Set the bowl down anyway."

"Whose drink is this? I'll put the bowl here beside it."

"Fresh glasses and wine coming up, once we're changed."

"And bandaged."

"I'm so worried over Henry. I think I'll sit out on the deck. Keep an eye out."

"He'll come back."

"Oh, I hope so."

"The little shit ..."

"It was my fault. Maybe I'll see him once everyone is inside. He must be shaking with fear out there."

Once everyone leaves Pat sinks into a chair. She feels terrible, responsible, embarrassed. She closes her eyes a few moments, staying her fretting, feeling the sun. Then beneath the chair she hears a soft mewing and feels Henry's fur as he curls around her leg.

"HENRY! Oh, Henry, there you are ..."

Henry proceeds to the food bowl.

50

THEY SIT IN Muskoka chairs on the deck of the cottage watching the dance of light on the water below. As the sun sets there is shadow play amid the trees. The air turns a perfect amber. The wind drops with the sun. Once the sun sets they will go inside as mosquitoes rise from their bushy lairs. Out on the lake a motorboat growls. Bats flit through the air. The two men don't notice them caught as they are within their own thoughts.

Both wear typical cottage clothing: T-shirts, shorts, sandals. They sip their drinks, rye and ice for Mel, vodka martini for Will. They don't talk. They have just completed negotiations. The result has been a horrific defeat for the younger man. He had thought to overwhelm Mel with his intellect only to find the older man possessed a set of tactics and an uncanny ability to derail each Will's best laid plans.

Will had arrived after Mel had called him, summoned him actually, once he'd heard his kids knew Will was providing assistance. Mel had made it clear on the phone that Will had to leave before Danielle got to him. Will felt he could handle Dani. Then Mel had levelled Will.

"They know you've been helping me. Give Dani a chance and she'll find the bottom of this quicker than you could believe. There are different kinds of intelligence, Mr. Baker: you have one type, Dani has another."

"Come on ..."

"Think about her for a minute."

"What about her?"

"What does Stan see in her? Why do you think a six-foot blonde has decided to live with a geek like Stan? You think *he* chose her?"

That this *old jock* would admonish him appalled him. The man was a nothing, his daughter a nothing. He answered the old fool's question with the obvious, not thinking it was rhetorical.

"Stanley is a genius."

"Of course you'd think that. You're a bit limited, Willy."

"Don't call me that!"

"Very touchy, just like Stan. What's with you guys? Look, there are different kinds of genius, like I said. Before he met Dani how did he dress? How did he behave? Think about this for a minute. She has moulded him."

"How could you know that? You never met him until she brought him home."

"I share a similar talent, Willy."

"I said don't …"

"There are *types* of people as well. There are the played and the players. Dani and I are the latter."

"That's ridiculous!"

"Really? Just a few seconds of overhearing a phone call and she was on to you."

He'd forgotten that moment, how quickly Danielle had picked up on it, how desperately sad were his excuses.

"Uh, yeah …"

"You have no idea what she's really like, do you?"

Will cannot believe he is hearing this. The old man is right.

"Even MJ knows you came to my house. He must have seen you coming or going at some time," Mel said.

"So, I helped you. That's not a crime."

"How do you know?"

Bombshell.

"What?"

"How do you know I'm not doing something criminal?"

"I work with you. I'd know."

"I thought you'd say that. Well, my friend, like it or not, you're implicated!"

"In what?"

"Don't you realize I know what you're doing under cover of helping me? Don't you think I know enough yet to recognize someone tinkering with the Dark Web? You think I haven't been on Exploit.in and Dark.0de?"

"What? Are you insane? You have no idea ..."

"I've been your guinea pig, haven't I?"

"Look, just what are you up to, Mel?"

"Another *what.* You've just proved to me Dani could unpeel you in minutes then find out more about me. I can't have that. So no more questions. You are to leave that house. Pack your stuff. Get on a bus to Toronto and then to Mactier and phone me when you get here. I'll pick you up."

"I am not about to alter my life at your request."

"It's not a request, Willy boy. If you know what's good for you, you'd best get up here before they know you're gone. And don't try to disappear into the States. If I'm arrested you will be listed as my accomplice."

"In what! I don't even know what you're talking about!"

"That's right. You don't. As I said, there are different types of intelligence. So get your ass up here and when you do I'll tell you what's going on and what the stakes are."

"How do I explain why I'm leaving?"

"Shit, Willy, write a note. They all know you're broke. Say you're going home to find a job. And *don't* rent a car. Take buses. Believe me, you don't want to leave a trail."

"I have responsibilities. I can't just ..."

"Leave them. You can, and you will, or you'll be facing ten years in prison."

"I'll leave tomorrow."

"Tonight. Be quiet about it. You can sleep at the bus depot."

51

WILL BAKER SPENT a two days in Toronto trying to establish his autonomy over Mel. He visited married friends who lived in the Distillery District with its old world charm of eccentric boutiques and restaurants.

He arrived unannounced, judging that without a warning his friends would have little choice but to take him in, saving what was left of his money for bus fare, and perhaps they'd join him in enjoying the kinds of restaurants which maintained his somewhat rotund figure.

As it turned out Josie and Robert Parker treated him to dinner that evening outdoors at Edulis, a top notch bistro patio inundated with greenery. The perfect place on a warm summer night. The next day found him visiting the Toronto Islands for a swim in Lake Ontario and an inexpensive hot dog lunch. That night the Parkers were working late so he took in Chris Nolan's *The Dark Knight Rising.* He stayed that second night at the Parkers' drinking a bottle of their *Chateau Malescot St. Exupery Margaux 2009* before going to bed pleasantly inebriated and delighted with his two days of liberation.

He should not have been.

He took the bus to Mactier from the terminal on Bay St., the building looking old and faded, the inside more like a barn filled with rows of plastic chairs than a transportation hub. There was every kind of low life. There was a tang of heavy duty cleaner in the air. He wanted out of it quickly. He went to the bus docks early just for the air and ran into the smokers. The bus doors opened not long after, saving him. No smoking allowed on the bus. The trip itself was pleasant enough. He spent most of it sleeping off his hangover.

He found Mel waiting for him outside the tiny post office in the village. They put his bags in the back of Mel's F150 and drove the five kilometres around the lake down Stewart Lake Road to the cottage. Mel said nothing at all as he drove, even when Will enquired about Dani.

Somehow the man has changed, Will thought. His face is harder. He looks more muscular. His strange eyes glitter weirdly in the sunlight. It seems he no longer considers Will an ally, which becomes clear when they arrive at the cottage, stow Will's bags and sit down across from each other at the dining table. Mel's laptop lies in front of him, the kind of overt symbol even Will Baker comprehends.

"Did you see Dani?" are his first words. They sound as hard as Mel looks. Will realizes he is dealing with a dangerous man. He decides to be careful, feel him out, find a weakness.

"I left when you told me."

"Where the fuck have you been then?"

"Toronto, with friends. I thought I'd enjoy some civilization before coming here."

"You're treating this pretty lightly, aren't you?"

"What?"

"Look, I'll give it to you straight. Me. Us. The fact that I paid you for services rendered. The idiocy of letting my daughter know ..."

"She guessed! I doubt she knows the truth."

"You guys are all alike; think you're the dominant beasts of the world. I got news for you, Son. You're a servant. A servant to your computers and apps and algorithms and all that shit. You spend more time in tiny rooms in front of screens than you do in real life with real people."

That this man would speak in this way: so patronizing, so superior. Will decides then and there to terminate the geezer's ego. He stands to speak. To his surprise the man rises with him and increases his volume.

"Don't interrupt! You don't get it, do you? You not only serve the machines, you serve the people who make them. They use you as their worker bee to help them take over society."

This is so unexpected Will has trouble sorting his thoughts to respond. He waits too long, losing the impetus.

"What are you talking about? You're a fucking neo-Luddite, Mel! You have no idea what I or others do for the *benefit* of society."

"We'll come to that. I would say you can't remember a single second in your life where you did something out of generosity. And as to your initial point, no, I am *not* a neo-Luddite, I am the actual *real thing*!"

Will finds it improbable this man even *knows* of Luddites.

"You think I've been up here vegetating all this time without you?"

"Really, I hadn't noticed."

"That's because you weren't looking."

"And what would I see if I had been?" Will said.

"A neo-Luddite is typically some guy who writes and talks a lot without doing much. A true Luddite takes on the System. I found out my own *family* comes from Yorkshire. I found out they were *real* Luddites!"

He grapples with something beneath his shirt pulling out an object on a chain. He holds it up, directly in front of Will Baker's eyes, so close if he chose he could punch it into one of them. Will has no doubt he would. His fear of the man is complete. He focuses on the object in front of his face. The hand holding it is rock steady. It is a hammer. A tiny pewter hammer. His gaze shifts to Mel.

"This little thing's two hundred years old, kid. Passed down over generations. I come from people who've been fighting this fight from the start! Now I've joined them. I've *become* a Luddite: destroyed property, threatened people with poison, and now I'm about to send these technological parasites something a little more explosive!"

"Jesus, Mel, what the hell are you up to?"

"If you looked up once in a while from your screens you might see!"

Mel opens his laptop and spins it so Will can glimpse the screen. Newspaper cuttings. Click. Chatroom talk. Click. Fiery photograph. Click. Ricin. Click. Dynamite in a box. Click. LUD. Click. Black screen. Mel closes the lid.

"Where does this come from?"

"From *me*, Will. I've discovered someone a little more hands on. Someone who didn't just talk the talk, he walked the walk too. He set out in his manifesto ..."

"Oh shit, you're not talking the Unabomber? Theodore Kaczynski?"

"Of course I am! Since he wrote it in the 90s I can see even now it's coming true. Most people think technology is merely things. They think they make use of them. They don't realize it's an entire system. It's a *single* thing. Like a creature! It grabs what it needs for its own expansion. It grows every day! It feeds off our labour and steals our minds. You smartass guys think it serves you but really you simply serve it and so will the rest of us if we don't stop it!"

Mel opens his laptop again.

Clearly he has prepared this presentation, thinks Will, and somehow he's got me tied in with it. This guy, he thought, could get me arrested. This man has the capability to trap me and use me. He's just lunatic enough that he might even kill me! What the fuck have I done?

52

"JUST LOOK AT this here, the highlighted part."

Will Baker already knows what he'll see: Kaczynski's words:

The system does not and cannot exist to satisfy human needs. Instead, it is human behavior that has to be modified to fit the needs of the system. This has nothing to do with the political or social ideology that may pretend to guide the technological system. It is the fault of technology, because the system is guided not by ideology but by technical necessity.

"Mel, the guy was insane!"

"Only because society says. I've been pushed as far as I can stand and now I'm pushing back!"

"Do you realize what you're saying? You haven't got a chance!"

"Well you'd better hope I do 'cause you're along for the ride!"

"You're crazy! This whole thing's crazy! You're holed up here like *he* was, in that cabin somewhere in Montana, and you're feeding off your own paranoia! I'm not coming with you!"

"Son, you already did. Don't think I'm stupid. I know I'm gonna get caught but when I am you've gotta realize you're already in this. The word I found is *complicit.* That's you. Complicit in your actions with me. You should never have let Dani overhear you. Now it's out and you can't put it back. Who taught me all this? You did. Who's working on the Dark Web? You are. Who helped me get those first addresses?"

"I thought you were looking for work! I'll deny it."

"Go ahead. How many times were you at my house? How often did you come up here? You think no one ever saw you? How often is my number on your phone and your number on mine? You think the cops won't see you're complicit?"

"I'm leaving, Mel. You're out of your mind!"

Will rises again from the table this time in a panic. All he wants is to get out, get away, get this monster out of his life. Mel smiles. His hand is instantly on Will's shirt collar. In the two seconds it takes to halt his escape a host of thoughts fly through Will Baker's brain. There had once been such promise to his life. Sent to special schools for the gifted, he had never been bullied by fellow students so this great hulk holding him now devastates him. He feels like a child. He has no skills to deal with persecutors. Protected by his parents' money and class pride he'd basked in his accomplishments which naturally turned to feelings of superiority.

He took a raft of scholarships and bursaries despite his parents' money. They felt he was destined to be illustrious. A doctorate meant less to him than fortune and fame and the app which dangled illusively in the thin atmosphere of Waterloo's student entrepreneurs. For the first time he found himself on a level playing field; indeed, for the first time in his life he was challenged. As he witnessed the success of so many others he felt himself drying up. When he met Stanley Best and those like him he began to know he would not be the stuff of his parents' his teachers' his colleagues' even his own, dreams. So, running out of money and time he had grasped at this one last endeavour: Pineapple.

Now he finds himself grappled by a monster of his own making with no chance of a way out. He has never felt this helpless this stupid this utterly lost in his life.

"Get ready to spend your life lookin' over your shoulder, Willy. When they catch me I'll name you. I mailed poison to people. How long do you think your sentence will be? Like I said on the phone, there's two types: the players and the played. I'm a player. Always have been. Now you know what you are. Sit down. Stop crying for crissake!"

"You can't do this to me!"

"Yeah, I can, Willy. But let's look at this another way. I'm gonna pay you more money. I sold my speedboat. I got lots of dough. Nobody knows where you are. Just stay out of Mactier and away from the neighbours. You should call your parents. Tell 'em you had a falling out with Stan. They'd believe that. I need to up my game, Willy, and you and me are gonna find ways to do it! I know I won't win but I'm goin' down trying."

"You'll take me down with you! I'll get sent to prison!"

He is sobbing, frustrated furious frightened. Mel smiles.

"That's the other part of the deal, Willy. You stick with me maybe 'til Christmas and I'll let you off the hook. Say I did it myself. Say I found a guy on the internet who helped me out from a distance, remote like. I'll lose my phone in the lake out there. I'll take it all on and you'll have money and be free to go on your way. No, that's not quite right. You'll never be free of the System. Ever. But now you know that. So pick your poison, Son."

"I … I'll stay with you," the devastated Will Baker replies, his nose dripping.

"I thought so," Mel says.

It happens quickly after that. Mel and Will have a busy month. Each targeted corporation is sent a small package with a bright red M-80 and one Silver Salute to Herbert Trimble, packaged carefully, nestled in shredded paper inside a four by four by four cardboard mailer. With each red tube is a newsprint page typed on Mel's old typewriter. The note is simple, just one word: *LUD*

Mel knew mailing gunpowder across the border would be impossible, so he keeps his list local. Ontario has both American and Canadian tech companies so he achieves what he wants and this time no internet nut can claim responsibility. The internet, of course, will light up once the news leaks. If it doesn't he is prepared to run the additional risk of leaking the news himself through anonymous Facebook and Twitter accounts.

Then it is a matter of packaging his messages and spending August and September driving to various destinations throughout southern Ontario, his packages going through Canada Post. Will Baker goes with him. The young man has little choice. He is bound in the web Mel has woven.

This night marks the last of the packages mailed. Together they sit on the cottage deck at sunset. Together they drink in the autumn air. Together, they are odd partners.

There are two kinds of people …

53

THE POLICE INTERVIEW nearly kills Gary Wilson. This big Asian detective shows up at the door asking to speak with him. Mona knows nothing so lets him in. Gary is in his basement library sorting his books. He has a job now at the Waterloo Library, mostly stacking as he learns the Dewey Decimal System. He has taken advantage of Erban's retraining and his love of books has brought him to a part time yet satisfying job. Mona's work and his own severance should serve them until his pension cuts in. He loves his new work. He is home on a day off when Mona shows up with the big detective. He has an English accent.

She introduces them and, rather than leave, takes Gary's reading chair. The detective and Gary take office chairs at his computer desk. Gary Wilson is frightened. He hopes he can make it through this without giving up the secret. Mona can read him like a book. He can see her looking knowingly at him. Can this detective as well?

"Sorry to trouble you, Mr. Wilson, there was a fire at Erban Industries as you know …"

"What?" Gary says, trying to look surprised.

"You didn't know?"

"I've been re-training. Pretty busy, y'know. Got a new job at the library."

Gary knows he's failed already. The limp excuse, the pretence of ignorance ... the guy can see right through him. Gary glances Mona's way. She rolls her eyes.

"That's good to hear, sir. Now, if we may ... you were employed at Erban. A foreman, if I have the paperwork right."

"Yeah, I was."

"How do you feel about what they've done?"

"Done?"

"The terminations. Moving out of town. Any of that get you angry?"

He has to get this right. He can see what the man is doing. Prompting him into something leading to something more. He has to alter his mood, has to use some truth with some well-placed lies.

"Well, of course I was. A few of us got a bit drunk over it. Then me and Mona took a good look. In the end it was a fair package. Gave us, me, a chance to get trained, maybe not anymore in factories but I took employment insurance and then as they posted jobs me and Mona would look 'em over. I always liked to read and this library thing came up. Mona said I should try. So I did and I got it. Part time only but maybe later it could develop."

With the truth he feels better. He's turned matters his way. Yes, he's hedged a few things but still seems to have satisfied the detective, or thinks he has, until the next question.

"I'm happy to hear that, sir. Why is it, Mr. Wilson, that you didn't answer my earlier calls for an interview? I've made three calls to this number ... this is your number, is it not?"

Time to lie.

"Yeah, that's it. I guess for a while I didn't want to talk with anybody ..."

"Not even fellow workers?"

"One or two maybe, but mostly no. You feel ashamed, detective, when you lose a job ... at least I did. So I kind of kept my head down. I figured your calls had to be about something I never knew nothing about, so I kind of ignored them. Shoulda known better. I'm sorry. 'Til now I had no idea about arson at the plant!"

"I see. Why would you call it arson, sir? I didn't mention that earlier."

"It was in the newspaper!"

"Yet you were surprised when I mentioned it.

"Yeah, I don't know. Really by that time the last thing on my mind was Erban ..."

"I see. Where were you on the night of March first?"

The directness of the question, the slight darkening of the voice and the lies he's already told catch Gary off guard. He struggles a moment. Drops the computer mouse from the desk just for a chance to bend down and give himself time. Too many memories splash through his mind. He pops back up. Sets the mouse on the pad. It's a pad from Erban. Shit. He still isn't ready.

"I, uh. Jeez, that's a while ago."

"He was out with a friend, Detective Khadri," Mona says evenly from the reading chair. "He was drinking. I don't know where. He came home around nine thirty. I remember 'cause I was upset he'd drink and drive. Is that what this is about? Did he hit someone, cause an accident?"

She has *saved* him! She's always been faster than him on the uptake. He breathes as the cop turns toward her. He's got to come up with something half true.

"No, not at all, Mrs. Wilson. As I said there was a fire at the Erban plant. It seeped inside and destroyed some equipment. While your husband was wrong to drive home inebriated, I'm not here about that."

He turns back to face Gary, who has found some composure.

"What was the name of the bar, Mr. Wilson?"

"It was the ONE, you know, on Highland."

"And who was with you?"

Jesus, now he has to name names. He can't do that. This guy will go after them. He thinks about who he knows is away. Still stalling.

"Oh, a coupla guys. Not sure. Quite a while ago. Uh, Peter Reitzel I think. Maybe Mel Buckworth. I can't be sure. I know I was wrong to do it. We were just comparing which way to go after we got dumped. We were pretty shell-shocked."

"I see. Did you leave before them, this Reitzel and Buckworth?"

"Uh, let's see. I think we all left together. Yeah. We did. It was cold that night."

"No one stayed behind? Did you leave them once you went to your car? Any idea where they might have gone?"

"Jeez, I don't wanna get nobody in trouble. I don't know. We all got to our cars. I figured everybody went home."

"And you got home here at ..."

"Nine-thirty," Mona says, cutting in sharply. "I was mad at him. I remember that!"

"I see. So Mr. Wilson, I have to ask ... is there anyone you can think of who might have held a grudge against Erban? It wasn't good the way things ended."

"No, it wasn't. I'm sure lots of guys would've taken a crack given the chance but really, arson? That's pretty big."

"Wasn't someone fired for trying to sabotage machines? Do you know who that was?"

"Not on my shift. I don't know that many guys on the other shifts. Sorry."

"We don't think the fire was meant to be so big. How do you think it started, sir?"

"Well, if anything the place was all cement, except the loading dock ..."

"Why would my husband know anything about how someone would set fire to a building?" Mona says sharply.

The cop turns to her again. She is a force.

"I have to ask this, Mrs. Wilson. It could have been common knowledge."

"Are you accusing him of anything?"

"Of course not. I just need to establish his actions that night."

"Well, he's not proud of them, I can assure you. I can also say he was here with me as of nine-thirty. What time did this fire start?

"Late, Mrs. Wilson. The early hours of March second."

"He was snoring by then. Kept me awake. He's not drinking anymore. So, have you anything more for my husband? Questions?"

"Not at this time. I'd appreciate it if he could stay in touch, however. In case something breaks with this situation."

"I'm sure he will, Detective."

Mona stands. The men stand with her.

"May I show you out, Detective?"

"Of course. Thanks for your time Mr. Wilson."

Gary says nothing.

Mona shows the man out with minimal conversation. She is back in three minutes.

"Gary, what the hell have you done?"

"I was with Mel."

"Naturally. I want to know all of it. Everything, do you hear."

"Yeah. Thanks for bailing me out."

"Now it's put me in trouble too. I can't believe you'd be fool enough to do something like that. What the hell happened?"

54

AMRIT KHADRI IS informed of a meeting at WRPS Headquarters. He is told to bring his file on Erban Industries. When he arrives, around two p.m., he turns off Maple Grove Road in the Gateway area of Cambridge, an island of big box stores and restaurants along the stretch of Highway 8 that separates Kitchener and Cambridge.

The headquarters building is impressive, with gleaming white walls enclosing expanses of blue tinted glass. A contemporary look to the age old business of policing from officer training to emergency response teams; the varied departments take up their spaces. They hum with activity during the day.

Once past the subtle outer defences—decorative stones, gleaming white poles, cameras covering every possible access—Khadri enters the foyer and approaches the desk to check in. The desk shrewdly takes the expanse of the foyer and narrows it into a hallway, though it doesn't look so because of the open space above the counter and multiple windows down its length.

Khadri finds his way to the proper conference room. There are people from several departments he knows from years of work but what is exceptional to Khadri is that Superintendent Bowen is present. He is a quiet man, slightly balding with a calm face and soft voice yet clearly in charge of this meeting, calling it quickly to order. Khadri takes a seat near the end of the table.

It begins with reports from *Investigative* regarding the sheer number of received mailings and details of the various corporations known to have been victimized. It moves on with a description of the contents: the M-80s, the old typeface, the moniker LUD and finally the point was made that none of them actually ignited, nor were they designed to do so. This is disconcerting, not knowing what to make of this crime which is actually no more than a threat. Why would someone go to all that trouble with these packages and not rig them to explode? Various theories are passed around the room including the tie-in with the earlier mass mailing of the rat poison letters, again from this LUD.

What alerts Khadri to his purpose at the meeting is finding the Superintendent looking down the long table directly at him and making the substantial point that one Herbert Trimble of Kitchener was the only *individual* to receive a second mailing.

"So, Detective Khadri, you've been on this file for some time now, am I clear?"

"I have, sir."

"You've interviewed Mr. Trimble?"

"Indeed, sir, since our deduction the fire at Erban in March was arson. I've spoken with Mr. Trimble twice: once at the site of the fire and once in the hospital where he was awaiting results of the white powder mailed to him. I've been in the process of reaching each former employee of Erban as they come available, though some have left the Region. I have yet to be able to speak with them all."

"Do you have anything then to work with?" the Superintendent asks.

"Not really, sir. No suspects. Until now it was just a guess regarding Trimble. This event seems to have certified that."

"I would say so. Staff Sergeant Thomas, would you re-arrange some schedules. Have two investigators join Detective Khadri in this. I think it's time to track *all* the Erban employees and interview each. Trimble is no coincidence. This LUD, one person or a group, seems to be escalating their actions. I don't want to wait for the next move. I think it will place more people in danger. Khadri, you'll have your partners by the end of the day. Prepare your file for each of them.

"I will, sir."

"And think a little more on potential suspects."

"Yes, sir."

"And Khadri ..."

"Sir?"

"You seem to have taken your time on this. I fear you haven't prioritized correctly. We'll deal with that when this is over but as of now this will be your only case. You will take the lead on it. Am I clear?"

"Very clear, sir."

"One more thing before we end this ... I want no news coverage. In case this LUD group gets its jollies from reading about its exploits. Backstrom, you and your people need to approach the media and request they hold off. Refer anyone from the press who doesn't co-operate directly to me. Anyone have anything else?"

They did. Further discussion from Intelligence requesting one of theirs on the team with Khadri, someone highly skilled, to assist. The unspoken comment in Khadri's mind telling him *you're not quite good enough, Constable Khadri. We'll take it from here.*

That is not going to happen.

Knowing this could be an all-nighter he calls Patricia to cancel their lunch. She has become a fascinating part of his life. More tennis. A few times to lunch. Once she dropped by his division in Waterloo. They have found they have interests in common. Tea is one. After their third tennis partnership he began to bring packets of loose tea to her: Yorkshire, rooibos, oolong, chai, and cardamom, even green and white teas. At times they would share tea together upstairs in the Waterloo Tennis Club.

They both enjoyed sports though his were cricket, which led to a good many gales of laughter as she tried to learn the rules, and football, the English type. He was a fanatic he told her, spicing their conversation with odd acronyms like UEFA, FIFA and FA. When she recognized them he was surprised. She told him about her own sports background. She told him about Dani's soccer. He said he'd love to watch Dani play but both knew it was too early for that and summer soccer was nearly finished.

She sounds disappointed on the phone. He feels disappointed as well.

These thoughts stay with him through his next hours. He spares no detail in his report. He knows he hasn't taken the Trimble thing seriously; his dislike of the man keeping him away. Now, with the size of the crime rolling over him he knows he must be at his best, ensure he provides the others with all he knows. He discovers the true extent of the ricin incident from Art Crozier, the veteran from Intel. Crozier had met with the FBI though neither had found any other clues. Still, the import of the LUD events begins to grow in everyone's mind.

Khadri also knows he's been given the lead so Staff Sergeant Thomas can keep an eye on his work. He will report directly to Thomas. It is not the best position in which to find oneself, he thinks. He is happy at least one part of his life seems to be working. Is it time to test it, ask her on a date? A dinner date. He picks an expensive restaurant in Waterloo. He calls once again. She says yes. They set the date.

He is just a bit giddy.

55

SUMMER FLOWS INTO a gentle autumn for Pat. She is becoming accustomed to being single because she is no longer alone. Despite Mel's refusal to answer her calls, texts or emails, she finds increased comfort with her children, and in another way with Amrit Khadri.

While Dani continues to live with Stanley, she finds more time to visit and often asks Pat to come over. It appears everyone, including Henry, has forgiven her the sin of outing the cat. She finds a delight in Stanley and Michael who, once they are accustomed to her, seem to relax into their natural characters: Stanley kind and slightly haughty, Michael gentle and musical and both, of course, profusely intellectual.

Dani, or *Danielle* in her new house, seems to have found a comfortable place with the two, capable of bantering back and forth with them. She is a young woman now in every sense: mature and more beautiful. She has grown slimmer from summer work and, since her confrontation with Mel, has become ever closer to Stanley. She has lined up her classes for her third year at UW. History is now her sole major, though she has added some undergrad computing courses on Stanley's advice.

MJ has all but moved out of the basement, his time no longer spent on his game; instead he has found new purpose and, guided by Stanley, is gearing himself for his imminent entry to Conestoga College. He too has lost weight over the summer and is nearly back to his former athletic physique. He has good genes. He looks vaguely like Mel, with a little of Pat's father thrown in. Sometimes it disturbs her when she catches a glance of him working, shirtless, outside on chores. He has lost his edginess too. He too has matured into a purposeful character much like his sister.

Life continues, Pat thinks, as she dresses for her third date with Amrit. They are going to the movies, something called *The Life of Pi*. There has been further tennis, each time agreeable and interesting. He'd told her a little of his early years: he, fleeing the void with his parents in England, they still living as though it was India. Choosing Canada for his future and getting student and work permits, then Humber College in Toronto. He had worked concurrently in a Bramalea carpet shop to support himself, the hard lessons from his days of poverty staying with him. Then the proud day he had attained Canadian Citizenship and his choice to join the police to find some stability, do some good, help some people and uphold the laws of the land he had married. He was hired by Waterloo Regional Police and then attended Police College near Aylmer, Ontario, becoming a constable.

He didn't speak of his work much, saying his current post as a

Detective Constable was often like her puzzles; just putting errant pieces together. Yes, she had told him of her puzzle infatuation. Perhaps her first venture at trusting a man since Mel. He calls her Patricia. His voice making the sound of her name delightful.

Their first date had turned into a comedy of errors. Rather than come to the house, Amrit had selected Jane L's. He'd heard it was a fine, highly reputable restaurant. It had turned out to be exceptional but not before each of them had turned up at different locations. Amrit did not often eat in high end restaurants so when he'd parked his Toyota in the lot beside Waterloo Town Square and walked to the place he'd *thought* he should be, he had found Jane L's was missing.

Meanwhile Pat, who lived near Belmont Village, had walked from her house to the restaurant; the *new* location in Belmont Village. She'd entered expecting him. He wasn't there though the reservation was. She'd sat for twenty minutes imbued with surprise then suspicion then self-doubt then a subtle trip to the restroom and a discreet exit. She'd turned west for home when she saw his car screech into the service lane beside her.

"Thank God," he'd said.

"Oh!"

"I was on King Street!"

"Why?" she'd asked.

"That's where the restaurant should be!" he'd said.

It took her a moment. Then relief gushed. He *could* be trusted.

"You didn't know they'd moved?"

"When?"

"In January."

"Oh!"

"You're sure you actually *are* a detective?"

"I'm a detective, Patricia. Not a gourmet!"

Dinner had turned out to be lovely.

Glancing at her watch she sees she is early. She thinks of being a kid when she would make a boy wait. Adolescent self-assurance. Now she is not so certain of herself. She peers into the mirror. The makeup has done its wonders. She recalls the days when she'd never needed it.

That recollection brings back Mel, the pair of them shining icons in high school. Waterloo Collegiate. Vikings. Red, white and blue. Bright cerulean skies red yellow leaves white hash marks on the playing fields Mel Buckworth a football running back she was field hockey and tennis.

Monica Martin now Mona Wilson appears in her thoughts. Double dating included Patricia and Mellor, Monica and Gary. Why did we shorten our names? Except Gary.

Her musing takes her back to the Harmony Lunch, a hangout in her early days. Pork burgers slathered with fried onions, the restaurant's aroma stayed on your clothes for hours. Still, it was a good place. No liquor. A good place for kids. And another type of human back then. She would watch the hippies: their bell-bottom pants, frayed jeans, maxi dresses; their tie dyed peasant blouses and ponchos; their chokers, headbands, scarves, and odd jewellery made of wood, stones, feathers, and beads. Many were from the universities just up King Street. Waterloo kids didn't mingle with hippies. She had never wished that kind of life for herself. When she wasn't dressed in a fashionable mini or shape hugging Tiger Brand athletic wear, her clothes were casual chic, consisting of sweat shirts, T-shirts, jeans and sneakers. Mona was like her sister then. She recalls Mona's penchant for craving to be hip, how she'd tried a shag cut once. The crew cut boys from school didn't like it. Gary and she had nearly broke up.

The delirium of adolescence. She smiles to herself, picks up her phone, taps contacts and Mona. She's tried a couple of times since Mel left. She's left messages but there have been no return calls. She wonders whether Mona and Gary know about the separation, then realizes they must. Things like that are never kept secret long. She wonders if they have chosen sides. The phone rings three times. She is about to hang up, no message this time, when she hears Mona's voice.

"Pat?"

"Hi, Mona."

She can feel the tension immediately; it comes through the cell like static voltage. It is in the breath Mona thinks Pat can't hear. It is in the years of sharing emotions like sisters.

"I'm fine," Mona says.

"That's good," Pat says. "I was thinking of you."

"Are you alright?" Mona says. She is inside her own conversation.

"Yes, I'm fine, Mona."

"Where is he?" Mona asks. Robotic.

"At the cottage. How's Gary?"

"Why would you ask?"

"What do you mean?"

"He's fine. He's not here."

"Oh?"

"So you won't be able to talk to him."

"That wasn't why I called."

"He's got a job at the library."

"That's wonderful."

"But he works odd hours. You'll have to call back."

"Mona, what's wrong?"

"Nothing's wrong. I'm fine."

"You sound like you're frightened."

"No. I'm not. Everything's fine!"

"Do you mind me asking ..."

"Please, don't ask me anything. You'll have to talk to Gary."

"I don't understand. I was going to ask about your kids."

"They're fine. They don't know anything at all. Okay? Please don't involve them."

"What? I'm lost here, Mona."

"I'm sorry. Sorry for you. I just want to put it behind us."

"What on earth are you talking about?"

Mona pauses. Pat is about to speak when she cuts in again.

"Oh God. I'm such a fool! You *don't* know. He didn't tell you?"

"Didn't tell me what? Gary?"

"Mel."

"What should he have told me?"

"Nothing. I jumped to conclusions. I'm sorry, Pat. I should go."

"Wait! Mona! What's this about? Did Mel threaten you?"

"So you don't know anything?"

"About what?"

"Just a minute."

Pat waits, half expecting a hang up. She hears liquid pour into a glass. She waits. She wishes she had the wine Mona is pouring. Why would she do that? Why is she so distressed? She was always high-strung. Pat remembers first meeting Monica at MacGregor School. Grade seven. Monica had moved from Elmira. A little girl with braids, freckles and red hair, frightened of the new school with so many kids. Patricia knowing it, and feeling a kind of purpose in helping the kid who looked so lost and anxious.

They have been friends ever since.

"Pat?"

"I'm here, Mona."

Mona speaks more slowly, less edge to her voice. She seems to have resolved something.

"It's alright," Pat says. "I thought you and Gary ... well, you know. People do."

"Pardon?"

"Take sides ..."

"No. It's not that. I thought you knew."

"Mona, for the life of me I have no idea what you're talking about!"

"Alright. You have a right to know. He's a bastard, really, Pat. I'm sorry but he is."

"Who?"

"Mel."

"He's very mixed up, Mona. I can tell you that much. He hasn't been the same since the plant closed. It keeps getting worse. Does Gary know? Has he talked to him?"

"Gary can't see or talk to Mel ever again."

"You've decided that?"

"Pat, listen, you need to understand this. It could come at you out of the blue and I don't want that happening. Do you remember last March?"

"Not exactly. So much has happened ..."

"They got drunk. Mel and Gary. Surely you remember."

"There was a lot of drinking back then. Me included. You'll have to tell me more."

"They got drunk, Pat. Really drunk. They were both so angry about the plant. They got so drunk they decided to go to Erban and set a fire."

"What? Oh, good God."

"They used gasoline. They only wanted to burn the loading dock. Like a kind of symbol or something. So stupid. Like kids! Remember that was when Erban was moving out."

"There was something in the paper ..."

"The fire seeped inside! They burned all kinds of stuff by accident. The news called it arson. Mel told Gary to keep it quiet. Just between them. They were gonna stay away from each other. Gary never heard anything from Mel. Nothing at all until we found out he'd left you. Gary got scared. The police showed up. I lied for him. I told the Detective that Gary was home with me. When the cop left I made Gary talk. He told me about it. The fire, I mean. I thought you were calling to get even with Mel, to tell me about this!"

"I would never do that, Mona. Heavens, what must you think of me?"

There is silence again on the other end, long enough for a long sip of wine.

"I'm so sorry, Pat. I thought you knew. I thought all kinds of things. I was so scared. Gary was scared. He still is. We never know from day to day if the police will come knocking!"

Mona is crying now, her voice tremulous on the edge of hysteria. Pat wants to let go, just go with her emotionally, but knows she cannot. Not now. Not with this. She holds the phone away from herself. Breathes. Tries to breathe.

"Pat?"

"I'm here, Mona."

"What can we do?"

Primal plea for help. How blithely things come at you; how sudden life's shifts. It is like water, on the surface so sparkling and placid, concealing the currents beneath which move the water yet seem not to, so subtle their hydraulic interchanges. She thinks of the tug of the undertow sucking the sand from beneath her heels. She thinks of the whispers at gatherings: the news people share below conversation. She thinks then of Mona and Gary living so tenuously over a drunken mistake. Yet that fire could be the cause of everything that came after. That it is quite likely what has created this new Mel.

No.

It was earlier, when the worry began with the rumours of Erban and the edginess crept into Mel's character. Then Dani and Stanley happened and Mel's hard response. Then Pat leaving their bed for her daughter's room. Why had she done that? Why had she chosen that tactic against her husband? Living in his daughter's room as if to say *he* had emptied it.

Currents and whispers.

They would fight about nothings. They would snipe at each other. For some reason neither of them could surrender in the way they once had: finding joy in returning to peace, finding ecstasy in the love flooding back, finding themselves as partners again, as lovers again as they had been for so many years.

Why hadn't he told her?

Yet she knew the answer already. By then they were nearly strangers. His lies must have come easily by then. She wonders how many he's told, building lies upon lies until his decision to leave her. Then she sees it has *all* been a lie. Rather than tell her and work it out he has swallowed the fire and driven her, and his children, away. What must it have taken to bear that burden?

More currents, more whispers.

What did it say that she had not seen it? Shouldn't she have perceived through the drinking the sports nights the computer the rage the fear finally the primitive slap? Shouldn't she have known driving his children away was his manner of protecting them, and her, from whatever it was he'd become?

How little we know of those we think we know most. The complexities are crushing. We live our lives in fragments. We all have secrets. It is finding those secrets that will bring him back. If it isn't too late. Yet now she is aware of his motives. A modicum of reason to the puzzle of Mel.

Closer to putting it together; all together.

"Pat? Are you there?" Mona's whimper from the phone.

"Yes. Yes. I'm here."

"What should we do?"

"What you're doing now, Mona. Take care of Gary. Thanks for telling me this."

"Yes but what ..."

"Nothing right now, Mona. You've given me lots to think through. I have to go."

"Okay."

Third edge discovered.

56

WITH SEPTEMBER WELL underway Danielle sees little of Stanley as the latter spends long days and nights at the Quantum Nano Centre. When he *does* come home he seems distracted. Too often he leaves the supper table with his meal cooling on his plate and goes into the living room where he spends additional hours gazing at what seem unreadable schematics on his screens. He has little time for either her or Henry. Henry has actually turned to her for comfort, his building affection having appeared after his *outing* by her mother and simultaneous desertion by Stanley.

She is sitting in the kitchen with Henry on her lap, Michael doing dishes after supper, Stanley not home yet again. Henry purrs. She absently scratches the top of his head while she worries about the end of something. She tells Michael. Michael says not to worry. Michael says Stanley is closing on his goals and his mind is taken up with them.

"But *you* don't act like that."

"I am not Stanley, Danielle," he replies, his Kenyan accent lulling. "You have your own doctoral work too, don't you?"

"I do, but my work is different from his. I work teaching machines to learn. I work in the world of classical computers and binary bits. Stanley's work is far more abstract."

"In what way?"

Michael sits down beside her. Henry opens his eyes momentarily. Dani strokes Henry.

"Stanley is developing a new platform for quantum computing based on scalable arrays of neutral atoms which can overcome the challenges to scaling of competing technologies. He is working on hardware to trap arrays of up to one hundred qubits, thus his nano interest."

"A hundred what? Oh, yes, the things in two places at once. Stanley's told me that much. I know a particle can be in quantum superposition. I have my own theory on that about humans."

"I'm not sure what you mean. Binary bits in classical computers, zeroes and ones, are like tiny switches either on or off: far too primitive to utilize quantum algorithms."

"Even supercomputers like the Sequoia and the Mira?"

"Yes. Goodness, you *have* learned, Danielle! So ... superposition. Qubits bits are subatomic particles. Picture a ball spinning in mid-air: the rotation axis of that ball could point in any direction. No off/on. Infinite multiples actually. Say you built a quantum processor with fifty qubits ..."

"They exist?"

"Not that size, not yet, it is part of what Stanley is working on. At any rate, *that* processor could make computations in, say, three minutes that would take a conventional supercomputer ten thousand years to solve."

"Stanley's doing that?"

"In a way. Look, I don't want to seem to patronize you ..."

"It's okay, Michael. I get it. The quantum computer is really Stanley. He's always balancing infinite multiples. I just wish he could be clearer about it."

"Hah! A fine way of putting it. He's working now with the Department of Combinatorics and Optimization."

"Never heard of it," Danielle says, laughing.

"Combinatorics is the study of discrete structures, and related algorithms. Optimization deals with determining the values of variables that maximize or minimize an objective. It's a bit complex ..."

"Stop! Please Michael! Stop!" Danielle says, giggling.

"There still have to be algorithms tailored for the neutral-atom platform."

"That too! Yeek!"

"Then, of course, there's the actual platform, could it exist ..."

"I'm sorry I asked!"

"Ha! So am I! I barely understand it myself!"

They have both broken into laughter while Henry, disturbed, launches himself toward his food bowl. It's not yet serving time so he sniffs the enclosed compartments. He uses a claw to try to pry open the one closest to him. Suddenly the machine dings and tuttles, opening. Too late for Henry. He has reacted with an astonished spring, straight up, once more smacking into the bottom of the counter. Down, hard, on all four paws. He looks at the two humans laughing. His look is so nasty, so Henryesque, that the two redouble their merriment. Henry leaves in a huff. Mister Walk-On-By once more, a quick, devastating glance as he exits.

It is in that moment of unrestrained joy that Stanley enters from the hallway. They haven't heard him at the front door, so noisy has been their delight. He has removed his jacket, being warm from the walk home. He appears slightly pale from all the time spent indoors. He seems troubled.

Danielle rises and goes to him. She raises her arms and holds his shoulders with her hands. She stays at arms' length, examining him. This adds to his perplexity.

"What's happened?" he asks, his accent as precise as Michael's Kenyan accent is casual. "Why are you looking at me like that?"

"Oh, nothing much," she says, "just that Henry and I have both been outed as Luddites!"

"Not really," Michael says from his seat.

"So what would you call it?" Danielle responds.

"I ... no ... you're right, Danielle ... good lord it was funny!" Michael laughs again.

"You're still examining me," Stanley says.

"I'm admiring you."

"Admiring?"

"Michael has been kind enough to explain to me something you never have."

"Really? What would that be?"

"What you do. A part of who you are I don't really understand but at least I have a sense of it now. It's the guy you are when you're away from me. He's a pretty impressive guy."

"Secrets, is it? He's giving away all my secrets?"

"Lover," Danielle says, "you'll just have to believe there are things in your life so beyond your scope it's kind of frightening. I bet I haven't told you my new theory!"

"Indeed. What?"

"The theory of quantum human character."

"I'm afraid you have me on that."

"I'm afraid I always will. Remind me to explain it some time."

She kisses him then. He loves her lips on his. Once again from the moment he entered the kitchen, he has felt unworthy of her. In her bare feet she is his height. Even unguarded she is beautiful with her thick golden hair tied up in a twisted bun, two long strands on either side of her face framing her cheekbones. It is in her porcelain skin and her smile through unvarnished lips of soft pink and her eyes, her eyes gleaming like diamonds glittering with her joy. He cannot believe this woman would settle for someone like him. He has come home on a mission, a fearful one, her beauty causing him augmented doubt but her welcome has settled him slightly.

"Come, sit down!" Michael shouts. "Henry once more has been terrified by his feeder. Hit the counter again!"

"And then there's me," Danielle says, seating Stanley at the table then sitting beside him. "I've just discovered from Michael ..."

"Revealing my secrets?"

"Nothing of the sort!" Michael responds.

"He told me about your doctoral work. Jeez, Stanley, why didn't you tell me more? You know I'm interested."

He is completely perplexed. He'd thought she would never want to know. Now she is laughing again, Michael laughing with her.

"It's not that funny," Stanley says, defensively.

"Oh, it's not your work. I just got the tourist's glimpse from Michael."

"I tried telling her," Michael says. "Made a mess of it."

"No, I don't think so. I just had a Henry moment, is all," she says.

"A what?"

"Just like Henry and his food machine, I am never, ever, *ever* going to comprehend quantum theory. I thought you were working with artificial intelligence."

"But I am, darling," he says. "Just look at the world around you. AI is all about. It's a way of understanding data, solving problems and making decisions that apply pretty much to everything. Think of Google Maps, Google Translate, Amazon and Netflix or the autocomplete on your phone."

"Oh my God," she says, laughing. "We're all slaves to our machines! What would I do without my phone?"

"And that's not the half of it," he says, building his elucidation. "It's exciting because of the range of problems it can be used to help solve, everything from self-driving cars, to robotics, to computers making medical diagnoses. Cloud computing has made vast power accessible. The internet can tap into the massive amounts of data needed to train machines. Algorithms for machine learning have developed in huge strides the past few years."

"That's not what you do," she says.

"It's what I do!" Michael says.

"Yes, well, I … you see, work in a slightly more theoretical field."

"No kidding," she says.

"I can explain," Stanley says.

"No more! Ah, here's Henry! My new best friend and fellow Lud!"

The cat returns from the hallway; again she can't help but notice his white T-shirt beneath the striped fur. This time he comes straight to Stanley, rubbing his leg with a jowl then a body curl. He ends up under Stanley's chair, glowering out at the two sarcastic types who'd made fun of him.

"Oh no," Danielle says, pouting, "now you're taking him back!"

"Not at all, darling," he says. "Actually, I came in with a purpose. You two have set me off track. Michael, would you excuse us?"

The mood shifts. Michael instantly senses it and rises.

"Yes, of course, I've got work to do," he says, popping into the living room/lab.

Danielle is perplexed. From the amusement of her quantum confusion she finds herself abruptly transported into a different atmosphere. That Stanley would exclude Michael doesn't bode well. Again her doubts begin. What does Stanley see in her? Is she like Henry to him? How could he love such a simpleton? What he says next cements her fears.

"I've been doing rather a good bit of thinking lately, Danielle," he says softly. It is as if he is suddenly another man. His words are no longer as confident. Even his look has changed, his eyes going just a bit sad and unsure.

"You see," he says, "we're not much alike, are we?"

"No," she murmurs. It is all she can do.

"So I've thought about how we get on together."

"What?"

"Live together. I've considered a slightly different arrangement."

Oh God, she thinks, *I don't want to lose him I don't want to lose him I don't I don't oh please something else why does this happen why do men leave my life?*

"I'm sorry I'm not smart," she says, trying to cover her panic.

"It's not that at all, Danielle," he says softly. "This is hard for me. I don't believe in soul mates or what have you but I do understand the common creed is that soul mates are often those of the same character, fitting together like man and mirror.

"I see. And we're not."

"No. We're definitely not."

"We're just too different. Is that what you're trying to tell me?"

"I don't subscribe to that doctrine, Danielle. I believe soul mates come from *completing* each other. They *can't* be the same with similar neuroses or fears or for that matter, goals. If they *were* the same how could they possibly help one another?"

"And I can't help you," she says. She is near tears.

"Please, dear, don't stop me now. I've rehearsed all this and I have to get it out."

He reaches into his pocket.

"What I'm trying to say is because we're so different I'm not sure you'll accept this. From the day I met you, you a kind of child I felt guilty of stealing, your father seeming to feel the same, yet then as time has passed you've become a woman in every sense of the word and I feel, well, it has made a deep impression and I want to be honest and open with you in every way I can. I want you to be honest with me as well. It's far too important now for us not to be. Do you understand?"

"I ... no, not really ..."

Her eyes glitter like stars. Tears twinkling.

"What I mean to say, Danielle," he says, moving forward in his chair bringing his hands together before him, "is, would you possibly consider, no, could you find it in yourself, no not that. Look, darling, what I'm trying to say is ... will you marry me?"

The small blue velvet box in his hand springs open and within it gleams, just like her eyes, the perfect sparkle of a diamond solitaire ring. She simply sits in her kitchen chair, stunned, facing him, staring at the ring in the satin folds of the box. His hands are slightly shaking. His fingers are white.

It dawns on her then that what she has heard is completely contrary to what she expected. Abruptly the world is a lighter, softer place, beautiful in its rightness, a place where she knows she can live happily. She can see Henry's green eyes peering up at her, she shifts her gaze to Stanley's hazel eyes, filled with doubt. He is troubled. Why should he be troubled? She cannot think of a single reason. The box snaps shut with an *edge on edge* clap.

"I'm sorry," he says, beginning to rise.

She realizes she hasn't answered.

"Oh no! Oh God no, Stanley! I mean YES! Yes! I *will* marry you! I'd love to marry you! I love you, Stanley. I love that we're different. I just wasn't expecting ..."

His face relaxes, his eyes come to life. He opens the box, takes the ring from its satin, and takes her hand in his.

"With this ring," he murmurs and just then, as he changes the grip of his fingers to put the beautiful ring on hers, he drops it.

Clatter on the tiled floor. Just a brief gleam before Henry is on it. He pounces like a cheetah (well, maybe more like a tabby) leaping out from under the chair batting the ring with his paw sending the ring skittling across the floor then flying after it whacking it, batting it like a juggler on the verge of catastrophe. Danielle shrieks as Henry knocks the ring through the doorway down the hall into the living room/lab.

She is on his tail. The little shit will not get *this* ring. Henry looks up, his eyes wide with panic. Then he is gone behind the old green easy chair in the corner, the one they all used to sit, resting their eyes from hours of staring at screens, the one they all call *the idea chair,* the one they had found on a boulevard and brought home half in and half out of the trunk of the car. She looks behind it.

No Henry.

"Omigod where's he gone? Where's the ring?"

"He's not there?" Stanley says.

"He didn't come this way," Michael says, on his knees.

"The little shit. He went behind the chair. Now he's not there!"

"Here we go again," Michael says, laughing. "Superposition!"

"He's got *my ring*!" Danielle squeals.

"What ring?" Michael asks.

"Her engagement ring. We're going to get married," Stanley says proudly.

"What? That's what you were doing? Well congratulations! That's wonderful!'"

"The cat stole *my ring*! Let's not fuck around here, boys!" Danielle says, her eyes glitter, this time with the kill.

"We'll find it!" Stanley says. "It can't be far."

"Unless the little shit knocks it through a register into the ducts!"

"Oh, damn! Where did he go?"

"Behind this chair!"

"But he's not there."

"He's not there?"

"No, he's not."

"He's not in this room. I can't see him at all."

"He *entered* this room!" Danielle's voice rises in pitch.

"Try behind the CPUs. He likes to lie there for the warmth."

"No. Nothing!"

"Where in hell is he?"

"Help me move the chair!"

"Move the chair?"

"Move the chair!"

"Okay. Though I don't see why. Michael?"

"Okay. I've got this side."

"Don't lift, just slide. We nearly put our backs out last time!"

"Right. Pull!"

The two men haul the heavy green chair away from the corner. Still no Henry. Danielle peers at the base, sees a tear in the backing, her hand pulls at it only to be clawed from inside."

"Ow!"

"What?"

"He's inside!"

"Inside the chair?"

"Of course!"

"You're sure?"

"He's there. I know you can't see him but he's definitely there!"

She holds up a bloody finger.

"Here let me try," Michael says. "Damn! Ouch! He's defending! He's clawed me!"

"Okay," Stanley says firmly, assuming command. Danielle, take the front, just push on it when we lift. Michael, we each take the back of the chair, tip it forward!"

"Of course!"

"Ready? Steady? Lift!"

The chair tilts and Danielle deftly rolls away just as it falls forward with a thump, upside down, its green cushion spilling onto the floor. And there, prone, naked to the world, guarding his stash, one hiss of challenge, is Henry. He glares at them balefully, surrounded by cotton balls tinfoil balls paper balls wine corks buttons a slice of mouldy carrot two pencils a silver laser flashlight (Will Baker's) various dust bunnies multi-coloured candies a shoe lace guitar picks (Michael's) a make-up brush (hopefully Dani's) two marbles (marbles?) Stanley's long lost school tie pin and there, glittering gaily amidst it all, the ring.

"The little shit!" they say simultaneously.

Stanley reaches for the ring. A yowl and a slash. He joins the walking wounded.

Danielle leaps through the air over the chair as only she could and lands purposely hard: feet spread apart, arms akimbo, eyes matching Henry's and screams like a banshee. Henry is gone in a cloud of dust bunnies. A disappearing act of no small skill. Danielle reaches for the ring, picks it up, blows the dust from it, and puts it on her own finger.

"I guess that means yes," Michael says, chuckling.

"I'm the happiest man alive," Stanley says, gazing at her proudly.

"The little shit," she says.

57

BY MID-OCTOBER THE air has turned cold. Yellow leaves wave from birch trees across the lake but otherwise the vivid colours of autumn have dropped and what remains is the green of spruce, hemlock and pine. They have taken the docks in off the lake and secured them, anticipating winter's ice. Mel would have done this with the kids. Now he uses Will, a petulant helper, even to splitting the wood for the woodstove that is their source of warmth.

Will Baker is humbled. He has realized how wrong he was about Mel. He had thought him once a mere factory drudge, a worker bee droning in the hive of mundane industry. Yet the man has mastered each step of an extremely steep learning curve with a resolve which Will finds second to none. From his early bumbling beginnings all it took was someone to show him a path, then the steps of that path, and he has since taken each with an obsessed motivation, one system at a time, resiliently to comprehend its basics, then continued until he has learned to manipulate these platforms beyond the norm. Working eighteen hours a day experimenting, testing, investigating the arcane, pushing until he had made himself ready for the next step.

It has been an uncomfortable revelation for Will. He had not really known much about Mel until the day he'd met him. He knew little of the former sports aficionado, the player who played beyond his skills because of that innate and unusual ability to focus. He is trapped in this strange symbiosis through his own underestimation.

Inside, the cottage is warm. The woodstove blazing, crackling. The two of them sit at the dining table, side by side, their computers in front of them. They wear T-shirts and track pants. Unusual clothing for Will but the hardware store in Mactier had only sweat suits on sale and a few heavy hunters' jackets. Mel purchased them. Will had complained. As usual the more daunting man prevailed.

"What the fuck d'you need dress up clothes for up here?"

"I have some pride," he responds, fondly recalling his navy blue Paterson sweater.

"You wanna stand out? You gotta look like regular people, I mean the way people look up here. Believe me, you don't want the Mactier gossips discussing you."

There is a bizarre tension in the room as each of them mouse and click through websites, mostly news or chat sites, in search of what they'd expected to explode into the public domain, yet remains unseen a week after the final package was mailed. Mel rises from his seat, his face flushed, eyes sparking like torches. He smacks a big hand down on the table. Everything jumps or vibrates, including Will.

"Where the fuck is the news?" Mel says, shouting.

"Maybe it's too early," Will says, trying to soothe him.

"Come on, Willy! Some we mailed a month ago! Somebody had to report at least one!"

"Maybe the news is being suppressed."

"In KW? Come on. How the hell can they do that? Somebody always leaks things, everybody knows that! It's not a big place. No, I'm wrong. It's a fucking part of the System now, a fucking technocracy! We're all in it."

"Calm down," Will mutters.

"You don't see it, do you? You think Kaczynski's crazy. You're so far inside the System you don't even know there *is* a System."

"Stop bitching, Mel. I've got an idea."

"What? What haven't we thought of?"

"There will be leaks, just like you said. We just aren't looking in the right places."

"Newspapers, TV, Facebook, Twitter ... come on!"

"You know a lot of these people, don't you? You said it was like a small town."

"I said *was*! I don't know everybody now!"

"We haven't looked for emails." For an instant Will Baker revels in transcending Mel's ignorance."

"What? Why emails?"

"Because, unlike you, most ordinary people do not obsess with learning about their computers. They use Word, Photoshop, YouTube, some games ... if those work, they don't trouble themselves with how they work. Emails are still the simplest method to communicate so most people use them."

"How do we get at people's emails? There's gotta be hundreds of people who should know about this! How do we find any one of them? Can you get past any of these tech companies' protection protocols?"

"I'd be crazy to try."

"Okay, let's hack the cops!"

"Jesus, Mel, you can be a real idiot sometimes. You *want* to get caught? Look, it has to be a personal email or a corporate one."

"But who ..."

"There was one package different from the others we sent?"

"Yeah, it had the Silver Star. I hope somehow he lit it up!"

"See? That's it. Not *they*, Mel, *he*. What was his name?"

"Herbert Trimble."

"Then that's our way in. Even if he didn't report it he'll have told somebody. You don't keep something like that to yourself."

"Okay. I get it. Can you do it?"

"It's gonna take time. A phishing scheme ..."

"Yeah, like sending him a fake link he can go to, something like that."

"But he could be a careful user. No. We need something more direct. We need to send him an email from someone he trusts. Something he'll click on before he thinks. He got kids? They're usually lazy about passwords."

"I don't know."

"But you've got his address. Do you have his email address?"

"Just the work email. He sent one to me about a meeting."

"Work would be good. Very good. We could spoof it. Create a mirror website. You have it?"

"It's on the computer at home."

"You have the same address now, here, as at home?"

"No. I got a new gmail account. That was Rogers, the other one."

"Okay, tell me and I'll get into your home computer. You got a password for it?"

"I did. It might be changed by now."

"Let's find out."

"Hack my own computer at home? I mean my family's computer?"

"Easiest way."

"I'm not sure. It's my family."

"It's the fastest way. They'll never know. Once I'm in I'll use a rootkit."

"A what?"

"A package of malware designed to avoid detection."

"Alright. So if you can do that, can I read my family's emails? I'd like to know how they're doing, y'know?"

"That's easy Mel, let's use your laptop. I'll put it up on your desktop as an ikon. You'll have all access all the time! What's your email address?"

Mel tells him. He can't help but be excited. An anonymous way into Pat and MJ, and maybe Dani. He would like to know how they are, what they're doing. He endures the heartache of his destruction of his kids' trust. Yet he knows that rift, and his separation from Pat, are necessary. He cannot turn back from his crimes. He cannot turn away from his newfound knowledge. He does this to save them. Still, it doesn't help the pain of missing them no matter how they've turned out. In the end he discovers their email addresses are terminated. The only viable one is his own.

Will tells him they've likely changed them on Stanley's advice.

Then Will begins another of his many hacks for Mel Buckworth, not knowing he has sealed his fate and even his sanity. He does it unthinking, as he almost always has. He does it for money. As he almost always has. It has almost always been easy.

Almost.

58

HAVING FOUND TRIMBLE'S work email and discovering it hasn't been discontinued, it is simple enough for Will to send him a work related message, to all appearances from Erban's head office. It bears Erban's logo. It uses like fonts. It is general enough. It enquires as to Trimble's current status. It asks him to click on a link then fill in the form on the Erban website. That is the line.

Then comes the bait. It mentions a bonus for his difficult and dependable work through the last months. All he has to do is click. There will be a letter of commendation. The bonus offered will be in the thousands.

It will send him to their Erban spoof site. The fake COO will ask him to await both the cheque and citation through regular mail. Meanwhile Will's load of malware will settle itself into Trimble's device. It takes a day and is done. Trimble has tumbled. They now can access at leisure his email. They will be the *man-in-the-middle*, a common hacker's term, intercepting Trimble's messages should he attempt to email Erban again. They are careful to take no active part. They merely stand shifts as Trimble sends and receives. It becomes quickly clear what has happened. It is clear too that Trimble has taken the bait. As Will puts it: *This is a fascinating thread.*

To: amrit.Khadri@wrps.on.ca 2012-10-11 06:22

Constable Khadri,

I am writing re our interview of last week re the package sent to my house. I again appeal to you to provide round-the-clock protection for myself and my family.

Regards,
Herb Trimble

From: herbertjtrimble@gmail.com

To: herbertjtrimble@gmail.com 2012-10-11 09:18

Hello Mr. Trimble,

I am sorry, sir, to again state that the WRPS does not possess sufficient manpower to fulfill your request. As you know, sir, we have put in place more frequent patrols past your residence and your children's school. We are investigating the origins of the package you received and will keep you updated as information develops

Sincerely,
Amrit Khadri

From: Constable Amrit Khadri
Investigative Services Branch
Waterloo Regional Police Service
200 Maple Grove Road, Cambridge, ON, N3H 5M1
555-570-9777 ext.828500
amrit.Khadri@wrps.on.ca
To receive our Media Releases, subscribe here: www.wrps.on.ca/subscribe

---

To: amrit.Khadri@wrps.on.ca 2012-10-11 09:22

Constable Khadri,

I must insist, Constable, that something more be done in my unique case. I have been the recipient of poison and now of a threatening explosive from this LUD. Surely you must have some idea as to the identity of this individual or gang of thugs terrorizing my wife, my children and myself. If I must I will appeal beyond your position, sir, to a higher rank.

Regards,
Herbert Trimble

From: herbertjtrimble@gmail.com

To: herbertjtrimble@gmail.com 2012-10-11 13:35

Hello Mr. Trimble,

My apologies for the delayed reply. Further work beckoned. I understand the anxiety you and your family must feel as a result of these criminal actions. I admit your case is somewhat unique but can say nothing further due to the ongoing investigation. It is your privilege, sir, to speak with our Executive Branch at your convenience.

Sincerely,
Amrit Khadri

From: Constable Amrit Khadri
Investigative Services Branch
Waterloo Regional Police Service
200 Maple Grove Road, Cambridge, ON, N3H 5M1
555-570-9777 ext.828500
amrit.Khadri@wrps.on.ca
To receive our Media Releases, subscribe here: www.wrps.on.ca/subscribe

---

To: amrit.Khadri@wrps.on.ca 2012-10-12 09:02

Constable Khadri,

Since you won't answer your phone extension I resort again to email. As I am sure you know your Staff Sergeant refused my request for protection. You indicated in your previous email that my situation was SOMEWHAT unique. You told me you would keep me updated on your investigation. It seems I am missing important information re other similar situations as well as sufficient protection.

What can you OFFER me further?

Regards,
Herbert J. Trimble

From herbertjtrimble@gmail.com

To: herbertjtrimble@gmail.com 2012–10–12 17:41

Hello Mr. Trimble,

I am sorry for having been out of the office at the time of your calls. I believe email is the best conduit for our exchanges. As to your situation not being unique, I can only say that other victims are in similar situations though I cannot reveal their identities. I have taken steps to have your mail monitored to obstruct any further suspicious packages or letters. As I indicated in our interview, should you suspect something please call police and do not open the article in question.

Sincerely,
Amrit Khadri

From: Constable Amrit Khadri
Investigative Services Branch
Waterloo Regional Police Service
200 Maple Grove Road, Cambridge, ON, N3H 5M1
555-570-9777 ext.828500
amrit.Khadri@wrps.on.ca
To receive our Media Releases, subscribe here: www.wrps.on.ca/subscribe

---

To: amrit.Khadri@wrps.on.ca 2012-10-13 09:09

Constable Khadri,

What am I supposed to do? You want me to move my family out of my house? What if someone plants a bomb in our garage? We keep everything under lock and key! My kids stay home from school more than they attend! My wife is on anxiety depressants! I am fuc I am tired of living this way! You've got to do something! What the hell is going on?

HT

From: herbertjtrimble@gmail.com

To: herbertjtrimble@gmail.com 2012-10-13 17:41

Hello Mr. Trimble,

Because the weekend is here might I suggest you take your family out of town on a small vacation? There is no investigative or preventative reason for this, I merely think it would give everyone a break from the tension. The investigation is proceeding apace. I have nothing further to report as yet. You told me in our first interview that you were being transferred to the USA with your work, did you not? Perhaps it might be fortuitous to make that move early; take yourself and your family out of perceived harm's way. Might that be a consideration?

Sincerely,
Amrit Khadri

From: Constable Amrit Khadri
Investigative Services Branch

Waterloo Regional Police Service
200 Maple Grove Road, Cambridge, ON, N3H 5M1
555-570-9777 ext.828500
amrit.Khadri@wrps.on.ca
To receive our Media Releases, subscribe here: www.wrps.on.ca/subscribe

---

To: amrit.Khadri@wrps.on.ca 2012-10-16 14:18

Constable,

Thank you for your helpful suggestions. What do you mean "perceived" harm's way?????? I AM THE VICTIM HERE! I have moved my family out of my house and into a rental property until YOU HAVE SOLVED THE CASE! I cannot move to the USA because MY EMPLOYMENT WAS TERMINATED by Erban Industries after I received a letter of commendation and promise of a bonus! I have nothing!!!! You have got to help me!

From: herbertjtrimble@gmail.com

To: herbertjtrimble@gmail.com 2012-10-16 18:52

Hello Mr. Trimble,

I recognize you are the victim of a crime. I apologize for my lapse in correct vocabulary in describing your situation. I have little to report at this time though the investigation continues apace. These matters often take some time, sir. I am sorry to hear of your termination of employment. I believe your idea of a rental is a very good one, though I will say with our increased patrols there was no reason for you to take this step. Our officers will continue to frequently monitor your premises and your mail. Perhaps a talk with our pastor here might help alleviate your, and your family's, situation. I can provide you with his number if you wish.

Sincerely,
Amrit Khadri

From:Constable Amrit Khadri
Investigative Services Branch
Waterloo Regional Police Service
200 Maple Grove Road, Cambridge, ON, N3H 5M1
555–570–9777 ext.828500
amrit.Khadri@wrps.on.ca
To receive our Media Releases, subscribe here: www.wrps.on.ca/subscribe

---

To: amrit.Khadri@wrps.on.ca 2012–10–17 14: 21

WHAT DO YOU MEAN TALK WITH A PASTOR????? IF I AM NOT THE ONLY VICTIM THEN WHY IS THIS CRIME NOT IN THE NEWS! WHAT IS WITH YOU PEOPLE????? CAN'T YOU GET THIS CASE RIGHT???? I AM ALREADY IN COUNSELING FOR YOUR INFORMATION! MY WIFE TOO!

From: herbertjtrimble@gmail.com

To: herbertjtrimble@gmail.com 2012–10–17 14:52

Hello Mr. Trimble,

I am sorry to hear this news. I am trying to understand your situation. I have spoken to my superiors and have been given direction to inform you that police are withholding information to the press due to the nature of the crime. They have also suggested a meeting at the Waterloo Regional Police Service Building, 200 Maple Grove Road, Cambridge at your convenience. That meeting will include a Superintendent, an Inspector and myself along with my investigative partners. Please call the number below, ask for extension 0828570 and arrange a time.

Sincerely,
Amrit Khadri

From: Constable Amrit Khadri
Investigative Services Branch
Waterloo Regional Police Service
200 Maple Grove Road, Cambridge, ON, N3H 5M1
555–570–9777 ext.082850
amrit.Khadri@wrps.on.ca
To receive our Media Releases, subscribe here: www.wrps.on.ca/subscribe

---

To: amrit.Khadri@wrps.on.ca 2012–10–22 09: 21

JUST FOR YOUR INFORMATION BEFORE OUR MEETING MY SON HAS RUN OFF SOMEWHERE OUT WEST. MY DAUGHTER IS SCARED TO COME OUT OF HER ROOM! MY WIFE IS ON SERIOUS MEDICATION. I AM THE VICTIM HERE! I WILL HAVE YOUR BADGE, KHADRI!!!!!!!!!!

From: herbertjtrimble@gmail.com

"Wow," says Will Baker, "this guy's off the rails. I think you're getting your message across."

"They're suppressing it! See? The cops said so! This guy is just one cog. I want the machine, the System," Mel says. He is furious.

"Mel," Will says, "what else can you do? You've got the answer right here. You can see the fear in these emails."

"Not enough. Not if it's suppressed," Mel says flatly, the blue light of the screens late in the night making their faces look roughly robotic.

"What the fuck are you talking about?" Will says. He has not shared Mel's frustration. They are not the same people. Their cultures are so differentiated the only entity connecting them is Mel's plot and Will's knowledge, Will's greed and Mel's need. One requires the other.

59

THEY STARE AT each other through the digital blue on that Saturday night, October 20. Outside is clear. A cold moon seems close. Inside is warm from the woodstove but murky with misunderstanding. They turn away from the screens and face each other.

"Well that thread tells you something, at least," Will says frankly.

"It was way more than that, Willy boy!"

"Look, I wish you wouldn't call me that."

"Too bad. You're in my life now with my rules."

"What did you mean *more than that*?" Will asks.

"Trimble's gone."

"He's fucked up is what he is! His whole family! Jesus!"

"He's left his house. There's no one there. Time to up our game!"

"How, for God's sake?"

"I don't want to kill anybody, Willy, I've told you that. But here's the chance to suggest it could happen, make them sit up and pay more attention. We'll build a fire bomb. They can't suppress an explosion on a quiet street in the suburbs. Like I said, it really is just a small town. Something like that gets around quick."

"Wait a minute, Mel. I didn't sign up for this!"

"No, you walked into it with your ego flying. So now you get to prove to me why you have that ego. You're going to get on your machine and find me instructions on how to build a bomb! I've got extra M-80s, so lots of gunpowder. I just need to know how to put it together and trigger it."

"I'm not gonna do that."

"Yes you are, Willy boy. You got no say. You don't do it, you know what will happen."

"This is a whole other league for crissake!"

"Shit, kid, for a bright guy you're a bit of a chump. What did you think I meant to do? You think I've poured my time, my work, my soul into this without some expectation? Did you think there was a limit to what I'd do? I have one limit. No murder. I'll bomb an empty house. Set the place on fire."

"What?"

"You'll come with me. I can't leave you alone, not with these stakes."

"You can't do that!"

"Watch me."

"Then fuck it! I'm leaving."

Will walks toward the door, grabs his coat, shoves his feet in his shoes and returns to the table to pick up his laptop. With that error, Will not departing at once, the force that is Mel Buckworth the athlete, strikes. As Will reaches for his laptop Mel's hands are swiftly again on his collars, yanking him violently upward. He finds himself staring into the fire of Mel's eyes. The younger man tries to push away. He cannot match Mel's strength. Mel literally picks him up off the floor and launches him backward through the air and hard into a wall. The collision knocks Will's breath out. Then Mel is on him grabbing his collars again like handles. Will Baker brings a hand up and slaps Mel's face. He has no idea what to do in this kind of situation. He has never, ever had to face a bully. He strikes out in his child-like way. It has no effect other than another slam into the wall and a forearm across his throat. With his free hand Mel simply reaches back, closes his fingers into a fist and sends it straight at Will's left eye.

Bam.

Stars.

The closest Will Baker will come to cosmological thought.

Mel drops his arm and Will slumps to the floor. As he returns to consciousness his hand automatically goes to his eye. He has yet to fully return from his astral journey. He has no idea how long it has taken though the sting and the bruised bone pain flare up. His other hand joins the first, hand on hand somehow in the hope that two hands will make the pain go away. The pain brings him clarity. When he recognizes what has just happened he cannot help himself. He starts crying.

"Oh, for fuck's sake," Mel says.

The cries turn to sobs.

Mel walks away allowing Will time to cry himself out and accept his place in this hierarchy of two. It takes twenty minutes. Mel spends that time looking out the window into the darkness of the lake. To look outside he must look through himself reflected in glass surrounded by darkness. It is a jolt to see oneself in the moment after violence. In sport there is little chance to take time to think. So much of it is immediacy, so much is training. You suck it up and you move on. Perhaps later when there is time you learn something: don't turn your back on an opponent going into a corner, watch for the spikes when someone slides into second base, lean into a tackle before you get hit. He should not have let the boy slap him. All the slap did was make him lose control and in an instant he has terrorized his partner.

Mel resolves never to strike him again. Fear is an effective master but too much of it leads to desperation. One does not take one's frustrations out on the tool. When the hammer hits your thumb you do not break the hammer. When you miss a fly ball you don't rip up the glove. When your stick puts in an own goal you don't break the stick. And this tool of his is quite delicate. It requires soft handling. When he hears sniffles and a shuffling as the young man rises, he turns.

Will blows his nose. Mel walks to the fridge and takes out a cold pack. He crosses the room handing it to Will. Will is trembling. Mel leads him to his computer. Mel opens it up in front of him.

"Password?"

"There isn't one," comes the frightened reply.

"Don't fuck with me, Will."

"It's my thumb print."

"Then do it."

Will brings his computer back to life. Mel hovers over him.

"Change the password."

"What?"

"To my thumb."

"What!"

Will Baker is utterly cowed. Nothing in his experience has ever prepared him for this weird reality. He is reduced. He cannot think. The pain is too fresh, too real. This is no game where one purchases health points. This is no game where one can start over. He is deep inside his new actuality. He changes the passkey from his thumb to Mel's. He will not be able to open his own machine without Mel's consent. While they are at it Mel shifts his own device over and has Will create the unique conditions for Mel's thumb only on that one as well.

"Okay," Mel says, "let's get started on finding the bomb instructions."

"I ... I can't see," Will says.

"You got two eyes. You just sit and tell me what to do. Hold the ice pack in place, dummy! Takes the swelling away. You never had a black eye before?"

"No."

"Jesus. Of course."

60

THEY DISCOVER THAT bombs can be simple things, particularly if they're not aiming to kill but merely to start a fire with a bang. The only moving part is a switch to create a connection from the power source to an initiator. The switch is of obvious significance. The bomb becomes lethal only when the switch is engaged and the circuit closed. They read about various types: mercury, mousetraps, pressure pads, kitchen timers, alarm clocks, toys' components, motion sensors, even toasters. They read about initiators: blasting caps, electric matches, bridge wires and those even more exotic. They read of combustibles: military C-4, dynamite, nitrate fertilizer, coal dust, propane, even wheat flour.

All too sophisticated for them.

They decide on the simplest of devices: a plastic container of gasoline, another of motor oil, four M-80s and two Silver Stars all linked by wire to a *burner*, a throwaway cell phone. They buy three of them: one for testing, one for the actual device and a third to call the second one: closing the circuit pulsing through wires setting off firecrackers igniting petroleum starting a fire. They might even get a few spraying rockets, a light show from the Silver Stars.

Will takes the lead on this. He understands circuitry, having experimented since he was a child. Mel paces the room. He stops to watch the latex gloved hands at work. He watches the soldering gun make connections with electrical wiring stolen from the deserted cottage where he'd found the rat poison. He sees the wires inserted into the firecrackers. The wires make a pretty tangle of red blue yellow and green. He looks carefully as Will connects the currently dead cellphone to a mini USB blade attached to the wiring through a connector.

When Will is finished they go outside. It is chill in the early morning air. Frost ices the ground. A thick fog like floating milk lies over the lake. No boats this day. Hardly anyone is around so late in the season.

Will has wired up a smaller version of the explosive: a single M-80 to a metre-long set of wires to the cell phone. He places the phone on one side of a tree, the firecracker on the other, the wires joining them in an arc on the icy ground. He turns on the cellphone.

Mel turns on another. He dials the number as Will joins him. They wait for a ring that never comes. What happens is the crack of the explosive. It sounds like a gunshot. Someone hunting duck or deer. It is a satisfying sound. Mel knows now his plan will work. Will then conjures up the real thing. The wired firecrackers are amalgamated by a compact copper wire connector. Will adds the oil product then the gas. It all sits on a plastic tray in the bottom of a laminated box, a delivery company box, familiar to people who look at front porches. The gas container is ancient, so worn as to be translucent. Finally he connects the cell phone, turned off until delivery, then stands aside for Mel to examine. Satisfied, Mel folds the box shut, puts a role of clear packing tape on top and carries it to the door.

It is the week before Hallowe'en.

They disguise the truck. Going into KW, Mel does not want someone he knows seeing him. They throw clods of earth into buckets of water and splash the goop onto the Ford. Black to mud brown. Once in the city they will blot the licence plates. The idea is to make the vehicle look like it's just come from off-road driving, thinking police will understand this and not pull them over. They cover the back with a tarp, the generic light blue polyethylene tied down, covering most of the sides and back. What they hope any one will remember is a dirty truck with a tarp. A work truck. At one point Mel thinks of spraying a decal on the doors but gives up the idea as too overt and too easily traced, removing the truck's anonymity.

Their intention is to drive south in the morning, find Trimble's house (they have the address from Whitepages) then spend the afternoon and evening observing it: driving by once, walking by twice. They have different clothes for each passage. They will wait until the early morning hours before setting the bomb in place and igniting it. The hole in Mel's plan is the drive back to the cottage. He does not want to make it at night. More police. Filthy truck. Obscured licence plates. They need a car wash to clean it but nothing is open that late.

They will have to stay the night. Prior to leaving, everything packed snugly into the back, Mel makes a phone call.

"Hey there, Wilson! How's it going?"

"Who's this?"

"Hasn't been that long has it? It's Bucks!"

"Oh shit. Hi Mel. I'm not supposed to be talkin' with you."

"What? Oh yeah. You heard about the separation."

"Yeah. A bit more than that."

"Sure. Life changes things, y'know?"

"Yeah. I know. Mel, I had a visit ..."

"Listen, Gary, me and a friend are coming to town. Gonna pick up some stuff at the house but I don't want to bother Pat. I can't stay there, of course, so I'm asking if we can stay at your place. You still got your trailer?

"Yeah, I do."

"In the driveway?"

"Yeah," Wilson says.

Mel bends the force of his willpower into his voice. There is something wrong with Wilson's voice. Still, he knows he can trust him. He knows the guy. Best friends don't stop being best friends.

"So we could use it! We'll be coming in late. I'm introducing this guy to the men's hockey league. Trying to get him on a team. It usually turns into a party. I don't want to put Mona out. We don't need anything. Just a place to sleep. You okay with that?"

"Sure. Oh fuck. Uh, just a minute."

Mel can hear muffled voices, high and low. There is a shuffling, scraping sound from the phone as if some kind of struggle is taking place.

"Mel Buckworth!"

It is Mona, her voice hard, tight. He's heard her like this only once or twice. It doesn't bode well. He decides to ignore it. Play the old friend.

"Hey there, girl! How are ya?"

"Why are you calling?"

"I ... hey, just to talk. I was hoping to use the trailer."

"You're an ass, Mel Buckworth. A selfish, shitty bully."

"Wait a minute here ..."

"You ready to go to police?"

"What?"

"About the fire."

"He told you?"

"Of course he told me. I'm his wife. You didn't tell your wife, did you! You left your wife for no goddamned good reason. You left Gary sitting here holding the bag! The cops were here. Now you've got the nerve to call and why? 'Cause you want to *use* him again. What are you gonna burn this time, Mel?"

This is far too close to the truth to pass off. Mona Wilson is furious. He knows her temper. He can only back down, apologize, make things right with her. He fears her more than her husband.

"Mona ... I'm sorry ... we got drunk that night. It all got outa hand. We can't go to police, Mona. We'll get charged. Even if we own up to it they'll still charge us."

"You think we don't know that?"

"That's what I mean. You want Gary in jail? You want everyone to find out about this? I'm just in town to pick up some clothes. Pat and me have settled things. She's gonna get a separation agreement. I'm not gonna contest it. Look, Mona, I just wanna slip into the house tomorrow and get some of my stuff. I've got no place to stay."

"Stay in a motel. Stay in a fucking tent, Mel. I don't care. Pat knows about the fire."

"What?"

"She called, trying to find out what was wrong with you. I told her everything."

"You *had* to do that?"

"You left my husband to face this alone. You abandoned everybody! What the hell is wrong with you, Mel! All that happened was you lost your job. Lots of people lose jobs. Did you know that RIM is going down? You know how many tech people are losing their jobs in Waterloo? Gary says you blame things on robots. That's just crazy as it gets, Mel. You need some serious counselling. I'm telling you this as a friend. It's the last thing I'm telling you as a friend 'cause I don't consider you one anymore!"

With that she ends the call. For a moment Mel's temper rises. He thinks to call her back. Give her hell. Then he thinks better. Now is the time for subterfuge. He calms himself, locks the cottage door and steps out to where Will is waiting.

"We're gonna go to Cambridge first."

"Why?"

"We need a motel for overnight. Somewhere we can get in without using ID."

"Where the hell would you find that kind of place?"

"Leave it to me."

"Jesus, Mel ..."

Will is clearly at the edge. His face is pale, his voice half an octave higher. Mel knows he must settle the boy. He forces himself to use a calm voice, pushing away the anger he feels in order to nurse the child by his side. Without Will, Mel knows, none of this could have happened. Mel has found a new purpose, discovered a different way to learn, unearthed a code to follow and achieved new skill-levels beyond his own expectations. None of it would have been possible without Will's weekend tutelage, the frequent phone calls and finally, the boy appearing just when he was needed most at the cottage.

He owes this boy more than money. The youth has empowered him in a world where he'd once been powerless. Will has to be coerced in these final stages but Mel has resolved to ensure the kid gets away. He has determined, if he isn't caught, to disappear off the grid. He will use Will one final time to get on the dark web and buy him a new identity, then set the boy free. He will burn the cottage to the ground so no trace of Will could exist. Then he will go north. Find work for cash in the Yukon. Live off the grid as do many people there. A subculture of Luddites, he thinks. He could find a place among them. Live peaceably after his war within a tribe of like minds.

Yet his war has not ended. If RIM is breaking apart it will leave empty buildings: targets, more LUD statements. He begins to envision attacks on others as well ... the Googles the Apples the Facebooks ... the future. Somehow, somewhere he must warn the world of the future.

61

MEL LISTENS TO tunes on the drive south. After a while of saying nothing, Will goes to sleep. Mel takes the 400 south where it joins 401 in the centrifugal mess of Toronto traffic. He takes 401 west to Cambridge, once the towns of Galt, Preston and Hespeler now become one sprawling city with Highway 24 serving as its main street. The road is filled with stoplights and traffic, either side nothing but mall after plaza after chain restaurant. About two kilometres along, right across from the Waterloo Region Police Service station, sits the Rocket Motel.

It squats on a rise on the east side of the street, a tawny brick two-storey structure in front of which are a bright red and white sign and on the other side of the driveway a six metre high silver bullet with scarlet red rocket wing tails; a comic monstrosity. A turn up the drive takes them around the house to a concealed parking lot with a strip of classic 50s style motel rooms. There are cars parked in front of a couple of rooms. It looks to Will like a low budget, very low budget, accommodation.

"What the fuck is this?" he asks.

"Open the glove box. Pull out that envelope."

"Jeez, how much money's in here?"

"Just stay in the truck. I'll be a few minutes."

Will would like to run. He wonders at Mel and whether the man sees the irony of what he is doing. His use of technology to destroy technology. Perhaps a cry for help, right now, or a run across the road to police would bring things to an end. Yet Will knows what will happen. If he turns, he will be charged as well, his life ruined. Mel may not be a genius but he is a master of manipulation. He has weaved his analogue web with skill and Will is the fly captured in it.

Mel avoids the office and goes to one particular room, knocking on the door. A woman answers. She is petite, has mid-length jet black hair and a curvy body encased in lycra-spandex. She is pretty, or was once; the life she has chosen has placed an unreadable mask on her face. Here, before him, is another player.

"Yes?"

"Noella, isn't it?"

"Yeah? Who are you?

"About a year ago, I was with a hockey party you were at. We met. You brought me here. We, uh, you know."

"I don't remember."

"My nickname is Bucks. You remember that? I left you quite a few when we were done."

"Nope. Sorry."

She tries to shut the door. Mel holds it open with one arm.

"Look Bucks, you can be in a load of shit if I want you to be," she grumbles, threatening.

"I know that. I just want to make a proposition."

"Like what? You gonna give me more bucks?" She laughs. Her teeth are not good.

"How about five hundred!"

"For what?"

She is defensive, though even the mask can't conceal her interest.

"You better come in," she says

Mel steps through the door, proffers the envelope which she quickly snaps from his hand, rips open, and starts counting money. She is fast. Experienced. She looks up at him.

"Okay, you got my attention."

"Me and another guy want to stay the night here."

"Then it's gonna be more if it's a threesome."

"That's not what I mean. You won't be involved. You give me your key. We'll be coming in late. We just need to sleep a few hours. Or if you can fix it you give me the key to another room. I can't use ID, that's why I'm here."

"Hey, I don't give a shit who you get off on. Some guys just need to stay in the closet."

"It's not that! It's ... something else. I can't tell you."

"Drugs? You running girls? What the fuck you doin' here, man?"

"I just want a room for the night! Okay, listen, I'll try somewhere else. It's just I remembered you, and this place. I'll take my money and go."

"Don't get so fuckin' shook up. I told you I don't care unless you're doing something way over the top. I can get you the room next door."

"How do I get the key?"

She slides across the room to a bureau. She wears fluffy pink bedroom slippers juxtaposed with her outfit. Mel finds the image comic but dares not laugh. She opens a small box on the bureau, pulls out a key and, holding it high, brings it back to him. Before she hands it over she takes a long, analytic look at him.

"You better tell me what's happening. I get flak from management I'm out. You got something planned. I can see it swimmin' around in those bright eyes of yours. What's up?"

"I can't ... it's not what you think. We're gonna play a Hallowe'en prank a little early is all. We live a long way away. We don't want to drive home all that way tonight. It won't affect you so long as nobody knows we were here. Alright?"

His explanation seems to satisfy her. She holds out her hand. He takes the key.

"What time?" she says.

"After two or three."

"You gonna be drunk?"

"No."

"If you are, if you make any ruckus, I call my friends. You won't like it."

"I know. Thank you for this."

"No skin off my nose. Don't talk to nobody either when you come back."

"I understand."

"You're up to somethin'. I can always tell."

"It's nothing that'll hurt anyone."

"Okay. You been here long enough. Take off."

Mel returns to the truck and shows Will the key, then starts the truck and pulls out onto Highway 24, headed through Preston into Kitchener. It is an easy drive. He takes King Street through Preston town centre, turns up Shantz Hill into the Gateway area where he once played hockey, then down Highway 8 to the Expressway. He takes the ramp to go west toward Kitchener's suburbs.

62

IT IS THREE-THIRTY in the morning: quite still, cold and quiet in this suburban enclave. The two men are dressed in black sweats, hoods up, balaclavas beneath. They stand in the shadows edging a neighbourhood park: some swing sets, a slide, one or two half buried tractor tires for kids to climb on. This is a substantial locality, a typical suburban series of curving roads and pie shaped lots with big houses. Several houses have Hallowe'en decorations, though at this time of night any lights have turned off. Illumination comes from streetlamps, one every half block.

Five houses away and across the street is the Trimble house, a single light on upstairs to simulate habitation. They know no one is there. Their reconnaissance drive by, then a walk in the evening have proven it. No other lights have switched on or off in any other part of the place. It is a yellow brick home, upscale though not ostentatious. Unraked leaves litter the lawn. The front porch is one step up from the lawn and the porch light is, fortunately, not lit.

They have left the truck in a school parking lot, deserted at night, and walked with their package along a short bike trail behind the houses to this park. Will holds the package. On command he sets it down. Mel opens it. He unscrews the cap of the gas container and punctures a hole in the foil top of the motor oil bottle. Finally he turns on the cell, then tapes shut the box. He hands it to Will.

"Okay, go to the front door. Right *at* the front door. No shortcuts."

"I'm not taking it. You do it! It's your plan."

"If they got cameras. I'm bigger than you. More recognizable. Look, don't argue!"

"You aren't gonna set it off when I get there?"

"Don't be stupid, Willy. If I did that there'd be DNA all over the place."

"Not when the gas catches. You'd burn me to death."

"Why would I do that?"

"Get rid of me. Get rid of my evidence."

"I'm not gonna kill you, kid. I told you I don't wanna kill *anybody*. Now go. And don't let the liquids spill or they'll short out the phone."

"I know that!"

"So go. No, wait."

Mel fishes in his pocket and pulls out a piece of torn cardboard twenty centimetres square. Scrawled in black is LUD. He places it on top of the box in Will's arms. He tears off a piece of the packing tape, attaching it to the sign.

"Put this up in the tree in the front yard, the side away from the blast."

"I'm not hanging around, Mel. Jesus, you have to do this?"

"Tape it up. Make sure it stays."

The shadow strolls down the street with its package, turns up the drive, sets the box on the porch. Every second seems like an hour for Will. He is not sure at all of Mel's sanity. What he's seen of the man has been frightening. He understands better why Dani was rejected the way she was. Mel has no toleration for differentiation. For a moment Will feels some pity for Dani then discards it, remembering it is she who actually put him in this place right now right here in the dark in the night with a bomb and a madman.

He sets down the package, carefully. He walks quickly to the tree, a skeletal maple with its leaves gone. He tapes the sign to the tree. He walks back to the park casually. When he arrives, Mel dials.

There is a sharp crack of the fireworks, a sizzle of silver light then a *whompf* as the gas catches and swiftly the box is on fire then the fire flows over the porch lighting up fallen leaves as it travels. It moves upwards as well melting the vinyl screen door. The fire licks at fascia. It burns yellow and blue it is beautiful as it consumes what it grasps.

The two men see it catch then are off down the trail then the winding streets to the truck. Mel starts it up, leaves the school yard and heads toward Cambridge by back roads. He is exultant. A veteran of arson now, he drives slowly and carefully.

When they pull into the motel, there are more cars. It is a busier place at night. Will marvels it hasn't been busted and shut down thinking he knows what is happening behind the row of closed doors. Their door is next to the one where Mel made the deal. They park the truck in a space distant from it. They enter the room. It is all cheap blonde furniture. There are too many mirrors on the walls. The bed itself squeaks when he sits on it. He thinks of bedbugs. They remove their black clothes and stash them in a duffle. They have street clothes for the next day. Each takes a side of the bed, each in his sleeping bag. Mel is snoring in five minutes. Will lies awake all night. He replays the crack, the sparkle, the gas lighting up ... over and over.

They decide to take back roads up to the cottage. They leave at ten in the morning, put the truck through a car wash and find a breakfast place on 24, each having the special. Mel looks around occasionally in case someone he knows might come in. Fortunately, on this righteous day there are no familiar faces.

Once back in the truck Mel turns on AM 570 awaiting news of their deed. Nothing. Too early yet, he supposes. They drive to Guelph, going north from Guelph to Fergus, then take the Marsville Road toward Orangeville and skirt the town. They lose the local radio signal. Eventually they are in the highlands around Mansfield and Everett. Will is entranced with the countryside, though most of the leaves are down. He has never really seen anything like it. Rolling hills, big sky, vistas that go on and on, farmsteads still operated by families, villages still vibrant with general stores and local merchants. It brings him out of the silent funk he's been in since the bombing. He starts talking when they turn north off Horseshoe Valley Road onto 400 then straight north to Mactier. In that hundred kilometres Will Baker sets off a conversation which will change his life. It begins when he jokes about the bomb.

"Real whizbang there, Mel. If I wasn't so scared I would've laughed my ass off. Shit, did you see that little sparkle light up just before the gas caught? For a nanosecond I thought we were gonna get the 4th of July. Wonder how much damage we did."

"I hope the news'll have it. We can watch CKCO tonight on satellite."

"Fuck! I've never done anything close to this."

"'Course you haven't. You were brought up to fit the rules. Maybe that's why you can't make an app. You gotta break rules."

"I'm breaking them now, Mel. Pineapple. Remember?"

"Maybe. Breaks the rules but Tor was already there before you."

"You've changed, Mel."

"Have I now."

"You know, when I first contacted you I had no idea I'd become Doctor Frankenstein!"

"Frankenstein the movie? How does that fit?"

"You don't know the book?"

"I never even knew there was one."

"Written by Mary Shelley in the early eighteen-hundreds. It's about this Doctor Victor Frankenstein who becomes obsessed with creating life. He accomplishes it using chemistry, alchemy, dead body parts and electricity. Ah, never mind, poor metaphor. Forget it."

"Poor what?"

"Let it go, Mel."

"No, I wanna hear. I always thought the monster was Frankenstein but you say he's not? So who's the monster?"

"You really want to hear this?"

"Yeah. Improve my mind, Willy."

"Alright. So in the book when Victor Frankenstein looks at the monstrosity he's created, the sight horrifies him when it comes to life. He runs away, abandoning the monster."

"So he was ugly, like Boris Karloff!" Mel says, laughing.

"According to the book he wasn't. Still, he was made out of human body parts so he must have been sewn together. I think there was mention of his eyes being white and horrible. Anyway, he's rejected by people because they think he's hideous. Inhuman. Yet he's actually a pretty bright guy in a monster's body.

"He finds a blind man who accepts him and teaches him how to act like a civilized person. Then after some time the monster finds Doctor Frankenstein again. Now he's learned to be human, taught to read, how to behave, be civilized; he tells how his life is lonely. He's alienated. He wants the doctor to make him a wife. The doctor promises, but backs out. This drives the monster insane. He ends up killing Doctor Frankenstein's wife. He murders other people as well. Anyway, Doctor Frankenstein chases him. He confronts him, I think, in the Arctic where the monster's chosen to isolate himself."

"Don't sound inhuman to me."

"Well I think Shelley's point is he *is* human. People *think* he's inhuman."

"And you called yourself Doctor Frankenstein. That makes *me* the monster."

"It was just a joke, Mel."

"How come you know this so well?"

"Well, I could say it's classic literature, but I read it in a different context. I read a partial proof at M.I.T. It's the original text but it's annotated for scientists, engineers and designers in robotics and AI. They don't necessarily understand allegories. This scientist wanted to remedy that."

"What's allegories?"

"Messages. Hidden messages."

"So you read it because it was being explained. Like Cliff's notes," Mel says, chuckling.

The sarcasm, particularly from a peon like Mel, no matter his *savant* character, scalds Will. Yet there is no way to strike back without retribution. Will rides with a bully, a monster of his own making. But Will has ever had a sharp wit. He uses it now to turn Mel away from his boasting.

"Not my game, all this creation," he says. "That would be *Stanley Best's* field. I find it fascinating, Mel, you're so hell bent on destroying technology yet you don't go after the guys who create it. Can you not see these people running the world? Even now they're taking over. In fact, one of them even took your *daughter.* He's turning her into one of them. But then you know that, don't you? You wanna burn something, try the Quantum Nano Centre at UW. That's where Stanley spends most of his time. That's the place where the future's happening. You wanna send a message that will really get society's attention? There's the place."

Mel doesn't answer.

The point of Mel's insurgency is to bring to light the plight toward which every human is headed. Inside it now, no one can see what it is or where it is heading. They either don't wish to look or are so vested in the System they can't bear to look. Then it dawns on him that every system has an order and most systems are based on a hierarchy and that hierarchy must have a summit. A simple summation of his research tells him: Carlos Slim *(Telmex)* Bill Gates *(Microsoft)* Larry Ellison *(Oracle)* Rupert Murdoch *(Fox)* Mark Zuckerberg *(Facebook)* Ma Huateng *(Tencent)* Elon Musk *(SpaceX Tesla)* Jeff Bezos *(Amazon).*

These are the alphas.

Even politicians serve. Given their modicum of hallucinatory power, they consider it real, again, not knowing or *choosing* not to know where *true* power rests. And Mel knows he can't get at them, these alphas. They have *all* the power, are *too* protected, so out of reach minding their System with all others merely the cogs.

Yet there is a way.

There is a place.

There is a person.

A metaphor, as Mel has just learned.

But it means a death. He wanders a moment into the unfamiliar realm of the metaphysical. Is he playing God with his vengeance? Is he a monster or is he a god? His brief glance into the ether is startling. It flits through his mind.

These thoughts compress into a few chronological moments in Mel Buckworth's life. He would never before have considered this epistemological train of thought. Furthest thing from his mind. It shakes him this time to recognize how far he has come. He is in so deep now he can't tell if he is man or monster.

Will, with the silence, concedes something as well. He knows he has gone too far having provided Mel a target. He should never have even spoken of Stanley or the Centre, the parallels being so obvious. He decides to stay quiet, spend his time looking out at the granite outcroppings, dark lakes and conifers of the Canadian Shield.

It is stunning country, beautiful and barren.

A place of gods and monsters.

63

DINNER AT THE Buckworth house: a special *engagement* dinner in the dining room: off-white stucco walls and ceiling, old mahogany polished, curving legs with claw and ball feet, sideboard and buffet and china cabinet glistening with antique coloured glass, the table covered in linen then lace, six upholstered hard back chairs around the table, the best Royal Staffordshire china and Cornflower crystal wine glasses, all passed down through the family, their worth unknown to Pat, Mel or the children but adroitly assessed by Stanley. He, however, remains quiet as Michael pops the cork on a Gosset 2012 Millessime accompanied by a cheer and hands clapping from the assembled celebrators. Stanley and Danielle sit on one side of the table, MJ and Michael opposite, Patricia at the tail ... the head chair remains ominously empty, the space at the back of everyone's mind.

Champagne flutes are filled and raised.

"Here's to the happy couple!" Pat says.

Tings of crystal ring around the room. Everyone comments on the wine's extraordinary quality. A good year for Champagne: exemplary maturity, acidity and grape health. Just before they sit Pat raises her glass again, bringing them all around to attention.

"So when is the happy day?" she asks.

"Oh, Mom, they just got engaged!" MJ says.

"Still, as mother of the bride I have planning to do."

"I agree," Michael says, smiling. "Best to nail this man down, Dani!"

"Danielle, please," Stanley says. "Her name ..."

"So do you have a date?"

"Not yet, Mrs. Buckworth ..."

"Please Stanley, call me Patricia."

"I actually prefer Patricia."

"Just don't call me Mother!" Pat says, laughing.

"Did you know Henry stole Dani's ring?" Michael says.

"Danielle," Stanley insists.

"What?" Pat says.

"I call him the cat burglar now."

"More the *cat bungler,* wouldn't you say?" Stanley says. "We did root out his hideaway."

"Still, he does have a way of disappearing," Pat says.

"And he's done it again," Danielle says. "We only hear him at night. We can't find him anywhere in the house. The little shit ..."

"Easy, darling. He'll come when the food runs out," Stanley says.

"So you haven't settled on a day, you two?" Pat asks again.

"Well, Mom, we've sort of decided we'll marry when Stanley gets his doctorate."

"Oh my, will that be long, Stanley?"

"It gives me impetus, Patricia," Stanley says.

"It could take forever, given his field," Michael says.

"Oh dear," Pat says.

"It's a quantum thing, Mom," Danielle says, smiling.

"The geek squad!" MJ shouts.

"Whom you have now joined as well," Danielle retorts. "How's it going there?"

"Conestoga? Great! Had no idea it was in me. I'm not the brightest in the class but I'm holding my own and every once in a while a certain future brother-in-law helps me out."

"Let's finish this wine and I'll fetch the meal," Pat says.

"I'll do it, Mom, you cooked!" Danielle says, rising.

"I'll open the red," MJ says, joining Danielle in the kitchen.

Pat begins to get up.

"Please, Patricia, stay on and chat," Stanley says.

The three partake of their Champagne. All of them seem at a loss to begin. Pat feels the weight of her ignorance. She has never had much chance in her life to exchange ideas other than those of sport, love, the weather, children's antics and dentistry. These young men, who they are, what they do, are yet another puzzle to her. She would like to know more, fit a few pieces together about her future son-in-law. As well, she is the hostess this time and it is her charge to make *them* comfortable in her home at her table. She takes a stab.

"I'm afraid you'll find me rather uneducated, guys. I'd like to know more about what you do. Would you mind if I ask a few questions? Don't be afraid, Stanley, they aren't going to be personal. Not yet!"

"Please, Patricia, feel free," Stanley says.

"Fire away," Michael says.

"So this quantum you do," she asks, "what exactly is it?"

"It's a theory, Patricia," Stanley answers. "It explains the nature and behaviour of matter and energy on atomic and subatomic levels."

"Oh, I see. Actually, I'm sorry. No, I don't."

Stanley launches a different approach. He speaks carefully, knowing he can sound pompous.

"Rather than deal with that, let's take the internet."

"Alright. That's something I know. It's made up of ideas!"

"It is, yes. But at a quantum level the information itself is abstract but all the data moving through cyberspace have mass. That mass has weight; not discernible, really, but if it were possible to measure it, it might weigh something like fifty grams, the weight of a strawberry."

"That small?" Pat says. "Good lord, Stanley, this is computers?"

"No, it's physics. Quantum computing is focused on developing technology based on the principles of quantum theory."

"So atoms and the like ..."

"Yes, using nanoscale devices. One nanometre is one billionth of a metre."

"That's incredible!"

"Just as quantum technologies exploit matter on diminutive scales they're dependent on advances in nanotechnology. Two years ago a research team used a high intensity short pulse laser to place an electron orbiting in silicon into varying states *simultaneously*. That's known as quantum superposition. No longer binary."

"That's important?"

"Rather than representing bits, particles represent *qubits*, which can assume multiple values. With the quantity of information on the internet and a neural network to categorize it, eventually devices will learn by themselves. Recall Michael's robotic research ..."

"Of course! That farming robot. Learning things on its own."

"That's right. So eventually an autonomous intellect will evolve; an artificial intelligence which will ingest all possible information. It would learn for itself, from itself, by itself ... not from human programmers."

"So they'll be smarter than us? These AIs? Isn't that dangerous, Stanley? Is anyone addressing that?"

"There are strategies being considered through the philosophy of computer science."

"Yes but how does it work? Philosophy is so ... human."

"It's concerned with ethical issues arising from the field of computer science, predominantly involved with software development, which is a very human thing."

"Oh really, this is too much to grasp. I feel silly."

"I've got it!" Michael chimes in. "Let me give an example from fiction. You've heard of Isaac Asimov?"

"I have!" says MJ, returning with the wine. "Science fiction guy!"

"So MJ, do you know Asimov's laws of robotics?"

"I do!" MJ smiles. Pat notes how much more at ease her son has become. For an instant she wishes Mel could see him now, then recalls it is actually Mel's actions creating this change. Her mind drifts through the conversation. Again she wonders what he is planning in his northern isolation. Since the end of summer there has been no communication. She wishes she had an inkling as to why he wants to protect them from himself. Because that *self* is so oddly different? Is it so very opposed to the character of the man she married and thought she knew? She hears her son's voice. She pays attention once more.

"A robot may not injure a human being or through inaction allow a human being to come to harm. That's the first law. A robot must obey the orders of human beings except where those orders would conflict with the first law. That's the second. And, a robot must protect its own existence as long as that doesn't counter the first or second laws!"

"Where on earth did you learn that?" Pat asks.

"Well I got it from reading his sci fi, but Stanley says it might be out of date."

"How so?" Pat says, turning to Stanley.

"There is the possibility of a zero-day patch."

"A what?"

"Zero-day is the moment when a vulnerability appears, unknown to the people responsible for patching or otherwise fixing the flaw. The fear is that at some point an AI device will discover that defect before humans do, then morph the patch in its own manner. At that point humans will lose control of the platform itself, unless it can be powered down."

And with that Danielle enters bearing a heaping platter of roast beef, potatoes and vegetables. MJ pours the wine.

"What were you talking about?" Danielle asks.

"Stanley was telling me what he does."

"Omigod! You're still awake?"

"It's fascinating, really. What I understand of it."

"What I understand is it takes him away from me way too often!"

"I can see someone being preoccupied with it," Pat says, sympathetically.

"I try not to be," Stanley says. "I just can't help it occasionally."

"Well not now!" MJ says. "Let's eat, drink and be merry!"

And they do.

64

IT IS AFTER the meal when the home phone rings. In that instant Pat thinks it might be Mel. The empty chair at the head of the table has loomed hollow throughout the dinner. Inside, Pat feels her daughter's engagement is somehow incomplete without her father there.

Mel was not a perfect man. He was far too driven in everything, mostly sports, though it had extended to his work as well. He had ensured their marriage would appear nearly perfect, no matter what circumstances arose in the varied clashes which mark all long marriages. He had tried to do the same with the children and succeeded mostly in the appearance of normal. Lost upon him was the tight control he held over his son in sports and his daughter's social life.

Their differentiations had rocked him. Pat had been mystified at his acquiescence in MJ's failure until she'd realized Mel too had failed in that part of his life. It was why, after his son's refusal to continue in sport and then college, he'd cosseted the boy. Good buddies. Same hierarchy. Man cave in the basement. It was also why, when MJ had proved more adept than him with the computer, Mel had turned on the boy. He resented his son surpassing him.

Dani had been a different story. She had truly transcended him but as his daughter she was not a threat to his alpha penchant. Because she *was* his daughter he had spent countless hours helping her through her dyslexia. He'd thought she'd inherited it from him. It was, Pat now realized, the introduction of a *man* into that equation of father-daughter, particularly a man of noted success and skills, which had upset Mel. The boys whom Dani had formerly dated had been high school kids as much in awe of Mel as was his daughter. Stanley was different.

"I'll get it," she says, thoughts of Mel in her mind. She had considered removing the landline but it served as a representation of Mel. It was the only phone he would use to reach her. She walks through the doors from the dining to the family room and picks up the hand set.

"Hello?"

"Pat?"

"Oh."

"You okay?"

"Yes ... sorry, yes Mona. I just wasn't expecting you."

"So he didn't get in touch with you?"

"Who?"

"Pat, Mel was in town ..."

"What?"

"He called here. Wanted to stay overnight in our trailer. I told him no."

"Why was he here?"

"He said to pick up some things from the house."

"I haven't found anything missing. Then again I haven't looked."

"Another lie. What the hell's gotten into him?"

"I wish I knew."

"There's something else ..."

"Okay? What? Mona, are you there?"

"I'm here."

"Can you tell me, please?"

She hears Mona take a deep breath. She finds herself not breathing at all.

"Pat, that week just before Hallowe'en a house was set on fire in Kitchener, like with a fire bomb, they said on the news. Gary watched it. He put two and two together. He called a guy named Oblauski. From work. You know, big, loud guy ..."

"I think so, yes."

"Well, he told Gary the house belonged to someone named Trimble."

"So?"

"Erban Industries! Trimble was the guy who fired Gary. He fired Mel too. Now there's a fire on his front porch? Just like the loading dock?"

"Oh, God."

"You better call Mel."

"He won't talk to me."

"Then get one of the kids ..."

"He won't talk to them either."

"This is getting way out of hand. If Mel did it, and I'm sure he did, Gary'll get dragged into it. What the hell is Mel up to?"

"I wish I knew."

"I can text him! Where is he anyway?"

"He's up at the cottage. I've tried texting too. Never get an answer."

"Well he'll answer mine! Once he knows what I know."

"Don't do it, Mona!"

"Why the hell not?"

"He's unstable. It's not like it's even Mel anymore. If he did *this* I don't know what else he'd be capable of. I'm afraid if he thinks you're an enemy he'll do something desperate."

"I'm gonna call the cops."

"Wait! Please. If you do they'll find out about Gary. Give me a week. Mel wants a separation. I'll get a lawyer to write one up then I'll use that to meet Mel and talk to him. I'll keep you and Gary right out of it."

"Okay, Pat. Just please be careful. Don't see him alone; make it a public place like a restaurant or something."

"I will, Mona. And thank you, thank you for calling me."

With that she mumbles goodbye, knowing it will be forever, pretending it won't.

65

IT COMES AS a shock when Amrit Khadri comprehends that Patricia, the woman with whom he has found so much joy, is the wife of an Erban employee. After their introduction she has always been Patricia with no last name. She has only once, he recalls, spoken of her husband and that was months before, at their first meeting. Since then he has called her Patricia, no last name. When her number comes up on his cell it is simply *Patricia.*

Yet here is the list for Erban Industries, each individual interviewed highlighted in yellow, those few remaining still stark black print on the white pages. One of them reads: *Mellor George Buckworth* along with his address, social insurance number, home phone and emergency contact: *Patricia Buckworth (spouse).*

He feels his pulse quicken. He rises from his desk and glances out the window, confused and confounded. There has been a light fall of snow, early this year and certain to disappear. It takes a few moments to regain his equilibrium. It comes to him then that despite his feelings for this woman he must break her world, disturb it at least, with a request for her husband's location. He has no idea what kind of animosity exists between them. He decides to call and ask for a meeting. Yet he doesn't wish to ambush the woman, watch her dissolve into tears or harden her face into a mask. His quandary is how to approach it. In the end, being who he is, it is the simple truth.

"Hello Amrit," she says. She sounds light and cheerful.

"Hello, Patricia," he says evenly.

"Don't you sound mysterious," she says. "Is something wrong?"

"Actually, I'm calling for a reason," he says, almost checking himself, "police business."

There is a hush on the phone. He can hear her breathe. It seems a lifetime and somehow it is *her* lifetime passing in the silence, until her voice comes to him again.

"This is about Mel," she says. Clearly she has been expecting this call, though not from him. They have made an island for themselves in the midst of the tumultuous world. They have carefully circumvented subjects which might have caused either discomfort. Under the guise of care they have become careless, not recognizing the depth of the human character when both should have known better.

"I'm sorry, Patricia. Your ... Mel ... is on a list of Erban employees. He's one of the few we haven't yet interviewed. If you'd prefer I'll have one of my partners talk with you."

"No," she says, "that won't be necessary."

"I don't want to do this over the phone," he says.

"No, I understand. You think I've been hiding him."

"Oh good heavens, no! I've not thought that at all! Honestly, it's just come up. It surprised me really."

"There's no need for someone else then. Can you just come see me? I'm at work right now but I'll be home in an hour."

"Why don't I meet you near your work? I don't want to intrude more than necessary."

"I see. Yes, of course. My husband isn't home if that's what you're thinking."

"I wasn't."

"Where do you want to meet?"

Not long after they are facing each other in a booth in Annette's Kitchen on Erb Street. It is a blink from the past, a diner with comfortable cracked vinyl seats and lots of privacy once they have received their coffee. The place has a storied history and Khadri realizes it is filled with Patricia's past. For a moment he thinks he has made a mistake by meeting her here. Her wan smile is so tired. Her eyes glance familiarly around the room.

"Lots of times spent here," she says softly.

"I'm sure," he responds.

"Mel was a big hit here. He had a bit of a thing with Annette's daughter. Her name was Terry. Italian with dark eyes. She was the only girl I ever thought I might lose him to. I had no idea I'd lose him this way. How is it you can know someone, marry someone, have his children, share his life and not really know who he is?"

"I can't answer that."

"Has he always had this other self and I missed it? How is that even possible?"

"In my experience people are complex. There are parts of their characters even they themselves don't know unless something happens to bring them forward."

"Like when they break the law," she says. There are tears glimmering in her eyes.

"Do you know where he is?"

This is the moment. This is the crux. This is the test of her love for Mel Buckworth. It is speak the truth now or forever live the lie. She uses a tissue to wipe her eyes, taking three seconds to make a decision.

"He's at our cottage up north. Sometimes he's away from there too. There's no way of telling. He doesn't answer his phone. He doesn't reply to texts. He's going through something I'm not sure of. I've heard things. I don't really know anything, Amrit. And I don't want to get him in trouble because people talk."

"We just need to interview him. It's a formality. If he won't answer I'll contact police up there. Where is he?"

"Mactier. It's a village. Our cottage is on Stewart Lake Road."

"So the OPP. I can get them to look in on him, request his presence for an interview."

"Oh, I wish this wasn't happening!" she says.

"Easy," Khadri pats her hand when he really wants to embrace her, kiss her. And he realizes that suddenly, startlingly, he has fallen in love.

She looks at him through her tears. She sees him alter his look, his soft eyes changing with emotion. He need say nothing for her to know he loves her. And in that instant the fourth edge of the puzzle is solved. She finds she loves him as well.

"I think there's a way you can meet him," she says.

She has stayed true to both men.

66

THE NEXT BOMB is built. It isn't much different from the first but is massive in comparison. Mel has purchased a soft tonneau cover. He's installed it on his truck to close in the back once the truck is packed. He and Will have also bought twenty polyethylene containers, different stores, all cash, and filled them with gasoline. There are four twenty-pound propane cylinders crammed in as well, along with Will's new wiring system. The activator switch is still a throwaway cell phone. The initiator more M-80's though this time they are wired inside five half-filled gasoline canisters. The two men imagine the payload enough to start a huge fire with the propane containers to increase the blast.

Mel has decided to use his truck to bomb a RIM building. He is worried he's used it too often for errands, for missions, even general transport. He knows it can be but a matter of time until some camera picks up his licence plate. This way, he hopes, he will delay discovery as the truck will be burned in the blast. Meanwhile he parks it up the road away from the cottage. It's November and there are lightning storms and its contents are potent.

After several tries Mel purchases a 2010 Nissan Rogue on Kijiji from someone willing to simply hand it over. It has old plates. He will get new stickers from dark web sources. Once the Ford has been parked in the place he has chosen he will set off the bomb, set Will Baker loose, take a bus back to the cottage to pick up his things, set fire to the cottage then drive the Nissan north, far north, disappearing into the Yukon. He has taken another page from Kaczynski.

He is packing his clothes and some personal articles, a photo of Pat and the kids, a great deal of cash, and set Will to the job of finding an abandoned RIM building when Will curses aloud from the kitchen.

"What's the matter," he comes out of the bedroom.

"I can't hack RIM! I told you I couldn't. There's a limit, Mel!"

"What, there's people better than you? Is that what you're saying?"

"RIM's encryptions are like military grade. Forget it."

"I just want an abandoned building. Why don't you try real estate sites?"

"Huh?"

"Real estate. They list buildings ..."

"Yeah. I didn't think of that."

"Sometimes it's not about your kind of smart is it, Willy!"

"Stop calling me that!"

"Listen, here's what you can do. Get on the dark web. Find a chat room with somebody who sells licence plate stickers. I need 2013s for the Nissan."

"That'll take time."

"Fine, a few days."

"It doesn't just happen, Mel, you know that."

"Use your Pineapple app."

"I'm having some trouble with it."

"Why? What kind of trouble?"

"I think there's a hack. I think he, or they, are trying to kill it."

"So stop them."

"I'm trying. You think these people are simpletons?"

"Why are they doing it?"

"Probably just to say they did it."

"That's not logical."

"Of course, it isn't. Humans aren't logical. Systems are."

"Get the stickers lined up. I'll find the real estate sites myself. This is gonna be our last run, Willy! After this we'll part ways, just like I said. You go south, I'll go ... somewhere else."

"Not soon enough."

"Just remember your part in this. You're a black hat now, Willy. In all the way!"

"Don't you find it ironic how often you use technology so you can destroy it? What does that say about *you* Mister Lud?"

"The more I learn the more I want to take it all down. Yeah, I know, you say I'm mouthing Kaczynski but here's a for instance: when I wanted to cut off my cable internet on a certain date, they couldn't do it! Oh, five or six of them tried the five or six times I called them and every time they'd tell me it was done on the dates I'd asked for. But then I'd get an email saying it was slotted for the date at the end of my billing cycle! Nobody could fix it! The system actually controlled them and they were too stupid to know it. I finally just left it and anyway I'm glad I did 'cause that's what we used to hack into my home."

"Mel, that's just inadequate operatives. It's all only as good as the people who program it."

"You're kidding me."

"Systems are made by humans, Mel. It's not like they do it themselves!"

"But they will! AI will! I know that much from my research!"

"Neo-Luddites and the nutcase Unabomber. Not the best testimonials."

"You and I both know people like Stanley are building them now!"

"Like I said. Welcome to the future, Mel, it's already here."

"I want to stop it!"

"Might as well stand in front of a moving train."

"What you see in AI is all good things."

"Of course. All the repetitive or dangerous jobs will be done by machines. What's wrong with that?"

"It takes jobs away! Mine was one of them! Ruined my life! I see robots running around guiding everything. There's no humanity to that!"

"It won't be used to replace people. Yeah, I see your point. But *eventually* it will help people do things faster and more consistently, create *new jobs* we can't even conceive, provide new insights that people can use to make decisions."

"Nope. What we'll have is a *System* of super-rich techies and have-not masses serving them; millions will be left behind. Or worse, you talk about machines learning to serve us but what happens when they learn too much, when they know *more* than us, when they turn on us and make us serve them?"

"You'd have to talk to Stanley about that, Mel. He's the guy on the bleeding edge."

"We're wasting time. You aren't going to stop me."

"I've just proved you can't prevent progress."

"Yeah, but I can warn the fuckers *making* this progress they better look out for people before their machines. You told me the other day I was inhuman. A monster."

"Mel, I was using a metaphor."

"Don't matter. I know what I am. I know these people who make these machines have created a System all for themselves. I can't hack them like you. If I could I would. It turns out you're not all that good anyway."

"Now just a minute ..."

Mel leans into Will, face to face. His eyes blazing. Once again Will feels a terror, staying quiet so Mel can talk the tension out of his brain. It is clear he is close to the edge. Will does not want to find where it leads. He knows an alpha dog when he sees one, and a mad dog as well.

"I have to be inhuman," Mel says. "Like them. You think they even considered the good of humanity when they were inventing their shit? *You* don't. You just look for money. Don't turn away from me, Willy! Pay attention! I have to become one of you for a while. You and Stan on the what?"

"Bleeding edge ..."

"Yeah, that. Him and all those other big shots. I can't stop 'em but I can make 'em think!"

Mel backs off as Will wipes spittle from his face then quietly turns to his laptop and goes to work on the threatened *Pineapple*. Mel opens his own laptop and boots it up. He checks his family's email as usual and as usual finds nothing on it. He taps to start on real estate sites when his cell dings a text message.

He glances down prepared to ignore it, then picks up the device, sees the headline then opens the text and reads:

Patricia:
SEPARATION AGREEMENT ... hi mel
i have papers for you to sign like you
asked will you meet me at mactier
library this Sat 17 at 1? i have other
news too let me know right away

The message sets him free from all circumstance. His family will be detached from him so protected from the havoc he knows will descend upon him. Now he is alone and there is a kind of freedom to it.

He feels nothing for Will, however. No gratitude for his guidance, no comradeship for his company, nothing that binds them other than their symbiotic association. He knows Will would turn on him in an instant, a mere mercenary in this revolt. He is a quisling by choice. No one Mel knows will weep for the boy. Perhaps his parents in far-away California.

It seems to Mel they never bothered to prepare him for real life. It seems they set him up, having smothered him with their affluent protection. Mel realizes he no longer requires Will's skills. He must discard him. Still, he has promised the boy his freedom and if anything he must be true to his principles, particularly now.

He types a reply into his phone. They will meet one last time. His Pat. The girl of his dreams since he dreamt of girls. Freedom does not remove the regret or the guilt or the pride or the pain or the anger or fear or obsession he feels. There is love too, not completely lost. Diminished perhaps. It is the one remaining emotion he must never lose for it is this passion driving him to protect his family, his friends, and his society from the systemic machine of the future.

67

PAT IS OVERWHELMED. She has spent the night sleepless, finding herself at work on two separate puzzles ... the obvious one is a very difficult Stave puzzle with swappable pieces that fit perfectly in more than one place or straight edged pieces that go inside the puzzle along with fake corners, and there is no picture to guide her.

Yet that is not the true puzzle. The jigsaw has no emotional strings. The other, the one inside her, the one of Mel, takes up her mind even as she fits the physical pieces together at four in the morning. The puzzle of Mel is like shattered glass, a crystalline puzzle hopeless to assemble as, once fragmented, even finding each miniscule shard is impossible. One cannot view anything clearly through shattered glass.

Each fragment she studies reflects not just Mel, but herself, and she too has changed. She thought the fourth edge would allow her comprehension of the remainder of the puzzle. She has seen their relationship now from four vantage points: herself, Mel, the kids, and Amrit. Now, she knows the *Mel puzzle* is most shattered of all. It comes to her that this is what she has missed all along: that the puzzle itself was not solvable, that it had more than two sides and four edges, that there are *no* sides and *no* edges. It is transparent translucent opaque reflective and refractive simultaneously with too much dusty silicone in the way to allow a reliable view. It was never two dimensional *bits*, never *this* therefore *that*, never simply *need* or *greed*. It is Stanley's *qubits*. There is an immeasurable dimension to human emotion.

She can no longer be passive. There are no answers but there are consequences. It is time now to make a selection from the choices available. At nine in the morning she calls George Buckworth. He gives her the name of a lawyer friend and arranges an appointment. George was always connected. By that afternoon she has arranged to pick up the separation agreement on Friday.

Her second call is to Amrit Khadri. She gets voicemail. She tells him she wants him to come north with her Saturday. She knows he will know what she means. She leaves a time of departure.

The third call is to Dani.

"Hi Mom."

"Dani, I have something to tell you."

"You want me to come over? I've got class at noon but I can be there by three."

"No, I want to tell you now while I'm strong and thinking."

"Mom, what's wrong?"

"I'm not waiting anymore for your father."

No response.

"Dani?"

"I don't think you should."

"But it's more than that."

"I know. He's different."

"I've found out he's done things, Dani."

"Like what?"

"He's dangerous. I'll explain later but now just listen."

"Okay."

"I will have a separation agreement by Friday."

"You … what?"

"It's what he wants. On Saturday I'm going north to meet him in Mactier."

"You just said he's dangerous! You can't …"

"I'm not going alone. I want you to ask Stanley to come."

"Stanley can't stand up to Dad …"

"He won't have to. I'll drive up with MJ and … someone else. I'm meeting your father at the library. Very public. You and Stanley will use your car and drive up with us. When we get to Mactier I'll park in front of the library. You and Stanley should park across the street behind the TD bank. When you see Mel arrive I want you to drive out to the cottage, use your key to get in and if he's changed the lock then break in."

"Christ, Mom, why?"

"I want you to search the place. Find out what your father is doing. Hopefully he'll have left his computer. I want you to steal that too. Then get out of there and drive the long way around, not through Mactier in case your father is going back to the cottage by then, and get home. Your place, not mine."

"What about you?"

"I'll keep him busy as long as I can. The other person I'm bringing is a police detective. He'll want to ask your father some questions."

"Mom! Police? What did Dad do?"

"I don't know all of it. I know he's committed arson."

"He what?" she cries out. "What are you saying? That Dad's a … oh, Christ I don't know …"

"I want to know if he's planning something more."

"Really? What about you?"

"Between your brother and a policeman I'm sure I'll be safe."

"Mom, are you sure of this?"

"Yes. I'll understand if you don't want to do it. I know it's a kind of betrayal."

"I'll bring Stanley, and Michael. Three of us can search faster than two."

"Alright, but warn them. Come here on Saturday morning, eight-thirty. It's a three-hour drive and I want to be in that library long before your father arrives."

"My god, Mom ..."

"I know, darling. I'm sorry. Believe me it's not just about separation. I'm not being the bitter wife. I think he still loves us but he's not the man we knew. Does that make sense?"

"Total sense."

"I love you, Dani."

"Love you too, Mom. You're very brave."

"I'll be safe, don't worry."

"That's not how I meant it."

68

THE MACTIER LIBRARY is a small yet spacious building. Its outer shell is deep red with white trim. It has the look of an old train station. Mactier was once a big railroad town, both CP and CN lines even now running through it. Inside, the library is painted mostly beige. It has a cathedral style ceiling, lots of windows and the stacks run along the walls on two sides of a focal centre point. That point contains a faux fireplace and four chairs covered in orange microfibre. At twelve-thirty that Saturday there are few people. The kids' morning workshops have finished. Only two or three browsers comb the stacks. A librarian with blue rimmed glasses stands behind a counter doing paperwork.

When they enter Pat goes to the desk. She asks if she might use the four chairs to conduct a meeting. The librarian asks if she would prefer a room. She says the chairs are for casual readers. Pat tells her she'll only be half an hour. She says she is meeting her husband. Something in the strain of Pat's voice speaks volumes to the librarian who tells her she is welcome to them. Pat removes her coat, Amrit and MJ doing the same. The three move to the chairs which sit at four points in a square in front of the fireplace. Pat is flanked by MJ to her right and Amrit to her left, the fourth point of the square awaits filling.

Outside is a blustery November day, micro-cells of rain coming and going with gusts of wind. The air is thick with moisture, not quite fog not quite rain, a permeable mist. Behind the TD Bank across the road from the library sits the Volkswagen Golf TDI parked in the rear lot. Michael gets out and walks past the bank, crossing the road into the hardware store where there is a small doughnut shop. He takes a table by a window overlooking the library's entrance. Stanley and Danielle remain in the car.

A pearl white Nissan Rogue drives into the gravel parking lot. It parks at the end of the row of four cars in front of the library. Michael sees a man, he assumes it is Mel, get out, look around, then walk through the library's entrance. Michael waits to be sure the man remains inside. He gives it five minutes then he is up and across the street and into the Golf. Stanley starts up immediately. Once on High Street, Danielle gives Stanley directions. The car leaves town heading for the cottage. It is a ten minute drive around the lake. When they arrive Danielle sees Mel's truck parked, not in the driveway, but in a grove of pine and hemlock just off the road.

"Michael, that's his truck! Are you sure it was him?"

"No I'm not. I've never met him. But this Nissan drove up and a big guy got out and went inside. It had to be him!"

"Michael, you can't be sure!"

"Well then *you* should have done it! Both of you know what he looks like. I only had your description."

"Never mind," Danielle says. "Pull into the driveway. I'll go in myself."

"Danielle," Stanley says, "your mother said your dad was unstable."

"Can't be helped. He wouldn't hurt me. Just wait here."

"There's someone in there," Michael exclaims. "I just saw someone through a window."

"Okay," Danielle says, then takes a breath. "Nothing to do but knock. I'll just say Mom's waiting and sent me to get him."

"Be careful."

"Back out of the driveway, Stanley. Park at the neighbour's place. I don't want Dad seeing you!"

"I assure you, darling, neither do I."

Dani walks slowly across the driveway peering into the windows of the cottage. It is a raised drive which can hold three cars and a boat. It is up a slope from the cottage. She steps off the drive then down a path of stone landings, moving toward a large rock where the path makes a turn. She stops a moment and places her hand on the cold, solid granite.

Sometimes in the midst of turmoil we yearn for our foundations. We require a return to an innocent age when so much was simple and its memories can quell the disorders we face. She remembers as a child climbing, what seemed then, a mountainous rock and sitting atop it feeling so proud until it was time to come down, when her dad would be there to lift her off her mountain and gently set her feet on the ground. Even as an adolescent, the long-legged girl with all the self-doubts, she would sit on that rock with everyone down at the water and worry how she could cope and fit in. Could she meet a nice boy could she have a good life would she ever be pretty how could she be normal when she was AC/DC or whatever?

Yet her dad was always there to help with homework, with sports, with answers to her questions. He had always been able to lift her down, or catch her when she fell. She'd eventually achieved her childhood dreams when she'd done well in school and knew she was pretty and had found a good man who would love her the way she had always wanted. Then why, why, did her father turn on her? Hadn't he wanted the same things for her? Why did he have to change just when she could meet him as a woman?

She steps around the rock to the cottage stairs. She climbs to the raised deck. She looks out at the lake through the trees. It is grey and windswept. Touches of foamy argent on waves' tips. She knocks at the door. Suspecting her father won't answer, she tries the handle. She opens the door.

69

MEL ENTERS THROUGH the library's alcove, double doors to keep the cold out during Mactier's harsh winters. He looks through the glass of the inner door. He sees Pat's blonde hair first, then his son, no longer the chubby slob from the basement, he sits beside his mother protectively. He's here not *with* his mother but *for* her, assuming the role of husband because the true husband is the villain in this. I am the villain, Mel thinks. For a few seconds he feels a deep regret. Did it *have* to be this way?

Patricia is slim again, almost like the girl from high school but for the worry lines on her face. It is an older face: more chiselled with much harder eyes. They fasten on him as he walks through the door. The two of them, Pat and MJ, sit in orange chairs. There is a stranger with them. He looks down at his phone. He's a big Asian guy who fills the chair and looks fairly fit. Mel wonders how they will manage this meeting with a stranger here. Mel takes off his jacket and drapes it over the one remaining chair. He sits directly across from Patricia: his son to his left and the big Asian to his right.

"Uh, sir ..." he says to the Asian who looks up from his phone but doesn't appear surprised. "I wonder if you could find another place. We've got a family meeting here."

"He's with me," Pat says.

Mel is stunned. He had not thought this of her.

"A lawyer?"

"No, Mel."

"You got a boyfriend? That's why the separation agreement?"

"Jesus, Dad," MJ says.

"Don't mind me, Mr. Buckworth. I'm just along for the ride. I'm not a boyfriend."

"Then who the fuck are you?" Mel turns on him and utters his soft, naked threat. Alpha dog. He turns his stare back to his wife.

"Let's get on with this."

"Mel," Pat says. "I've brought the papers you've asked for. We need to talk about who will live where, who's going to get what. Are you coming back to Waterloo?"

"What happened to your email?"

"What?"

"Your email. I've been reading ... I tried to get hold of you. You didn't answer."

"After you left home Stanley advised us to get new addresses. We all have Gmail now. What were you reading?"

"Nothing. You could have told me."

"How? You weren't responding."

Her voice has an abrasive note, the sound of experience maybe, or maybe the sound of fed up. Either way, she makes it easier to pretend not to love her. He has gathered his new persona and will use it to crush any thoughts impeding him. None of them know he is protecting them, delaying the onset of systemization and the termination of their humanity. None know he is shielding them from the repercussions of his actions.

"You have the agreement? You got a pen?" he asks.

"Can't we talk this through a little?" she replies. "Mel, perhaps you don't want to see me anymore but MJ and Dani love you. They both need their father."

"Why would you say that now?"

"Dad," MJ says, "you pushed us away. We were getting along up here, remember? Then suddenly you just weren't you anymore. What the fuck, Dad? What's the matter? It can't just be the job. Nobody else went off the rails ..."

"People keep those things hidden. People have secrets. You'd better get used to it, Son. The System forces certain behaviours ..."

"System?"

"... And once somebody steps out of bounds the System discards them. What are you doing now? You back in sports?"

"No, Dad, I'm in school. I'm taking computer studies."

"Really?"

"You got me into it! Your obsession! If you hadn't left home we could have shared it. We could have made a team again."

"Yeah, well MJ, it would have come to a head at some point, you and me."

"And you were afraid it would be me who ended up the winner?"

"Tell you what, MJ, we'll go over to those computer stations and I'll show you who's boss. I haven't been lazy up here."

"Mel, you're talking to your son!" Pat says. "This isn't a game! Nobody competes!"

"Really Pat? It's *all* competition! Didn't we do it most of our lives? You think Stan's not competing? You ever take time to hear him talk?"

"As a matter of fact, I have," she says.

He ignores her response, locked in his own.

"Stan's out there in some stratosphere where only people like him can reach. He's part of a cyber System that one day will overwhelm us! They've got us all constantly using devices, becoming more and more dependent. They've got us thinking there's only one kind of intelligence. They supply information on the internet and block the things they don't want us to see. They've even gone after kids! You ever hear of the teams that go head to head playing first shooter games in cyber tournaments? MJ?"

"Yeah. Of course."

"They call 'em E-sports. Video games played professionally. That's what you were doing for a while there, wasn't it? You dreamed of being one of those guys."

"Dad, it was just a game."

"Which you played all the time. Don't tell me you didn't believe you could do it, be one of them, make the big money. Nobody spends that kind of time without some goal in mind. Sports taught me that much."

"Okay. Maybe."

"I played the wrong sports."

"What are you talking about, Dad? You played elite everything."

"But not professional. Never good enough! So what did I do? So I *could* play sports I dumped everything else for a fucking job as a wire weaver. A robot can do that job. So what did *you* want? King of *Mortal Combat*? World champ of *Quake*?"

"Don't turn it on him," Pat says. "They were your dreams and your disappointment."

"How do you know about these games?" MJ says. "You were never ..."

"Never interested. Correct. Didn't see the point. I'm a bit clearer now. You'll never know why. Or maybe you will but by then it'll be too late. You're gonna settle for a service job? Computer repairman?"

"Yeah."

"Stan helping you still?"

"What of it?"

"You're settling for second rate and he's allowing it. Computers are gonna repair *themselves* in ten years. Stan's part of that. You'll become just another wire weaver, tossed into the bin with the rest of the garbage!"

"Leave him alone, Mel," Pat says. She leans forward to make her point: "Any two people can suffer the same circumstance and neither reacts the same way. Take you and Gary Wilson. He's *working* now. He's not obsessing about being left behind. He's not blathering about a System ..."

"I wouldn't compare me to Wilson. There's things you don't know."

"So assume I don't. Do *you* have a job yet?"

"Oh, I do. Not like Wilson. Mine is more a mission."

"So why so mysterious? What are you doing?" Pat asks.

Mel ducks the question. A two second pause.

"Let me sign these papers."

"As you keep saying, society's changing," Pat says, even as she hands him a pen and watches him sign away his old life. "MJ is part of that change, so are Dani, and Stanley ... they'll *adapt*, Mel, in their separate ways but they *will* adapt. That's the new world you haven't quite figured out."

Mel begins to feel trapped, not ready for an assertive Pat. He changes the focus to regain his advantage.

"What's this guy doin' here? Who are you? What's your business in my business?"

"Mel, show some class," Pat says.

"It's alright, Patricia," Amrit says softly.

He looks into the fiery, sparking eyes of Mel Buckworth. Even he is a trifle shaken by them. Still, Amrit knows why he's here. He has been trained to look relaxed when he anticipates action.

"I've no business yet, Mr. Buckworth. Nevertheless, Pat's a friend, not a *girlfriend* but a friend. I'm just going to sit quietly."

"Hell of an accent you got there, buddy," Mel says. He is not ready to back down. There is something about this man he innately doesn't like. "You don't sound Indian."

"I'm Canadian."

"You don't sound that either."

"Emigrated from Britain. Any more questions?"

"After this maybe you and me can settle up outside."

"Mel!" Pat gasps, appalled by her husband.

"Where's Dani?" Mel asks. "Why isn't she here? Too busy being the geek fashionista?"

"You should tell him, Mom," MJ says.

"Tell me what?"

"I don't think so, MJ," Pat says

"What is it? Where's Dani? Let's hear it!"

"Promise you'll keep your temper," she says evenly.

"Of course I will!"

"Mel, our daughter is engaged to be married."

"What the fuck? She's too young!"

"Calm down, Mel. She's the same age I was."

"Yeah, look what happened there!"

"You need to settle down, Mr. Buckworth," Amrit says quietly.

"It didn't have to happen to us," Pat says. "I didn't do that, Mel. I've thought about this a long time. I've thought about hardly anything else. What *did* I do to drive you away? What *could* I have done to help you? Where and when did it all go wrong? I don't feel guilt anymore. I've come to see how complicated we are. Like the choices we make: sometimes not knowing why we made them, yet deep inside knowing anyway if we look hard enough. I've looked, Mel. I know who I am."

"She's throwing her life away!" he says.

"Like I did?"

"Is that what you think?"

"Not at all. It's been worth it, Mel, even the heartache. But I no longer define myself by you. I am finding who I really am. I wish you could too."

"You don't know what you're facing. You don't know what's gonna happen to the kids, or *their* kids in the future!"

"And you do?"

"Once these machines take over, we're done. They'll be smarter than us, faster than us, stronger than us, and they'll be immortal. What will they need with us then, when they start to know they're alive? We might have built them but by then they'll be building themselves. So what use are humans?"

"You should sit down, Mr. Buckworth," Amrit says.

"Shut the fuck up!" Mel yells.

"Sit down," Amrit says, quiet but firm.

The softness warns Mel this man might be more than he seems. He sits again. He signs the last of the papers. He ends his marriage.

"We should talk about what you want," Pat says.

"You keep it all. I don't want it."

"You're going to change your life that much?"

"It's changed already."

Mel rises and grabs his coat.

"Not quite yet, Mr. Buckworth," Amrit says.

"MJ," Pat says as she too stands, "come outside with me, please."

Mel can see his son caught in the crosswinds of fidelity. How does a boy make a choice like this? He watches the tears form in MJ's eyes. He can feel the pull and push inside the boy.

"Go on, Son. Maybe later we'll get together," Mel says, lying.

"He's a cop, Dad," MJ nods toward Amrit.

"I was going to tell him, MJ," Amrit says. "Please go outside with your mother."

"You brought a cop with you?"

Mel stares down his wife.

"You assaulted her once," Amrit says.

"How does he know that?" Mel says.

"MJ," she says, beckoning. She no longer looks at Mel. He watches them don their coats and walk out of his life. In that moment he is triumphant. In the teeth of the enemy sitting beside him he has rescued his wife and son. It is hard for him not to smile.

"I'm a detective, Mr. Buckworth. Waterloo Region Police Service. My name is Khadri."

"Why are you here?"

"I need to ask you some questions."

"Like what?"

"You worked for Erban Industries."

"That's not a question. Cut to the chase."

"Alright. Where were you on the night of March first?"

"How the hell would I know? Back in March? Look what's happening to me. I'm getting divorced! I hardly remember last week."

"How about before Hallowe'en, October twenty nine?"

"Up here, my cottage."

"Really."

"Yeah. I got a guy stayin' with me. He'll vouch for me."

"Do you know a man named Herbert Trimble?"

"Why should I?"

"You worked for Erban Industries. Your wife said you lost your job."

"Okay. Yeah. There was a guy, Trimble."

"Who terminated your employment?"

"So?"

"We are interviewing former Erban employees. Circumstances I'm not authorized to discuss. Would you be willing to come to Waterloo for an interview?"

"Don't see why."

"It would help us considerably."

"You gonna arrest me?"

"I have no cause. I just need to ask a few questions."

"Think I'll get a lawyer before I see you again."

"That is your prerogative, sir."

"I know it is."

"You'll come down Monday?"

"I said I'd like a lawyer."

"That's fine."

"Tell me one thing, detective?"

"What's that?"

"You like bein' a cog in the wheel?"

"I beg your pardon?"

"The System. You serve the System. You're so inside it you don't even know what it is."

"There is a justice system if that's what you mean."

"I'm leaving now. I'll be in Waterloo. Monday."

"Police Headquarters. You know where it is?"

"Yeah. Gateway. Sportsworld Road. Used to play hockey out there."

"Ask for me when you arrive. Here's my card."

"Jesus, just like a machine, aren't you?"

"I'm afraid I don't take your meaning, sir."

"Never mind, Khadri. I'll see you Monday."

70

WILL BAKER IS furious. Pineapple is fractured. It is clear Mel has been reckless, ignoring Will's preventative measures. Malicious code is erasing data and simultaneously stealing information from his site. Mel must have clicked on a false URL or been hacked while in a chat room.

Now Pineapple is juice.

He doubts whether Mel used Firesheep or off-the-record-messaging but he can't bypass Mel's encryptions. He knows five significant hacking languages: Python, C/C++, Java, Perl, and LISP, each representing different approaches. He has found fingerprints of numerous individual black hats. He is being gang hacked. At this rate even Will's talents will fail against so many cyber rivals. The dark web's inhabitants are making it plain that Tor will remain the *only* router in their shady dominion. All others to be shredded.

Will has been desperately tapping code and trying patches. He curses each gif or graphic flashing up, mocking his site, months of work gone. He slams his laptop shut as though the physical action will end the metaphysical torture. He is done, his invention trashed, reduced to nonsensical code. He is crying. He is a child again. Why is it this far along in his life he has become the target of bullies?

Then comes the knock and then the door opens.

"It's me, Da … Will! What are you doing here?"

"Hello, Dani. I live here. I'm a prisoner."

"Is my Dad here?"

"Not at the moment."

"Just a minute."

Dani steps outside and waves. Will looks through the dining room window and sees the familiar Volkswagen pull into the driveway, then Stanley and Michael get out. He wonders could anything worse happen, then wonders when Mel will return.

"Dani, you've gotta get out of here. Your Dad told me he'd be back soon."

"What's the matter, Will?" she says. "You don't look good. Are you sick?"

"I told you I'm a prisoner."

As he says this Michael and Stanley enter.

"I don't see any chains," Stanley says.

Will stares at him, chin quivering, then lets go the pent-up emotions of months.

"Look, you guys don't know Mel Buckworth! He's insane. He's modelled himself on the Unabomber. He's blackmailed me into helping him: making bombs, hacking, all kinds of shit. I'm a criminal now and it's your fault, Stanley!"

"How can that be?" Michael asks.

"Stanley introduced me to Mel!"

"He did not!" Dani says.

"And you set it up! Dani, you told me he needed help, told me he would pay. Stanley, you told me I owed the house money ..."

"I had no idea what you were doing."

"Then why the hell didn't you ask? You overheard me on the phone, Dani. None of you stopped me. None of you tried."

"Come now, Will," Michael says, "no one's here now. You can walk away,"

"He's blackmailing me. He's got me like a spider in his fucking web. He says he's going to save the world! He got this shit from Kaczynski!"

"Who's that?" Dani asks.

"Never mind. If he comes back I don't know what he'll do!"

"He's my father. He won't hurt me."

"Doesn't mean he won't kill *us*!"

"Why?" Stanley asks.

"He thinks you've enthralled his little girl. He thinks you're a dirt bag. Worse. A *geek* dirt bag. He thinks every time you touch her it's some kind of perversion! Now he's thinking you're part of something he calls the System, the very thing he wants to destroy."

"He was coming around."

"You can't see anything! Any of you! You think he's *dear old Dad* and you two think he's just some dumb jock. He *pretended* to like you because he *used* you. That's what he *does*."

"He's not like that," Dani says.

"How would you know?" Will answers. "You haven't seen him in months! He kicked you out, didn't he?"

"That's ..."

"Then he turned on MJ and then his wife!"

"Will ..."

"You don't know anything. Nobody does! I created an app for the dark web!"

"What are you talking about?" Michael asks.

"He used it for all kinds of criminal shit."

"Look, Will, you're clearly a victim here," Stanley says. "Why not come with us?"

"He'll crucify me! He's had me by the throat since the minute I met him. Dani, why didn't you tell me your father's a sociopath?"

"He's not."

"Yes, he is! He's mailed poison packages to people. He's committed arson. He made me plant a bomb at some guy's house! Now he's got a truck bomb that'll blow up a building. He's gonna kill someone and I'm afraid it's gonna be me!"

"Just come with us," Stanley says. "We'll go to police."

"Then my life is fucked. I'll still be involved, have a criminal record. I won't be able to get back home, back to the US."

"Where's his laptop?" Stanley asks.

"In his bedroom. All the proof you need is right there but you won't get past his encryptions. It's so wound up in protocols there's no backdoor."

"You did that?"

"He made me do it!"

"Surely you're smarter than he is!"

"There's another problem we have. We think we're the smart ones. There's different kinds of smart! He's incredible. His focus. He saw me do everything and learned it. You think he knows nothing about neural systems. He knows so much more than you'd ever believe ..."

"You taught him?"

"I gave him direction. He taught himself. The guy hardly sleeps."

"I know that much," Dani says.

"You know nothing," Will turns on her. "He could be back any time. You don't want to face him."

"I'm not leaving without his computer," Stanley says.

"I'll look," Dani says and is off down the hall.

"What got you into this, Will?" Michael asks. "You had everything going for you."

"You think I'm greedy, don't you? You think I wanted to make an app just to make the money but it's way more than that. You guys don't have parents expecting you to be the best. Mine think they're special, so why not me? I've been pushed all my life. It's not about money. It's about reputation. *Distinction.*

"The one thing my parents *don't* have. The one thing they wanted from me. You don't know what it's like to live that way. Every success not quite good enough unless you transform into Einstein or Hawking or Jobs or Gates? Every time I went home I was met with the same anxious looks.

"You all thought you knew me. You *can't* know me. We work to create artificial intelligence when we don't even know the extent of our *own.* What's the iconography of the mind? What about parts of the brain we don't seem to use? What makes a saint or a psychopath? What makes a savant different from a genius? Go ahead, tell me!"

"I can't," Stanley says. "No one can."

"I've got it!" Dani returns from the bedroom.

"Come with us, Will," Stanley grasps Will's arm. "Whatever's happened ..."

"So *you* think! The brilliant, bleeding edge Stanley Best. I feel sorry for you. You spend so much time chasing theory you can't see reality."

"I have a sense ..."

"You can't help me. I have *one* way out."

"What are you talking about?"

"If I leave with you I'll either go to jail, have a criminal record or spend the rest of my life looking over my shoulder. I can't do that. I've worked it all through. So you guys just go. Go now."

There are no goodbyes. They leave the cottage walk up to the car, get in, start it up and back out. They drive down Stewart Lake Road, turn onto Highway 612 North and when they reach the Lake Joseph Road they turn south. The road takes them around Mactier rather than through it. In a matter of twenty minutes they are headed for home on 400 South.

When they have departed Will Baker takes action. He dons his coat, takes the keys to the F150, then walks up to the truck. It takes him five minutes to prepare then he starts the truck and follows down Stewart Lake Road turning right on Highway 612 but rather than continue to Lake Joseph Road, Will turns left on Healey Lake Road. This road twists and turns but Will drives carefully, passing Hellangone Lake on his left. It is beautiful on this November day. Visible through the bare trees the water is leaden but for small whitecaps whipped by the wind. A shower passes, pattering its shimmer along the lake.

At the curve in the road just after Hellangone there is a gravel pit, unused now. It looks vaguely like a New Mexico desert. Will drives along a weedy lane into the pit and wends his way through the mounds of gravel into a valley between two ridges. The shower from the lake has passed here as well. The crushed granite sparkles like diamonds; like Mel Buckworth's eyes.

Will Baker parks. He sits a moment looking outside.

He picks up the cellphone and dials.

And finds his way out.

71

MEL BUCKWORTH KNOWS it is nearly over. He has met the first of the forces against him. The System's agents will ultimately bring him down.

He could run but Khadri has seen the Nissan. He considers hopping a train out of Mactier, wondering how far he might actually get.

Detective Khadri, mild, inquisitive, knowing more than he should, would have little trouble finding him. Mel is sure once at police headquarters he will be uncovered. Once the interrogation begins it will not end until all is revealed; like peeling away the onion.

Or not.

He has realized now the impossibility of *knowing*.

There have been changes in each of his family members. The algorithms of social custom replaced with new more dexterous ones, his family shattered by differentiation. They have all diverged far from the routine roads they once travelled. He is no longer the base of his brood but the *other*, the one who is outside the norm.

He does not hear the blast from the gravel pit. The weather is cold. The truck windows are up. He arrives at the cottage and he sees his F150 gone, Will Baker with it. He had thought he'd controlled the boy in their strange symbiosis. In the end who has any control? He finds his computer gone. He understands Patricia has played him. Someone came here, likely Dani, enticing Will away, taking the truck and computer.

His secrets will not remain with Will talking and Stanley blowing past his encryptions. The police will consider him unstable and even dangerous. He has, after all, threatened the System they've sworn to protect. Indeed, he has threatened one of its agents.

He spends that Saturday night watching hockey yet not seeing it. He has *lost* sports now, the way of life he'd once chosen in his blithe ignorance. He'd been a version of binary: off-on, this-that, black-white, ignoring the greys and the in-betweens. Before the game ends he turns it off. He sits at the table with pen and paper trying to devise his Manifesto.

He needs to leave something behind: a message explaining his efforts to obstruct the System as it rolls inexorably over humanity. He recognizes new social calibrations have altered the twenty- first century. Gender roles, economics, even families have changed. Scientific success, religious beliefs and political propaganda have been re-defined. Cogs in the mechanism, people lose their souls as the System devours them, having no further need of their service. Technology creates social bureaucracies with Systemic world views far different from human acuity. Actually, only a very few humans will ever enjoy this logical luxury while the rest are diverted with *correctness* or subsumed as chattel.

And then, of course, there is the mind. Immeasurable in any sense it is the enigma employed to grasp self-awareness. There is no metaphor for the mind. Each person constructs an elaborate edifice of persona to make us recognizable to others. Yet if Mel has learned anything he knows there is nothing but our own perceptions of what we wish to believe. Space and time are our minds' creations, so *all* elements are in superposition existing in simultaneous states.

Like thoughts.

Like dreams.

Like what we call existence.

72

THE NEXT DAY finds him in the Mactier hardware store. There is gossip in the coffee shop. A blast in the pit out on Healey Lake Road. A truck burned beyond recognition. No one will say anymore but Mel knows.

So now he has killed someone.

Finishing his coffee he crosses to the library. The librarian is a different woman. He requests use of a computer. He sits down and finds what he needs quite quickly. No Onion routers no Tors no Pineapples just plain Google Search. He had thought to print out instructions. It is so simple he finds he won't need them.

He asks the librarian to use the phone. Long distance. Explaining he lost his cell while fishing. After the laughter and condolences she lends him hers. She has cross Canada calling. She asks if he would use one of the small rooms so he can talk. It *is* a library after all. She leads him to one. It has tube chairs and stacking tables. There are pieces of children's art on the walls. Some remind him of Dani's early doodles, the stick people she made. Two of them always had eyes that glittered.

He has one item left to use. Stanley Best's phone number, written down during the surreal weekend when everything changed. Just pencil on paper. As he dials he marvels at his own changes. He hears the *brrrr* in the phone. After two repeats the connection is made.

"Yes, hello?" Stanley says, pre-occupied.

"Hey there, Stan. You got my laptop?"

"What? Mel?"

"Thought I wouldn't call you?"

"We've opened your files and auxiliary memory. You've kept trophies, I see. What on earth do you think you're doing?"

"Trying to stop characters like you."

"Like *me*? Of course, Danielle ..."

"Not anymore. I want to meet you."

"I'm afraid not. I'm aware of your truck."

"It's gone. Will Baker blew himself up. So were you with Dani? Was he there when you got there? What the hell did you say to him?"

"We asked him to leave with us. He wouldn't. He was very confused. Blew himself up, you say? Good God!"

"I used him. I didn't expect him to die. Then again, how can we know?"

"What?"

"You of all people should understand that."

"Mr. Buckworth, why not turn yourself in? You can talk to police and sort it all out."

There is a rustle on the phone. It is changing hands.

"Mel?"

"Pat? Why are you there?"

"He's with *us*, at the house."

"Shoulda known. Quite a trick you pulled in Mactier."

"What is *wrong* with you? What have you done? Arson? Poison? Letter bombs? Amrit ... Detective Khadri, took your computer for evidence but Stanley uncovered enough."

"Amrit, is it? I have to say *that* surprised me."

"We had dinner a couple of times."

"You sure he's not using you?"

"That's coincidence."

"Believe what you want, Pat. It's really the only freedom you have."

"You need help, Mel."

"I thought once I had control. Now I know it's a sham. This whole year's proof of that. I did some research. I went back two hundred years. Turns out I'm descended from Luddites."

"Just give up. With what they know now ..."

"I am the Luddite of my own life, Pat. That life is a shambles. I'm coming to Waterloo tomorrow. Khadri must have told you. I'll be arrested. Before that I'd like to see my family."

"I don't think so, Mel. You're dangerous."

"Yeah. I can see how you'd think that. We can't really know each other at all, can we? Despite our programming we don't always behave according to plan. Not *my* ancestors anyway!"

"You're rambling. Listen to yourself."

"You have any feeling at all left for me? I need to make amends to the kids. What if it's public? So you'll feel safe. In the open so there won't be cops."

"I don't know."

"I'm asking you to trust me. It can be on our street in front of the house on the sidewalk."

"Not with your truck. I heard about it."

"Truck's gone. Just me. Alone."

"Mel."

"Please, Pat. If I ever meant anything to you ..."

"You ... did. You do. Alright."

"Tomorrow at noon then. Please pass the phone back to Stan."

"Why?"

"I want to make sure he's not there."

"He's going to be part of our family! Did you hear me yesterday?"

"I did. I'm glad."

"What?"

"She'll be one of the safe ones with him. He's gonna be a Systemic power."

"Meaning?"

"Just an ask, Pat. Put him on."

The rustling sound as the phone changes hands. Stanley speaks, his voice unsure.

"Hello?"

"They'll want you to stay with them. I've set it up. I'll wait ten minutes then call you again. Say it's an emergency. Work. You got a problem you gotta work out at the Quantum-Nano Centre tonight."

"Why?"

"I have a Manifesto. I'm gonna give it to you. Some people *matter*, Stan. You're one of them, or you're gonna be. If anything's true in this world it's that. You'll be my messenger. Meet me at the doors on the ring road side of the building. Clear?"

"Yes."

"I'll call you again."

He hangs up. He goes to the desk. He asks if he might make one more call.

"Of course, sir," the librarian says, smiling.

He calls back. Stanley answers, fakes a conversation. It ends with: "What time then?"

"Eleven-thirty tonight," he answers. "No police, Stan. I want your word."

"Yes. You have it. I'll be there."

With that he disconnects. He returns the phone to the librarian. He crosses back to the hardware store. He buys a hunting vest, end of the season sale. Colombia bird vest, yellow shoulders, beige net body with cargo pockets. He buys two rolls of grey masking tape, two water bottles, a six volt battery and a universal remote. He buys electrical wires: red, white, and black.

Then he drives south.

73

INSIDE THE QUANTUM-NANO Centre is a wide hallway bisecting the building. A single practical staircase climbs to a second floor crossover, the bridge made of dark glass and light wood. On his right is the orange translucent wall of the nano lab, to his left are glassed in offices. He feels a sense of being in a large space. There are no furnishings whatsoever in this hall.

He wears a navy blue raincoat, jeans and boots. He is watchful for signs of police. His eyes glitter like lasers. People pass through the atrium, distracted minds in the midst of conversation, one or two others glance at him, wondering. He employs the remote as if it were a cell phone. Talking to air. He appears a man impatiently waiting. He does not trust Stanley to come alone. He is sure the man is a coward.

Then Stanley Best enters at the opposite end of the atrium. He sees Mel immediately. He walks toward him. No hesitation.

Another mistake I made, Mel thinks. That's what Dani sees in him.

As Stanley advances he removes his gloves, tuque and scarf then unzips his coat. He battles the *fight or flight* response. Primordial. Everything in his mind screams *panic* yet he continues forward.

"Hello Stan," Mel says softly.

"Hello sir," Stanley replies.

"So you don't remember my name?"

"I do."

"Use it. You came here. I think that gives you the merit."

"Alright. Hello, Mel."

"You're a brave man for showing up."

"You said you had no intention of harm."

"And I don't, but I know you don't trust me."

"I have little choice. I have news for you, sir, about Danielle."

"I know already. You're going to marry her. That's a good thing."

"It isn't just that ..."

"Not now, Stan."

"It's important. Very ..."

"Don't try to distract me. I came here to give you something. I need to get this clear and correct."

"Your Manifesto ..."

"Yeah, but I'm no writer. So I want you to remember what I say."

Mel reaches into the raincoat's pocket. For an instant Stanley's brain bellows *run!* Mel withdraws his hand and holds it out, his palm open. Resting there is a miniature hammer, glinting pewter in the soft light.

"This has been in my family for *two hundred* years. It's been passed, father to the first son of each generation. MJ should get this but I'm going to change the equation. I want *you* to take it. I want you to have another one made just like it. I want you to give this one to Dani and the other to MJ, or vice versa, that will be up to you. When you and Dani have children I want you to ensure they *each* have one. I want you to ensure MJ does the same: that this tradition will continue as long as there are Buckworth descendants, male or female, whatever their surnames. Pat should know this as well."

"This ... this is astonishing," Stanley says, receiving the ornament.

"What you *do* isn't right you know. I want you to understand how I feel about that. It's not personal, not just about you, but what occupies you. You play in this quantum world of yours but you're nearly blind to it. You think to build a machine more complex than anything known to the human race. Yet how can you build a human equivalent without knowing humans themselves?

"How can you match evolution? Oh, I *get* it. We have to think we're special to give our lives meaning but you, especially, must know we're not. We're microbes on specks in infinite space and inside us there are lives going on: viruses, bacteria, the microscopic particles you want to play with. Why don't you be a doctor? You could do it. Why don't you learn the human brain instead of trying to build an artificial one? You'd still be a success."

"You're losing me, Mel," Stanley says.

"Look, I noticed when I put my hand in my pocket you wanted to run. If you had then none of this, what we're doing now, would have happened. Yet you stayed. Did that surprise you? Did you know you had courage?"

"About Dani—" Stanley says but is cut short.

"To my thinking humans are the true unknowns: never exactly the same, changing instantly with each interaction and sometimes within the same one. I read about quantum superposition and how it applies to physics. So why shouldn't it apply to human character? I think of my kids. They aren't the same anymore. Aren't you, at your base, *really* at the base, still who you were before you built your personality? And do you know who *that* was back then? It's all quanta: memory flashbacks, déjà vu, nightmares, daydreams, perceptions."

"It seems you've changed as well, Mr ... ah, Mel."

"I know I have, but you surprised me tonight by coming here. I'll bet you were, as they say, of two minds about coming. That's superposition right there, isn't it? That's what you study? You apply it to subatomic matter. You should actually study yourself."

"I'm trying, Mel ..."

"Someone has to remind us we're running blind. That's why I gave you that hammer. It's a model of a Luddite Enoch. They lost, of course, the Luddites. Technology won. Maybe it does improve life in the long run and then again maybe it's just an illusion.

"In the world I perceive you seem bound for big things. I'm grateful you love my Dani. I'm thankful she'll be part of the *privileged elite*. My son won't make it but you will. I can't know for sure, of course. I had no idea what I could learn in a year until I'd done it. I think now I wasted my life, except for this part of it. The thing is: no one knows. No one can."

Mel stops speaking. The silence in the hall's space is deafening. They simply look at each other, man to man. It takes a moment for Stanley to realize Mel is crying. His eyes are so bright they conceal the tears until tears appear on his cheekbones.

"This ... is your Manifesto then, sir?"

"One part of it. There's another part. You don't really understand this, do you?"

"Sorry?"

"Do you have your phone?"

"I do."

"Call the police."

"What?"

Mel removes his raincoat and lets it drop to the floor. Beneath he is wearing a bomb vest. Yellow shoulders, mesh body, cargo pockets filled with shapes, what looks like plastic bottles of fuel, red cartridges, a six volt battery and a maze of coloured wires running to and from each pocketed explosive, silver grey duct tape holding it all together. He looks to Stanley like a cyborg.

Mel lifts the TV remote above their heads.

"I *am* the Manifesto, Stanley. I will die here in this science temple of yours. It's the only way to focus attention on my campaign. It's the only way for me to win! Once this place goes up, it will be news. No one can ignore me. I don't want to kill you, so walk away and call the police."

"Daddy!"

The voice comes from above him. The crossover. From this glassine perch Danielle peers over the edge. Her eyes glitter.

"Dani! Why are you here?"

"Didn't Stanley tell you?"

"Tell me what?"

"I'm pregnant, Dad. I'm going to have a baby."

Suddenly the world shifts and Mel Buckworth is faced with transformation, with the very change he has spoken of. There, on the glassine crossover, his daughter's eyes shine with love, fear and joy simultaneously. Up there are two beings in one.

His eyes centre on Stanley.

"Why didn't you tell me?" he murmurs.

"You didn't give me time," he replies. "She just took the test last night."

"You're cunning. This is a ruse."

"No sir, it is not."

"I was afraid you'd hurt Stanley but I heard you, Dad!" Danielle says. "You don't have to do this! You can give yourself up! Constable Khadri is here! I brought him."

"You? *Betrayed* me?" Mel says so softly only Stanley can hear.

"Put an end to this! Please!" Dani pleads. "You're going to be a granddad!"

"Dani, you're ..."

"We're getting married! Please, don't do this. Walk me down the aisle!"

That life is so infinitely erratic so utterly unpredictable so very, very, very strange that even when you think you have all the answers there are only more questions one cannot fathom. He lowers the remote though it stays in his hand.

"Khadri! Can you hear me? If she's here you're here!"

Amrit Khadri emerges from behind the staircase leading up to the crossover. He is at its base on the atrium floor. He wears a three quarter length wool overcoat. He does not look as harmless as in the library. His Glock 17 is pointed directly at Mel.

Yet Mel smiles. Some things *can* be anticipated. The System does indeed work. He is sure now his message will be delivered.

"Please put that device in your hand on the floor and step away from it."

"I can't do that, Khadri."

"You'd kill your own daughter?"

"You've used my daughter. This pregnancy lie ..."

"It's no lie."

"Why didn't Pat tell me?"

Danielle has run down the stairs and now stands with Khadri. He holds her by her arm, the Glock in his other hand. She looks flushed, beautiful, precious.

"She doesn't know. I just found out myself."

Mel turns to Stanley. The young man perceives a change in his eyes. It is an odd light, like nothing he's seen before. It is as if Mel is looking inward and the diamond flash has become moonstone.

"Walk away now, take my daughter with you," he says softly. "You're responsible now. Take care of her. Take care of your child. Remember my words."

"Mel, please," Stanley says, begging.

"Go now!"

Stanley backs away toward Khadri. At the same time Danielle moves urgently forward.

"Mel, please put down the device."

Khadri's voice is calm.

"Daddy!" Danielle is sobbing. Stanley prevents her from passing him. She fights. She slaps him hard with one hand while pushing away with the other but Stanley refuses to loosen his hold, a half-clutch half-embrace even as she slaps him again. He tells her he loves her as she curses him.

There is no comparing the two kinds of love inside Dani inside this instant.

"Take her out of here, Stanley," Khadri says. "Go."

"Dani," her father says. "Just go. I'm doing this for you. I need you to know it, Dani. I need you to know I love your mother. I've never stopped. And you and MJ. But you couldn't be part of this."

"Daddy please!" she cries. "It's not what you think! You can get help!"

"Stanley, move. Don't resist him, Dani. Just don't!"

The couple moves away: the daughter reluctantly, her lover protectively. They struggle but Danielle is suddenly drained. Stanley steers them toward the wall partially sheltered by the staircase. He has no idea how big this bomb is. They move down the wall to the doors at the opposite end.

"Let them get out of the building," Khadri says.

"That's the plan," Mel says.

"Why?"

"Someone has to stand up, make people think."

"Put down the device."

"I can't do that."

"I don't want to kill you."

"But you will if you have to."

With the sigh of a closing door at the opposite end of the atrium, the sound of police sirens seeps through. Mel raises the remote.

"You don't want to run, Khadri? You'd die for the System?"

"Of course I do but I can't let you do this."

"Of two minds then?" Mel Buckworth chuckles.

"Put it down, Mel, save us both."

"In THREE, TWO ..."

A single shot spits from the machine in Amrit Khadri's hands.

Mel Buckworth never hears it.

The atrium echoes.

74

AMRIT KHADRI ADVANCES toward the body prostrate on the floor. One shot to the head. Blood fans out from a pool where Mel lies. There are spatters on the wall. The blood and body disturb the atrium's logical symmetry. The echo has brought heads to windows. The temple's tranquility has been disturbed.

Khadri has never killed anyone. He feels disbelief he could take a life. His guilt merges with the relief that he is alive and has done his duty and the pity he feels for Danielle, Pat and MJ and not a little for himself for he knows this will stay with him for the rest of his life. All in the same instant. All his varying synapses entangling into multiples of emotions, they are in and of each other. They are inseparable.

The remote has fallen and broken open on the terrazzo floor. Khadri looks carefully at the remote, searching for the batteries that power it. His heart sinks.

There are none.

There never were.

Manifesto.

SOURCES

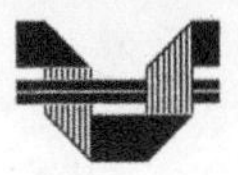

To Save Everything, Click, The Folly of Technological Solutionism
Evgeny Morozov, Public Affairs, Perseus Books Group, 2013

Googled, The End of the World as We Know It
Ken Auletta, Penguin Press, 2009

Amusing Ourselves to Death
Neil Postman, Viking Penguin, 1985

THE Glass Cage: Automation and Us
Nicolas Carr, Norton, 2014

The Bomb Maker
Thomas Perry, Thorndike Press, 2018

How to Be a Cat
Mark Leigh, Michael O'Mara Books Ltd., 2016

Notes toward a Neo-Luddite Manifesto
Chellis Glendinning , 1990, retrieved on May 1, 2014 from www.jesusradicals.com/wp-content/uploads/luddite-manifesto.pdf

Industrial Society and Its Future
Theodore Kaczyinski, Friday, Sept. 22, 1995 editions of Washington Post

ACKNOWLEDGEMENTS

MY THANKS TO

Diane Eastham
Lianne McClean
Richard French
Doug Hyslop
Mark Torrance
Jan Sebald
Doug Blakey (Watsec Cyber Risk Management)
Constable Ashley Dietrich (Waterloo Regional Police Service)
Raymond Laflamme (Institute of Quantum Computing University of Waterloo)
Mike & Ophelia Lazaridis Quantum-Nano Centre
Nancy Silcox
John Oughton
John Drudge
David Menear
James D. A. Terry
Dorothy Sjolholm
Henry the House Cat

AND

The many, many friends, students, professors, scientists and researchers who took the time to talk with me regarding my research for this novel.

AND

Michael Mirolla for his guidance, patience, and the mettle to trust me with this undertaking.

"No Limits, No Borders." That's the truth!

NOTE

The Mike & Ophelia Lazaridis Quantum-Nano Centre which plays a central part in this novel was not opened until 2013, whereas I have it running in 2012. My apologies to those who are upset over this tinkering with history. It is a novel after all and the symbolic status was simply too good to ignore.

ABOUT THE AUTHOR

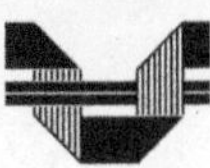

Once a teacher, award winning playwright, theatre director and adjudicator, Brian Van Norman left those worlds behind to travel the planet with his wife, Susan, and take up writing as a full time pursuit. He has journeyed to every continent and sailed nearly every sea on the planet. Brian is the author of three previous novels: *The Betrayal Path*, *Immortal Water* and *Against the Machine: Luddites,* the first in a trilogy of *Against the Machine* novels. His base is Waterloo, Ontario, Canada though he is seldom found there.

This book is made of paper from well-managed FSC® - certified forests, recycled materials, and other controlled sources.